Trudi Johnson

From a Good Home

From a Good Home

A NOVEL

Trudi Johnson

FLANKER PRESS LIMITED
ST. JOHN'S

Library and Archives Canada Cataloguing in Publication

Johnson, Trudi Dale, 1955-, author
From a good home : a novel / Trudi Johnson.

Issued in print and electronic formats.
ISBN 978-1-77117-525-8 (paperback).--ISBN 978-1-77117-526-5
(epub).--ISBN 978-1-77117-527-2 (kindle).--ISBN 978-1-77117-528-9
(pdf)

I. Title.

PS8619.O4842F76 2016   C813'.6   C2016-901654-4
                                               C2016-901655-2

PRINTED IN CANADA

MIX
Paper from responsible sources
FSC
www.fsc.org   FSC® C016245

This paper has been certified to meet the environmental and social standards of the Forest Stewardship Council® (FSC®) and comes from responsibly managed forests, and verified recycled sources.

Edited by Robin McGrath   Cover Design by Graham Blair

FLANKER PRESS LTD.
PO BOX 2522, STATION C
ST. JOHN'S, NL
CANADA

TELEPHONE: (709) 739-4477   FAX: (709) 739-4420   TOLL-FREE: 1-866-739-4420
WWW.FLANKERPRESS.COM

9 8 7 6 5 4 3 2 1

Canada   Canada Council   Conseil des Arts   Newfoundland
         for the Arts   du Canada   Labrador

We acknowledge the [financial] support of the Government of Canada. *Nous reconnaissons l'appui [financier] du gouvernement du Canada.* We acknowledge the support of the Canada Council for the Arts, which last year invested $153 million to bring the arts to Canadians throughout the country. *Nous remercions le Conseil des arts du Canada de son soutien. L'an dernier, le Conseil a investi 153 millions de dollars pour mettre de l'art dans la vie des Canadiennes et des Canadiens de tout le pays.* We acknowledge the financial support of the Government of Newfoundland and Labrador, Department of Tourism, Culture and Recreation for our publishing activities.

For Albert, with deep appreciation.

From a Good Home

CHAPTER 1

Shortly after 7:00 a.m., Hannah woke to the familiar cries of seagulls and became suddenly aware that she would likely never forget this day. She raised her head to meet a gentle breeze of cool sea air across the nine-patch quilt on her bed. She pushed back the frayed edge of her quilt's green satin binding and winced as her eyes met the glare of the early morning sun casting a silvery glow on the ocean waves only fifty feet from her bedroom window. Looking down beyond the window ledge, she smiled as dozens of pink fireweed danced among the rocks. She wondered when she would see them again after today. *Do they have flowers in St. John's? Of course they do, but not these old flowers that grow whether anyone tends to them or not. Likely flowers that are planted and taken care of.*

Hannah loved the smell of the fresh air. Despite her mother's warning that she would "catch her death," most nights, in the darkness, she would struggle to pull up the wooden-framed window in her bedroom until it loosened and a draft blew in. Hannah rarely got sick, and she doubted whether the salt sea air could cause a cold. *If it did,* she often thought, *we'd be all dead by now.*

The sun was well up over the horizon, so Hannah was not surprised that Frances, her older sister who shared her bed, was up and gone. Frances worked down harbour, cleaning and cooking for the minister's family. She worked long hours but never complained because the pay was good. And their father, a fisherman since he was twelve, always said it was important to find a way to "keep body and soul together," so the girls worked, too, if only to show their brothers they could work just as hard as they did.

Today, Hannah was going to prove to her family how hard she could work, how brave she really was. At the age of seventeen, she was going to leave her home in Falcon Cove, a small fishing community on the northeast coast of Newfoundland, and travel for the first time to work in a city she had never visited, for people she had never met. She convinced herself that she would do a fine job and her mom and pop would be pleased. And her brothers would never again make fun of her or say she was spoiled.

She let out a loud sigh and thought how her life had changed so quickly in only a couple of weeks. She smiled as she thought about her grandmother's words. "Life happens that way, my dear. You don't have time to think about it. Or get ready for it. And that's a good thing," she had said. But Hannah did think about it. Every minute of every day since her father came home a month ago to say that the Sinclairs, a prestigious family in St. John's, were looking for a young maid from the outports to work for them. Her father had added that young outport girls were thought to be hard workers, and with a wink of his eye he added that truer words were never spoken. The family, he said, needed a young girl to do housework and, most of all, to care for their two-year-old daughter, Emily. Hannah's mom had laughed out loud as she pushed more wood into the stove to help the baking bread along. "They only have one child? And they want someone to look after that child? Just the one?" she had asked in total disbelief, a tinge of disgust in her voice. Her husband felt obliged to comment, though he rarely talked about others. "Hettie, maid, they're busy people, I s'pose. That's all I know. They want somebody."

And her mother let out that delightful laugh again and said, "And what am I, James, if not busy?" She only called him James when she wanted to make a point. Usually, it was simply Jay.

Hannah's father had turned to his three daughters, Frances, Elsie, and Hannah, at the supper table that night and asked which one of them would be willing to go to St. John's to work. Hannah had not hesitated. Everyone turned to look at her in surprise. She was the last one they expected. After all, Hannah rarely spent much time at the other end of the harbour. She was always within calling distance of their house. But she quickly nodded and told her father that she would. And just as quickly, she was running down the path that led from her back door to the water's edge, a path worn by generations of neighbours and children, to her friend Adelia's house to tell her that she was moving to St. John's. She would be working for an important family, she explained, and she didn't know when she would be back, likely not until next summer. Adelia, for the first time in her life, was speechless at the news. Even in their brief eye contact that evening, neither girl acknowledged the emotional reality of Hannah's decision. They just swallowed hard and agreed to write as often as possible.

By the next day, she had realized the depth of her decision. She delivered the news to her relatives with a laugh and a shrug of her shoulders, but deep inside, she shook with fear as she prepared to leave on Friday morning. It was not the work she feared—she was used to work—it was the loneliness, being away from her brothers and sisters, Mom and Pop, her grandparents, Adelia, and even the wildflowers, now seemingly waving goodbye to her in the breeze. She twisted in the bed, tugged her nightdress up across her knees, and wondered why her mother hadn't called her to get up yet. Perhaps she didn't want to face what was to come that day. Perhaps her mother didn't want to say goodbye to her daughter as she climbed aboard the steamer to St. John's, to face a twenty-four-hour journey into an unknown life.

Hannah squeezed her eyes shut and tried to imagine what awaited her at the Sinclair house, but couldn't. *Will I wake to the sound of the sea and the foghorn? Do they even notice the sea in St. John's or is it always too noisy? Do men like Pop come in from fishing?* Hannah rubbed her stomach gently, hoping it would ease the flip-flop feeling she had there. She had promised her family and she couldn't let them down, no matter how hard her stomach hurt. She'd take Falcon Cove with her, if only in her heart.

* * * * *

AUGUST 8, 1995, SHORTLY AFTER MIDNIGHT

"The house is yours, you know that."

The words came in a hoarse whisper from the frail figure lying in a bed of white linens. Charles Sinclair squinted at his daughter, who sat stoically near his bedside, delicately fingering a handkerchief edged with blue embroidered flowers. Her tightened throat prevented her from speaking, so she nodded in acknowledgement.

His few words were the most he had spoken in several days. "I have provided for your sister," he continued, but looked away. "It's only fitting." His breathing was laboured and shallow. He closed his eyes in exhaustion and relief. He was not afraid.

"Of course," she managed in a whisper.

His daughter peered at him in the darkened room, watching his chest slowly rising and falling underneath the layers of sheets and woollen blankets. She struggled to commit his face to memory. So fragile. Hardly the man she cherished in her childhood memories: tall, strong, full of life and energy. An image of him as a young man flashed through her mind. She remembered how he used to reach to open a door before his feet had caught up with him, an idiosyncrasy she proudly thought to be symbolic of his drive to succeed. She smiled briefly at the memory, but this was quickly replaced with sadness at the realization that it was all over now. For the past few months, he had sat downstairs in his favourite chair looking around the room and marvelling at how much he had achieved, all he had worked for. But he knew then it was all in the past. He would stare at his hands, hands that had counted so much money and made sure all the Queen's pictures were facing the right way. He had asked, "What's after this?" But no one, not even the clergy who visited once a week, could provide him with an acceptable answer.

She stood up from the small, round teak chair, allowing the striped cushion to fall, and bent to kiss him ever so lightly on the forehead. Straightening his pillows and tucking a blanket in place across his chest, she whispered, "Good night, Father. Sleep well."

He opened his eyes for only seconds and looked at her. He thought how much she resembled her mother. Her beautiful face had the same clear complexion. She sat and pulled an ivory-coloured afghan across her knees. For a brief moment, she wondered about her sister, asleep down the hall.

His breathing laboured into the night until, shortly after 3:00 a.m., the house fell silent.

* * * * *

Jeanne Sinclair had never liked her sister. Truth be told, Jeanne did not like much. She particularly disliked poorly prepared food, shoddy clothes, loud noise of any kind, small talk, and house guests. But her dislike of her sister featured prominently on the list. She did feign a fondness for her, at least in public and when speaking to friends, but most things about Emily irritated her. Emily's hands were always clasped together in front of her, even while she slept. That bothered her. Jeanne wondered if a game that their nanny had taught them had stayed too long with Emily. It was the game that required children to recite "Here is the church, here is the steeple, open the doors and see all the people," while holding their hands together with fingers interlocked. Other things about Emily irritated her, like the awful pearl earrings that she seemed to wear all the time. Jeanne wondered if they had left her ears for the past ten years. Emily claimed that they were a gift from her former (Emily never said *ex-*) husband, but Jeanne believed deep down that the man never would have bought them if for no other reason than that they were ugly and no one except Emily, not even a man, would spend money on them. She slurped her tea. That bothered Jeanne, too. And, above all, she always seemed to get along wonderfully with Kurt, and Kurt had always "felt for her," as he said, back when he and Jeanne were married. Yes, everyone seemed to pity Emily and care for Emily and side with Emily, and, oh, it was always all about Emily. Emily had personality, her mother reminded everyone on numerous occasions, especially Jeanne. Emily had had a difficult time raising a son on her own. Poor Emily. And perhaps that's what bothered her the most about Emily. No matter what she did, or said, everyone *felt* for Emily.

This morning Jeanne was exceedingly tired, physically and emotionally, and certainly not in the mood for Emily. The last few months had increased the strain, and this day was the breaking point—the day Jeanne knew had to come.

The night had been a long one. When the end came, neither sister spoke. Jeanne sat on the edge of the bed clutching the pillow as Emily sobbed quietly next to her. Without speaking, Jeanne dressed and left the house, returning to her own home, alone, on Exeter Avenue, where, with the help of a milligram of Ativan, she slept until early morning. No one questioned where she was going or whether she was all right. She was used to that. In fact, she preferred it.

Now, in the morning hours, as she sat in her solarium at the back of her house, lightly spreading butter over a whole grain English muffin, cutting it into eight even pieces and leaving them on the plate to get cold, she thought of contacting her son, Joe, and her daughter, Lauren. The worst for her was to come. She hated public displays of emotion. She felt they were inappropriate and embarrassing. She knew she was contrary to a world that relished public birthing and public grieving. For the next few days she would speak to people she hardly knew, say things she didn't mean, and keep every fibre of emotion restrained within her. At least, she hoped, by the end of the weekend, Emily and her son would be gone, leaving her to cherish privately her memories and her father's possessions.

* * * * *

By 8:00 a.m., the sun was sufficiently up over the Southside Hills in St. John's to dry the concrete steps and the grey interlocking pavement bricks of the semicircular driveway in front of the imposing structure of the Steffensen home. A slight westerly breeze moved the leaves of the Norway maples, horse chestnuts, willows, and lilacs standing protectively on the front of the expanse of lawn, perfectly manicured and maintained. Rows of border flowers, purple, red, pink, and white petunias and impatiens, edged the lawn, drawing a thick line between the grass and the bricks. On either side of the steps marking the entrance grew dozens of pink roses in full bloom and, behind them, the August flowers as they were known here, rows of pink, yellow, and red gladiolus, just maturing.

Kurt Steffensen steadied his Minton china cup of steaming hot coffee on one of the small white wicker tables of the veranda. A tall man of striking attractiveness by anyone's standards, he was dressed in a distinctive quality, denying any subscription to fad, holding instead to classic tailored lines. His hair of thick light waves showed no sign of receding, although some strands of silver confirmed his fifty-eight years. Taking a quick survey of his surroundings, he noted that the rose bushes on the eastern side of the veranda had been victimized by last night's wind and would need attention. There was a peacefulness here—their home tucked away from the world but still within the city, guarded by the natural and the artificial, trees and gardens, concrete and brick.

He knew it was time for work but opted to take his coffee cup and sit comfortably on the veranda facing the garden for just a precious few minutes.

"Kurt? Are you still here?" called a soft voice from inside.

"Yes, Jaclyn. Outside," he responded.

He heard her approaching footsteps and then felt her hand on the back of his neck. "I thought you were gone to work already," she said.

"No, I thought I'd enjoy the lovely morning, if only for a moment or two." He sipped his coffee.

"Yes, it is nice. And so it should be after last night's heavy rain." She tucked her shoulder-length brown curls behind her ear and moved to the railing to stand in the sunshine. Jaclyn was nine years younger than Kurt, though assumed by many to be much younger.

They had met over eleven years ago at her art gallery in the west end of St. John's when he wanted paintings by local artists for the executive suite in his newly renovated offices. Theirs was a comfortable relationship, and their home a sanctuary.

"Listened to the news this morning while I was making coffee," Kurt said. "Charles passed away last night, so I should expect a call shortly. Jeanne has likely called Joe and Lauren already." Jeanne was Kurt's ex-wife. They had remained on somewhat civil terms since their divorce fourteen years before.

Jaclyn took in the news. "I guess it was coming, wasn't it? He's been sick for a while." She sighed and thought briefly of her own father and their strained relationship. "Still, it must be difficult for Emily and for Jeanne to lose their father."

Kurt allowed his wife's calming voice to overtake the thoughts of more recent conversations with Jeanne regarding her father's health. He knew there would be talk of inheritance and he knew, more than anyone, that it would not be easy.

Jaclyn turned back to him. "I'll be at the gallery all day, if you need me. And we should go to the funeral home tonight." She knew he would go, if only for his son and daughter, for whom he would do anything.

"Thanks, Jaclyn, I *really* appreciate that."

Kurt stood, wrapped his arms around her waist, and kissed her gently. "Well, I'd better get to work, pretty lady. I'll see you for lunch."

Jaclyn watched him as he headed down the concrete steps to his car. She thought how he exuded unwavering confidence. In his thirty years in business he demonstrated acumen to perfection. Today, he was the wealthiest man in the province, and ranked well up there in the eastern part of the country. Most men in his position would tally up the favours owed by others, but Kurt enjoyed only the company of a select few, family and those whom he considered as close as family.

He turned his deep green Jaguar left onto Waterford Bridge Road and headed east toward downtown. He adjusted the visor to block the sun over the hills to the southeast. *Such a quiet, clear morning*, he thought as he passed businesses on Water Street. *This is why I live here*. Despite his extensive travels, St. John's remained his home, a city clinging to the rocky edge of the North Atlantic facing its past to the east but eagerly anticipating the benefits that would come from newly found oil reserves. Moments later, as Kurt drove into his marked parking spot near a sign that read Steffensen Publishing and Printing, he wondered about life at the Sinclair house this morning. He paused before getting out of his car and looked at the striking red brick building in front of him that was his own. *Deaths and funerals and inheritance have a strange way of bringing to the surface some things that are better left alone*, he thought. He prayed that this would not be the case now.

* * * * *

Just a few city blocks away, in the Martel house on Stoneyhouse Street, Lindsay woke early and welcomed the cooler air. She threw back the pale blue cotton sheet and sat up. *The humidity's gone*, she thought. *Thank heavens. Perhaps there is something to this notion that the weather changes here in St. John's after the first Wednesday in August.* As she was from the west coast of the province, she had only heard townie lore from her husband, who was born and raised in St. John's. Summer weather ended with the annual rowing regatta, or so everyone said. But when September temperatures exceeded those in the rest of the country, local residents were convinced that was why they lived there, and relished pointing that out to visitors.

She took a quick glance at the clock radio that signalled 6:46 a.m. and decided she'd done enough lazing around in bed. She got up, being careful not to disturb Steven, on vacation from his job as a provincial engineer. His greying hair was all she could see above the sheet pulled up tightly around him. She envied him. He never found it too warm or too cold. Never saw the point, he would say. For Lindsay, on the other hand, the temperature was always wrong. She had blamed it on hormones, but now that she had recently turned fifty-six, she wondered how much longer she could use that excuse.

She tied her pink cotton bathrobe around her waist and headed down the carpeted stairs. The window in their bright yellow kitchen faced the clear eastern sky and the room warmed quickly in the rising sun. Lindsay opened the patio door off the dining room to allow Mollie, their tricoloured collie, to go outside. She poured water into the coffee maker, emptied a package of coffee into the brown plastic cup, and inserted it, flicking the switch. She opened the door of the breadbox and pulled out a loaf of whole wheat bread and sighed as she sliced it. *When did the world turn against white bread and ruin my mornings?* She switched on the small clock radio to the right of the stove and heard a feature on housing starts in the city, on the rise because of the potential oil boom.

"Finally, in the news this morning, well-known St. John's businessman Charles Robertson Sinclair passed away last night at the age of eighty-five. Left to mourn are his two daughters, Emily and Jeanne, and a large circle of family and friends. The funeral service is scheduled for Friday morning at eleven a.m. from the Anglican Cathedral . . ."

Ah, Lindsay thought as she poured her coffee, *poor old dear. If Phyllis were here, she'd probably say he'd gotten his trial over.* Phyllis was Lindsay's sister-in-law, who tended to see everything in life through one lens: a dark one. Lindsay spread a thick layer of three-fruit marmalade across the two half slices of toast and wondered how she could burn off the calories during the day. *Fifty-six and I'm still feeling guilty about calories. Will I ever stop doing that?* She clicked off the radio, took her coffee and remaining half slice of toast, and joined Mollie on the back deck. She gingerly lodged her breakfast on the small wooden table and went back to the kitchen to get a thick towel to wipe the heavy dew off the Adirondack chairs.

Moments later, Lindsay heard her daughter's familiar voice. "Mornin'! Lovely one." Lindsay nodded. Sandi was tall and slender with a pretty smile and glistening brown eyes. She was dressed in taupe shorts and a peach T-shirt, her hair was towelled dry, and she carried her hairbrush, which was rarely far away from her. Sandi sat in the orange chair next to her mother and propped her bare feet up on the rail. She leaned back to put her face up to the sun, which was peeking through the trees in the eastern sky. "Any news this morning?"

Lindsay brushed the crumbs from her fingers. "Moose accident out in Salmonier. No one seriously hurt, thank God. S'posed to be cool in the evenings right through to the weekend. And a local man, Charles Sinclair, passed away."

Sandi kept her face to the shining rays and closed her eyes. "Who's Charles Sinclair?"

"Businessman for years. Old money, and lots of it. He owned stores on Water Street back in the days when that was the only place to shop. In later years, I think he was involved in shipping. I'm not sure, but your father would know. Anyway, he passed away last night."

"Ah, too bad. That'll likely be a big funeral. Did he leave a wife or children, grandchildren?"

"His wife predeceased him, according to the announcer, but he has two daughters. I'm guessing they'd be in their fifties."

"Well, we won't have to worry," Sandi said with a chuckle and leaned forward so that the legs of the front of the chair rested on the deck. "Not like we'll inherit his money."

"True." Lindsay stood to deadhead a basket of petunias. "So, you're meeting this young woman, Sara, for lunch?"

"Yep. Sara Russell. At a place down by the Newfoundland Hotel called Steffensen Publishing. Then we're going to lunch, likely somewhere downtown."

"Where does she work at the university, Sandi?"

"Engineering. She's a naval engineer."

"Impressive." Lindsay smiled and surveyed the backyard and wondered which of the two men of the house, Steven, or their son, Jordy, would she volunteer to mow it.

* * * * *

"Good morning, Doris! Beautiful day." Kurt greeted his longtime assistant and friend, seated at her desk not far from his own office door.

Doris McKinlay was the epitome of efficiency and organization. Kurt was always glad to see her because he knew that without her, his day would be both chaotic and humourless. For over thirty years, he had relied on her sensible opinions, although Doris always looked surprised when she was asked for them. And in his mother's absence, she kept him humble.

Kurt had started his publishing company with money given to him by his maternal grandparents and some he'd saved while in university completing a degree in English. The eldest child of two academics—his father, Christian, an English professor, his mother, Catherine, a sociologist—Kurt had developed a passion for books and wanted nothing more than to publish them. Soon after graduation, he got his wish, opening his publishing and printing company, at first on a small scale, but within a few years expanding it to a profitable business. Shrewd investments over the years had made him a wealthy man.

Widely respected for his contribution to the community, Kurt had a reputation for taking care of his employees, and anyone who walked into Steffensen Publishing could see why those who were fortunate enough to work there stayed and put everything into the company. He rarely complained of the headaches or the hours. He loved the work and it showed.

Kurt's sharp memory and attention to detail endeared him to his employees. He acknowledged them all as he passed their offices on the way to his own on the third floor. Everyone who had ever worked for him either admired and respected him or hated him. The latter, threatened by his commitment to a full day's work and standards of excellence, did not stay around.

Doris stood at his side placing letters in front of him to be signed. "Too bad about dear Mr. Sinclair. Heard it this morning on the radio."

"Hmmm. He's been sick for a long time. I have to phone Joe and Lauren."

"Before you do, you might want to call Jeanne first. She phoned about ten minutes ago."

"Thanks, Doris. Talking to Jeanne, always a good way to start my day."

Doris, recognizing her employer's sarcasm, quietly closed the door behind her.

Kurt pushed the papers away, wondering again why obligations to ex-spouses never seemed to end, and reached for the phone. He spoke briefly to Leah, Jeanne's housekeeper, before she passed the phone to Jeanne.

"Jeanne? I'm very sorry to hear about your father. How are you?"

She ignored his inquiry into her state of health, as she believed it to be superficial. "The doctors were right this time when they said just a few days. He was so weak. It has been very difficult. Not much sleep for any of us." Her voice faded momentarily. She paused as she regrouped. "But he's gone, and we move on."

"Again, I'm sorry, Jeanne." He marvelled at her usual form of faltering only momentarily. "Is Emily with you?"

"Here in town. But not staying here. She's at Father's house with that son of hers." She sighed heavily. Her disdain for Gregory, Emily's son, was obvious. "I haven't been able to reach Joe. He's at some work site."

"Okay, leave it to me. I'll track him down. Is there anything else I can do?"

"No, all the arrangements have been made."

"All right. If there is, just let me know. I'll be here all day, except . . ." and then he remembered, ". . . for lunch. In the meantime, I'll drop by the funeral home after supper."

"Yes."

Kurt hung up the phone and, before taking another call, asked Doris to phone Joe's assistant, Diana, and leave a message for his son to drop by Kurt's office before lunch if he could. He would tell him the news, if he hadn't already heard it, and ask a favour at the same time.

* * * * *

Joe Steffensen received his father's request when he checked in at his own office across the street from Steffensen Publishing around 11:00 a.m. Knowing his father appreciated his schedule, he made a

· few phone calls, checked with his fellow architect, Michael, and told him he was heading over to see his father for a few minutes. He hurried across the street and found his father in his office.

"Good day." Kurt looked up at Joe, then glanced at his watch. "Time for lunch? I'm meeting Jaclyn at the Hotel in a few minutes."

"Wish I did. But it's an impossible day, Dad. I'm just finishing a couple of projects. And I have a heritage house that I'm restoring on a very tight schedule." Joe pulled along a chair, sat back comfortably, and placed his feet on a small table in front of him.

Kurt hesitated a moment and rubbed his hands through his hair and around the back of his neck, as if to demonstrate that the topic he was about to discuss brought him as much physical anguish as it did mental. "You got the news about Charles?"

"Yes, I heard it on the radio shortly after seven, and I phoned Mother about an hour ago. She wanted me to come over, but it was impossible at the time because the contractor was waiting. Lauren was with her."

"Charles meant everything to her. It'll be very hard for her to adjust. With Emily living up in Wolfville, there's really no family around for her, except you and Lauren. 'Course, not that she and Emily were ever very close."

"I imagine there'll be a huge funeral," Joe commented, looking out the large window behind his father at the working harbour.

"Oh, I'm sure. Even those who didn't know him claim they did." Kurt chuckled. "I remember Dad once speculating if the size of a funeral was directly proportional to the size of one's heavenly reward."

Joe smiled at the reference to his paternal grandfather, Christian. He could not help but reflect on the differences between his two grandfathers. "Have you talked to Granddad and Grandma in Halifax?"

"Not yet. No one home. I called and left a message."

"Will any Sinclairs be flying down from the mainland?"

"No doubt." Kurt sighed. "There's a host of cousins in Markham." He turned in his maroon leather chair. "Charles Robertson Sinclair," he said with emphasis. "Never easy to get along with, to put it mildly."

He let out a chuckle. "The only thing he ever liked about me was my bank account. It was so much like his, I guess, except, of course, his money was crumpled; mine is crisp. But, then, he always thought he had the edge over me. How many times did he tell me how easy it is to make money these days as compared to what it was like fifty years ago when he started?"

"Now it doesn't matter," Joe observed.

"Indeed."

"I wonder what Mother and Emily will do about the house?" Joe shifted his feet. "That's quite a place. Emily's been talking about renovations for years. God knows it needs work. I doubt that any substantial repairs have been done."

"I have no idea," Kurt said. "Depends on who inherits the place, I s'pose. That person will decide."

Joe wondered momentarily at his father's remark, since it seemed obvious to him that the two daughters would equally inherit the estate. But he dismissed the thought quickly.

"Are Emily and Gregory staying with Mother?"

"Emily's been staying at the Sinclair home ever since the doctor checked out Charles a couple of weeks ago and found his condition deteriorating. Gregory's only been here a couple of days. Jeanne will be content to put them both on the plane, I'm sure. Unfortunately, knowing Gregory, he'll want the will read immediately just to see what's in it for him."

"I assume you mean whatever Emily gets, Gregory gets?"

"Exactly," Kurt responded. "That house was originally owned by Virginia's family, the Bolands, so they'll come out of the woodwork. I'm sure Jeanne will be devastated to see anyone else live there in the house where she grew up. Although her memories have always been rather selective—about everything, for that matter." He was alluding to his ex-wife's perspective on their marriage breakup but did not elaborate, knowing that his son understood.

"Mother already has a house," Joe declared.

Kurt smiled at his son sardonically. "Joe, a Sinclair house beats a Steffensen house any day; you should know that. Maybe she'll use one as her summer home," he said with a smile. "Anyway, on a serious note, the funeral is Friday at two o'clock."

Joe stood to leave. "Okay, I'll clear my schedule."

"Oh yes, just one other thing before you go. I talked to Lauren just before you got here. She wants us to meet at the funeral home, too. Tonight, around seven. I said I would, and I'd mention it to you."

Joe looked at his father and then away. He was going to make the point that Charles never cared much for either of them when he was alive, but he knew his father needed no reminding of that. "I'll meet you there."

"Thanks, Joe. Talk to you later." Kurt's tone reflected his relief. He knew it would not be easy for any of them and no one, not even Kurt Steffensen, would spend too much time in the company of Jeanne Sinclair without a witness, even at the best of times, and this was certainly not one of those.

*　*　*　*　*

Worried that Sara would be waiting for her, Sandi was relieved to find a parking spot in front of Steffensen Publishing. She had never been inside the unique building, although she had walked by it once and peered into the wide foyer behind the double glass doors. She stood on the busy sidewalk and observed the passersby, but after ten minutes there was still no Sara. Glancing at her watch again, she turned to the entrance of the building and decided today was her chance to become familiar with the interior.

So bright and airy, all natural light, she thought, as she pushed back the right glass door and held it for a young man who was exiting. The plants, indoor trees, and fountain immediately grabbed her attention. *But an unusual design.* In front of her, the expanse of the foyer led off in three directions. At the far end stood a pair of glass elevators and a directory. She stepped quickly to catch one of the two elevators.

The doors opened again, this time on the third floor. She found herself at the end of a skywalk to her right and a lounge to her left.

The lounge was decorated in shades of blue with splashes of plum and white. Flowering plants of a variety of sizes, shapes, and colours adorned every corner and crevice, and local art filled the walls. The intersections of the hallways were marked by alcoves with small tables neatly laden with books and magazines. *Nice place to spend the after-noon reading,* she thought, as she turned right, slowing down only long enough to observe her surroundings. Then, checking the time, she hurried across the skywalk, with its ceiling-to-floor tinted glass on either side. Some of the windows were open and a gentle cool breeze blew in. Looking through the glass, she took in the expanse of executive office space with walls of glass bricks and wooden beams. *What a place! Kurt Steffensen sure knows how to pick a building for his publishing company. Okay, there's Editorial over there.* She turned corners and followed the doors to the end of the hall, looking for the name of Ruth Ann Pike. It was not to be found. She came to another intersection of halls, a large open area that was alive with activity, and veered slightly left to ask directions. The young man behind the counter had the face of an adolescent boy. He was short and wiry and he was desperately trying to present an air of self-confidence that would suggest he owned the place.

Farthest away to her left was a huge glass-topped desk with papers and folders neatly organized. An older woman, with cropped light brown hair, sat staring at a computer monitor with great concentration and typing furiously on the computer keyboard. On her right shoulder rested the telephone receiver, and she carried on a conversation as if idle. The nameplate on her desk read Doris McKinlay. Behind her, two large doors of birch framed the engraved name, Kurt M. Steffensen. A title was not listed; it was not necessary. Everyone in the building knew him. Everyone in the province knew him.

Sandi stepped to a counter and immediately caught the attention of the young protege. "Hi, I wonder if you could give me some idea where I could find Ruth Ann Pike's office. I'm supposed to meet a friend there for lunch at noon and it's already . . ." She glanced at her watch. "Good grief, fifteen minutes past." Sandi could tell he was frazzled and was reluctant to add to his tasks.

Politely, but with marked hesitation, he replied, "Oh yes, well now, as soon as I find out myself."

"You mean even the employees can't find their way around?" Sandi laughed.

He was obviously relieved at her response and breathed a heavy sigh. "I'm sorry. I'm new here. But just a minute, I'll check my directory." He hauled a laminated floor plan of the office building from underneath a pile of paper. "Was that Pike?"

At that moment, Joe left his father's office, closed the door behind him, and glanced at Doris working at the computer just a few feet away. She turned quickly to acknowledge him with a smile. In front of him, at the counter, stood a beautiful young woman with a smile unmatched by any he had ever seen. Her dark eyes sparkled. Long brown curls cascaded down her back. Forgetting his need to hurry back to his own office, he stepped forward.

"Excuse me, but if you're looking for something or someone, I can help. I know the building."

Sandi turned and welcomed the prospect of competent assistance. She looked up slightly to meet blue eyes the colour of a summer sky. His face was wreathed with tousled thick blond hair, swept back at the sides, with just a little covering the top of his ears. His smile revealed the whitest teeth. A wave of infatuation swept from the top of her head to her toes. She prayed it didn't show.

"Thanks, I'd really appreciate it. I'm supposed to be meeting a friend at Ruth Ann Pike's office."

"No problem, I'll show you. Come with me."

Sandi felt the light touch of his hand on her arm as they headed off in the opposite direction from where she had come, and a tingle followed the earlier wave. She walked with her guide for several minutes down a long corridor and noticed that several employees spoke to him or nodded in recognition. She assumed he worked there and in an important position.

"It's my first time in this building. It's beautiful, but it is a very strange design," she commented.

"You think so? I thought it was quite innovative and comfortable. What do you think is wrong with it?" His blue eyes glistened as he smiled at her.

Sandi hoped that he wasn't noticing her stare. *It's the eyes. No, maybe the blond hair. Perhaps the shoulders?* She finally managed, "Well, I don't know much about building design, but it's quite different, the layout I mean. Like the architect couldn't make up his mind. Or her mind."

"About what?"

"About whether it should be compartmentalized or open and spacious."

"So he allowed for both."

"Perhaps. Bit of a contradiction, don't you think?"

"Trying to please everyone, allowing for private meetings and open communication, when needed."

"Okay, that's one way of looking at it. But I do love the glass and all the plants and flowers. Even if the rest of it is strange."

He changed the subject. "So you're meeting a friend. Does she work here?"

Sandi shook her head. "No, a friend who had some business with Ruth Ann this morning. We are on the same committee at the university. We decided to meet downtown, and since she wasn't sure where she would be and when, I decided to meet her here. Her name is Sara Russell."

"You're kidding!" He stopped and laughed. "How long have you known her?"

"Just a few weeks. I met her at the university. Why? Do you know her?"

He grinned and looked away. "Perhaps better than anyone. We grew up together. We go back a long way . . . as friends."

Sandi noted that he emphasized *as friends* and wondered why.

"Sara and I went right through school together. She plays a mean game of squash." They stopped in front of a door with the name R. Pike—Editorial Assistant on it. While he spoke, Sandi tried to memorize every detail of his appearance so she could later recall them for Sara. Tailored navy blue cotton pants and a French blue Oxford shirt.

No chains, no earring, no visible tattoos. His jewellery was limited to a watch on his left arm. It looked like a Rolex. No rings, particularly on the left hand. She noted that. *This guy has nothing to prove and no one to impress.*

The office door was open slightly, but there was no one in sight. Across the hall was a small waiting area with chairs of plush plum upholstery and light wooden armrests. Sandi turned away from the door. "I guess I may as well wait here. Thanks so much for your help." She gave her most beautiful smile and turned her head ever so slightly to look up into his eyes. She longed to ask him some personal questions, but she refrained. He paused, still looking at her, then spoke finally. "You're quite welcome. It's been a pleasure. So long." He, too, wanted to ask her some questions, beginning with *are you seeing someone*, but he resisted. As he turned and walked away, she wondered if her budding friendship with Sara Russell would ever put her in his company again. She sat and gazed at the pilot boat heading out the entrance of the harbour.

"Sandi! Hi! I've been looking all over."

Sara's voice startled Sandi back to reality. Sandi stood to meet her friend as she walked into the lounge. She had beautifully styled short, dark hair and deep brown eyes. Despite her small frame, she had a real presence.

"Sara, I got lost. What a spot this is!"

"Really something, isn't it? I worked here when I was a student. Loved it. Anyway, I dropped off the stuff for Ruth Ann and there's no problem to get it done when we need it, so let's go to lunch. There's a great place down the street and it shouldn't be too busy today."

They made for the crowded elevator, and when they reached the main floor, they headed across the foyer and outside, where a warm westerly breeze blew gently up Duckworth Street. Sandi recounted her trip through the Steffensen building, which was, as it turned out, the longest way around. "Well, I knew something was wrong when I saw an office door with Kurt Steffensen's name on it."

"You *were* lost."

"Steffensen. Where does that name come from?"

"Northern Europe. Specifically Norway. But Kurt is a Newfound-lander. It's his father who's from Norway originally, though he and his wife, Catherine, live in Halifax. Catherine is a Newfoundlander, as was her family for several generations. Her father was a businessman and her mother . . . well, let's just say she was what today we'd call an activist. She was big into women's rights."

"Interesting. By the way, I ended up with a guided tour to Ruth Ann's office. He was a friend of yours. A great-looking guy, deep blue eyes . . . unfortunately, he didn't tell me his name. Clothes that are a perfect fit. Seems like everybody knew him. He told me you went to school with him and that you're long-time friends."

"Blond hair?"

"Yep."

Sara laughed as she pulled open the restaurant door. "Sandi," she said, shaking her head, "you had quite the escort."

"Really?"

Sara's eyes lit up. "That was none other than Joe Steffensen, Kurt's one and only son."

"You're kidding!"

"He's an architect. You haven't been long in St. John's, but believe me, you'll hear his name as much as his dad's. He designed the build-ing you just got lost in."

Sandi came to a halt. "No, Sara, tell me that's not true." She put her hand up to her face. "Would you believe I just insulted him about the design of the building? I told him that the architect couldn't make up his mind."

"Don't worry about it. I'm sure he didn't take offence." Sara waved her on.

"So that's Joe Steffensen. He certainly won't want to talk to me again."

"I wouldn't say that."

"So, let me guess, he's gay."

"Nope."

"Okay, then he's married with kids in daycare."

"Nope." Sara laughed and shook her head. "Not yet."

Sandi and Sara settled comfortably at a small round table in front of the window. A white curtain halfway up the frame provided them with privacy from passersby outside.

"I remember you telling me that you live close to the university?" Sara asked.

"Yes, on Stoneyhouse Street near Churchill Square, but I hope to find my own place sometime during the winter, when things settle down. How 'bout you?"

"Not too far away, on Portugal Cove Road. Got an apartment. My family lives across from you on the other side of the Square, but the truth is, I don't exactly get along with them. I moved out as soon as I started university, with a lot of help from some friends, Kurt being one of them. That's a long story." Sara sat back, sighed loudly, and stared out the window. "Then, I made the biggest mistake of my life. I married a total jerk."

Sandi's eyes widened in surprise at her friend's assessment but couldn't help but laugh at the description.

"Sorry, Sandi. Forgive me for being cynical. I'm going through a divorce right now and it's not pleasant."

"So, when will the divorce be final?"

"Now, there's a question. I dunno. I guess when the lawyers make enough money. I really wish it were all over now, but it looks like it's going to take a while. Raymond figures he's entitled to everything. I'm letting my lawyer handle it all and, of course, I've got Kurt and Quentin around to give me advice, fortunately. I don't know what I'd do without them."

"Quentin?"

"Quentin Henderson. He's a lawyer and a good friend."

"How long have you known him?"

"Since we were four. We're all the same age. In fact, I sat next to Joe in kindergarten at Brenton Elementary School. Alphabetical order, R and S. There's a fourth, by the way. His name's David Gilchrist. He's a cardiac surgeon here now. So, back in school, Quentin and David were across the table, G and H. In those days here, the kids you started kindergarten with, you pretty much ended up with through school. In high school, we deliberately chose the same classes for our own sanity. They've been my three closest friends all my life."

"Three guys."

"Yeah. Great, hey? Speaking of men, last week when we had coffee, didn't you mention something about a guy you lived with in Halifax?"

"Yep. Shawn and I lived together after Christmas till I moved here. We've known each other since we started university together. Then he went off to medical school. He's got a practice now in Halifax."

"So, what happened?"

"I got the faculty position at Memorial. And there was nothing available at Dalhousie or any other university. I could have gotten contractual work, sessional stuff, but MUN advertised a tenure-track position, so I applied."

"You had to leave Shawn. That must have been rough."

"It was when I left, but that was four months ago. A long-distance relationship wasn't going to work. Anyway, enough of that. Tell me more about your three friends."

Sara placed her napkin across her lap in preparation for the plate of cheeseburger and French fries being placed in front of her, and reached automatically for ketchup. "The four of us depend on each other a lot. We spend a fair bit of time together. To be honest, I can't imagine my life without them. It was hard when Joe and Quentin were in Halifax in university and David was in Boston doing his residency."

"Joe Steffensen seemed really nice, the few minutes I spent with him. Although stupid me had to insult his architectural design. My mother would tell me I speak before I think. I guess with his family's money, he's had it easy."

"Financially it was easy. His father owns that publishing company outright. And he owns a lot of other stuff, too. Made money investing over the years: oil, hydro, land, you name it. So there's money there, and Joe is doing really well with architecture. As a renovator, he does a lot of research into original design and historic materials. He's even won national awards already." She bit down into the cheeseburger and watched it fall apart in front of her on the plate, then proceeded to construct it again. "We, the four of us, practically grew up at the Steffensen house. I needed to get away from home, David's parents are both doctors, so they were never home, and as for Quentin, well . . . both his parents were killed in a car accident when he was fourteen."

Sandi looked up from her chef salad. "Oh my, how sad!"

"He doesn't talk about it much, but it was terrible, Sandi. I remember it like yesterday. Tony and Celia were on their way home on a Sunday afternoon, on the highway just east of Whitbourne, when it happened. They weren't killed instantly, but they died in the hospital shortly after." Sara spoke quietly and with obvious remnants of pain. "It was really rough on Quentin and his sister, Stephanie."

"How tragic! But Quentin did fine getting through Dal law school?"

"Yes, there was some life insurance money. Actually, not many know this, but Kurt was the one who paid for most of Quentin's education and helped him set up a law practice when he graduated. The boat I designed that I told you about? He's giving me warehouse space to build it in. And he's been really helpful through this divorce mess."

"What about his wife, Joe's mother?"

"Ex-wife. They're divorced. Kurt married again. Jaclyn is a nice lady, quite gracious and gentle. But Jeanne, Joe's mother, never had a lot of time for any of us. We always had the feeling we were messing up her precious house. Granted it was a beautiful place and we were there all the time, four teenagers plus Lauren, Joe's younger sister, and her friends. Kurt never seemed to mind. Must have been a distraction from Jeanne, or better yet . . ." Sara's eyes sparkled with the thought, ". . . a source of irritation to her."

"What does Joe's sister do?"

"Lauren's a lawyer. Looks like her grandmother Steffensen. The guys tease her mercilessly sometimes for being, shall we say, well looked after. But she's the centre of the universe for her father and her husband, Alan. She and Alan were married three years ago."

"I've read Alan's columns. Great stuff! Do Joe and Lauren get along with their mother?"

"They're civil most of the time, until she tries to run his life or

Lauren's, then it gets nasty. I think it was one of the things that ended Kurt and Jeanne's marriage. I remember when Lauren decided she wanted to be a lawyer. Jeanne wanted her to stay home and find a young man. Instead, Lauren went to law school and met Alan, who was doing graduate work with Christian, Lauren and Joe's grandfather. Jeanne's never liked Alan, for whatever reason. Not sure she needs one. They've all sort of gotten accustomed to her, Sandi, like people do with mothers. You learn what to say and how to say it. Tone is more important to a mother than content."

Sandi laughed and shook her head at her friend's candour. "Good point. So, neither Quentin nor David are married?"

Sara laughed. "No. Never have been. I think if either one of us would be married it would be David. He deserves someone wonderful, but he spends most of his life at the hospital. So I guess he figures that wouldn't be fair."

"And Quentin?"

Sara laughed. "There's only a few of us on planet earth who can put up with him. I'm not going to attempt to describe him to you. You'll have to meet him." Sara grinned at the failed attempt to categorize Quentin. "But Joe, he's a great guy. He's got high expectations of himself and of everyone else around him. He's self-confident about his work, but he hasn't been successful when it comes to relationships. He needs someone like himself."

"Don't we all," Sandi commented, pensively.

* * * * *

The news of the passing of Charles Sinclair spread quickly around the city, but in the community of Falcon Cove, a four-hour drive from St. John's, word of his death was either not heard or ignored, as it did not have any impact on lives there. With one exception. Reverend Carrie West picked up a copy of the St. John's *Telegram* on her way home from a nearby community on Wednesday afternoon and saw a "special obituary" at the top of the second page. She glanced at it and tossed it on the passenger's seat. At home in their kitchen, she read the story to her mother, Hannah, whom she had lived with in the family home for the past four years. She spoke softly. "He passed away at home, it seems. His two daughters, Emily and Jeanne, were at his bedside. The funeral is Friday at the Cathedral at 11:00 a.m." Carrie looked up from the paper and focused on her mother, who was sitting across the kitchen table finishing a crossword puzzle in the local TV guide. She studied her mother for some visible response, but none came.

"I'm sure it will be a large funeral," Carrie commented.

"Yes, no doubt," came the only reply.

"Are you all right, Mother?"

"Yes, fine," Hannah answered. But Carrie knew otherwise.

CHAPTER 2

Hannah slipped quietly onto the nearest wooden chair in the kitchen of the Sinclair home. She twisted around and ran her fingers up and down the spindles that formed the back of the chair. "Mrs. Sinclair leaves lights on, even when she leaves the room. Can you imagine, Mrs. Green, leaving lights on?"

Alva Green smiled. Alva had worked for the Sinclairs for four years, and before that for the Boland family. She was in charge of the household, and she and her husband, Lawrence, had been the first to greet Hannah when she arrived at the wharf in St. John's two days ago.

"This place is very different from Falcon Cove, Hannah," she said, as she picked up the silver creamer and gently buffed its surface. "You'll have to get used to it."

"It is *so* different. We don't have electric lights or running water, either. Or the kind of food like you have here. Nothin' about this place is like Falcon Cove. Nothin'," Hannah said wistfully, as she looked around the kitchen. She wondered what her mother would think of the oak wainscotting and deep green paint, the lined curtains that covered the windows from the ceiling to the floor. The kitchen, she decided, was larger than the whole downstairs of their house in Falcon Cove.

"Hmm. By the way, you're Methodist, aren't you?" Alva asked, glancing up from her task to check the time.

Hannah nodded.

"Good, then you can come to church with Lawrence and me on Sunday."

"Thank you. That would be nice. I saw the church when you and Mr. Green picked me up and we drove back here. I recognized it from a picture Mrs. Blake—that's our minister's wife—had. She told Adelia and me that it's called the mother church, Gower Street. Mrs. Blake is from here and she's so proud of her home church, as she calls it."

"Yes, that's right, it is. Who's Adelia?"

"She's my best friend back home. We've always been friends. 'Course, Adelia's not at all like me. Adelia just goes through the days. Nothin' ever bothers her. And she's never afraid or lonely. Once, when we were just kids, we were copying down near the bridge, and Adelia went too far out and got stranded on a pan of ice, and I had to go get Pop and my brother Toby to come rescue her. All she did was laugh. I told her she'd live to be a hundred because she never has fear in her heart."

Alva laughed at the inflection in Hannah's voice that sent the last syllable of each word high into the air. "Good for her. Adelia sounds like a lovely friend girl to have."

"Mrs. Blake said there's nothing to be afraid of, anyway, if we remember the story of Daniel in the lion's den."

"Mrs. Blake is right."

Hannah paused to think on that and declined to admit that she was afraid, sometimes, anyway, even when she thought of Daniel. Then, she stood. "I almost forgot. Mrs. Sinclair wanted me to dust the shelves in Mister's room after I got Emily to sleep. Where would I find a cloth?"

Alva pointed to the cupboard by the back door. "In the bottom drawer." Preoccupied with her polishing, she neglected to tell Hannah to wait until the Sinclairs were gone out before she ventured into the study. Hannah was gone before she could mention it.

At the end of the hallway, Hannah stood momentarily at the

large wooden door, then gingerly turned the shiny brass knob and slowly pushed it open. She hadn't been inside the room and was curious about it. She was surprised to find two lights on, and even more surprised to find Charles Sinclair sitting behind the desk at the far side of the room, between two tall, heavily draped windows. The desk, made of deep mahogany, was covered with papers and ledgers on top of a black leather ink blotter. A lamp with a brown shade shone across the desk. The sound of the door caused him to look up.

Hannah stood frozen in the doorway. "Oh, I'm very sorry, sir. But Mrs. Sinclair said to dust the shelves in here, and I thought while little Miss Emily was asleep I'd take care of that, but I didn't know you'd be here, and I'll leave again . . ." she gasped for breath.

"It's fine," he said with a half smile. "Hannah, isn't it?"

"Yes, sir."

"Go ahead, Hannah. You're not bothering me."

"Thank you," she replied weakly, and went about her work.

At his desk, Charles momentarily laid down his pen and watched the young girl as she methodically moved the cloth across the leather-bound books on each shelf. *Good worker*, he thought. *Rare these days. And a pretty smile.*

"Do you like it here, Hannah?"

She kept on dusting as she answered, "Oh yes, it's a beautiful house."

"I meant, would you rather live in St. John's than in your home? Falcon Cove?"

She stopped and turned around to face the desk. "I haven't really thought about that, sir. St. John's is a big place and it has so much. I met a girl who lives a few doors down. Her name is Caroline and she says she's going to take me lawn bowling. Can you believe it? I've never been." She shook her cloth. "But I miss my family."

"You are close?"

Hannah didn't understand the question. *How can a family not be? But then there's that crowd down harbour.* She feigned an answer. "Yes, I guess I am."

"Then you are very fortunate."

Later that night, as she lay in bed, Hannah's mind raced through the events of the past two days, of meeting the Sinclairs and the rest of the staff. It was all so different from what she was used to. Warm rooms. Lights. Fruit and vegetables she had never seen before. Linen tablecloths, shiny crystal and silverware. She would have to tell her sister, Frances, that women like Mrs. Sinclair had a separate drawer full of gloves, day gloves and night gloves. Frances would be impressed with that.

Tonight's encounter with Charles Sinclair left Hannah puzzled. He looked so hurt when he made that comment about her being fortunate. She wondered why. She turned in the bed, closed her eyes tightly, and prayed for everyone at home. Then she opened her eyes and thought of Adelia. She smiled and folded her hands over her heart under the layers of the softest sheets and blankets she could ever imagine. "I hope my fear goes away soon, Adelia," she whispered in the darkness, "because if not, I'm afraid my heart will burst."

* * * * *

AUGUST 1995

Joe's memories of his grandparents preoccupied him as he drove to the funeral home that evening. As a child, he and his younger sister, Lauren, visited them with their parents on Sunday evenings. His grandfather regularly complained that they were messing up the house, making too much noise, or causing unnecessary work for the household staff. Their grandmother, Virginia, insisted that Lauren sit and be quiet. Joe's most vivid recollection was his first Christmas Eve home from university. His mother asked him to have dinner with the Sinclair family and he gave in reluctantly, only because Lauren begged him to come along. His grandfather was especially belligerent that night. Over a dinner of overcooked stuffed cod, Joe listened as Charles criticized him for choosing a career of "drawing houses" instead of business "like a man." He remained silent at the dinner table, staring at a spot in front of his plate, but, when the meal finished, he followed his grandfather into the living room, and privately told him exactly what he thought of him, his business, and his opinions. The conversation became loud and nasty. Lauren suggested that they leave and quickly got their coats as their mother stood quietly by the door. Charles never forgave Joe for that display, and any affection that Joe had for his maternal grandfather all but disappeared.

Now, as Joe searched for a parking spot at the funeral home, he thought about them both, Virginia, a grandmother who never so much as hugged him in his life, and Charles, who had taken every opportunity to remind him that he could never live up to the Sinclair name. He greeted his mother and Emily just inside the frosted glass doors and quickly sought out Lauren and Alan on the opposite side of the room. Kurt and Jaclyn stood nearby, admiring an arrangement of flowers sent from Steffensen Nurseries in Halifax, a business owned by Kurt's brother and sister-in-law, Peter and Katie.

Moments later, Sara, Quentin, and David arrived together and searched for familiar faces as they entered the room. Quentin paused to speak to several people who knew him, including the Sinclair family lawyer, Jonathan Hamlyn. When he joined them on the far side of the room, Jaclyn immediately sensed Quentin's discomfort at being in a funeral home. Through the past eleven years, she had come to know and understand Quentin as well as anyone could. He was, first and foremost, a brilliant lawyer, having graduated top of his class from Dalhousie Law School with a specialty in contract law. But Jaclyn also saw a young man who was forced to grow up quickly at the age of fourteen, and since that time railed against change at every turn. Perhaps he had earned the right to be that way. She knew he had a steadfast sense of loyalty to the few whom he counted as his friends. Ironically, he also had the type of personality that drew everyone, even strangers, to confide in him, and he held their deepest secrets.

"Ever notice how clean funeral homes are?" Quentin asked, looking around the room, struggling to find some humour in the situation. "Place is spotless."

"What would you expect, Quentin? Not like they should be going for a lived-in look." David's dry wit was the predictable follow-up to Quentin.

"No, but everything is so precise. Even the tissues stand up in the same formation in every tissue box. See that? Who has that job of ensuring the tissues stand up? Is that a stressful job, I wonder?" He smiled, raised an eyebrow in wonder, and moved closer to Jaclyn and Sara.

Meanwhile, Joe poked Sara's arm. "The woman you met down at Dad's office today." He sighed heavily. "Beautiful. Long dark hair. Tall. Who is she?"

"Ah, you mean Sandi. I wondered how long it would take for you to ask," she said with a grin. "Her name is Sandi Martel. A doctorate in political philosophy from Dalhousie."

"Dal? Really?"

"Yep. But the family's from here. She works at MUN. Just got hired tenure-track in the spring."

"Look out, here comes the family politician," Alan said, only loud enough for those closest to him to hear. Joe's conversation with Sara was cut short when he noticed his cousin, Gregory Sinclair, bustling through the crowd toward them. Kurt had once dubbed him "the politician," despite the fact he was a medical doctor, simply because Gregory could work a room with amazing superficiality. The title had stuck.

"Uncle Kurt!" Gregory made it more of an announcement than a greeting. His booming voice filled the room. He followed it with a hefty handshake and nodded to the others. "Greetings, all," he puffed, out of breath as he spoke.

Short and stocky, Gregory bore little resemblance to the Sinclair family. He had inherited his looks from his father, a man whom Emily had met over thirty years ago. Joe and Lauren had no recollection of him, as he disappeared from all of their lives shortly after Gregory was born. Gregory's hair, a version of a brush cut, was greying prematurely. He was stuffed into a navy blue suit, white shirt, and blue striped tie. His fat cheeks spilled out over his collar. When Gregory spoke, he rocked back and forth on his feet and rested his hands on his suit lapels. After thirty-six years, he had become a caricature of himself.

"Gregory, nice to see you," Kurt said quietly, hoping his volume would be contagious.

"Grandfather looks at peace," Gregory pronounced.

Quentin glanced at Sara, rolled his eyes, and turned away.

Gregory surveyed the room and acknowledged those he considered important to know with a nod. Then he turned back to survey them all. "By the way, now that we are here, I was wondering, actually Mother and I were wondering, have either of you seen Grandfather's pocket watch? He always had it with him. Mother thought it would be nice to put it on him in the casket while he is here, and then I would take it, of course, as the eldest grandchild." He gave Joe a sharp look on the word "eldest."

David, standing nearby, shook his head and marvelled at how quickly Gregory, like many family members, vied for personal items of the deceased only a few hours after death. "Gregory, perhaps you might wait until after the funeral before you start inquiring about your inheritance," he said softly, always the voice of reason and sensibility. "This is, after all, a difficult time for your mother."

"Oh, well . . . yes . . . I was only just saying . . ." He seemed at a loss for words, as if he were learning for the first time what was appropriate to say in such circumstances. He regrouped quickly, strode across the room, and bellowed at the minister, "And how's the good reverend this evening?"

Kurt turned to his daughter and son-in-law. "Unbelievable. The boy missed his calling."

Lauren covered her laugh and Alan nodded. "I think he missed his century. He would be more at home in an Edwardian parlour."

* * * * *

On Friday morning, a cold easterly wind whipped across the concrete steps of the Anglican cathedral as Kurt and Jaclyn walked through the crowd of several dozen mourners. Kurt glanced up to see that the restoration work on the old cathedral was finally finished, after years of ugly scaffolding. Inside the cool sanctuary, they slipped quietly into a long line of pews halfway up the aisle and turned around to greet Joe, Quentin, Sara, and David. Jaclyn pulled her jacket around her and turned back to the others.

"Quite a crowd," she whispered.

Kurt nodded and responded with a serious tone. "I guess they were afraid not to come."

"Afraid?" Quentin asked.

"In these social circles, Quentin, what you don't do is more noticeable than what you do."

Quentin smiled at the observation and sought to divert his mind by focusing on everyday things. He thought back to his last conversation with Charles Sinclair, two years ago in a downtown law office, a conversation he had never shared with anyone, not even his good friend and confidant, Kurt. He now wondered if it was time for the contents of that conversation to come out. He forced the thought from his mind and leaned over to Jaclyn. "Looking lovely this morning, Ms. Peters, albeit navy is not your sexiest attire."

Jaclyn fought back a laugh, given her surroundings, and chose not to make eye contact with her young friend. Instead, she whispered, "Not here, Quentin, don't make me laugh here. But you look quite attractive in a navy suit. It appears that we match." Kurt turned back to Quentin and nodded at Jaclyn's approval.

In the front pew, Jeanne sat stoically, focusing on one leg of the communion table in front of her and trying desperately to block out where she was or the reason for being there. She had said very little to her sister on their way to church. Sitting on her right, Emily squirmed and adjusted her skirt unnecessarily, like a nervous habit.

"Jeanne," she whispered, "there are so many people here. Isn't it wonderful? Father would be so pleased."

Jeanne gave Emily a puzzled look and chose not to respond. Instead, she turned her head to look over her left shoulder. It took a minute, but she finally made eye contact with Kurt. He nodded briefly, but his face remained expressionless. She turned back, refocused on the table leg, and let her mind wander back to the beautiful sunny day in July 1957 when she and Kurt were married. Just a few feet from where she was sitting now, she had stood next to him and they exchanged vows. She was dressed in the most beautiful gown she had ever seen, bought in Montreal. It was full-length, ivory taffeta, accented by a bouquet of white roses, her favourite flower. Seeing Kurt in a black tuxedo took her breath away. She wanted everything to be perfect that day. And it was. She had fussed with the hairdresser to copy the side part worn by the actress Grace Kelly, whom she admired. She had touched up her makeup repeatedly until she was satisfied with the final stroke of red lipstick. She remembered Virginia, sitting in the first pew with an expression of amusement. Only Jeanne knew at that moment what Virginia had found so amusing.

The night of her wedding had been like no other in her life. She and Kurt danced well after midnight in the ballroom of the Newfoundland Hotel. Her midnight blue satin going-away dress with ribbon lace detail was the talk of the room. In those precious moments, no one else existed, just her and the man she adored and vowed to love forever.

Twenty years later, Kurt decided he could no longer live with her and was gone. He had told her there was no other woman and she believed him. Just a glib comment that their lives were no longer compatible. His friends were not her friends. He didn't like the way she tried to shelter their children.

And today she sat again in that church, feeling as alone as she had on the day he left.

She inhaled deeply to instill a measure of calm and tried to listen to the scripture, to the prayers, and finally to a carefully crafted eulogy given by Jonathan Hamlyn. She smiled and nodded in thanks to him when he finished. Shortly after, the minister dismissed the congregation with the words ". . . that you may do His will, working in you that which is pleasing in His sight, through Jesus Christ, to whom be glory for ever and ever."

The mourners slowly filed out through the large front entrance behind the family members. When Kurt edged closer to her, Jeanne kept her head down. She did not want to hear his voice, not now, not today.

"Jeanne," he spoke softly, "if there is anything you need done, just call. Joe, Lauren, and I are here for you. You know that."

She did not want to look at him as her eyes moistened. "Are they coming to the cemetery?"

"Yes, of course," he replied. "As am I. And Jaclyn."

"Thank you," was all she could manage.

Outside on the steps, Kurt and Jaclyn could overhear conversations of Sinclair family and friends behind them. Kurt recognized several of Charles's in-laws, relatives of his late wife, the Boland family, in attendance. Their talk was of inheritance, speculation on the contents of the will, and the fate of Charles's many business interests. Jaclyn leaned closer to Kurt and whispered, "Isn't that just a little crass and cold-hearted? Talking about the will?"

Kurt placed a protective arm around her waist as they walked across the parking lot, and he opened the passenger door for her. He whispered back with a broad smile, "Robert Frost said it best: 'And they, since they were not the ones dead, turned to their affairs.'" Inside the comfort of the car, he continued, "And not to upset Mr. Frost, but when 'their affairs' involve a few million dollars, this bunch will turn real fast."

The cemetery in the east end of the city was situated on the side of a steep incline overlooking a lake. As it was quite old, it was now the centre of a city block, surrounded on all sides by roads, hemmed in by asphalt and sidewalk that prevented its expansion. It was edged with trees that had grown much higher than the two-storey houses nearby. Fog, which had stationed itself outside the harbour throughout the morning, had made its way in, across the lake and now across the graves. Jaclyn shivered and wrapped her arm in Kurt's. Next to her, Lauren pulled her summer scarf tightly around her neck and brushed a stray tear from her cheek.

As the brief service began, Kurt focused his attention on Jeanne, stationed directly across from him, staring off into the distance, her muscles tight and her lips pursed. He had come to know her facial expressions over the years. He could see that she didn't want to acknowledge what was happening, that she was, as she used to say, simply enduring the inevitable. *How well I know you, Jeanne Amelia Sinclair,* he thought. *You are struggling so much against your feelings, railing against reality, resisting the emotions as . . . what? Unbecoming? Unnatural? You are more stoical than anyone I've ever known. You deal with this with such finesse and swiftness that most people would envy you. With not as much as a quiver. Self-restraint perfected and, yet, bereft of passion.*

To Kurt's left, Sara looked up from a final prayer to find that Quentin was no longer by her side. Her sudden looking around aroused Joe's attention. Then, as she looked up at the top of the hill to the right by the black wrought iron gate, she saw him looking down at a large grave in front of him. She remembered. They were the graves of his parents. She motioned to Joe that she would take care of it and quietly slipped away along the narrow grassy pathways up the steep incline. He did not look up but felt her presence.

"Quentin," she whispered, "the funeral's over. We can go."

"You know," he said, as he stared down, "sometimes, I can't remember their faces. I remember everything else, like sitting in the back of the car with Stephanie on our holidays. Every two hours they changed drivers. Dad taught Mom to drive just after they were married. He was proud she was such a good driver. Sara, sometimes I dig out the photos just to see their faces. Just so I'll remember."

Sara wrapped both arms around his left arm and placed her head on his shoulder. "I know, Quentin, I know. And you have such warm and wonderful memories of them. That's so much more than most people can say. Come on, now. Let's go home."

Rather than face the others, Sara turned with him in the direction of the gate and left. The sun was bright now and the wind calmer. Inside the car, it was warm. Sara watched him slowly start the car and fix his seat belt in place. She waited for him to speak. Finally, as he edged forward in the heavy traffic of Friday afternoon, he asked, "You coming back to my place, or did you want to go home?"

"Whatever you want. I don't have anything special to do. But I understand if you want to be alone."

Quentin did not answer but reached for his sunglasses and headed his car down Empire Avenue toward his own house. He needed the company of a good friend.

* * * * *

Friday evening, on returning to her father's house from the cemetery, Jeanne sought refuge in the quiet study and left Emily and Greg to handle mourners who were standing quietly in the living room, the hall, and even the kitchen. Alone, sitting there in the study, staring out at the park through the tall window, she thought about her father and the last few months of his life. *I know I was his favourite*, she thought. *He told me that, so many times.*

She looked down at her hands, which had always been so supple and manicured. Hands, the first tell-tale sign of age. Her father had said so often, "You're such a lady, my Jeanne. Look at these fine, delicate hands." She remembered their quiet times. On Sunday evenings, they would sit together and read by the fireplace in the living room. In the warm days of summer, the opened window would draw in the light westerly breeze and the smell of lilacs and roses and earth from the garden. There would be little conversation, but promptly at 4:00 p.m. she would slip quietly out of the room to arrange for tea. It would be served strong, as Charles had liked it, and Jeanne would dilute hers with extra milk. Those afternoons were the oasis of her week, a time when she was completely isolated from the world and nothing, it seemed, could go wrong. But now, she realized with a gasp of breath, she would not hear his voice again.

She squeezed her eyes shut and rested her head on the back of the chair. Kurt's words, spoken so softly to her today, played over and over in her mind. She clenched her hand tightly, pushing the emotions of hate and love together in her fist. She thought of the first time she'd seen Kurt Steffensen, when he stood tall and strong at a New Year's party at Government House. She had longed to meet him because his name had quickly travelled through their small social circle, St. John's elite who knew each other's secrets but rarely spoke of them, and who judged the rest of the community with a well-honed arrogance. The name Steffensen had not been familiar to her. It was not an old St. John's family, and they were certainly not acquaintances of her parents. But it didn't matter because he had a sophisticated charm that she had only read about as a teenager. It didn't matter who he was or wasn't, as long as some day she would be his wife. Then, and only then, would those whom she met at social occasions acknowledge her as one of them.

For the next few months she had been captivated with Kurt and held her breath in disbelief when he proposed to her. Marriage, she was told, was all she should want: two children, a son and a daughter, the perfect family, and her father steadfastly there when she needed him. In those years, she remembered, she had control over her life; she was able to make things happen despite Kurt's attempts to bring home people she didn't care to know. Now, it all seemed to be happening around her without her participation or her provocation.

She opened her eyes and came back to the reality of Kurt today at the funeral. He was just as handsome, just as charming, but no longer with her. She looked back down at her hands interlocked in anger at the thought. So much had changed. So much. She shook her head as if to shake the sentiment away. *No,* she thought, *I deserve more than that from this life.*

"Jeanne," a male voice interrupted her thoughts. She turned her head to see Jonathan standing in the doorway. Tall, thin, and always impeccably dressed, he had been the family's lawyer as long as she could remember and always there when needed. "Can I get you something?"

"No, no thank you, Jonathan. I'll be fine."

He stepped into the room, out of earshot of those in the hall. "I know this may not be a good time to mention it, but I just spoke to Emily. She would like to take care of the reading of the will as soon as possible, say early next week, if that's okay."

"Of course." Her words had double meaning. *Emily's true colours*

*are coming through now. Father has only just been buried and she wants
the will read.*

"Fine, then, I'll get back to you. In the meantime, I think it best
. . ." There was hesitancy in his voice as he looked briefly around the
room. "I think it best that you and Emily get together privately and
talk about the house, the furniture, and so on. Perhaps you can come
to some decisions on your own."

"Decisions?" Jeanne was perplexed at his suggestion.

"Yes. Please, just talk to Emily. I'll get back to you."

She nodded and turned away, and heard the door close. *The
house*, she thought, *my father's house*. It felt so good just to sit there
in the quiet of his study, to see his papers and his books as he had left
them, as she would leave them. If they would all just leave her there, in
the security of that haven, in the house that he had said would be hers.

* * * * *

Distant thunder rumbled across the north side of the bay from
Falcon Cove that evening. Strong southwesterly wind all day had suddenly died down in the late afternoon and abruptly changed to an
easterly direction, dropping the temperature quickly and stirring up
an electrical storm off the coast.

In her bedroom in a corner of the second floor of their home,
Hannah sat on the edge of her bed and looked out toward the small
islands nearby and the red and white lighthouse that stood tall in
the distance, though no longer in use. Memories of Charles flashed
through her mind. She remembered his voice, his eyes, his whisper,
the smell of his pipe tobacco, and his heavy woollen suit. *How strange
the things one remembers from so long ago.*

She stared down at the round gold piece, turned it over and over
around her fingers, and imagined for a few brief moments his fingers,
thumb and forefinger, reaching for it regularly throughout the day.
The Hamilton pocket watch had large numbers around the outside, a
twenty-four-hour time on the inside, and even a one-minute smaller
clock at the bottom. She remembered asking him how something so

small could do three things at once and he had just laughed and tucked the watch away in his vest pocket. Now she wrapped her right hand around it and squeezed so hard that the little clasp hurt the base of her middle finger. A tear slowly found its way to the edge of her cheek until it dropped on her light cotton blouse. "Goodbye," she whispered.

* * * * *

Over the past three years, a tradition had grown. Every Friday night, with rare exception, the same group of six—Joe, Quentin, Lauren, Alan, Sara, and David—met to have dinner at one of their homes. Relaxation was valued over the food. They vented their frustrations and challenged each other with the most unusual story of the week, whether in their own lives or something they had read or heard.

Tonight it was Joe's turn to host. With the rush of the day behind him, he prepared baked Atlantic salmon, drizzled with butter and lemon, placed six baking potatoes in the oven, sliced a loaf of multigrain bread, unwrapped brie, and tossed together his sister's favourite spinach and strawberry salad. By 7:00 p.m., the six friends were sitting around the dining room table in front of a large picture window overlooking the city's east end. In the distance, they could see Steffensen Publishing and, to the right, Signal Hill, the Battery, and, above it all, Cabot Tower, watching over the city and the Atlantic Ocean beyond.

"I really don't like funerals," Lauren said, as she carefully moved a large portion of the salad to her dinner plate.

"No one *likes* funerals, Lauren." David broke open his baked potato and gingerly scraped out the inside. After late rounds at the hospital, he was glad to have the chance to unwind.

"I know that, David. But what I mean is, I can't help but get upset, no matter who it is. And frankly, I wasn't that close to my grandfather. I watched Mother today and Aunt Emily. I don't think either of them shed a tear."

"Some people prefer to grieve in private, Lauren."

Quentin returned from the kitchen with more butter because,

in his view, there is never enough butter for baked potatoes. He had changed from his blue suit to his favourite casual attire, blue cotton pants and a striped blue and yellow rugby shirt. The colour blue was Quentin's signature. "That's one explanation, Blondie," he said, using his favourite nickname for her. He plopped two tablespoons of butter in the middle of his steaming potato and sprinkled it generously with salt and pepper. "What an event that was today! At one point I hardly knew who they were talking about. Enough praise to get Charles through eternity, I figure," Quentin quipped.

Lauren took a small sip of white wine. Gingerly returning the glass to its place on the table, she shook her head in disgust. "I don't know what you were expecting, Quentin. Okay, so the man never cared much for us, especially after my parents' divorce. But his daughter, who had been married for twenty years, had been left alone. Some would say he had every right to be upset with Dad, given that he left his wife after twenty years."

"Yes, there she was, left to fend for herself, to eke out an existence, in that two-storey, four-bedroom house on Exeter. Rough living. Say nothing of the thousands in alimony." Quentin's blatant honesty was not what Lauren wanted to hear.

She continued. "Houses and money do not compensate for hurt, Quentin."

"Sara," Joe said, wanting to change the topic, and taking a mouthful of salmon.

"Yes, Joe." She answered just as emphatically, with a grin, predicting what was coming.

"You didn't get a chance to finish your description of the friend you met at the publishing company. Greg interrupted, remember?" Joe laid down his fork before he continued. "I met her briefly and I forgot to introduce myself. But I did show her around the building."

"Oh yes, she mentioned that to me."

"Oh, she did?" His deep blue eyes lit up as he made a poor attempt to hide his enthusiasm.

Quentin continued. "Oh God, Sara, did you have to say that? There'll be no end to this. You know what he's like."

"Well, she said you showed her to Ruth Ann's office when she got lost."

"Is that all she said?"

"What else do you expect her to say? That she wants to have your baby?"

"Just tell me everything you know about her." He picked up his fork and resumed eating.

Sara sighed and refilled her wineglass. "I met her a few weeks ago at a committee meeting in the university, the local Canadian University Women's group. She teaches political philosophy. She's pretty bright, and the stuff she's doing, the research, is great. Apparently, her dissertation won a national humanities award."

"Impressive. And I notice she's not married. At least she's not wearing a wedding ring."

"No, she's not."

"Well, c'mon, then, Sara, tell me more. Is she seeing anyone now?"

Sara was reluctant. "Joe, I don't want to gossip. Sandi is a friend and I'm just getting to know her. I don't feel right talking to you about her personal stuff."

"Sara, for God's sake, I'm not asking for intimate details, just, is she serious about anyone? That's all."

"I believe that's covered under the Freedom of Information Act," Quentin interjected, without looking up, and clearly enjoying his meal.

"Okay, okay, relax. She was serious about a doctor in Halifax."

"Was?"

"Well, he's there and she's here. It's kind of difficult to keep up a long-distance relationship. I think she lived with him for a while. But now that she's back here, I think it's over. At least that was the impression I got when I had lunch with her."

"Back here? Is she from here originally?"

"She was born here, but she grew up in Halifax. Her mother is from Corner Brook and her father is from St. John's. Her father is an engineer with the provincial government. They moved back here last year, I think. Her mother taught primary school in Halifax, but she's retired after about thirty years. Sandi's got one brother, Jordy. He's likely younger, 'cause he's still in university. There, that's all I know."

"So, do you think she'd consider seeing someone else now that this thing with the doctor is over?"

"I can't say. You could ask. What have you got to lose?"

Quentin had just taken a bite of his salmon but still asked, "His ego?"

"Actually, I'll be talking to her on Monday. She's coming over to my place on Monday night. We have a proposal to work on. If you like, I can mention that you want to see her again. Or better yet, why don't you drop by?"

Quentin finished eating and sat back. "There you are, all set up, Joe. What more can you ask for? God, some men have it so easy. Then again, some need to have it that way."

"Thanks, Sara. I'll be there, Monday night." Joe ignored Quentin and the round of *ooohhhhs* from others at the table.

* * * * *

On Sunday morning, Jeanne was relieved to say goodbye to the last of her cousins who had come from out of town for the funeral. Although it was lunchtime and she hadn't had any breakfast, she didn't have much appetite. She forced herself to sit at the small round table set for her in the solarium, but her lunch was soon interrupted by the arrival of her sister. Emily was clearly overdressed for the season in dark pants and layers of matching blouse and cardigan. Jeanne noticed for the first time that she had given up colouring her hair.

"Emily. I wasn't expecting to see you today. You said you wanted to rest."

"I thought you were coming down to the house."

"No, not today. I prefer to stay here." Jeanne responded without making eye contact.

Emily slipped off her sweater and joined her sister at the table, while Leah, Jeanne's housekeeper, hurriedly set another place. "I told

Leah I would have some lunch, if that's okay. I hate to eat alone. Gregory left this morning on that awful early flight. I feel like I've been up forever. I had breakfast with him early."

Jeanne chose to ignore her sister's speech. Only Virginia had been able to get Emily to stop droning on and on, and only then by firmly stating her name with a slight inflection on the last syllable.

"It was a wonderful funeral, Jeanne. Beautiful."

"Mmm." Jeanne hoped a disinterested tone would deter Emily's third recap since Friday.

But Emily continued. "Everyone said Father would be so proud of us, you and me."

The word struck Jeanne as an odd choice. "Proud?"

"We handled everything well, didn't we?"

"Oh." Jeanne wanted to tell her how Charles had planned every detail meticulously since Virginia's death, but she chose not to break the delusion.

"I hope when our time comes, we can do the same for each other."

Jeanne wondered at the absurdity of the statement, but again let it go.

"This is wonderful soup, Jeanne. Delicious. By the way, I spoke with Kurt at the service. He was quite gracious. Of course, he always was a kind and gentle man. He's always been quite gracious to me. His wife—Jaclyn, is it?—she extended her condolences. I thought that was quite civil, don't you? I mean, she didn't have to. She didn't have to say anything. Goodness, she didn't have to attend the funeral home and come to the funeral, but she did."

Jeanne had avoided looking at her sister to this point, but the last comment forced her eyes to meet Emily's in a cold, hard stare. It had no effect.

"Yes, quite civil, I think." Emily answered her own question. "Well, she could have been nasty. But, then, I suppose most people aren't nasty in such situations, are they? I mean, they tend to rise above the petty . . ."

Jeanne closed her eyes, shifted in her chair, and realized only a response would halt the babble. "Civil, yes, Emily, marvellous. And gracious, just wonderful people, she and Kurt. The perfect couple." Her tone was cutting, but Emily, oblivious, moved on.

"You talked to Jonathan Hamlyn, I suppose?"

Jeanne laid down her spoon after just one taste of her cream of asparagus soup. "Yes, he said he's fine with having the will read and the estate taken care of as soon as possible. I thought you'd be anxious to get away, to go back to your home. Is Monday okay?"

Emily nodded. "Fine." As was her custom, she tried to read her sister's feelings by staring into her face. She had not learned yet, even after all these years, that Jeanne was opaque. "I know it will be painful. I just can't bear to hear of all of Father's possessions being scattered. I just can't bear it." Almost instantly, she began to sob.

Jeanne looked across the table in amazement at the person who was wiping her eyes with a napkin and wondered if Emily wasn't in need of some kind of therapy. Perhaps it was the last remnants of menopause. Jeanne could not understand why women allowed their symptoms to be so visible. What ever happened to suffering in silence? "Emily, I hardly think there's any scattering to it. It's just you and me. I can't recall Father ever talking about leaving anything to anyone else. Perhaps a few items, sentimental things, but, really, I don't know what you're upset about."

Emily tried to regain her composure. "Yes, but it's still Father's things, and Mother's, of course. Most of what's in that house belonged to Mother."

Jeanne looked away and said quietly, "I'm not sure one can distinguish between the two in terms of possessions. They were married for over fifty years. By law, everything was jointly owned."

Emily broke apart the soft dinner roll on the side of her plate. Her hands were shaking. She returned the two pieces to the plate without eating them and needlessly wiped her fingers in the white linen napkin. As she did so, the words "Not necessarily" were spoken, clearly and distinctly.

Jeanne was startled. "What exactly does that mean?"

Emily swallowed and took a deep breath. "Actually, that's why I came to see you this morning. I thought it was time."

"For what?"

"That you knew." She faked a cough. "Gregory suggested I should wait until the reading of the will. That way, there'd be no dispute, no question. But then, he doesn't understand how close we are, how you and I can talk so easily and honestly to each other."

"Dispute about what?" Jeanne pushed away the plate holding the soup bowl. "For God's sake, Emily, out with it. You act as if you have some great revelation. You sound like you know the contents of the will already."

"No, not all of it. Just about the house."

"The house?"

"Yes, it's mine."

"It's what?" Jeanne stood abruptly. Not willing to look across the table at her sister anymore, she walked to the other side of the room.

"I'm sorry, Jeanne. I really am. I know that maybe you thought somehow Father would leave it to you. After all, you've been living here, you looked after him, but you must understand." She stopped suddenly and resumed eating, but watched Jeanne as she paced.

Jeanne turned and looked at Emily in total disbelief. "Emily, what are you saying? I've never heard such nonsense. The house is yours. Where did you ever get such an idea? Father would never . . . Stop eating and explain yourself!"

Emily obeyed. "The house used to belong to the Bolands—Mother's family. You know that."

"Yes, but what does that . . . ?"

"You asked me to explain. Of course, once Mother and Father were married, the house became theirs. But the Bolands wanted the house to be passed on to the eldest daughter. That's how Mother explained it to me."

"That's ridiculous."

"It was a tradition in their family. It goes back several generations." The words trailed away.

Jeanne felt ill. She placed her hand on the armrest of the nearest chair and turned to sit. She stared blankly at the floor. "Whatever the Bolands wanted or did not want, it became Father's to do as he wished once Mother died. He would never have left the house solely to you regardless what his wife thought."

"He did, that's all I can say. He must have had reason, Jeanne, although I don't know what it could be."

"How long have you known?"

"Since Mother passed away."

"That's almost two years ago, and you never told anyone, no one at all?"

"No. I just told Gregory last night. I felt you should know before the will is read so it wouldn't be a shock."

"A shock? And what do you suppose it is now, for heaven's sake?"

"At least it gives you time to deal with it before we see the lawyer."

Jeanne, still reeling from the news, wondered how she would face the legal confirmation of this in the morning. "And what about the things in the house? What about Father's books, the furniture, the paintings, those exquisite rugs?"

"The house and its contents are mine." Emily whispered as if she didn't want the rest of the world to hear.

Only a few seconds were spent in silence but it seemed to Emily like an eternity as she waited for her sister's response.

Jeanne felt her heart pound. Her stomach wrenched at the thought of her sister owning it all. *That twit, Gregory, sashaying through the rooms of my father's house, the proud owner, the possessor. Emily has won.* All those years of bickering between the two of them . . . Jeanne was the stronger-willed of the two, always able to get her own way, subtly manipulating Emily to do her bidding. Behind her back, Emily had the advantage, and now she would use this advantage to claim the family home, right when Jeanne was at her most vulnerable. She wanted her out of sight. Finally, she spoke, "And what . . . what are you going to do with it all?"

"With the house? Oh, I don't know." Her vague response only served to irritate Jeanne more. "Gregory suggests I sell it. The windows need work, especially to sell it, don't you think?"

Jeanne had had sufficient time to allow the significance of this conversation sink in. She was bursting inside with rage and spite. *The windows,* she thought, *damn the windows, and damn you, Emily.* Her heart pounded wildly, and she momentarily focused on that comforting bottle of Ativan in her night table upstairs.

But Emily was still talking about the renovations, oblivious to Jeanne's mood. Jeanne sat away from her, with her chair facing the garden of roses on the far side of the deck outside. There seemed to be nothing left but her garden. Emily drew a breath. "I guess I could just close it up and come back and forth sometimes, but then the place will fall down if someone doesn't maintain it. It is the family home, after all. Others in the family may want to use it. Perhaps Greg would want to stay in it for a while."

Jeanne cringed and clenched her fist at the idea of her father's house being used as a hotel by Greg and his friends. She felt her legs beginning to shake and she forced them to stop. Deep breathing was not working. *That avaricious son of Emily's,* she thought, *swaggering around, betraying everything that was my father, violating my home. He'll probably fill it with tacky carpeting and functional furniture.* She found herself reeling at the prospect. *Clearly, something has to be done. Something. Anything.* She would not stand by and watch what was rightfully hers being taken away by a sheet of paper. But in order to do so, she had to be careful, very careful, to keep the door open.

"Emily, there are some things I would like to have, from the house." She forced a polite tone.

"Why yes, of course, Jeanne, whatever you like, you know that. And perhaps Joe and Lauren would like to have a small item, some of father's books for Joe, perhaps, and a picture for Lauren. Whatever you wish. Now, I must go. I have some people coming in this afternoon and I must see that everything is prepared." She stood. "Thanks for the lovely lunch. Leah is such a wonderful cook. I wish I had her with me."

Certainly. I bet you would, thought Jeanne. *Is there anything else?* And to think how often Virginia had said, "Jeanne, if only you had Emily's personality." She wanted her gone. Aloud she said, "Yes, well, goodbye. I'll see you in the morning at Jonathan's." She called out. "Leah, get Emily's coat and show her out, please."

Emily left, satisfied that the worst was over. Jeanne sat back in her chair, rested her chin on her thumb and forefinger, and considered her options. She had to be cautious, but somehow she would have to find a way to make Emily understand and accept that the Sinclair house was hers, rightfully hers, to take care of for her father's sake and for her own sake. Emily would have to see that. But how would she do that . . . without anyone learning the real truth about her father?

CHAPTER 3

"Hannah?"

"Yes, sir," she answered quickly. Hannah turned from her place at the end of the kitchen table to see Charles standing in the doorway.

"Mrs. Green has you cleaning the good crystal, I see."

"Yes, it's for that special dinner tonight. The platter is for dessert, blancmange, I think it's called."

"Uh huh." He walked to the far corner, opened the cupboard, and took out a large bottle filled with brown liquid. "Speaking of special things, would you like to see something I brought back from Montreal?"

"Yes, sir," she answered, and stood up, but was hesitant to join him at the counter.

"Well, then, come here." He beckoned to her. "It's called Coca-Cola."

"That's a strange name," Hannah commented.

"Indeed, it is, for a strange drink. Would you like to try some?"

"Oh my, no, sir, I couldn't possibly. You see, Pop says I should never drink spirits. He says we should keep our wits about us, in case our Blessed Saviour should call upon us to do something for Him."

Charles laughed. "Does he say that? Is your Pop a wise man?"

"Yes, very wise. And a good Christian."

"And are you a good Christian, Hannah?"

"I go to church every Sunday."

"Does that make a person a good Christian?"

"It helps," Hannah quipped.

Charles threw his head back in laughter. "Oh my, that's good to know," he said, still chuckling. "Here, try a little. I promise you it doesn't have alcohol in it." He passed along a small glass with the brown, fizzy liquid filled almost to the top.

Hannah picked it up and tried to sip. It was not like anything she had ever had. But with Charles standing there, she felt obliged to try it. She gagged on the first mouthful. "Oh, I'm sorry, that's not good."

"No?"

"No, sir. Awful. I think I'll stick with tea."

Charles laughed again, and quickly swallowed the contents of the glass as Hannah watched, wide-eyed. She wiped her hands in her apron.

"I think I'd better get the crystal done, before Mrs. Green comes back."

"Of course," Charles responded, and placed the bottle back in the cupboard. He turned back to her. "You know, Hannah," he said, in a whisper, "you have beautiful skin. Clear as the crystal you are shining. Did you know that?"

Hannah looked up from her work at the table. She had never heard such words before. No one had ever said she was pretty. But to be called beautiful—her heart skipped a beat. "I . . . ah . . ."

He laughed again. "It's okay. My guess is you're not used to compliments." He placed his glass near the sink and walked to the doorway, stopping only long enough to say, "You make me laugh, Hannah. You're the only person who makes me laugh." And he was gone.

Alone in the kitchen, Hannah struggled to focus on shining the glasses in front of her. *What did he mean by that? I make him laugh. Is that a good thing?* She tidied the table and placed the crystal vase and glasses back in their appointed spot on the sideboard. *Of all the things I have to remember to tell Mom when I get home, that's certainly not one of them,* she thought.

* * * * *

AUGUST 1995

Jeanne was anxious to beat the Monday morning downtown traffic on Duckworth Street. She pulled into a parking spot only half a block from the law office of Stanley, Hamlyn, and Whiffen, a two-storey grey stone building, the oldest law office in the city. She thought carefully about her mission as she climbed the stairs and ran her hand up the mahogany rail, darkened and uneven from years of wax build-up. She was relieved to see her lawyer sitting behind his desk in the corner office. He rose immediately when he saw her, straightened his tie, and slipped on his grey tweed jacket.

"Thank you for seeing me early, Jonathan. I wanted to speak to you privately, before Emily arrives," she said, and settled into one of two chestnut Victorian Club armchairs stationed in front of his desk. "This is personal and I want it to go no further."

"Of course, Jeanne." Jonathan moved his folder across the desk and settled back in his leather chair. He knew all too well that any directive coming from Jeanne Sinclair was to be taken seriously.

"I spoke with my sister yesterday. She has the impression that Father's house is hers. I know she must be mistaken." She crossed her legs, straightened her linen skirt, and clasped her hands on her knee. "It's just not possible," she said, shaking her head for emphasis.

Jonathan twisted uncomfortably in his chair and then leaned forward to rest his arms on the desk. He gave a slight wince. "I'm sorry, Jeanne, she is correct."

There was a marked silence.

"I don't understand!" She clasped both armrests with her hands.

"Why would Father do that to me?" She struggled to keep her voice low. "I took good care of him. Emily has been living away. Listen to me, Jonathan, he told me the night he died that he left the house to me. Now this!" Her voice pleaded for an explanation.

"I know, Jeanne. I know it's not what you were expecting. And I am so sorry. Emily is the eldest daughter, and that was your parents' wish, or at least that is what was said. He did, however, leave you a sizable inheritance."

Jeanne sat quietly, forcing back her disappointment and disillusionment, though Jonathan knew she was hurting deeply.

"Is there something I can get you? Tea, perhaps?" he asked in a half whisper.

"No, thank you," she said, taking a deep, calming breath. "I accept what you are telling me. Obviously, I have no choice. But, that being the case, there *is* something I would like you to do."

"Certainly, if I can. What is it?" He had known her since he began practising law and had always admired her inner strength, more so in the past few weeks than ever before. He had never witnessed anyone who was able to regroup as quickly as Jeanne Sinclair.

"I would like you to keep the details of the will to a minimum. There is no need to indicate to Emily where *everything* is going. After all, if it doesn't affect her, it won't matter, will it?"

"Jeanne, as you know, she has a right to see the will. I intended to give you both a copy today."

She held up her hand. "No need to do that, Jonathan. I'll take mine now. And please, refrain from giving a copy to Emily until it is absolutely necessary, and only if she requests it."

"Jeanne, I know what you are trying to prevent."

"Yes," she interrupted. "Indeed you do. And if you want me to continue to give you my business and, more importantly, you want to continue our friendship, you will do as I ask—for now. I promise I will give her the will later."

"And should she ask? What should I do?"

"That's unlikely to happen. At least right now." She raised her head and looked at him directly. "I am asking you." Her look was sufficient to remind the lawyer that her father had paid a large amount of money to the firm over the years and there were secrets on both sides of their arrangement that needed to be protected.

"As you wish," and a quick nod of the head was enough to assure Jeanne that she was in control.

Emily arrived moments later in a taxi, and true to his word, Jonathan gave only the details pertaining to their inheritance. To his surprise, Emily did not ask for details. Jeanne sat perfectly straight, giving no visible response to what she was hearing.

"Emily," Jonathan explained, "if you need advice regarding the current housing market, I would be happy to give it to you. There should be no problem selling it now."

Jeanne wondered at his assessment of the market but did not openly question it.

"Thank you. That's very kind." Emily smiled and nodded with complete satisfaction. "I'll have to give that some thought."

"Of course," he replied.

Thought! When, in heaven's name, have you ever had a rational thought! Jeanne stood and gathered her blazer and purse, fighting the urge to speak.

Outside, standing on the sidewalk in the bright sunshine, Emily faced her sister with an expression of pity. "I hope that wasn't too painful for you, Jeanne. I know it must be difficult to . . ."

"I'm fine," she interrupted, but refused to make eye contact. "I will drop you off at your house. I have things to attend to at home." Except for a quick goodbye as Emily got out of the car in the Sinclair driveway, Jeanne remained silent.

Once at home, Jeanne phoned Lauren with the news about the house and left a message for Joe, asking him to come by in the evening. She feigned a headache to Leah and retired to the comfort of her bedroom. As she lay on her bed, tears streamed down her cheeks and stained the pristine white embroidered pillow covers. She inhaled deeply with every third breath. Mindlessly, she studied the Irish green toile pattern on the wall facing her. The overwhelming disappointment. How could her father, the most

important person in her life, deny her the one possession she valued most?

* * * * *

The sun in a deep blue morning sky shimmered on the water in
Falcon Cove harbour and made the sea look like it had been spread
with cast aluminum. Carrie locked the heavy wooden door to Bethel
United Church, strolled down the main road toward her home, and
enjoyed the heat on her face and arms. Surprisingly, the wind was
calm. Spying a couple of smooth beige stones with flecks of pink
and grey, she bent down to pick them up for her rock garden. She
peered out at the expanse of the harbour and shaded her eyes from
the bright sun with her left hand. *Home*, she thought, *this will always be home*. She breathed deeply and welcomed the salty fresh air
into her lungs. Down the road, around the bend of the harbour, she
could hear the moaning buzz of chainsaws cutting wood for winter
stoves. In the opposite direction, on Saunders Point, several summer
residents were raising their small boat, a rodney, from the water,
with the help of two young local men. They would store their oars,
ropes, and anchor in the shed, then begin the painstaking task of
scrubbing off the algae from the bottom with a mixture of vinegar
and water. She smiled and telepathically suggested that they accept
a challenge and stay for the winter. But she knew that as Labour
Day approached, they would pack their SUV and drive to the mainland ferry to leave the island behind in the bleak winter months. By
the freshly painted white fence of her front garden, she tossed the
two new additions near her rock garden and stepped onto the small
wooden bridge in front of the side door of the house. She heard her
mother's voice inside and, as she entered the kitchen, saw her hanging up the phone.

"For me?"

"No, for me," Hannah answered.

"Oh, good, I'm beat." She dropped her jacket on the back of the
chair and stretched her arms. "Spent most of the morning at the sc-

niors home. And the rest of it on the phone checking out the cost of
building supplies. Renovations on the church hall won't come cheap."
She stopped to look at her mother, who was fussing unnecessarily at
the kitchen counter. "You okay? Not bad news, is it?"

"No, no, not bad news, Carrie." She sighed deeply. "Just a lawyer from St. John's. He said his name is Mr. Hamlyn. Nice fellow.
Very soft-spoken." She did not add that his voice had a familiarity
about it.

Carrie poured tea and sat at the kitchen table that had been crafted from juniper many years ago by her Uncle Toby. She knew it would
take a while for her mother to get to the point if she intended to do
so. She waited.

"He said he represents the Sinclair estate."

"Oh?" She hoped for more.

But Hannah deliberately changed the topic. "I finished the cap
I was knitting for young Jake, Carrie. Looks nice, doesn't it?" She
proudly placed the boy's cap of blue, white, and red stripes on the
centre of the kitchen table.

"Yes, it's cute. He'll love his team's colours." Jake was a neighbour's
son, who ran errands and, most importantly, shovelled snow for them
all winter when he wasn't obsessing over his favourite hockey team,
the Montreal Canadiens. "I've got a meeting tonight and I have some
things to do to get ready for it." She rubbed her hand through her
short dark curls.

"I have lunch ready. I just have to heat up the fish cakes."

"So, what did the lawyer want?" She risked the question.

Hannah opened the cupboard for two dinner plates. "He just
wanted me to know that there's some money left for me in the will.
He didn't say how much and I didn't ask. It will be a while before I
get it, though. There's a lot of paperwork. Funny, he didn't make a
comment about me being in Charles Sinclair's will. Just told me that
I was."

"He has no right to make a judgment, even if he knows," Carrie
commented. "He's obligated to keep it to himself."

"Good. No one needs to know," Hannah said in a half whisper, and brushed the few crumbs from the placemat in front of her. Not wanting to elaborate, she left the room, saying, "While dinner warms up, I'm going to put the towels away upstairs. Keep an eye on the fish cakes, will you?"

She climbed the stairs, knowing that she had not told Carrie that Mr. Hamlyn had asked about the pocket watch. And she had not told Mr. Hamlyn that the watch was upstairs in her jewellery box.

* * * * *

On the same Monday morning, Sara found Sandi working in her office at the university.

"Dedicated, aren't we?" she asked, after tapping lightly and pushing the door open.

Sandi's office in the arts atrium of the university, though tiny, was organized and inviting. Three pink carnations in a spray of green divided the telephone from a large notepad and a photo of Halifax's Public Gardens. Sandi looked up from her work and smiled. "Good mornin'! I'm trying to get as much done as I can before the term starts."

Sara sat in a large wooden armchair on the other side of Sandi's desk. She smiled warmly. "Then I won't keep you, but I'm here to tell you, or warn you, depending on how you look at it," she said with a laugh. "Joe Steffensen wants to see you again, and I told him to drop by my place tonight."

"Sara, don't kid me about such things. I'm especially fragile these days."

"I'm serious."

Sandi sighed. "It's just that I've made a promise to myself to stay out of relationships for a while. Right now, I don't need the stress. I didn't exactly part on good terms with Shawn, the last man in my life."

"He didn't want you to move here?"

"No. Even bought a house in Bedford to coax me to stay, believe it or not. He figured if I stayed around, something permanent would come up at one of the universities in Nova Scotia. I just wanted to get to work."

"Okay. But Joe's not Shawn. He just wants to be friends, that's all. I assume you could use one of those?" Her eyebrows raised with an accompanying grin. "He's the kind of person who restores one's faith in human nature. Perhaps you need that right now."

Sandi wasn't totally convinced, but she laughed and looked out the window. "You make a good sale, Ms. Russell. Okay. Besides, he's not hard to look at, I'll give him that. That blond hair. I've always melted over men with blond hair."

"Is Shawn blond?"

"Nope."

"So, you'll be over tonight for supper?"

"All right."

"Good. I'll see you around six."

* * * * *

The sun flickered through the tree branches as Joe turned into the Steffensen driveway that evening to pick up his father.

"This shouldn't take too long, I hope," Kurt said, as he got into the car and reached for the seat belt.

"No, it won't. I have somewhere else to go later."

"Oh. Do I know her?"

Joe smiled at his father's observation. "Didn't you for one moment think I was meeting a client?"

"Nope. You look like a man on a much more desirable mission."

"Actually, I'm going to drop in on Sara and a new friend of hers. Just a casual thing."

"I see." Kurt smiled to himself, knowing well that, for his son, that was not possible.

Getting every green light on the parkway, Joe made it across town in a few minutes, turned onto Exeter Avenue, and pulled into the familiar driveway of the house where he had grown up. He rang the doorbell and turned to look around the front garden, flawlessly groomed by professional gardeners. When the door opened, both men were surprised to find that Jeanne answered it.

"Jeanne," Kurt said. "Leah not in this evening?"

"Family wedding this week. Please, come in."

They followed her through the foyer, up six steps to a hall, and directly out to the back of the house. The place was impeccably neat, as usual. One door was opened to the patio deck and the setting sun sent its last rays through the room into the hall. Through the picture windows, they could see the garden in bloom, a tapestry of foliage and flowers framed by two red maples in the back corners. The grey stone wall along the back was lined with mature rhododendrons and rose bushes. Pots of lavender and spearmint interspersed with begonias and verbena edged the back walkway. Nearest to the windows, rectangular pots of pink, purple, and white petunias decorated with ornamental grasses welcomed the late afternoon sun.

Jeanne studied the two men carefully. They seemed to be more alike every day. Kurt sat a fair distance away on the same side as Joe, facing the garden. "How have you been?" he asked her quietly.

"I'm managing. Why?"

"I just asked. Now that everyone is gone . . ."

"Emily is still here. Not here, as such. She's staying at Father's, or, I should say, at her house."

"At her house?" Joe asked.

She nodded without expression. "It's the reason I asked you to come by. I wanted you to hear it from me. Emily got the house and most of its contents." She stared at a spot on the rug beneath her feet. "All the years I took care of him and this is how he repays me." Her voice quivered. Then she said in a whisper, "He even told me the house was mine, the day he died."

Joe glanced at his father and back to her. "Mother, I don't understand. Did your lawyer give you any kind of an explanation as to why Grandfather would do that?"

"The house was originally owned by the Bolands and your grandmother inherited it. Your great-grandmother Boland inherited it all from her father, along with most of the land on Forest Road.

Mother and Father owned it jointly, of course, as the family home, and they decided that Emily would get the house, as she is the oldest." She glanced at Kurt, who was studying her carefully. "I did receive a sizable inheritance, but I don't care about the money. It can't make up for the house." She turned to look directly at Joe. "I wanted you to know, I'll be altering my will to make absolutely certain that this inheritance will go to you and Lauren equally when I'm gone. There are several personal items to deal with as well."

"Whatever you want. I don't really care for any of it."

"I want you to start caring, Joe." Her voice rose in anger. "I want to make sure that Emily doesn't get anything else she doesn't deserve. That idiot son of hers, Gregory, has already shipped the beautiful teak sideboard that was in the dining room back to Nova Scotia. Anyway, as I said, your inheritance and Lauren's will be secured along with the proviso that the money is to be further inherited by your children, should you ever have any, not to be inherited by your wife. The same is true for Lauren. There's hardly a need for Alan Matheson to get any more than he's already managed to. You do understand?"

"Sure." His flippant tone only served to irritate her more.

"Jonathan Hamlyn said it'll be a few months before it's all settled. Something about probate. Emily wanted to go back home to Nova Scotia, and she thought it would be all taken care of before she left, but he explained that these big estates take time."

She sounded cold, precise, and calculating, and Kurt knew it was her way of hiding her true feelings. "Jeanne, at the funeral home last week, Gregory mentioned something about a pocket watch. Said he couldn't find it or his mother couldn't find it. Do you know anything about that?"

"No, I don't have it. It's not that it was valuable, but I would have loved to have it. My guess is that Gregory has it and won't admit it."

"Just as a point of interest, what does Emily plan to do with the house?"

"I don't know and I don't really care. When I left the lawyer's office this morning, we parted hardly without speaking. Emily was like someone who had won the grand prize."

In fact she had, Kurt thought, but declined to say it aloud.

"She already has a house in Nova Scotia," Jeanne pointed out.

"And you have one here." Joe waved his hand around the room.

"It's not the same," she said dismissively.

"No, of course not," Kurt observed with a sigh.

His sarcastic response was the tipping point. "I don't know what I'm going to do. I really don't." There was a raw desperation in her voice that surprised Joe. Up to now, she had been stoic in her demeanour, but suddenly that changed. She was breaking her own code of keeping her emotions to herself.

"Seems to me like you don't have many options, Mother. Granddad was of sound mind. It's up to Emily, and Gregory, I guess, to decide what happens to it all."

She stood and walked the length of the solarium. "I plan to go down to the house as soon as Emily leaves and take some things I know Father would have wanted me to have."

"Be careful, you'll be trespassing on her property and taking things that don't legally belong to you," Kurt advised.

She stopped. Just his tone released the pent-up rage inside of her. She could feel her heart pounding and her legs beginning to tremble. She wanted to scream at Joe, *See, there it is, that's how he scolded me all those years*. But she knew it would be in vain, because he was a reprint of his father. Instead, she glared at Kurt. "I don't give a damn what it is."

"Okay." He withdrew, dismissing it with his hand and not wishing to get into a shouting match.

But his quip spurred her on. She walked back and forth, visibly shaken. "I'll not have her or that greedy son of hers take what's mine. She has the house but, by God, she won't have what's in it if I have any say in the matter. I put nothing past Gregory. He could claim the lot before his mother dies!"

"I doubt that," said Kurt, without raising the volume. "Perhaps it would be better for all concerned if the house was sold."

"I will never stand for that. I grew up there."

Kurt twisted in his chair, rubbed his hands across his eyes, and sighed. "The two of you have never gotten along, Jeanne. At best, you were civil in your father's presence. Legally, the house and its contents belong to Emily. Perhaps you should just find a way to let it go. Stirring this up could get you more than you bargained for."

Joe wondered at his father's observation, but believing the conversation to be going nowhere, he glanced at his watch and stood. "Dad, I'd like to get going, if it's all right with you. I don't think we can solve this problem tonight."

"Agreed." He stood and moved toward the door. "Jeanne, I'm sorry about the house." He looked directly at her. "You know your father had no choice."

Only her eyes acknowledged his comment. She turned to her son. "Thank you for coming. I may need to see you in a few days about some other things."

"Fine, just give me lots of advance notice. I'm really busy. It's that time of year."

"Of course." She closed the front door behind them. "God forbid you should let your mother inconvenience you even for a few minutes," she muttered to herself.

"We're not used to that kind of emotion from her," Joe said, backing out of the driveway. "Guess it's all been too much. Dad, what do you think Emily will do with the house?"

"If she's smart, she'll sell it. Or try to. God knows I wouldn't want to try to dump that place in the market we have now. If anyone's thinking of buying a house in this town, they'll put their money into something better than that place. It needs renovations."

"It's amazing what family members do for the sake of an inheritance, as if being someone's child entitles you to it all. Mother and Emily will allow this to destroy what little relationship they have. A house that neither one of them needs."

Kurt laughed. "Yeah, and the funny thing about all of this, Joe, is that I'll bet somewhere right now in the afterlife, Charles is sitting back with one hell of a smirk on his face, watching the two of them battle it out to the finish. He got control even beyond the grave. Now there's power. Perhaps the only time he truly managed to have it. And the tragic part is the two of them are foolish enough to entertain him."

Joe pulled into the driveway of Kurt's home. "Have a good evening, Dad, and say hello to Jaclyn for me. Thanks for coming with me tonight."

"Glad to be of service. Good night. Oh . . . and good luck with the young lady," Kurt replied, as he got out of the car. As he watched his son drive away, he chided himself for not divulging the real reason why Charles left the house to Emily.

* * * * *

Joe arrived at Sara's apartment just as they had finished supper. "Good evening, Sara, I see you're going minimalist these days," he commented with humorous sarcasm as he surveyed her apartment filled with boxes and books. "You don't mind if I recommend it to some clients, do you? Perhaps use your place as a showcase?"

"Give me a break, Joe. I don't know what to do with all this stuff. And don't say throw it out. That's the line Ray used to use first when we got married, and I would have preferred to throw him out. I certainly would have been better off."

As she spoke, Sandi came from the kitchen, wiping her hands in two paper towels. "All done, Sara."

"Thanks. It's likely the tidiest that kitchen's been since I moved in."

"Hello, Sandi. We meet again. I can see Sara has managed to take advantage of your good nature to have you clean up her apartment."

Sandi laughed. "No, that's not it at all. I just put the dishes away." She moved forward. "It's nice to meet you, Joe. By the way, have you eaten?"

"Just a sandwich," he said pitifully.

"We could get you something."

"That's okay," he said with a broad smile, "I'll make do with these peanut butter cups," and reached for the bowl on the coffee table.

"I'll get you a piece of cheesecake," Sara said.

Sandi sat across from him and crossed her long legs. He wanted to tell her she looked sensational in her yellow minidress, but remembered Sara's cautionary advice to go slowly. He longed to speak to her privately, so he called out to Sara and asked for a coffee.

"Sure, okay. But you don't usually drink more than one cup a day," she responded, and reached for the empty coffee pot.

"Yeah, I know. It's a special day. Go on, then." The words came out of him almost without thinking.

Joe moved to a chair next to Sandi. "I'm sorry for being so bold. It's just that I told Sara I wouldn't stay long, and I didn't want to go without having a chance to speak to you alone."

"Oh?"

"Sara tells me you've been seeing someone in Halifax. A guy you've known for a while."

"That's right."

"So, do you still see him?"

"No, I'm not much for long-distance relationships. It was difficult, and we're both finally accepting the inevitable. At least I hope so."

Joe convinced himself that there was only one way to do this. Straight out. In a rare moment, he felt weak in the knees and his pulse quickened. "Would you consider seeing someone else?"

Sandi immediately drew back. "Oh, I don't know, Joe. To be honest, I really need some time . . ."

"I see," Joe said, rethinking his words. *That was dumb.* He hesitated momentarily, leaned forward in the chair, and rested his forearms on his knees. "We could just go out to dinner, then, as friends. Sara and I are friends. I force her out to dinner with me from time to time. I mean, it's better than eating alone." He grinned.

She looked at him and found herself wanting to say *Yes, absolutely, anything you want,* but instead she simply said, "Since you put it that way, and you do understand that's all it can be, I'll have dinner with you sometime. Thanks."

Joe sat back with satisfaction of having achieved his goal. "Great."

And on that word, Sara returned with a fresh pot of coffee. "So, did I miss anything important when I was *driven* out of the room?" She stared at him when she said the word "driven."

Joe poured the coffee. "Sandi and I just decided to have dinner together some evening. Perhaps later this week?"

"Sure."

Sara passed him his coffee, accompanied by a look that said *you owe me.*

"Joe, I heard that your grandfather Sinclair passed away recently," Sandi said. "I'm so sorry. It's tough losing a granddad. My Granddad Martel passed away two years ago."

"Thanks, Sandi."

"Are your paternal grandparents still alive?"

"Yes, living in Halifax. They were both profs at Dalhousie. Retired now."

"Of course. I should have made the connection." Sandi's eyes lit up. "I've heard of them. And Jeanette Steffensen's your aunt? In the English Department at Dal? I heard she's a great teacher, as were her parents. I should have known they are your relatives. After all, how many Steffensens are there in eastern Canada?"

Joe laughed. "Not many. What about your family? Sara said you were born here."

"My parents moved us to Halifax when I was little for my father's work. My Grandma and Granddad Martel were from St. John's, and my mother's family lives in Corner Brook. Actually, Grandma and Granddad Mackenzie moved to Corner Brook after they got married."

"From where?" he asked.

"Granddad's from the west coast, but Grandma Mackenzie is from a small community in Bonavista Bay, the north side. A pretty little place called Falcon Cove."

* * * * *

Shortly after eleven o'clock that night, Jaclyn came out of her dressing room and searched a small cabinet near the fireplace for a book she wanted, but couldn't find it. She was too tired to look for it elsewhere. As she straightened up, her eyes caught the pictures that lined the mantel on top of the hearth. She smiled as she studied the picture of Joe, David, Sara, and Quentin that was taken when they were six. In the frame next to it, a pretty three-year-old Lauren smiled back at her. Kurt was sitting comfortably on the left side of their king-sized bed, engrossed in a magazine article he had wanted to get to for some time. She walked to the bed, slipped off her robe, and laid it over the cedar chest next to the footboard.

She sat on the edge of the bed and turned around to speak. "This business about the Sinclair house, Kurt. It must be devastating for Jeanne. And completely unexpected."

"Devastating, yes. Unexpected, perhaps." He folded his magazine and placed it on the night table and settled under the sheets. "Jaclyn," he said with a sigh, "when I was married to Jeanne, she used to complain about her father. He pontificated on everything from business to politics to church and didn't have a charitable bone in his body. All of a sudden, this past week, it's like he did no wrong. Amazing."

"It's possible that Jeanne talked negatively about her father around you, thinking that's what you wanted to hear. She may have been desperate for approval."

"Somehow, my love, I can't imagine Jeanne wanting to do anything to please me." He turned back the sheets and welcomed her next to him.

"Still, you don't seem to be surprised by all of this."

"It was originally the Boland house. He abided by his wife's wishes."

"I understand that, Emily being the eldest daughter. I didn't know the man, but from what you've said about him, he could hardly have been ordered to do something."

"Actually, my love, he had no choice."

She turned to adjust the pillows, lay back on her side, and ran her hand across Kurt's chest. "No choice? A man in his position?"

"Even men with the power and influence of a Charles Sinclair can have their choices narrowed by circumstance."

Jaclyn turned her head to look at him with a puzzled expression. Kurt took her hand and kissed it tenderly.

"This has to be kept in this room for now, Jaclyn, please."

"Of course."

"Let's just say that Charles committed a serious indiscretion early on in their marriage."

"Another woman?"

He nodded.

"So, Virginia insisted that Emily get the house. It was her way of punishing him?" she asked.

"Indeed. It was the only way she could."

CHAPTER 4

A wide band of fog lingered outside the harbour, waiting for the sun to go down that Saturday evening. Joe reached for his jacket in the hall closet, headed for the door, and grabbed his wallet and car keys as he left.

The traffic was light as he drove up Military Road and down Bonaventure Avenue. The cool mist of fog had not yet reached Churchill Square and he needed to turn on the air conditioning in his car. Joe parked on the street in front of the Martel home, and as he walked toward the house he noticed the rows of nasturtiums in full bloom edging the stone walkway. He remembered his Aunt Katie recently saying that nasturtiums should be the provincial flower in Newfoundland because they grow on rocks and stay around until the snow falls. Joe had just reached the front door when Jordy opened it. The tall, slender young man was dressed in jeans and a striped polo shirt. His hair was lighter than Sandi's, but just as thick and wavy.

"Hello, I'm Joe Steffensen. I'm here to see . . ."

"Sandi. C'mon in. I'm her brother, Jordy. Nice to meet you, Joe."

Mollie came bounding out to investigate this stranger, and Joe bent down to play with her. It would not be the only scrutiny Joe would be the subject of that evening. He followed Jordy into the living room with Mollie close to his heels.

"Beautiful dog. What's her name?"

"Mollie."

Joe laughed. "That's great. Mollie? So she's Mollie the collie?"

"Yeah, I know. We're simple folk. Not much imagination. You can't expect much from the middle class these days. We're being taxed to death."

Joe appreciated his dry wit. "Well, Mollie-the-collie, you are special," he said, and the canine raised her head to encourage the scratching underneath her chin.

The living room was both comfortable and tastefully decorated and, in a rare moment, he did not evaluate the place with an architect's eye. He studied the photos, starting with Sandi and Jordy's graduation pictures on the mantelpiece. There was a photo of a happy older couple, whom he assumed to be their grandparents. "So, Jordy, what are you studying at university?" he asked.

"I'm finishing up an MBA. Got a business degree from Dal, with a side order of music."

"Interesting combination: music and business. Well done!"

"Thanks. Hopefully it will lead to a job."

Seeing Lindsay walk into the room, he stood to introduce himself.

She straightened her light cotton pants and brushed back her fine brown curly hair. "Nice to meet you, Joe," she said with a smile. Sitting on the edge of the piano stool, she scrutinized the young man whose upbringing and bank account were quite evident. She also noted the fine film of dust on the mantel and immediately apologized for the state of the living room.

Upstairs, Sandi reassured herself that this was nothing more than a casual dinner and she was not preparing to impress anyone. Out of her limited wardrobe she chose her favourite dress, mainly because of its colour, deep purple. It would make her feel comfortable and relaxed, and that's just what she needed. *Besides,* she thought, as she slipped the tank chemise over her head, *the guy seems obsessed with colour. I trust royal purple will be acceptable.* She picked up her purse and hurried downstairs in time to hear her mother blame the mess in the house on Mollie.

In the restaurant, Joe and Sandi were seated at a table over-looking the east end of the city. The dining room was spacious and arranged in three tiers of tables. Each table was distinctively dis-tanced from the others to provide some degree of intimacy. Their table to the far left provided the best seclusion. At night, the lights were dimmed enough to enhance the city lights just below. "I de-liberately asked for this table when I made the reservation," he ex-plained. "It's a view I don't get very often, but I see the harbour and Narrows all the time from my office and from the balcony of my apartment. If you like, I'll show you after dinner. Is this your first time here?"

"No, but it's been a while. Jordy and I used to bring Mom and Dad and our grandparents out on Sundays for brunch years ago, when we'd visit in the summertime."

"Your father's parents?"

"Yes."

"You miss them a lot."

"Every single day." She sipped her water to ease the lump in her throat. "How about you? Do you miss your grandfather?"

Joe hesitated. "My grandfather's life revolved around his work, Sandi. He never had much time for family. But I have two other grandparents who make up for that. I am more of a Steffensen than a Sinclair. By the way, Jordy looks a lot like you, except his hair is lighter. Martel or Mackenzie?" he asked.

"Most people say that Jordy is a Mackenzie, while I'm a Martel."

"Jordy is an unusual name."

She grinned. "I chose it. I was five when he was born, so Mom and Dad gave me the responsibility of naming him, sort of a way to get over the crunch of not being the only child anymore. It was the name of a character in a book I loved. What about you? I know where Steffensen comes from, but 'Joe' . . . are you named after someone special?"

Joe nodded. "A man that my dad worked for when he was in university. In the summers he came here and stayed with his grand-parents, Grandma Steffensen's parents, the Thorburns. He worked at a printing press for a man named Joe Ivany and learned a lot about the business. He really admired Joe, and when he passed away suddenly during the year I was born, Dad decided to name me after him. I have no idea how he managed to convince Mother. 'Cept that he did go along with my middle name, Sinclair."

When the waitress returned to take their orders, Sandi chose oven-roasted chicken with pears and brie and Joe ordered a seafood bake. "Can't be of Newfoundland and Norwegian ancestry without ordering seafood! And the thought of having salmon, scallops, cod, and shrimp on the one plate is great," he explained with a grin.

"They have a wonderful selection. Must be terrific for tourists." Sandi sipped her wine. "Sara said your parents divorced about fifteen years ago?"

Joe nodded. "Yeah, I can't say it was unexpected. I've always gotten along with my dad, my mother not so much. She always wanted me to work with her father. Frankly, I'd sooner be unemployed." He reached for the butter and spread it lightly across a warm slice of bread. "My mother is all about appearances, Sandi. Doing the right thing, what will people think, that kind of thing. She barely tolerated Quentin or Sara when we were growing up, and that's always been a source of tension between us. For her, they aren't in the right social circle."

"Your father's certainly well respected here in the city. I mean, Steffensen Publishing has a reputation as one of the best places to work in eastern Canada, if not in the entire country."

"Dad has always taken very good care of his employees, and they're loyal to him."

"Jordy's doing research on management styles and leadership for his MBA. He'd enjoy talking to your father, no doubt. And what about your work? I understand you've won national awards for your designs?"

Joe looked surprised. "How did you know about that?"

"I have my sources," she answered with a smile.

"Ah, of course, Sara."

"No, not at all. My dad. He remembered reading about it a while ago."

"Curious about the man his daughter's having dinner with, hey? Dad's little girl?" he teased.

"No, I'm not going to admit to that." She could feel her face flush.

"And speaking of awards, Dr. Martel. I understand that your dissertation received a national honour. Congratulations!"

"Oh yeah. That. No big deal. They have to give it to somebody. I think an east coast university was due," she said in all modesty.

Joe thought how beautiful she looked in her deep purple dress. She owned the colour, no doubt about it, although he imagined that she would look good in anything. Her accessories were simple. Her natural long curls were swept back on the left with a simple gold clasp, the hair on the right fell around her face, and her makeup was understated.

"So, tell me more about yourself. What do you do in your spare time? Although you probably don't have much."

"The day I completed my Ph.D. defence, my supervisor said to me, 'Now the real work begins; get tenured.' So that's where I am these days, teaching in the fall, full courseload, trying to write some articles, and going to committee meetings. To be honest, I am starting to come to terms with the realities of academic life. Rather disillusioning, to put it bluntly."

"That's what my Aunt Jeanette says. She's wrestling with the English Department at Dal. You two should get together and compare notes. Apart from university work, what else is in your life?"

"Well, when I was a student, I played volleyball on the university varsity team. Now, when I can, I play tennis in summer. Just recently got into photography. I walk a lot, usually with my mom and/or dad since I left my best friend, Jennifer, in Halifax. I'd love to run, but I hardly have the body type."

"I see nothing wrong with your body type—that would stop you from running."

Sandi could feel her face redden and willed it to stop. She tried to get away from the topic. "I'm an avid sports fan—watch baseball and hockey all the time with Dad and Jordy. And Jordy and I spend a lot time on the keyboards. I play the flute, too."

"Well." Joe was impressed. "I can see you're idle most of the time. Perhaps you should look for some hobbies to get your mind focused," he teased her.

"Oh, just something to keep me from being bored. I'm not a party person and I really don't like bars. Half a glass of wine puts me to sleep. Other than that, Joe, I'll give you some idiosyncrasies only if you give me some of yours. My favourite colour's purple, hence the dress. I break the spines of books as I read them. I have trouble opening cereal boxes, or at least Jordy complains that I do. I love manicures, pedicures, and facials. And I'll even confess to following one daytime drama with my mother. It's our bonding time. And, someday, I hope to write a murder mystery. Right now I'm content to read them by the metre. So, the truth about Joe Steffensen? Go ahead."

"I'm nowhere close to being as accomplished as you. But, like you, I tend to avoid noisy parties. I love to snack on chocolate-covered macadamia nuts, so I pay for it by playing squash with Quentin regularly. My father likes to golf, so from May to September I golf on weekends with him, although I never keep my score, which drives my dad over the edge. Sail when I get the chance. I enjoy music, too, but only to listen to. I have *no* musical talent. I read voraciously, a habit I came by honestly given my father's and grandparents' occupations. Other than that, I live and breathe architecture. Designs are always on my mind, except for the past couple of hours, of course."

"So, to ask a stereotypical question, your favourite colour?"

"Green. Oh, and since I *am* the son of a publisher, I have to report your spine breaking to the book cops. It's my duty," he added with a smile.

The evening passed quickly. They talked comfortably about Joe's designs, Sandi's research, sports, politics, travel, books, and family. Shortly after eleven, Joe reached for the bill and dismissed Sandi's attempt to contribute. "So what about that view from my balcony, want to see it now?"

Sandi looked at her watch and could hardly believe that four hours had passed. "Okay, for a few minutes."

His apartment was as visually appealing as the publishing company, with its mixture of colour and texture. The light hardwood floors set off the large stone fireplace and deep green sofas. Birch beams ran the length of the ceiling. The fully-equipped kitchen had white and plum granite countertops and white cupboards filled with twelve-piece sets of traditional fine china, modern dishes, and stemware. On the counter between the living room and dining room, a large crystal bowl filled with chocolate-covered macadamia nuts sat at arm's length from the computer. "Joe, this place is gorgeous! I can see why Sara was so complimentary about it. What an interesting blend of colours, blues and greens and reds, all rich shades!" She slipped off her coat and laid it across a dining room chair. "You designed it yourself?"

"Actually, I renovated the whole building a few years ago, the summer after I graduated. The top floor was vacant, so I worked on it and moved in. My grandmother bought the china and Aunt Jeanette gave me the modern stuff."

Captivated by the style, she peeked into the master bedroom. A wall of windows faced the southeast, overlooking the hills and the ocean. From floor to ceiling, the other three walls were filled with books, magazines, and CDs. The bed was king-sized. "Unique headboard. Where did you get it?"

"My great-grandfather hand-carved it. We had it shipped here from Bergen, Norway. The mattress is white goose down." He wanted to add, "You're welcome to try it," but refrained and chose instead to invite her to the balcony. The fog had captured the city, but the lights of the harbourfront were still visible, creating an eerie effect. The air was damp and salty and there was a faint smell of diesel fuel from the working harbour.

"It's not a good night for a view, Sandi. You'll have to come back."

"Sure," she responded, and realized she had just committed herself to another evening with him. "I had a wonderful time tonight. Thanks for inviting me and thanks for dinner."

Joe switched off the light on the balcony to sharpen the contrast.

Only the lights from the living room shone through the doors. Sandi stood, both hands clasped to the railing. She glanced at him. "Joe, you're staring at me."

"I'm sorry. It's just that you have the most beautiful smile."

She was embarrassed. "Thanks," she said, looking away.

They gazed at the harbour in front of them and at the lights leading out of the city. "I have to confess," Joe said, "it's going to be difficult to keep this at the friendship level."

"You mean you don't want us to be friends?" She asked, knowing well what he meant.

"Yes, of course I do. It's just that . . ." Sara's strong advice to be patient reverberated through his head.

"What?"

"Nothing." He sighed, wanting to wrap his arms around her. "I really enjoyed this evening. I hope we can do it again sometime soon."

"That would be nice," she said with that irrepressible smile that awarded him a measure of relief.

* * * * *

On Sunday evening, Jordy tore himself away from watching the ninth inning of the ball game on television to have dinner. Plopping a large spoonful of butter on top of his mashed potato, he asked his sister if she was going out with Joe again or whether it was a one-time thing.

Steven smiled and scooped up the rest of the potatoes, all the while keeping an eye on the base hit being scored in the background. "Not every woman gets a chance at a second date with Joe Steffensen, I s'pose," he said with a wink at Jordy.

Lindsay welcomed the opportunity to discuss the topic. "I thought he was quite nice," she began. "He wears his money, I could tell that. I couldn't help but notice the Rolex watch on his arm. Impressive. And his socks stay up."

Steven stopped mid-bite. "What? His socks stay up! You sized up his socks, Lindsay? Did you do an underwear check as well?"

She smiled as she reached for the butter dish. "Father always says you can tell the wealth of a man by whether or not his socks stay up or bunch around his ankles."

Steven made eye contact with his son and nodded his head toward Lindsay. "We obviously shop at the wrong stores, Jordy. Wanna make an impression—be careful where you buy your socks." He turned his attention back to his daughter. "So, Sandi, are you going to tell us? Your mother is dying to know about your date."

Sandi sighed loudly. "May I point out here, since you are all talking about my life, that it was not a 'date,' Dad? People don't date anymore. The word died in 1965. Joe and I have a mutual friend, Sara Russell. We met the other night at her place and decided it would be nice to go out to dinner. And that's exactly what we did. We're just friends."

It was exactly the response Steven expected, but Lindsay ignored any hint that commentary on Sandi's love life was off-limits.

"Oh yeah! I've heard that 'just friends' routine before," she remarked. "And my guess is, from the way Mr. Steffensen looked you up and down when you walked into our living room last night, friendship wasn't exactly on his mind." Lindsay punctuated her words by pushing back her empty plate.

Knowing the best possible reaction for this, Steven and Jordy, who always had some kind of unique telepathy, prompted Lindsay to describe what it was exactly that Mr. Steffensen had on his mind. Lindsay forced back a smile to make her next point. "Fine, I won't say any more about it," she said, and stood to take the dinner plates to the kitchen. "Why do I always have to apologize for stating the obvious?" She left a relieved Sandi shaking her head.

A short while later, Sandi ran to catch up with Steven on his way out the door with Mollie.

"I thought you had reading to do; otherwise, I would have told you where I was going," he said.

"I need the walk," she responded, zipping up her jacket.

They headed up Stoneyhouse Street, turned up Maple, and crossed Pine Bud Avenue in the direction of the Square.

"I understand that Joe Steffensen made quite an impression on you."

"He's a nice guy, that's all, and he's not like Shawn."

"That's good to know." Steven had never held back on his judgment of her former boyfriend.

"We talked all evening and it was like five minutes. He wanted to hear all about my research. And he knows so much about art and architecture. Travelled a lot. He told me about growing up and his parents' divorce. To be honest, it was the most relaxing time I've had in years."

"All of that and he's good-looking?" Steven's eyes twinkled.

"How did you know?"

"Your mother. Down to the minutest detail." He laughed and moved Mollie's leash from one hand to the other. "So, are you going out with him again?"

"We're going for a walk on Sunday afternoon if the weather's nice."

"I see."

"You don't sound pleased."

"No, I'm fine," he mused. "I shouldn't judge Joe. I've never met him. But he clearly comes from money."

"So? He never talks about it. Okay, so he looks the part . . ."

"Sorry, Sandi, I grew up in this town when everyone knew their place. And place was defined by old money and people who didn't mind letting you know it. I guess it's left me with preconceived notions of the rich."

"Grandma and Granddad Martel certainly had nothing to be ashamed about. Granddad was proud of his years on the railway. They both worked very hard all their lives and their children did quite well."

"True, but they didn't have the pedigree, that's what I'm saying. I guess I'm just a little bitter."

"It's funny you should say that. Joe told me that his mother is all about appearances. What people will say, that sort of thing. I'd hoped people were long past that nonsense."

"Not if it helps define who they are, my sweet."

"Anyway, Dad, as far as Joe and I are concerned, it was just a dinner. We're friends, that's all."

"Okay, but just to be clear so I'll know for future reference. He picked you up here and took you to dinner, told you his life story, listened to yours, paid for dinner, and then you went back to his place?" He struggled to keep from laughing too much.

"Yes."

"I can see where that was definitely not a date."

"Why don't you believe me? I can be his friend, can't I?"

"Sure, but for the life of me, there must be something wrong with the man if all he wants to be is your friend."

"I think you're just a tad biased."

"Maybe I am, but I'm not blind, and neither is he." Steven chuckled as they rounded the corner. "Let's hurry. It's getting dark and chilly at the same time."

* * * * *

On Friday morning, Jeanne entered the empty Sinclair house to an eerie silence. She slipped off her coat and hung it in the hall next to the mirror as she had done so many times before. Gregory had left several copies of the *Globe and Mail* spread out on the mahogany dining table. She gathered them immediately and placed them in a recycling bin near the kitchen door. Looking around the room, she noted the silver service, Royal Doulton china, and Waterford crystal, once immaculately clean and sparkling, were now tarnished and dusty. *It's a wonder Emily didn't ship that off to Nova Scotia*, she thought.

The room sparked childhood memories. She reached out and touched the dining room table. She remembered how she would sneak downstairs late on Saturday nights and peer through the half-opened door at a group of well-dressed men, each with a glass in hand. She'd have to hold her breath to keep from coughing from the cigarette and pipe smoke. There were doctors, judges, clergy, and politicians—men of wealth and power and secrets. Sometimes they talked in hushed tones, but her adolescent ears caught every word. Through the French doors, in an adjoining room, their wives gathered and spoke the names of women whom she never knew. Their words were often derogatory and condescending. Occasionally, they would laugh and share stories of their travels and the books they had read. Those were the times Jeanne enjoyed the most. No one ever knew that she heard their stories. No one ever knew that she shared their secrets. Little did they know that one day, sooner rather than later, they would all need caregivers like her father did. And the caregivers would give them little deference because deference was no longer given, despite the fact it was still expected by them.

Now Jeanne pulled her cotton sweater tightly around her as she felt a chill race from her neck to her feet. She reached to turn up the heat and crossed the hallway to her father's study. The smell of stale furniture wax and dust permeated the room. She sat at his desk and ran her hands across the surface in a swirling motion. The edge of the desk was worn and scratched. She surveyed the room. She sat back in the large, wooden chair that creaked when she moved and turned her attention to the desk in front of her. In the bottom right drawer she found a small wooden box with an unusual silver latch. It was unlocked. Curious, she raised the lid to find a stack of cancelled cheques that she removed and studied carefully. She sifted through them twice, checking the dates. *Just as I suspected*, she thought. She tucked them into her large leather handbag, returned the empty box, left her father's study, and headed upstairs to the master bedroom. There, she straightened the two sets of drapes and checked to see that the windows were tightly closed.

She returned to the downstairs, gathered her coat and purse, locked the doors, and returned home. Later that afternoon, in the privacy of her bedroom, she looked again at each cancelled cheque, noting the dates. She was interrupted by a phone call from Jonathan Hamlyn.

"Jeanne, Emily phoned me yesterday and I wanted to touch base with you."

"Oh? What did she want?"

"Well, it's a little dicey, Jeanne. She wants full disclosure of the will."

"She used the words 'full disclosure'?"

Jonathan laughed. "Well, no, but it's what she meant. She wants a copy of the will. She's entitled to it, of course." He cleared his throat. "We have to tell her, about the money and the settlement your father made. I'm just wondering, should I tell her? Or do you prefer to do so?"

Jeanne took a short, stuttered breath. *And so it begins.* "Go ahead, Jonathan. Tell her what's in the will."

"Really? You know he left Mrs. Hannah West some money."

"Yes."

"Okay, then." Jonathan was surprised. "I should tell you as well that I have spoken to Mrs. West. I mentioned that there is a bequest, but I didn't tell her how much. And I did say it will be a while before she receives it."

There was silence on the other end of the line, and Jeanne considered the words she had just heard. A knot twisted in her stomach. Finally, in barely a whisper, she managed, "And her response?"

"Oh, not much. She just thanked me for calling. Is there a message that you want to give her? I could put you in touch . . ."

"No, absolutely not!"

"I'm sorry, Jeanne. I know this is difficult. I didn't know if you wanted to bring closure."

She ignored his suggestion. "Jonathan, if you talk to Emily about the will, or give her a copy, you need not mention their relationship. I mean, there is nothing in the will to indicate what happened. She was a friend of the family, that's all."

"I understand." He paused. "Jeanne, I should tell you. Your father sent her money from time to time over the years. I wasn't sure you knew."

"I know. Thanks for everything, Jonathan. I'll be in touch." She hung up and returned to the papers in front of her and carefully bundled them. She secured the cancelled cheques with an elastic band, dropped them into a brown envelope, and sealed it. The envelope remained unmarked, and she placed it where it would never be found.

* * * * *

Jeanne arrived at Steffensen Publishing that afternoon shortly before two. She went with a purpose, determined not to become emotional as in her last encounter. She hated showing Kurt her weakness, as she saw it. Outside his office, she stood with perfect posture in front of Doris McKinlay's desk, next to the ever-present vase of fresh flowers. She waited patiently for her to hang up the phone. "Doris, I'm here to see Kurt." She had little regard for Doris, and the feeling was mutual. Even when Jeanne and Kurt were married, she always sensed that Doris did everything she could to prevent Kurt from talking to her during the workday. When their divorce was in the works, Doris became even more protective.

"I'm sorry, Jeanne, he's very busy today. This is not a good day at all. He has meetings all afternoon."

"I see. And will these so-called meetings bring about world peace?"

"No, I expect not."

"Then tell him I wish to speak with him. I will only be a few minutes. And it's important."

"Yes, I'm sure it is. One moment."

Doris tapped on Kurt's door, entered, and closed it behind her.

"Jeanne is here. Sounds important."

"Always is," he said, without looking up.

"I told her you are busy, but . . ."

"It's okay, Doris. I'll see her. Was she nasty to you?"

Doris smiled. "Just going with her strengths, is all."

Without a glance, Jeanne passed Doris in the doorway, then stood and waited while the door closed behind her. "I know you're busy. I don't come here often. But this is important. We won't be overheard, will we?"

"No, Jeanne, we won't. Please, sit down." He motioned for her to sit on a sofa by the window. He remained at his desk, and momentarily glanced at the photo of Jaclyn in front of him, looking for solace. "As you recall, I hired the best architect in the country to design the place. I've no doubt he made the rooms soundproof. Now, what's this all about?"

"I spoke to Jonathan this morning. Emily has asked for a copy of the will."

"Didn't both of you review the contents with him already?"

"Yes, but Jonathan only told us what was in it, what we needed to know. He didn't actually give her a copy."

"At your request."

"Yes."

"Of course," Kurt quipped, "and he would do anything for you."

She ignored his comment. "I was concerned about some of the bequests. Now she wants him to send it to her. My guess is that it's not Emily but Gregory who wants it."

"They're entitled to see it."

"I know that."

"Well?"

"Father left money to Hannah. Not a big amount, in my view, but no doubt a substantial amount in her eyes."

Kurt wanted to contradict her by suggesting that Hannah might be a millionaire by now, but why prolong the conversation any more than necessary?

"And he put it in the will?"

"Yes. Fortunately, he doesn't state their relationship. I was worried about that because Father mentioned to me several times last summer that he left money to that woman. I assumed he put it in the will. But he had the good sense not to identify her."

"So what's the problem? Your secret appears to be safe."

"It's unlikely Emily will ask questions. She would never question Father's wishes. But I put nothing past that son of hers. I expect he'll hire someone to investigate who she is."

"Jeanne, you've been watching too much television."

"I don't watch television, Kurt. You know that."

"So what do you want to do? Tell Emily the truth? That your father left a sizable sum to a woman now living in a small community in
Bonavista Bay? Ask her to keep it to herself?"

"Do you think she would?"

"I have no idea. Emily is, to say the least, unpredictable. But with
something this sensitive, something that puts your father in a bad
light, it's likely she'd stay quiet. As I recall, Emily has always suspected
that your father had a relationship, albeit brief, with some other woman. She may not assume it was Hannah West. And even if she did, she
wouldn't say anything about it."

Jeanne sat for a moment in the silence of the room. *I don't want
Emily's pity*, she thought. *I don't want anyone's pity.* She searched for a
way to keep Emily quiet, and at that moment she felt more alone than
ever. The only person she knew who could keep Emily quiet upon
request was sitting across from her. Slowly, she looked up and met his
eyes.

"Kurt, would you ask her?"

"Pardon?"

"Would you ask her? Tell her the truth about Father and ask her
to keep it to herself. It's unlikely that Emily would do anything for me
if I asked. And yes, you're right, she would protect Father, but we all
know that if she would listen to anyone, it's you. She thinks you sit at
the right hand of God. If you would just tell her that Father left money
to some woman named Hannah West and we prefer it didn't get out.
Just leave it at that."

"Hold on. Just a minute." He sat up straight and gave her a stern
look. "I've been party to this cover-up for a long time. I have no desire
to compound the lies. It won't make any difference for her to know
that Charles left some money to a Mrs. Hannah West. Jeanne, for the
love of God, people don't care about that stuff anymore. Charles was
no different than a lot of other married men . . . or women, for that
matter."

"It makes a difference to me, Kurt."

"Why? Because that's all you have, memories of your father?"

His words hurt her to the core. She felt a sudden cold shiver spread from her shoulders through her arms to her fingertips. She fought the lump in her throat and her quivering lips. "Why?" she whispered. "Why do you try to hurt me? Does it make you feel good?" The words tumbled out, and she felt her throat tighten. As much as she railed against it, the emotion she had kept tightly reined for so long came pouring out. Her eyes brimmed with tears.

Across from her, at his desk, Kurt sat aghast. He wondered which persona of Jeanne's he was seeing today. He stood, reached in his pocket for his handkerchief, and passed it to her. Without speaking, he crossed the room, poured a glass of water, and laid it on the coffee table in front of the sofa.

She wiped her tears, sipped the water, and then cradled the glass in her lap. She did not look up. To do so, she knew, would cause her to make the greatest mistake of her life, to rest her head on his shoulder and beg for comforting. But she would not ask Kurt for that. Not now. Not ever.

"Jeanne, I'm sorry. I didn't mean that in a hurtful way. I'm just suggesting that it would be better, healthier, for you to move past your father's indiscretions, to put it all behind you, our marriage included, and find something for yourself for today. You have no reason to believe that anything more will come of this. Take one day at a time. As Mother says, that's how we get them anyway. It'll be forgotten once Emily and Gregory get the house. They won't question his actions."

His words did not provide the comfort he had hoped.

"I can do without your analysis, Kurt," she said, suddenly feeling a renewed sense of energy. "As far as Emily is concerned, Father's last connection with that woman, if she believes Hannah was the woman he had a relationship with, was over fifty years ago when she left the house for the last time. But the date on the will is two years ago. That means that he was thinking about her still, that even before his death he was thinking of her. What does that say about my father?"

"Jeanne, don't you think when the time is good, in the next few weeks, we should tell Joe and Lauren about Charles and Hannah? After all, Charles is gone; Virginia is gone."

"No," she said, emphatically. "It's bad enough that she took his money." She realized that she had hoped in vain. Kurt would not help, no matter how much she believed she deserved his help. She stood to leave, but paused momentarily. "There's absolutely no need for Joe and Lauren to know what their grandfather did."

"They probably already suspect it. There have been rumours."

"Which we are not going to confirm." She gathered her purse and coat and moved toward the door.

"What about Emily? What are you planning to do?"

"I'll deal with it," she said, and closed the door behind her.

Doris came into the office to find Kurt standing at the far window looking toward Signal Hill. "Everything all right? She looked very upset."

Kurt sighed and turned back to his long-time friend. "I never know with Jeanne, Doris. Seems the estate of Charles Sinclair is stirring up a lot more dust than is warranted."

"Well, I've yet to meet a person who hasn't had turmoil as a result of inheritance. We went through hell in my family. My brother still doesn't talk to me, and it's been ten years since Dad died. All because I gave away my father's snow blower to the man who lived next door. Bless his heart, he used to come over and blow out the driveway when Dad was sick. Maintained the machine every year. So when Dad died, I told him to keep it. But my brother felt I did wrong. Said I should have consulted him." She straightened the folders on Kurt's desk and placed them in a neat pile on the left. "Personally, I think there should be a law that says when you die everything goes to a charity of your choice. No family. Period. No arguing."

Kurt laughed. "Sounds like a good idea, Doris. I must have Quentin change my will. I had planned to leave everything to you."

"Get to work."

"Yes, ma'am."

* * * * *

It was rare for Lindsay's parents, Edna and Stuart Mackenzie, to make the long drive from Corner Brook to St. John's. But Lindsay's sister, Sharon, wanted to do some fall shopping and decided to bring along her parents to get them out of the house before the winter set in. They arrived at the Martel home on Sunday evening.

The next afternoon, while Stuart slept in the family room, Lindsay encouraged her mother to take her knitting and join her on the back deck. For the next half-hour, Edna talked about people at her church, most of whom Lindsay only vaguely knew, but she listened anyway because she knew that her mother rarely had someone's full attention. When she paused, Lindsay asked questions to encourage her.

She passed her mother a cup of hot tea. "So, how's everyone in Falcon Cove? You mentioned the new minister. A woman?"

"Yes, and she's a lovely lady. Her name is Carrie West. What kind of tea is this, Lindsay?" She laid down the cup and picked up the second knitting needle.

"Green. I got it in a specialty store in the Square. It's good for you."

"It's very nice, but don't serve it to your father. You know how fussy he is about his tea. What was I saying? Oh yes, the minister. This is her second year back home. You're not going to believe who her mother is."

"Who?"

"Hannah West. She was Hannah Parsons before she married Marshall West. Poor man, passed away a few years ago. Terrible struggle with cancer. I remember my friend Frances, Hannah's sister, telling me all about it. But the Lord rewarded him by bringing him home early."

Lindsay avoided the theology of that statement by shifting the topic.

"So Reverend West grew up in Falcon Cove. That's nice. She knows the area."

"Yes, and she went off to university. Sharp as a tack, they say. Got a good education. I think Frances said that Carrie spent years in northern Ontario on several charges, but then when poor ol' Marsh died, she wanted to come home to be with her mother. A good Christian."

"Yes, of course." Lindsay looked away and focused on the hanging baskets of petunias along the deck to keep from laughing. "Well, it's nice for Carrie to be back here."

"I only heard her that one Sunday when we were home in July, but, Lindsay, let me tell you, that lady can pray like no one else. I felt like I was sitting with our Saviour Himself. She's wonderful with the older people in the congregation."

"That's great. Just what they were looking for, wasn't it?"

"Yes, and it's about time. Everything today is geared toward youngsters. All that music and jumping around the altar. Good heavens! In my day the altar was sacred. Here they are now, up running around the communion table. It's ridiculous."

Lindsay could not help but laugh at her mother's assessment of the changing times in her church. "Carrie's mother, Hannah, she's younger than Frances and you?"

"Yes, not by much, a couple of years. Pretty girl, she was, when we were growing up. Lovely. Quiet little thing. Frances says that Hannah spends a lot of time with the seniors at the home, Serenity by the Sea. They're having a lot of trouble with that senior citizens home, you know. Needs a lot of maintenance and repair. But heaven knows when or how they'll raise money for it. And they're hoping to build a new church hall in Falcon Cove, since that other one collapsed in the windstorm."

Lindsay added more milk to her tea, which she had deliberately made strong to please her mother. "Did Hannah ever work?"

"She came in service here in town a few years after me." Edna continued to knit and look at her daughter at the same time. "Poor maid. I felt sorry for her. She only stayed a year or two."

"Where did she work? What family?"

"You've heard of them. The gentleman who just died. Sinclairs. Charles and Virginia Sinclair."

Lindsay looked up from her cross-stitch in surprise. "Really?

How interesting! I didn't know who they were until recently. Actually, Sandi just met his grandson, Joe. He's a Steffensen. His grandfather is Norwegian. That's where the name comes from. His father owns a big business here and his mother is a Sinclair, born and grew up here."

"So this young man that Sandi knows, his grandfather is Charles Sinclair?"

"Yes."

"Well, my dear, if he's anything like old man Sinclair," Edna warned, "tell Sandi to run away and keep on running. The grandfather was bad news."

CHAPTER 5

Thanksgiving weekend approached with the forecast of a potential hurricane for the east coast of Canada. Joe persuaded Sandi to join the Friday night group and offered to pick her up on the way to Lauren and Alan's home on Nottingham Place in the city's west end.

"Alan, your home is beautiful," she said as she slipped her jacket on a hanger in the huge hall closet. Her host looked like he had stepped out of an LL Bean catalogue. He was well over six feet tall with broad shoulders and dark curly hair.

"Thanks, Sandi. The architect was easy to work with." Alan nodded at Joe with a grin. "The rest is Lauren's touch."

"How long have you lived here?"

"Since we got married, three years ago. C'mon, everyone's in the living room."

She committed to memory every detail of home decor, as she knew her mother would be quizzing her the next day. It wasn't difficult because the colour and furniture fit together in a seamless and appealing pattern.

She followed the two men down the hall and made a quick study of the beautiful living space. Two large sofas of taupe suede faced each other in the centre of the room and were lined with a collection of brightly coloured striped cotton cushions. A large stone fireplace with granite hearth was centred in the back wall. There were four smaller tables and a coffee table of light teak and tinted glass. The walls, a creamy off-white, were a wonderful backdrop for a collection of beautifully framed paintings and photos. Another seating area in the far corner had a large flat-screen TV and a collection of neatly piled VHS tapes. Lauren referred to them as her "comfort tapes," to use when she just needed to escape the real world.

Sandi looked at the photos across the mantel and observed that the Steffensen gene was clearly dominant. "Joe, I think you look more like your grandfather than your father."

Joe nodded. "Yeah, everyone says that. Dad's a Thorburn, more like Grandma." Sandi returned to her comfortable armchair. "Lauren, I just love your house. Alan said the architect was co-operative."

"Yeah," she laughed. "Actually, we just told him what to do, didn't we, Joe?"

"I even agreed to the one thousand shades of beige." Joe shuddered.

"Not beige." Quentin scolded him. "Remember that Friday night with the paint samples? There's bisque, cream, toast, wheat . . ." He gave his best imitation of Lauren.

Lauren ignored Quentin's mocking. "I hate dark houses, that's all. They give me the creeps," she said, tossing her long blonde hair. "I appreciate the colourful pillows and other stuff during those unending weeks of rain, drizzle, and fog in the spring."

Sandi smiled and recalled Joe's description of his "well looked after" little sister over dinner one night. But as she listened to Lauren talk about her work during the evening, she imagined that in legal circles she was a force to be reckoned with. She had already met Quentin and David, but for the first time she appreciated the accuracy of Sara's earlier descriptions of them. She wondered what the four of them were like as children and teenagers.

The dining room table was set in aqua-coloured dishes and Scandinavian-styled cutlery. The arrangement of flowers in the middle of the table was a gorgeous blend of yellows, oranges, reds, and browns, highlighted by sunflowers and burgundy mini-carnations.

As they passed around the spinach salad made with goat cheese, honey-roasted pecans, and raspberries, Sara asked if there was news on the Sinclair house.

"As a matter of fact, I had a visit this morning from Emily," Joe responded. "She flew down on Wednesday, as she explained, to get the gardens ready for winter."

Sandi and Sara exchanged looks that questioned why someone would fly to another province to make a garden ready for winter, especially when the house wasn't being lived in. Joe continued. "She said something about Gregory coming here this weekend for a conference at one of the hotels. So be forewarned, everyone. He's in town."

"The conference on reproductive health," David explained. "Meeting at the Delta Hotel, I think. I assume that's where he'd be going. It's his area."

Joe nodded. "Anyway, Emily wants the house renovated, and she wants it done tomorrow morning," he said sarcastically.

Quentin was shaking a generous amount of Parmesan cheese on his crepe. "My guess is Gregory is behind this. He likely wants to put the place on the market as soon as possible and get the money for it."

Sandi was taking in the conversation with interest. "I take it Gregory is her son?"

"Sorry, Sandi," Joe said. "We're talking about people you don't know. Yeah, Gregory Masters is my Aunt Emily's son. Best described as a pompous ass. His father financed his way through medical school out of guilt for leaving them both behind. His father and mother split up years ago."

Lauren shook her head. "In any event, Joe, I don't envy you taking this on, the house, I mean."

"I haven't done it yet, Lauren. Michael and I are meeting Emily at the house tomorrow morning to look at what she wants. A lot of things have to fall into place before we commit to that. I s'pose I could always give it over to Michael. He likes a challenge."

Quentin poked at his salad. "I think you should take the job yourself," he said definitively.

"Why?" Joe asked.

"It's money in the bank. It's another demonstration of your reno-vating style."

Joe raised an eyebrow. "Have you considered doing TV ads for Steffensen Architects?"

Quentin ignored the question and continued picking at his salad, his least favourite food group. "Gregory has no idea about renovations or how much a sheet of drywall costs. He won't argue the bill, and he wants it done as soon as possible. Besides, you know there's money there to pay for it."

"Guess so," Joe said, "but is it worth the aggravation? That's what I have to decide. There's a lot of restructuring to be done. Besides, they say it's never good to work for your relatives." He noted Alan and Lauren's inquisitive look. "Of course, there are exceptions," he added with a laugh.

Recalling an earlier conversation with her mother, Sandi waited for a break in the conversation to ask a question. "This is slightly off topic, everyone, but my grandmother Mackenzie told Mom recently that a friend of hers from Falcon Cove—that's where Grandma was born—came in to St. John's many years ago to work in service with a family. She said that the young girl went to work at the Sinclairs'."

"Really?" Lauren asked.

"Her name was Hannah Parsons. Hannah West now. Did you ever hear your mother or grandparents mention that name?"

"No, can't recall that name," Joe answered. "You, Lauren?"

She shook her head. "But then, if she left before Mother was born, well, she wouldn't have heard anything. Our grandparents wouldn't be too attached to someone who worked for them. She would have been considered the 'help.'"

"Just thought I'd mention it. Apparently, she was only young, just seventeen, and she only stayed a year or two. My grandmother worked in service for three years with another family."

"Those women were made of different stuff," Sara observed. "Can you imagine what it was like to come in here at that age from a small outport community and move into a huge house with a bunch of strangers?" she asked. "The expectations on those girls must have been enormous."

Lauren nodded. "Absolutely. And I know they're my grandparents, and they're both gone, but believe me, this Hannah you mentioned, Sandi, likely didn't have an easy time of it with them. My heart goes out to her."

* * * * *

Saturday morning began with a vengeance. The wind had increased during the night, and by dawn it was accompanied by torrential rain. Joe pulled up in front of Michael's house on Dublin Road at eight forty-five and waited for his architectural partner to lock the door to his house and run to the car.

"If this is a tropical storm, what's a hurricane like?" Michael wiped the rain from his face with his hand and tossed his black leather-covered notebook in the back seat. "And this is only the beginning. Supposed to get worse throughout today and tonight."

"Yeah, it woke me up a few times last night." Joe manoeuvred through an intersection, avoided potholes in the pavement, and headed down Forest Road. "Michael, I have no idea what to expect here. I suggest that we don't agree to anything until we get a really good sense of what we're up against. I have the plans to the house but haven't studied them carefully, so God only knows what we'll find. On top of that, my Aunt Emily, as Sara would say, is peanut butter shy of a good sandwich."

Michael laughed. "I take it Sara loves peanut butter."

"Sara would eat newspaper with peanut butter on it."

He pulled into the long paved driveway of the Sinclair home. They peered through the rain at the large stone and brick structure that sat in the middle of an acre lot surrounded by mature trees and gardens. A black wrought iron fence, worse for wear, marked the perimeter of the property.

"Was that the servants' quarters, Joe?" Michael pointed to the attached building behind the main house.

"Years ago, yes. I have no idea what's in there now. Guess we'll soon find out. Notice the conservatory on the front. And would you believe the place has ten working fireplaces?" He turned off the car. "One more thing. Whatever we do, Emily'll want it done for free."

Michael gave his business partner a sharp look. "We're doing this *pro bono*?"

"Not on your life. If we do it at all, someone's going to pay. C'mon." They dashed through the gate to the front door, rang the doorbell, and prayed that it worked as the rain poured down on them.

Emily opened the door and stood back, seemingly surprised that it was raining. "Joe, there you are. Good morning. Please come in."

"Emily, this is my associate, Michael Preston. Michael, this is my mother's sister, Emily."

"Nice to meet you, Michael. You both come highly recommended. Please take off your jackets. Gregory is in the living room," she said, and closed the door tightly.

Gregory was standing by the window, sizing up mahogany window sashes and pretending he knew something about the structure of houses. His arms were folded across his chest, and as usual he rocked back and forth, heel to toe, toe to heel. When Joe and Michael entered, he turned and walked immediately toward them with a hand outstretched. His voice boomed loud enough to be heard next door. "Joe, it's good to see you again. Didn't think we'd see each other so soon after Grandfather's funeral, eh?"

"No, no, I guess not."

"But then, I didn't know the house would be ours, did I, Mother?" He glanced at her with a firm look and spoke with a chastising tone. She was standing by the stone fireplace, forcing a smile.

Interesting choice of words, thought Joe. *Ours*. He turned his attention to his aunt. "Emily, you think it is best to renovate before putting the house on the market?"

Gregory interrupted. "Actually, Joe, the renovations are my idea. I want to get the most we can for this . . . place," he said, deliberately avoiding the word he was thinking. "I know the estate isn't settled yet, but the will states explicitly that the house and its contents belong to Mother. And what's hers is mine." .

Joe looked at Michael with an expression that communicated the project was definitely going to be more difficult than he first thought. Michael gave a half smile in acknowledgement.

* * * * *

Shortly past noon, Jeanne pulled back the drapes, looked at the torrents of rain, and saw Emily hurrying up the stone walkway. She was dressed in a dark green trench coat two sizes too big for her, the tail of which almost reached the ground, flapping and twisting around her legs in the high winds. She struggled to keep the hood up and tightly clasped around her face. Jeanne hurried to the door with Leah close behind.

"Emily, what in heaven's name brings you out on a morning like this? And how did you get here?" Jeanne ushered her in and closed the heavy door behind her.

Puffing to catch her breath, Emily explained. "Gregory. He flew in last night. He has a meeting downtown, so I asked him to drop me off here. I didn't want to stay in that house in this weather. The electricity was blinking. Besides, I thought it better to spend the afternoon with you. He'll come by for me when his meetings are over later this evening." She had unwrapped her rainwear and handed it over to Leah, who hung it up by the door and quickly ran to place a towel underneath it to catch the dripping rainwater.

"Leah, I guess this means Emily will be here for lunch."

"Yes, of course," she answered, knowing exactly how her employer felt about that prospect. She left to set another place at the small table in the corner of the solarium.

A few minutes later, after fixing her hair, Emily joined Jeanne for lunch. "Why are we eating out here this time of year?"

"I like it here. And it is heated, Emily. It's not like we're in the garage."

"Oh, no, of course not. And it is such a pretty room." She studied the furniture as if she was trying to commit it to memory. "I've always loved this house, you know. So . . . comfortable."

They sat and Jeanne listened to Emily prattle on about the weather and the electricity while she poured tea. Emily checked the pattern on the Royal Albert Rose Cottage cup and saucer in front of her to see if they matched. "Oh Leah, would you mind making me some toast? Multigrain, if you have it. Gregory says that's better for me than white. But I don't know. What do you think? Lightly buttered. I didn't have much for breakfast. Gregory bought those pastries—danishes, I think they're called. Horrid things. All fat and sugar. Thank you."

Jeanne turned the conversation away from Emily's eating habits, as they were, after all, inexplicable. "Did you see about the gardens?"

"Oh yes, the gardeners will be in next week, the first fine day, to pull up the summer flowers and cover the shrubs and so on. I gave them explicit directions."

"I see," Jeanne responded mindlessly, straightening the cuff of her blouse and adjusting her gold watch strap.

"I think I told you we are planning to renovate the house. Joe and his friend were over this morning to look at the place. They said something about a new roof and new windows and entrance. And they went on about plumbing and electrical work and supporting walls. I think that would 'raise the resale value,' or at least that's what he said. That's why I'm having the garden taken care of as well."

"Joe's friend, as you call him, is Michael, Emily. He's his business partner. He's an architect, too." She moved the fork through her salad searching for the pieces of tomato. "So you said resale. Then you've decided to sell it?"

"Yes, Jeanne, what else is there to do? You have this lovely home here, so you don't need it. I thought for a while about moving here, but, frankly, I have so many friends back in Wolfville, and the weather is awful here."

Jeanne resisted mentioning that Nova Scotia had experienced the full brunt of the hurricane yesterday and it had been downgraded to a tropical storm by the time it reached the Avalon Peninsula. But she knew that Emily would never accept that.

"And I talked to Kurt about it. I called him at home. He was all for it."

That statement piqued Jeanne's attention. She returned her cup to the table. "Kurt? What ever for?"

"Well, I figured he's so knowledgeable about the market. He thought I would get a fair price for it. He's so kind to help. Honestly, Jeanne, it's too bad you couldn't hold on to him."

"Indeed." Jeanne altered her tone to one of indifference, but in her mind she wanted to throw the tea at her sister.

"I'm so glad you agree. Of course, I'm not selling it for a bargain. We'll hold out until we get what it's worth, and then some."

"In the meantime, what do you plan to do about the furniture, dishes, linens? They'll be in quite a state with carpenters going in and out."

"Of course! I never thought of that."

"Then why don't I have the more fragile pieces moved up here? I could store them downstairs until we can pack them well enough to ship to your home."

"Jeanne, that is so kind of you. Thank you very much. I hope it's not an inconvenience." She poured extra oil and vinegar across the salad bowl. "You know, I've been thinking a lot about all those beautiful dishes at the house. Remember that Spode porcelain set? It's all there, you know. It's likely worth a lot. What are we going to do with it?"

"It's your decision, Emily. It doesn't matter to me. After all, they're only dishes."

"I believe they belong to our whole family." Her eyes widened. "Perhaps Lauren would like to have some. I don't have a daughter. And Gregory, he doesn't seem much interested in women, for some reason."

Jeanne smiled behind her water glass. *If you only knew.*

"What do you think? Should we offer some of it to Lauren?"

"Lauren doesn't have much interest in old things such as antique dishes. Her house is ultramodern. I can't say those things would fit in very well."

"Oh dear, young people today . . . how about Joe? Does he have a woman in his life? Someone serious, I mean?"

"Not that I know of."

Emily seemed exasperated. "Oh, I'm sure he would tell you if he did. You're so close. Then, what about Kurt's wife? She's a lovely lady. Quite gentle. Offered to do what she could when Father died and when Mother passed away, too, as I recall."

"Emily, I'm sure she and Kurt have more dishes than they'll ever use. Let's just leave it for now. I'll talk to Lauren."

Leah returned and placed the toast and a small glass dish of marmalade on the table in front of Emily.

"Leah, you go on home now before the weather worsens. Emily and I will clear up."

Leah nodded and received a tell-tale glance from Jeanne as she left the room.

Emily scooped a heaping tablespoon of marmalade onto her toast and took a large mouthful. Jeanne looked away in horror. Once she swallowed, she continued. "Have you heard anything about the rest of the estate? It certainly is taking a long time."

"No. There are many investments and other assets to uncover, taxes, that sort of thing."

Emily squirmed in her chair. "I read through Father's will. And Gregory did as well. We were wondering about that money he left to a Mrs. West. Who is she?"

"I have no idea."

"It seems kind of strange, don't you think? I know Father was a generous man, but to single out one person to receive such a sizable sum. He must have had good reason, I suppose, but for the life of me, I can't imagine what it is." She paused and wiped her hands in the linen napkin. "Jeanne, I have to ask, between you and me, do you suppose it might be a woman that he had a relationship with?"

"As I said, Emily, I have no idea. Just let it go. I'm sure we'll all manage quite well without that part of the bequest."

"Oh, why, yes, of course. Just saying, that's all."

Minutes passed as the two sisters ate in silence.

Emily regrouped and pressed the issue despite her fear of her sister's reaction. "Jeanne, Gregory is headstrong like his father. He gets an idea in his mind and he won't let it go. He wants to find out about this Mrs. West. Would Jonathan know about her?"

"As far as I'm concerned, it's no one's business. And whatever Jonathan knows, he's not at liberty to say," Jeanne explained with an authoritative tone, but not knowing if it was accurate. "My point is, I don't think this should become a public thing. Besides the fact that this woman could go public with her relationship with Father, if indeed there was one, it would be terribly embarrassing for you and me, and she might also demand more than what she's getting. If we have to go to court to protect our inheritance . . ."

"Oh my, no! I couldn't possibly have anything to do with courts. They publish all that court news in the newspapers now, you know."

"Good. Then there's no need to pursue this or talk about it any more. After all, you and I agreed a long time ago that there are some things that our children are better off not knowing about. Gregory, for instance, would be humiliated if he ever knew about his father and those fraud charges. You know what I am talking about." Jeanne knew that reminder would finish the topic quite nicely.

"Of course. I'll try to talk him out of it."

"See to it that you do. Do whatever is necessary to persuade him otherwise." Her tone indicated that her directive was not open for further discussion.

They finished their meal in silence. "Jeanne, if it's all right with you, I think I will lie down for a while. This low pressure is bringing on a migraine."

"Choose whichever one of the guest rooms you would like. Make yourself comfortable."

A short time later, Jeanne pulled back the Belgian lace curtains in the dining room and watched the rain running down the glass. *Tomorrow evening,* she thought, *and those two will be gone.* She closed the French doors and reached for the phone. She opened her notebook to the number for a moving company she had contacted earlier in the week and dialled it. Their answering machine came on, so she left a message to be at the Sinclair house on Forest Road by 9:00 a.m. on Monday.

She walked quietly upstairs and found Emily in a guest room at the end of the hall wrapped in a pink cashmere blanket on the bed, apparently asleep. Jeanne stood in the doorway and stared at her sister. The last two years had taken their toll, she thought. She looked ghostly pallid. She pulled the door closed quietly and ran her hand down the sturdy oak railing on the stairs as she returned to the first floor. The wind gusted and heavy rain beat against the living room window. She sat in her favourite armchair, picked up her Mary Wesley novel, turned on the lamp, and tucked a tartan throw over her legs.

But it was a challenge to concentrate on the words. Her mind wandered to Virginia in the hospital only two years ago, her father's last days, and Emily's inquiry about Hannah. *Emily*, she thought, *I could tell you more, if I knew you could handle it. I could tell you about my wedding day, thirty-five years ago, when Virginia told me she was not my mother. And the day I met my mother, the day she stood in this very room and begged me never to tell. Yes, Emily, there is so much more that I could tell you, but not now and not ever, if I can help it.*

* * * * *

"Mother, what are you doing?" Carrie turned the corner to her mother's bedroom door and noticed the room in an unusual state of disarray.

"My mother used to say, 'better the day, better the deed,' so I figured with this weather, it's a good day to clean. I'm getting rid of clothes I don't wear anymore."

Carrie laughed, and sat on the bed. "I'd prefer to sleep on a day like this. I was just talking to Aunt Iris and she suggested, and I quote, 'staying in the bunk.'" She looked around the room. "Which pile is the giveaway one?"

"On the chair." Hannah had taken everything out of her small closet and was returning the items she wanted to keep. On her dresser she had laid out several items of jewellery to give away.

"You keeping the stuff in your jewellery box?"

"Oh yes. Not much there. Just my life membership pin from the United Church Women, Grandmother's ring, and a few necklaces and brooches given me over the years."

Carrie picked up the small white box. Its corners were worn and there was a spill mark from many years ago. "You could use a new one," she observed.

"That one'll do me fine, Carrie. I don't have the Queen's jewels."

Carrie slowly opened the box and looked lovingly at the items inside. In the bottom, Hannah had tucked the church bulletin from her husband's funeral service. Carrie picked it up and noticed a large item underneath loosely wrapped in tissue paper. She removed the paper and was surprised to find a man's pocket watch. She held it up and turned to her mother. "Who owns this? Dad certainly didn't have anything like this that I can remember. It looks antique."

Hannah turned to see what her daughter had found. She stopped, laid a silk blouse on the bed, and steadied herself on the nearby chair. "It belonged to Charles, Carrie." She gently took the watch and ran her thumb across its face. "He sent it to me along with an old hymnary he had. It was just after Christmas last year. His note said he wanted me to have it because, according to him, I was the only person who would cherish it. He wanted me to have the book because I was the only real Christian he ever knew—so he said. Mind you, I could never use it, because it's Anglican." She stopped, and smiled. "I used to sing hymns while I worked, and he liked that. And I was always fascinated by that watch."

Carrie was surprised by her mother's sudden candour. "I had no idea he was in touch with you."

"It came in the mail one day with a brief note. My guess is he knew he was not well. I was just as surprised then as I was when I got that call from Mr. Hamlyn. Believe me, Carrie, I never went looking for anything." Her voice was reduced to a faint shaky whisper.

"I know that. It's okay. He obviously wanted you to have it. Nothing wrong with that." She watched as Hannah placed the watch back in the jewellery box, lowered the lid, and waited for a click to indicate it was closed.

Carrie walked to the window and looked out across the bay. The wind was churning up whitecaps, and sprays of white were lashing against the shoreline. She could see the tiny boats bobbing against each other at the nearby wharf. She wondered whether any of the summer residents would lose their makeshift wharves in the storm. Wind gusts made the house strain and creak. She prayed it would die down before dark.

"You've never talked about him before." She watched as her mother returned to tidying her shelves. "His passing really affected you, didn't it?" she asked quietly.

"Yes, I suppose it has. And I've just been trying to put it out of my mind."

"Would you like to tell me about him?"

"No."

"Why not?"

Hannah paused. She collected some favourite books off the floor and placed them back on the top shelf of a bookcase, one by one. Her hymn book and Bible were used as bookends.

"Because I feel like I would be betraying your father." There, for the first time, she uttered the words aloud.

"Mother, don't be ridiculous. You hardly knew Dad while you were living in St. John's. When you were growing up, you said you'd speak to him occasionally on the main road, getting mail, in Sunday school, that's all."

"What I did was wrong, Carrie. *Wrong*. And I made a promise to myself a long time ago that I would never let that story get out. It's not fair to anyone. No one should have to pay for my stupidity."

Carrie sighed and shook her head. She ran her hands across the yellow flowered polyester bedspread that had become crumpled with all the clothes spread across it. "I really wish you wouldn't be so hard on yourself. You were a young girl, only seventeen years old. He was an older man, a man of money and social position. Your employer, for heaven's sake. He should have known better. If there is anyone to blame here . . ." She stopped, not sure how far to go with this.

"You'd better get back to your Meditation for tomorrow, Carrie. The day is wearing on and, you never know, we might lose power."

Knowing her mother as well as she did, she realized that the topic of conversation for now had ended. She would have to leave it to her mother to revive, if indeed she ever wanted to do so. Perhaps some evening over a game of Scrabble, she'd get to the truth.

* * * * *

At the Martel home later that evening, as she cut up vegetables for supper, Lindsay asked her daughter how Joe's meeting had gone with his aunt.

"Emily wants to sell the house and Joe suggested that renovations would make it more saleable," Sandi explained.

"That old place? Good grief, it'll need a lot of work. But if anyone can fix it up, Joe can. Personally, I'd suggest putting a match to it. What about Joe's mother, Jeanne? Does she get a share of the house?"

"From what I understand, she got money, but that's it. Joe said something about the house being originally in his grandmother's name. According to Charles's will, they wanted the house to go to Emily, presumably as the eldest daughter, and money went to Jeanne. Kind of strange since Jeanne spent so much time there. But that's the Sinclairs." Sandi took tomatoes and cheese from the refrigerator to make a salad. "By the way, I asked Joe and Lauren about the young woman, Hannah, and they had never heard of her. Lauren said she was likely gone and forgotten by her grandparents. I got the impression they didn't treat their staff very well."

"She may have been gone and forgotten by them, but Hannah is alive and well and living in Falcon Cove." Lindsay sought the bag of carrots from the refrigerator crisper and passed it to Sandi at the counter.

"She only lived with them a year, didn't she? Perhaps they were nasty to her and she couldn't take it."

Lindsay stopped at the kitchen counter. She turned back to Sandi and pursed her lips. "Sandi, I don't know if I should be telling you this, but . . ."

"But what?"

"I was talking to Mother last night and I mentioned that you were gone over to Lauren Steffensen's for supper. Mother didn't have kind words for Charles Sinclair, believe me. She told me that, according to Frances, her sister left the Sinclairs because she had a baby."

"Really?" Sandi responded. "So she went back to Falcon Cove and had the baby?"

"No, she had the baby here in St. John's. Then she went home."

"Do they know who the father was?"

"Yes, but I'm hesitant to say." Lindsay got her daughter's full attention. Sandi stopped, laid down the knife, and stared at her mother. "Who? Is it someone we know?"

Lindsay nodded. "According to Frances, the father was Mr. Sinclair."

CHAPTER 6

Mid-October brought an unusual stretch of milder weather on the east coast. Hannah sat at the kitchen table watching carefully as Emily ate her porridge without spilling any.

"Mrs. Green? Do you suppose it would be all right for me to take Emily to the park? It's just up the street."

"Mrs. Sinclair believes that Emily is too young."

"She's almost three! I think the reason why she's so fussy about going to bed is she doesn't get enough fresh air. Maybe it would help."

"I don't know, Hannah. You can ask. It certainly is a nice day for it." She laid down the bread pans long enough to look out the back kitchen window. The large maples had turned yellow and red and a few leaves had dropped in the garden. Overhead, the sun shone brilliantly in a deep blue autumn sky.

"Then, I will ask. Is Mrs. Sinclair around?"

"I believe she just left," Mrs. Green answered while she rubbed the tops of the bread loaves with buttered parchment paper.

Hannah stood, wiped Emily's face, and reached for her little hand. "C'mon, Emily, let's see if we can make this a special day." Surely, Emily's father would give her permission, she thought.

The door to the study was opened, and Hannah stood and

watched Charles as he worked at his desk. *His shirt is always so white and neatly ironed. And he is a very handsome man.* Charles looked up to see her standing in the doorway.

"Want something, Hannah?"

"Ah, yes, sir, I was just wondering if it would be okay for me to take little Emily to the park. I think it would be so good for her to get some fresh air. Maybe it would help her sleep better."

"I see nothing wrong with that. Just watch her carefully." He looked down at the little one standing still next to Hannah. "Do you want to go to the park with Hannah?"

Emily nodded.

"Then, go ahead. But be a good girl. And listen to Hannah."

Emily nodded again, and they were off.

To no surprise, dozens were strolling through Bannerman Park. Hannah brought a blanket and Emily's doll for her to play with. For the next hour, they sat under a large maple, and Hannah tried to teach Emily the colours around her.

When they entered the side door of the house, Emily ran to her mother with a handful of maple leaves. Virginia quickly ushered her to her bedroom and asked Mrs. Green to make sure Emily's hands were cleaned. She scowled at Hannah. "Where did you go, young lady?"

Hannah was taken aback. "I . . . ah . . . took Emily to the park. We weren't gone long. Mister said it . . ."

"Don't make excuses. You should have asked me first. Do you understand?"

Hannah nodded, her throat tightened in emotion. "I'm sorry," she managed weakly.

"Just don't ever do that again." And with that directive, Virginia turned and headed upstairs, leaving Hannah standing distraught in the hallway. She fell into the hall bench next to the mirror and lowered her head. When she heard footsteps, she looked up to see Mrs. Green walking deliberately downstairs. "I told you," she whispered, "Mrs. Sinclair doesn't want Emily among people. She might catch something."

"But she's not sickly. She's strong. And she wants to play," Hannah explained with tears forming in her eyes.

"Hannah, let it go for now. Just remember to check everything with Emily's mother from now on. She's in charge." She headed for the kitchen.

Hannah stood slowly and turned at the end of the bannister to go upstairs. She would have to try to make it right. She glanced in the front room and saw Charles sitting in the corner chair enjoying his pipe. He was staring at her, and he beckoned for her to come in. She moved through the doorway.

"It looks like I got you in some trouble."

"It'll be all right."

"I will speak to my wife. I will explain that I gave you permission." He inhaled, then blew out a long puff of smoke. "Not that it'll make much difference. Virginia has the final say." He sighed, and Hannah heard him quietly add the words "in everything," though she was sure he didn't intend for her to hear.

Later that night, in the stillness of the house, Hannah lay in bed, feeling very much alone, and unable to sleep. Even Mrs. Green was upset with her. Would they send her home? Her stomach churned as she thought back on the cold hard look that Virginia had given her. *Why is she so angry at me?*

Finally, after an hour of restlessness, she pushed back the blankets, got out of bed, and in the darkness reached for a dressing gown. She tiptoed through the doorway and down the stairs, mindful to avoid the sides of the steps that creaked. She turned at the bottom and was startled to hear a voice.

"Who is it?"

She turned back and looked into the front room to see one light and Charles sitting in the large corner armchair. The table in front of him was scattered with newspaper. "Just me, Hannah, sir. I'm sorry to disturb you. I wasn't feeling well, and Mrs. Green left a tonic for me in the kitchen."

"It's fine, Hannah. You did not disturb me. Are you quite ill?"

"Oh no, sir, just a stomach upset, that's all." She moved in through the door of the study. "You are up late."

"Yes, finally getting time to read the local paper. There's a lot go-ing on in this world, Hannah. And a lot going on here."

"Yes, sir, there is."

"Please, why don't you sit down and keep me company? It will help settle your stomach to sit for a while."

Hannah hesitated, but his warm smile was the only comfort she had received that day. She sat on the sofa next to his chair. There was a stark silence between them. The clock on the mantel ticked away the seconds and minutes. The last embers of the fire flickered. Hannah stared at them, searching for words to hold a conversation. "My pop says we're in for some big changes here in Newfoundland. He thinks we haven't been treated right."

"There's a lot going on across the waters, Hannah. Newfoundland can hardly be important right now."

"I s'pose. Still . . . we're people."

"Your father doesn't like the current arrangement, then. The Commissioners."

"My pop doesn't like able-bodied people not being able to find work."

"Things will turn around," Charles reassured her, "but I don't know when."

"If you don't know, then I'm sure I don't." She shook her head and rubbed her stocking feet across the rug in front of the chair. She felt a chill go up her back, but she struggled not to shiver.

"Do you like working here, Hannah?"

"Oh yes, very much. I hope what I did today doesn't . . . well, doesn't change that."

"No, no, of course not. I spoke with Mrs. Sinclair. She worries, that's all. About our little Emily. One of Virginia's sisters died when she was just about Emily's age. Our Emily was named for her."

Hannah's eyes widened. "Oh my, I had no idea. I am so sorry. I promise I will make sure she is not harmed."

"I'm sure you will."

Hannah stared at her feet, wondering if she should not excuse herself and return to bed. "I should go back to bed now," she said.

He smiled warmly. "Hannah, you are a treasure."

She turned her head and met his eyes. "Thank you," she whispered.

"And you have a lovely smile," he added. "You are one very special young lady. I hope the world always treats you kindly." With that, he touched his fingertips to her cheek and held them there.

Hannah held her breath and for a moment the events of the day disappeared. She no longer felt alone or afraid.

* * * * *

OCTOBER 1995

It was darker than usual for early afternoon in October. Joe switched on a kitchen light and poured half a mug of cold tea down the drain. He rinsed his Fitzsu mug and put it in the dishwasher with the others. His habit was to use a clean mug once, then place it in the dishwasher. By the end of each day, there was usually a full line of coffee mugs on the top tier of his dishwasher.

Joe had decided to become an architect after he had travelled to Europe as a teenager with his family. His instructors in the school of architecture in Halifax had praised his natural affinity for design, but it was his skill at renovation that helped him to excel. By the time he completed a six-month work term in Oslo, he had already gained a reputation for unusual colour combinations and a unique style. His allegiance to heritage design was devout. He spent hours pouring over photographs and experimenting with materials in an attempt to restore a structure to its original design. By now, just a few years after graduation, he was gaining national attention as a first-class architect.

Now he stood at the granite counter and braced both hands against its edge, stepped one foot back, lowered his head, and thought about the renovations. He knew Quentin was right about the guaranteed money, but how would he ever deal with Gregory? He needed a sympathetic ear. Returning to his computer, he noticed that the monitor was blinking and, fearing a power outage, shut it off as he reached for the phone.

In her office at the university, Sandi had shifted some boxes of books and was reaching for the bottle of furniture polish when the phone rang. She was surprised to hear Joe's voice.

"You tracked me down," she said with a laugh.

"Yes, your dad said you decided it was a good day to work."

"Actually, I'm cleaning my office. It gets dusty, and there's some stuff that was shipped from Halifax that I hadn't opened."

"Could you use a break? I need to run something by you. I'll take you somewhere for coffee?"

"I'll be finished here soon. How 'bout I drop by your place? I'll pick up something on the way along. Frankly, I'm not fit to be seen out in a restaurant. I've got on my old jeans and sweatshirt."

Joe laughed. "I'm sure you look great. Come by when you can. I'll be here for the rest of the afternoon working on a design. It's not good outside, so be careful," he advised.

* * * * *

At home, in his study on Sunday afternoon, Quentin hurried to finish typing. Sitting beside him, Kurt read carefully through the fine print of a contract and rechecked some numbers.

"Almost done, Kurt. Good thing, too, 'cause we're probably gonna lose power." He stopped and looked up. "Do you hear a car?"

Kurt laid down his papers, got up, and left the study to look out a living room window across the hall. "It's Sara," he called back to Quentin, and hurried to the front door to let her in. "Miss Russell," he greeted her, feigning formality with a smile. "What in the world brings you out today?"

"No power. At least none up my way in Airport Heights. Lost it during the night, and they're saying it won't be fixed until tomorrow."

Quentin came through the hallway to the front porch to meet her. "So I have a house guest?"

"Yes, you do." She dropped her bright red sports bag on the floor and hung up her coat. "But I come bearing gifts. I stopped at Tim's and bought your favourite. Least I can do for a free bed." She placed a cardboard box of Boston cream doughnuts on the small glass table next to the door and followed them back into the study.

Sara curled up in her favourite armchair of buttery soft leather in a beautiful deep shade of persimmon. She and Quentin often fought for it whenever she visited, and Quentin usually gave in. She tucked her feet underneath her and leaned on the armrest. "Anyone hear from Joe? He was supposed to meet with Emily and Greg down at the old house yesterday morning."

Kurt nodded. "I talked to him last night. He's debating whether to take it on."

"Speaking of Sinclairs, Quentin, did you ask Kurt about the young girl Sandi was talking about last night?"

"Nope." He stared intently at the computer monitor.

"Kurt, Sandi told us last night at dinner that her Grandmother Mackenzie, who lives in Corner Brook, actually grew up in Falcon Cove on the northeast coast. Years ago she came in town to work *in service*, I think they called it, and her friend did, too. Her friend worked at the Sinclairs'. We figure it was when Emily and Jeanne were small."

"Oh yes," Kurt said, taking in her every word, but offering little response.

"Her name was Hannah somebody. I think Sandi said Parsons, didn't she, Quentin? Ever hear Jeanne mention her?"

When there was no answer, Quentin glanced at Kurt sitting in the chair facing him. Since Quentin could remember, he'd had an uncanny ability to read Kurt's face. In business negotiations they only had to make eye contact to communicate what he wanted. At that moment, Quentin noticed the look of concern on Kurt's face, like he was turning something over in his mind, and he wondered why such an innocuous question would cause him to be evasive. Figuring he had good reason, he decided to step in.

"It was a long time ago, Sara," he said dismissively. "I doubt anyone would remember some young woman who only worked with them for a few months. They certainly wouldn't have kept in touch, would they, Kurt?" He gave him the question, already knowing the answer.

"No, not likely," he managed weakly.

Quentin stood as the printer finished, took the pages from the tray, and placed them in a large manila envelope. "Here you go. Done." When the envelope was gone from his hands, he reached for some Hawkins Cheezies that usually left his hands a brilliant shade of orange. "Time for coffee and a Boston cream?"

Kurt stood to leave. "Thanks, Quentin, but Jaclyn's expecting me, and she would not be pleased to hear that I was eating doughnuts. I must get home before the weather gets worse. Thanks for doing this today. Much appreciated."

"Take the parkway. Some of the side streets are flooded," Sara advised.

Closing the door behind Kurt, Quentin took the box of doughnuts from the table and walked behind Sara toward the kitchen.

"Kurt seems to have something on his mind," Sara commented.

"Just business. You know what he's like when there's a business transaction involved. Total focus. He hasn't gotten where he is by being distracted." But Quentin knew otherwise.

* * * * *

Alone in his apartment across town, Joe grabbed a handful of chocolate-covered macadamia nuts from the bowl on the counter, sat at his desk, and brought up the computer file he wanted. He reminded himself to click "Save" with every change. The doorbell startled him. *Sandi.* He was surprised to see his mother.

· Jeanne slipped off her raincoat and passed it to Joe. Surveying the room, she noticed the computer screen and stacks of paper on either side of the desk. "You're working?"

"Yes. As long as the power holds."

"Then I won't take much of your time. I understand that Emily and Gregory have hired you to renovate the house?"

"I gave it a lot of thought. Gregory phoned earlier this morning, and I told him I could design the basic renovation, if that's what he wanted. There are some things that have to be brought up to code. To be honest, he's not anxious to spend much money. He probably expects me to do the design work for free."

Jeanne sat on the sofa closest to her. "No surprise there. Do you think it will sell?"

"Not at the price they want for it, but then, don't quote me on that. They might have a completely different version when they talk to the realtor, poor soul."

"Joe, if you agree to do it, do whatever you think is best. And makes sure he pays you *well*."

He raised his eyebrows in surprise at that last comment. His mother rarely mentioned money.

"Okay, anything else?"

"Just to let you know, I'm having some of the furnishings and dishes moved to my house tomorrow morning. I thought you should know in case you want to send in the contractor right away."

"I thought Lauren told you that you might get in trouble for doing that. You know that Gregory would relish a legal battle."

"Yes, but I have the perfect excuse now. The renovations. In fact, Emily is quite appreciative of my offer to store things in my basement."

You're good, he thought. *The perfect ploy.*

"You and Lauren are welcome to come over and take whatever you want." She was studying the room as if looking for decorating flaws.

"I can't speak for Lauren, but I don't think I want anything. Even if I did, I don't have room here."

"No, but I could hold on to it, until you find a bigger place, perhaps a house of your own. Lauren has already agreed to come over and look through it with me."

Joe stared at the woman in front of him and wondered about her motive.

"Mother, why are you so determined to keep those things away from Emily? You know that legally she owns it all. You don't have the right to pass it out to me or Lauren or anyone else."

Jeanne sat at the end of the sofa, her posture perfect. She answered his question with a half-truth. "Why am I doing it? Because those dishes meant so much to your grandmother, Joe." In her mind, she continued, *They symbolized everything she believed she was. And I want to destroy every last one of them.*

"Okay, then. I'm sure Lauren will help you, but . . ."

The doorbell interrupted them. He was glad to see Sandi, but soon realized she was not her usual self. "Hello," she said as she entered slowly, but stopped short when she saw his mother.

Jeanne immediately assessed the young woman: breathless, red-faced, and dishevelled. Her long brown hair hung in a mess around her face, rainwater on the ends dripping onto her shirt. She was not impressed. She said softly, "Have we met?"

Joe came to the rescue. "No, you haven't. Mother, this is Sandi Martel. Sandi, this is my mother, Jeanne Sinclair."

Sandi restrained herself from looking down at her opened jacket and rumpled blouse. She knew the wind had played havoc with her hair, and she tried weakly to smooth it to some kind of order with her fingers. She could not help but stare at the attractive woman standing nearby in her exquisitely tailored clothes, flawless makeup, and perfectly coiffed blonde hair. *Had she beamed over from her house?* Her perfume was glorious, and surely she looked no more than forty. Sandi managed a weak, "Hello, it's nice to meet you."

Jeanne nodded. "Has something happened? Your hand . . ."

Sandi quickly covered her reddened hand. "No, no, just a small accident. I'm fine, thank you."

From an angle, Joe noticed that it was not fine, and sought a way to dismiss his mother. "Perhaps we can talk about this later, Mother. The house, I mean. I'll talk to Lauren as well."

Jeanne collected her things and moved to the door. "Yes, of course. I'll be in touch. Good evening, Ms. Martel."

"Nice to meet you." Sandi did not follow her to the door, but walked to other side of the room, took off her wet jacket, and laid it across a chair.

Joe closed the door behind his mother and returned to her quickly. "Sandi, what happened to your hand?"

"I'm sorry, Joe," she said, breathlessly, her gestures emphasizing the point. "I had no idea your mother . . . My God, what does she think of me? I'm a state. I left the Arts building. It was torrential rain and a storm of wind. I got soaked walking to the parking lot even with my rain jacket on, the hood wouldn't stay up, my hair was flying all over the place, I had an armload of stuff, I opened the car door, and I couldn't see because of my hair, and the wind took the door and it slammed shut on my hand. Good grief. I come here to face your mother for the first time, of all people."

Joe was laughing. "I'm not laughing at your misfortune, just at the way you describe it. I'll get some ice for your hand."

"Thank you. If you don't mind, I'm going to rake my hair in your bathroom." She grabbed her purse and left the room.

"I'm making some tea," he said, as she came out of the bathroom moments later. "And here's an ice pack for your hand."

"Thanks." She gathered up the box she had laid on the juniper table by the door. "I dropped by the bakery and picked up some chocolate mocha cake that I know you like." In the kitchen, she opened a cupboard that held eight Wedgwood china mugs, neatly in a line. Preferring them to the modern ones, she took two mugs and placed them by the stove.

"Are you all right? Perhaps we should have that hand looked at."

"No," she said, placing the cold package gently on her hand. "It'll be fine. Looks worse than it is. So, you wanted to talk to me about something?"

"Grandfather's house, or, I should say, Emily's. She and Gregory want me to renovate it, and, frankly, I'm worried about taking it on. I just told Mother that I would, but it's never a good idea to work for family."

"Joe, as long as you're the architect, they'll go along with whatever you suggest. Gregory may not like the price, so make sure he understands up front how much it'll cost."

"Ha, you share Mother's advice. Anyway, I have a new design

for the front entrance worked up, if you wouldn't mind looking at it in a few minutes, after I have a piece of that cake. I just want a second opinion. Something 'bout this whole business has me put off."

"Sure, be happy to." She sat on the sofa, placed her heels on the coffee table, and listened while Joe described his mother's plan to move dishes to her own house.

"Joe, I hope you don't think I am prying into your family, but I found out more about the woman who worked for your grandparents."

He laughed. "Believe me, Sandi, I don't consider it prying. Nothing would surprise me about the Sinclairs."

"This might. Mom mentioned to Grandma on Friday evening that I was gone to dinner with you over at Lauren and Alan's place. That's when Grandma brought up the topic of Hannah again. She said that Hannah had a baby while she was working for your grandparents."

"Really? Jeez, that must have been tough. Just getting a job, working for a few months, and then having a baby, with little or no support."

"Exactly. And she was so young."

"Did she go back home? To Falcon Cove?"

"Apparently, but not before she had the baby."

"I remember Grandma Steffensen told me once that her mother, she was Susannah Thorburn, used to help out and donate clothes, sheets, that sort of thing to homes where single women went to have babies in St. John's. So it's likely that young Hannah would have gone to one of those homes, the one for Protestant mothers, I imagine, because they certainly would have been segregated by religious denomination back then. I'm assuming Hannah was Protestant, because it's not likely my grandparents would have hired her otherwise."

"We don't know where she had the baby. Then again, the father might have had something to say about it. But I'm just guessing."

"The father? You know who he was?" Joe's eyes widened. "Wow! That's interesting!"

Sandi nodded and reached across the table to touch his fingers with her hand. "That's what I wanted to tell you, in private. From what I understand, the father of Hannah's baby was . . . your grandfather."

Joe sat back and looked away at the rain lashing against the balcony doors. Suddenly he laughed, an uproarious laugh, one that Sandi did not expect.

He shook his head. "Sandi, I've got to say. I thought it would take a lot to shock me, especially when it comes to family, but this one tops it. Grandfather! Charles Sinclair! Whoa! Now imagine if that got out. The Sinclair sisters would stroke out."

"I'm certainly not going to tell anyone. There's something else. Hannah has a daughter living with her in Falcon Cove now."

"Yes, I remember you mentioned that. She's a minister."

Sandi nodded. "Her name is Carrie. I don't know if this is the same child we're talking about. It could be. She goes by the name West, if that means anything."

"She could have taken her mother's married name."

"I thought you and Lauren should know. After all, this is your grandfather we're talking about. I didn't expect you to take it so lightly. It means that he cheated on your grandmother."

"No surprises there. There's been a rumour to that effect for years. I'm not going to ruin our evening with a litany of my grandfather's wrongdoings."

She collected their mugs, brought them to the kitchen, and walked over to the balcony doors to look at the harbour stirred up by strong winds. "The weather's a lot worse than the first night I was here. Remember?"

"Absolutely." He joined her by the doors.

"Joe, I remember that you wanted to say something to me that night, but you stopped yourself. What was it?"

He paused and turned to look at her. "When I told you that it would be difficult to remain just friends, I wanted to say it was because . . . friends don't kiss. And I wanted to."

"Ah, I see."

"It's just that Sara's been lecturing me about not putting pressure on you, and even my grandmother in Halifax told me on the phone that I need to be patient."

"And your patience has run out?"

"No, no, I'll wait, as long as I need to, Sandi."

She wrapped her arms around his neck and turned her head to rest on his shoulder. She could feel the warmth of his chest and his hands touching her back. "Well, then, let's change the rules about being friends, shall we? Besides, you've waited long enough. I know I have."

* * * * *

A pool of water had accumulated at the intersection of Rennies Mill Road, so Jeanne slowed down as she made the left turn. Her thoughts were on the new woman in Joe's life. She made up her mind right then to find out about the Martels before Joe's obvious infatuation went too far. Turning left on Exeter, she faced the full brunt of the rain, and turned her wipers to maximum. The tires sprayed the sidewalk. She wondered whether Emily and Gregory's flight would get out early in the morning before the movers arrived at the Sinclair home. She had not anticipated a backlog at the airport due to weather when she had booked them.

Inside her front porch, she shook the rain off her coat, slipped it off, and sat on the bench in the hallway to remove her shoes. She thought about Virginia and her precious dishes gathering dust in that empty house. As a young girl, she was never allowed to touch them, although she wanted to. She had spent a lifetime trying to meet Virginia's standards, but she was never good enough. One of her earliest Christmases with Kurt, when Joe was a baby, she had spent hours planning the dinner menu and finding the most beautiful arrangement of flowers for the dining room table on Christmas Day. Everything was perfect, she thought, but not in Virginia's eyes. Alone with her in the dining room that day, Virginia took the opportunity to cut to the quick using words that Jeanne had never forgotten. "Not bad, I suppose, Jeanne, for a girl whose mother is from the bay. After all, you can give a person wealth, but you can't give her class. That's something you'll never have. Not with the blood of a fisherman's daughter running through your veins."

CHAPTER 7

"The days are shorter, Carrie. Evenings are closing in earlier," Hannah observed as she pulled up the zipper of her fleece-lined jacket to the top. They made their way gingerly around the puddles of the dirt path from the cemetery to meet the main road in Falcon Cove. On Thursdays, Carrie's day off, the two women walked the length of the community, regardless of the weather. They often detoured onto the cemetery road and visited Marshall's grave, as they had done this afternoon.

"Carrie! Hannah! Wait up!" came a voice behind them. They turned around and saw Hannah's sister-in-law, Iris, waving to them from her front doorstep. They opened the wooden gate to the walkway of her home, a pretty white bungalow, meticulously kept. Green baskets decorated each window outside, though the flowers had been removed for the winter, leaving just the soil. White crocheted curtains hung on each side of the front door and trimmed the front windows. The front garden was dotted with colourful lawn ornaments.

"Lovely day, Iris. What's up?" Hannah asked.

The small, grey-haired woman stood in the doorway, her cardigan pulled tight and her arms folded across her chest. "I phoned your place and there was no answer. I just wanted to let you know that a few of us are going over to the church to clean tomorrow morning. Toby was over there this morning and said that some of the windows are leaking a bit. Says it would be good to get them tight before winter sets in." Toby was Iris's husband and a skilled carpenter. "He hopes to get to it next week, if the weather holds and he gets that shed he's been working on finished."

"Thanks, Aunt Iris, and thank Uncle Toby for me," said Carrie.

"Time to come in for a while?"

"Thanks, but another time. We left a chicken in the oven, and that was over an hour ago. We'll drop back later."

By the time they reached home, they had decided on the food needed for the annual fall church dinner. "You know, Carrie, if your father were still alive, he'd have those windows done already," Hannah said, walking into the house through the side door. She hung up their coats in the small hall closet and closed the folding door. A warm smell of savoury roasted chicken and root vegetables filled the kitchen.

Carrie had noticed that her mother was especially quiet at the cemetery. Now she looked at her wistfully. "You've been thinking a lot about Dad lately, haven't you?"

Hannah nodded and sighed heavily. "It'll be two years next week. What they say isn't true, Carrie, about time being a great healer. It's not. I don't feel any better than the day I left the hospital. The day he died." Mindlessly, she opened the oven door and took the cover off the roaster. Satisfied that the chicken was cooked, she turned the button to "Off" and laid the pan on top of the stove.

Carrie took butter and mustard pickles from the refrigerator and placed them on the kitchen table. Her mind debated whether she should ask the question she'd been wondering about for some time. She paused and took the risk. "Mother, would you tell me something . . . did Dad know? About the baby?"

Hannah stopped what she was doing. "Yes," she whispered. "He knew. I told him a long time ago. You were just a baby yourself."

"What did he say?"

Still with her back to Carrie, Hannah fought the lump in her throat and searched for the right words. "Just that if it ever came up, we would deal with it, that's all. He didn't judge. He didn't get angry. Just, 'If it ever comes up, we'll deal with it.' That's all he said. I had no idea how we would deal with it. Not with his family, Toby and Iris, Frances, the children, everybody in the community all knowing about it."

Carrie meticulously placed forks and knives in their proper places. "Did he know who the father was?"

"Yes, I had to tell him. It was only right."

"And that didn't make him angry?"

"Carrie," she said, with a slight scolding tone, "when can you remember your father ever being angry?" She placed the cut-up chicken on a dinner plate and laid it in the centre of the table.

Carrie smiled at a precious memory. "Never."

"Exactly. His mother used to say you could cut off Marsh's left arm and he'd still say he had a good one left, and say a prayer for the person who cut it off."

"Did you ever see Charles Sinclair get angry?"

"Oh, yes, many, many times. Not at me, mind you. But he was a wealthy man, Carrie. Lots of people relied on him for their livelihood. And he depended on them to work hard, you know, to keep the business running." She poured hot water into the red teapot and placed it on the warming element of the stove. "I read one time back in the sixties that he used to drive around St. John's in a Rolls Royce, the only one in town, with his own chauffeur. Imagine. Everybody knew who it was when they saw that car."

"Lots of money." Carrie provided a statement rather than a question.

"Hmm, he did."

"Have you thought about what you're going to do with the money he left you when it comes?"

Hannah made eye contact with her daughter for the first time in the conversation, and there seemed to be a mischievous glint in them. "Someone has to pay for those windows in the church, Carrie. It might as well be Charles Sinclair."

* * * * *

"David, you have two Thanksgivings, don't you?" Sandi asked as she sat at the dining room table at David's house on Friday night.

"Uh huh. And very different ones at that, Sandi. We were at my mother's parents' last Monday in Clarke's Beach. Very comfortable, good laughs, lots and lots of food. My grandmother figures I don't eat between the times I visit her, so she made me what she assumes are all my favourites. I didn't need to eat at all on Tuesday, especially after the bakeapple cheesecake with clotted cream on top I had Monday night. I think my left ventricle slammed shut on that one."

Sandi chuckled. Joe had mentioned David's passion for health and fitness, and she admired how well he stuck to a workout routine. "And you see your other grandparents in Boston in November?"

"That's the plan. But I don't know if I'll get time off this year. Mother and Father will go, for sure, although Mother insists that I have to go with her for support. Grandmother Gilchrist gives a whole new meaning to *contrary*." His expression indicated he was tired of family politics. "I had a patient a couple of years ago who described her grandmother as so crooked, they'd have to screw her in the ground when she died. That pretty much sums up my Grandmother Gilchrist."

Quentin sat back and momentarily closed his eyes. "Hmm, I'm still thinking about the bakeapple cheesecake with clotted cream. I don't suppose your grandmother sent me any?"

"In the freezer. For that 'lovely young man, Quentin.'" David shook his head as he repeated his grandmother's sentiment.

Sara leaned over to Sandi. "Quentin's got older women all over the place taking care of him."

"Ah, sometimes it pays to be an orphan," he quipped. "I must send your grandmother a thank you."

Joe put down his fork. He had been quiet up to this point, thinking of a way to broach a delicate topic. He knew it would be a shock for his sister. "Speaking of grandparents," he began, "we've come across more information on Mrs. Hannah West."

Lauren looked up from her meal.

"Apparently, she did have a relationship with Grandfather." He paused and looked around the table. "And . . . ready for this? They had a baby."

Lauren's eyes widened. "What? A baby? You . . . are . . . kidding!"

"Nope," Joe interrupted. "Hannah had a baby."

Not surprisingly, Quentin's response was one of laughter. He shook his head. "Well, well, Charles had a looove child," stretching the word "love" out for several seconds. "This is rich. Didn't know he had it in him, as they say." He poured a generous amount of gravy over his baked chicken. "Thanks for the gravy, David. I know you made it under protest."

At the other end of the table, Lauren's furrowed brow indicated she did not see the humour. "Funny as it may be," she began, "the child we're talking about is our aunt or uncle, Joe. I'd like to know where he or she is. Sandi says that Mrs. West has a daughter, Carrie. It could be her."

David spoke seriously and raised his hand slightly for emphasis. "Careful, Lauren. These things can get messy. You're really opening a can of worms if you start looking into it, as much as you want to find your long-lost aunt or uncle. Remember, your mother's entangled in this. She may not be as enthusiastic as you are, if at all. In fact, given how the whole thing tarnishes her father's reputation, well . . ."

"I know that, David. I appreciate what you're saying. Mother and Emily will be quite upset, I'm sure."

"Not exactly shining to begin with," Joe added. He sat back, rested his forearm on the table, and swirled his wine in the glass. "To complicate matters, I had a call from Gregory this morning. It was one of his regular calls to see how the renovations were going. Just before he hung up, he asked me if I had ever heard of Hannah West."

Joe had everyone's attention. "It seems her name was mentioned in Grandfather's will."

"What?" Lauren asked. "Good heavens! Why? I mean, it's not common knowledge. Why would Grandfather want all of this to come out now?"

Joe shook his head. "All I know is she received a sizable sum of money. No explanation given. No mention of their relationship."

Lauren picked up her fork and resumed eating her salad. "There's only one way to find out about all of this," she said with a deliberate tone. "I'm going to ask Mother—outright."

Joe wanted to dissuade her, but chose to let it go for now. "Okay, Lauren, just tread lightly." He looked to Quentin to change the topic of conversation, and he did. Later, on their way home, he noticed that Sandi seemed unusually pensive as she looked out the passenger-side window and ran her finger along the top of the door.

"Say goodbye to Portia," Joe said, using his nickname for his car. "She's going into winter hibernation tomorrow." When Sandi didn't respond, he looked at her. "Hey, you all right? Got something on your mind?"

"What? Oh, I'm fine. Yes, Portia is going to bed for the winter." She patted the door frame. "I was just thinking about all this business with Hannah and your grandfather. I hope it doesn't lead to trouble in your family. I'd never forgive myself. Neither would Mom. Dad said we should stay out of it. Perhaps he's right."

"Why?"

"I've only known you and your family for a few months. And, as Dad says, it's none of our business. Besides, like David said this evening, it might open up wounds that can't be healed. I can imagine your mother will be upset when Lauren brings it up."

Joe turned right off Elizabeth Avenue and headed toward Stoney-house Street. He reached out to squeeze her hand. "Sandi, first of all, we're hardly just acquaintances, are we?"

"Well, no." She looked at him with a smile and rubbed his hand.

"I heard enough about my grandfather when I was growing up, not much of it good. So don't give it a second thought. Besides, it's unlikely Lauren will get what she wants from Mother. She's an expert at keeping things under wraps. If she wants to keep it where it is, believe me, that's where it'll stay."

* * * * *

The following Thursday was the first opportunity Lauren had to have lunch with her mother. They agreed to meet at Pier 17, a long-standing, popular restaurant in Churchill Square. She pulled out the grey cushioned chair and dropped her handbag on the floor. "This is a busy spot."

"Yes, I guess so," Jeanne answered mindlessly, while she checked to see if Lauren's scarf matched the colour of her blouse. Jeanne had a habit of surveying a restaurant only once when she entered to see if there was anyone she knew. After that, she kept to herself.

Jeanne decided to wait until they ordered before she sought information from Lauren. "So tell me about this Sandi Martel. Has Joe been seeing her long?" She picked her way around the feta cheese in her Greek salad.

"They met in August."

"I had no idea. Where did they meet?"

"Through Sara, actually. She's quite nice. She joins us for Friday night dinners and I've been over to her place for lunch. She lives just around the corner from here. On Stoneyhouse."

"Does she work?"

"She's a professor at the university, and she's very talented. As is her brother, Jordy. You should hear him play piano."

"I met her briefly." She laid her fork down and braced for a predictable reaction from her daughter. "She doesn't seem like Joe's type."

"Now, Mother, stop right there. Don't pass judgment on one brief meeting. The last thing Joe needs to hear is your disapproving tone."

"I haven't said anything to him," she said defiantly.

"And let's keep it that way." Lauren waited a few minutes while they ate in silence, then decided it was time to risk a sensitive topic. She sipped her water. "Joe mentioned that you've moved some of the dishes and furniture from Grandfather's house."

Jeanne nodded. "Just a few small tables and the dishes in the cabinet. The good items. I told Emily that I thought it best to get those things out of the way of the workers who are replacing the windows and painting and so on. She thought that was a wonderful idea. Quite grateful to me, actually." Jeanne lifted her napkin to her lips to wipe imaginary food from them.

Perfectly played, Lauren thought. She took a chance on the next question. "While we're on the topic of the Sinclair estate, I need to ask you about someone who worked for Grandma and Granddad years ago."

"Oh. Who would that be?"

"Well, her name is Hannah Parsons, or it was at that time. Her married name is Hannah West."

Jeanne stopped mid-bite. Her perfect application of Estée Lauder makeup could not hide her shock. Her only hope was that Lauren didn't notice under the twinkling ceiling lights of the restaurant. She reached for her water and took two sips. She searched for a way to dismiss the topic. "Mother and Father had a lot of staff over the years, Lauren. Why do you ask about her?"

"Lindsay Martel mentioned to Sandi and Joe that her mother grew up in a community called Falcon Cove. She came into St. John's to work with a family when she was a young girl, and so did her friend, or, to be accurate, a sister of a friend who worked with Grandma and Granddad. She didn't stay much more than a year or two."

"When was this?"

"I think Emily and you were only small because part of her job, according to Lindsay, was to look after the little girls."

"I certainly don't remember her, Lauren, if that's what you're asking. Why would I, if I was just a toddler? And I never heard her name mentioned."

"Oh, that's curious."

Though anxious to let it go, Jeanne could see that Lauren had more to say on the subject. "What is?"

"I don't know how to say this exactly."

"Out with it, Lauren. Gosh, you remind me of Emily, stumbling over words. I would think someone in your profession would be more articulate."

"It's not that I don't know what to say, I'm just wondering how you're going to take it. You see, the story is that Hannah got pregnant."

"Lovely," Jeanne commented in her best sarcastic tone.

"And that Grandfather was the father of the baby." *There, I've managed to say it out loud in front of her.*

"Lauren, since when have you taken to gossip? Surely I raised you better than that. Have you started watching those silly daytime dramas in your spare time?" Although she kept her voice low, it was laced with rage. Her lower lip quivered.

"There's no need to get upset with me. I'm just asking."

"You are doing more than asking, young lady. You are defaming the name and character of a wonderful man, your grandfather. I am appalled that you would even suggest such a thing. And if that's all that this Lindsay Martel has to do, spread malicious lies about a person she never met, then I would suggest that you and Joe stay as far away from her and her family as you can."

"This is not Lindsay's fault, Mother," she said in hushed tones. "She just asked an innocent question."

"There's nothing innocent about it, and you know it. It's terrible gossip. Obviously she's just jealous of our family, that's all. Where does she come from?"

"Corner Brook, but that hardly has . . ."

"Ah, enough said." She punctuated her words by laying her napkin across the plate and sitting back.

Exasperated, Lauren decided not to mention that she knew the woman's name was in the will. They finished eating in silence. A short time later, she glanced at her watch and mentioned that she had an appointment. She took the plastic folder with the bill inside. "I'll pay for lunch, Mother. I invited you." She stood and walked to the counter at the front. As Jeanne gathered her purse and sweater, she heard a voice.

"Jeanne, good afternoon."

She looked up to see Jonathan Hamlyn approaching the table. "Jonathan, how are you?"

"Fine, thanks. As a matter of fact, I have your name on my list for today's calls."

"Oh?"

"May I sit down for a minute?"

Jeanne looked around to see if anyone was observing. She did not agree with conducting legal business in public, but could hardly refuse. "Yes, I guess so. But be brief. Lauren is waiting for me."

"Certainly. I just wanted to let you know that I received a letter last Friday from your nephew, Gregory. Says he is looking for information regarding the whereabouts of Hannah. He noted that she received a sizable sum in Charles's will. He also inquired about the pocket watch. I'm just wondering how you want me to respond." Jonathan smoothed his moustache over and over, not knowing what to expect.

"Leave it to me, Jonathan. I'll get in touch with Gregory and take care of it."

"Very well."

"As a representative of the family, I would hope that this remains confidential."

"Jeanne, you know I would never break a confidence with you. Surely you know that."

"Yes, of course, Jonathan. And I appreciate that."

He nodded and left, and Jeanne made a mental note to phone Emily as soon as she got home. Obviously Gregory needed a reason to drop this investigation.

Jeanne joined Lauren at the counter and waited as she put on her coat and scarf. "What did Jonathan want, Mother? Have they settled Grandfather's estate?"

"Not this year," she said with biting sarcasm. "Just the usual questions about income tax, that sort of thing. By the way, I'm going to the Bahamas for a couple of weeks. Leaving on Sunday. I thought you should know."

But Lauren knew as well as anyone could when her mother was being evasive. She could tell from the way the colour drained from her mother's face when Jonathan was speaking to her that something was happening and that she and her brother were deliberately being left to wonder.

* * * * *

"This will likely be one of our last Sunday walks, Joe, given that the weather is changing. We're going to have to come up with something else to do on Sunday afternoons."

"I'm sure I'll think of something."

Sandi laughed at his cryptic suggestion. "Let's make this one a challenge."

"So where are we going?"

Sandi smiled and looked to the sky overhead. It was overcast and the clouds were heavy. "It's not too bad. I have the perfect place."

Less than fifteen minutes later, they were at the top of Signal Hill, a St. John's landmark overlooking the city, used by the British in the eighteenth century to defend the town from the French. Joe related the story of the construction of Cabot Tower to Sandi as he parked. There were only two other cars in the parking lot.

"Okay, so where are we going? To the Tower?"

"No." Sandi stared at him, wide-eyed. "That's not a walk." She moved over to the edge of the paved sidewalk and stood next to the three-foot stone wall that edged the entire parking lot. She looked down the side to the hill and then at Joe, who was still standing by the driver's side of his car. "Down there." She pointed to the cliff that separated them from the ocean.

Joe walked over to her, leaned on the top of the wall with one hand, and looked down, way down, at a narrow walkway beneath and a small expanse of flat grassy land protruding out into the sea. There was a fine, cold mist in the air and the wind was picking up.

"You're kidding, right?"

"No."

"Sandi, I can't get the car down there," he joked.

"C'mon."

With that, she sat on the top of the wall and threw both legs over and stood on the other side. He hesitated.

"Joe. Come on." She held out her hand for his.

"I thought you were afraid of the ocean."

"I am. But we're on ground here."

"One false step and we won't be."

The initial decline was sharp, but walkers had created a pathway of smooth stone and packed earth. Joe was relieved that he had worn his hiking boots. He held her hand tightly, more for his own security than hers. Their walk, despite the wind, was reasonably comfortable. The trail that accommodated only one person at a time brought them around the base of the steep hill, along the edge of the narrow passage into the harbour. They stopped for a while on a bridge overlooking a deep gorge and watched the waves wash the jagged rocks beneath. Soon, they looped back toward the incline where they had started. Sandi was the first to feel a few flakes of snow landing on her face. She looked overhead and noticed the heavy grey clouds moving across the sky. White precipitation covered the western end of the city in the distance. Sandi called back to Joe. "We'd better hurry. Looks like we might get caught in the snow or hail, whatever that is toward the west."

She had no sooner spoken when heavy ice pellets pounded down on them. Sandi stopped, turned to Joe, and buried her face in his shoulder to avoid the sting of the hail. He held her tightly and brushed the hailstones from the back of her hair as they landed. As the wind whipped up around them, the cold grains found their way to the back of his neck and inside his shirt.

Two minutes later, the hail stopped as quickly as it started and the sun returned. Joe brushed the remaining beads of ice from his shoulders and head. Sandi shook her hair and wiped the melting hail from her face and hands.

She laughed. "Well, that was lovely."

"Yes, marvellous." He grinned at her. "Let's go before it happens again."

They hurried back up the hill, but not before another dwigh of hail repeated the performance. By the time Joe put the key of his car into the lock, hail had accumulated on the windshield.

Sandi shivered in the passenger seat. "Let's just get somewhere warm."

"The closest warm place is mine."

Minutes later, in Joe's apartment, Sandi slipped off her jacket and hung it by the door. She looked down to find her jeans soaked through from the top of her knees to the bottom. Water dripped from her hair and a chill ran down her back.

"Sandi, you'd better dry off. I'm going to change and make something hot."

She went into the bathroom, slipped out of her wet clothes, and exchanged them for one of a stack of large white bath towels sitting on the shelf. She cleaned up her makeup and looked in despair at her wet hair in the bathroom mirror. She left the room and searched for a hair dryer in Joe's bedroom. Meanwhile, Joe had changed into dry clothes and was making coffee in the kitchen.

It was the first time Sandi had been in Joe's bedroom since her tour of the place in August. She ran her hands over the hand-carved headframe and recalled Joe's description of how his great-grandfather had made it for his new bride. The mattress was high and puffy and covered with a teal green tartan duvet that looked so warm and inviting, Sandi couldn't resist. Keeping the towel tucked securely around her, she pulled back the duvet and slid underneath. She pulled off the towel she had used for her hair and dropped it on the rug next to the bed.

Joe appeared in the bedroom door just in time to see her nestling beneath the duvet. He held a cup of steaming hot coffee in each hand. Sandi looked up at him, embarrassed.

"It looked so warm and I'm chilled, Joe. Sorry, I couldn't resist."

He smiled broadly. "No complaints here. Glad you find it warm." He walked over to her, sat in the chair beside the bed, and lodged the two cups of coffee gingerly on the night table. "You'll never be warm with wet hair. Here, you sit up and I'll dry your hair."

She held the duvet up around her body with one hand and turned back-on to him with the help of the other. She felt the heat from the dryer across the back of her neck and around her face. With his free hand, he moved his fingers through her hair, pulled it back from her face, and allowed the warm air to permeate each handful of curls. Then, he lifted the back of her hair to expose her neck. Sandi felt the warmth of the dryer first and then his soft kisses. Turning off the dryer, he dropped it to the floor. She sat back, with her eyes closed, and heard him speak softly. "How about we get rid of this towel? It's a little damp."

When she complied, he threw the towel on the floor. She clasped her hands around the back of his neck and responded to his kisses. Looking down into her beautiful brown eyes, he smiled. "Sandi, do you realize I've been wanting to make love to you since the first day I saw you standing in front of Dad's office?"

"Really? That's amazing. So have I."

He looked away with feigned exasperation. "Well, my darling, what have we been doing for the past two months?"

Sandi tilted her head and ran her hand through his blond hair. "I think they call it foreplay," she said with her beautiful smile.

* * * * *

On a Monday afternoon in mid-November, Kurt and Quentin sat in the meeting room of Steffensen Publishing and faced two stacks of legal-sized file folders on the table in front of them. The spacious room held a large, rectangular wooden table, beautifully polished, and comfortable soft-cushioned armchairs. A set of glass pocket doors separated the room from Kurt's office.

Glancing at his watch and noting it was 5:28 p.m., Kurt reached for the next file folder and sighed. "Can't complain, Quentin, I guess. Lots of work, but I sure could use a break."

Quentin was never one to complain about workload. He just did what he needed to do according to a deadline, whether it took a three-hour or a fourteen-hour workday. "Ah, we'll get though it, Kurt. It's always like this in the fall." He reached for his legal pad. "By the way, on a totally unrelated topic, did Joe mention to you more news about that woman, Hannah West, and Charles?"

Kurt had stood and walked through the double doors to his desk. When he heard Quentin's question, he paused. "And the baby? Yes, Joe told me last Saturday."

"Bit of a shock, wasn't it?" Quentin laughed, but noticed that

Kurt was forcing a smile. He studied his face and saw the same reaction as he had the night that Sara had brought it up.

Finally, Kurt stood and stretched. "Yeah, that was a long time ago. Long before I knew him." He tried to change the subject. "Perhaps we should call it a night and pick it up early tomorrow morning."

"Not a problem. I'm going to take some contracts home with me, anyway." Quentin took four file folders and stood to place them in his leather briefcase. He thought about letting it go, as Kurt apparently wanted, but something deep inside told him not to. Slowly he walked across the room and closed both doors. He didn't want to take the chance that someone else was still working. "Kurt?"

"Yep."

"There's something going on, isn't there?"

Kurt looked up. "Why do you say that?"

He pulled along a chair and sat. "Gregory has read Charles's will, and when he called Joe on Friday morning, he asked if he knew a Mrs. Hannah Parsons West. Apparently, she got a bequest."

"I see," Kurt said solemnly.

"This issue has come up twice, and both times you have shut down. You've never actually come right out and said that you've never heard of Hannah Parsons, which sets me to thinking that . . ." He hesitated, because the last thing he wanted to do was to accuse the man he admired of lying.

"That I'm not being honest with you, or with Sara?"

"I guess you could say it's none of our business."

"And you know damn well you would be wrong. You're both family." He sighed, tossed his pen on the desk, and walked over to the window. Outside, thick snowflakes fell on the brick pavement stones in front of the building. "Quentin, I made a promise to someone a long time ago. That person begged me to keep some information to myself. And she had good reason. If I tell you any more, then I will put you in an awful position of knowing something that Lauren and Joe do not. And when they do find out, and I have no doubt that someday they will, they will hold you accountable. The very last thing in this world I want to do is jeopardize your relationship with them."

"But by keeping it to yourself, aren't you risking the same thing?"

Kurt returned to his chair, sat, and rubbed both hands across his face. "I know, Quentin, I know. But I made that decision a long time ago, and I have to live with it."

"Lauren wants to pursue it. You know her—what she's like."

"I know. Look, the only thing I will say is that we don't know Hannah Parsons because she doesn't want us to know her." He shook his head in frustration. "But, for the life of me, I don't know how to keep all of this from Lauren."

CHAPTER 8

The aroma of freshly brewed coffee greeted Lindsay on Saturday morning when she arrived to serve morning coffee at a large downtown United Church. She had intended to be a patron, but at the last minute her sister-in-law, Phyllis, called to enlist her help. In the large hall, a dozen women from the congregation spread Christmas tablecloths and napkins on rectangular tables and filled them with plates of sweetbreads and cookies, milk jugs and sugar bowls, and small plates and cutlery. Sprigs of holly tied with red tartan ribbons in small glass vases served as centrepieces. Red, white, and pink poinsettias decorated a raised platform at the front. Laughter and chatter filled the room.

In the coatroom, Lindsay slipped off her coat and scarf and exchanged her black dress boots for soft, navy flats. New to the church, she studied her surroundings and thought about the generations of people who had walked the halls of the historic building before her. The place was worn-looking, but, in Lindsay's view, it was a pleasant worn, as it marked a wonderful commitment of time and energy.

"Lindsay, I'm so glad you could make it," Phyllis greeted her. "We're really pressed for servers, what with that awful flu bug that's going around."

"Not a problem, Phyllis, glad to help." She placed her china teapot on the counter near one of the shiny stainless steel stoves in the kitchen.

When the doors opened to the public shortly after 10:00 a.m.,

Lindsay poured coffee from a large aluminum urn on the counter into a Country Roses coffee pot and brought it out to those who were waiting at the first table.

Shortly before eleven, Phyllis touched Lindsay's arm as she was walking through the doorway with a pot of hot water in her hand. "Lindsay," she said in a half whisper, "have you met any of our special guests?"

"Not today, but I've met a few before. There are several I don't know."

"Then you must meet one person in particular, the woman at the end of the table with short brown hair." Phyllis pointed to the table nearest the stage. "See her? She's from Falcon Cove, where your mother's from."

Lindsay wanted to say, *Yes, Phyllis, I know where Mother is from*, but her mind went in another direction. "Really? Is she the minister?"

"Yes, Reverend West. Carrie West. Lovely person. I told her I'd send you over to meet her. Go on, then. Introduce yourself." She waved her hand in the direction of the table.

Lindsay wondered if all teachers directed everyone's life like Phyllis did. Since Lindsay had been a teacher, it was a genuine concern. Jordy had accused her of nagging on several occasions, and she had always denied it. Anxious to meet the woman, she waited for the numbers to dwindle, then made her way to the front table. She waited for a break in the conversation. "Excuse me, Reverend West? Hello, I'm Lindsay Martel. My sister-in-law, Phyllis Martel, told me that she had met you and that you're from Falcon Cove."

A pleasant smile turned to greet her. "Yes, that's right. And Phyllis mentioned that your mother is as well, Lindsay. Edna Saunders, married Stuart Mackenzie?"

"Yes, that's right!"

"She knows my mother, Hannah, then."

"Yes, she does, but I believe my mother is a few years older. She went to school with your Aunt Frances."

"Of course. Well, it's so nice to meet you, Lindsay. The morning coffee is marvellous."

"I'm glad you enjoyed it. My best to your mother. And Merry Christmas!"

"I'll be sure to tell my mother that I met you. Merry Christmas!"

Lindsay walked away, wishing she could ask the woman who her father was, but, knowing that prospect was ridiculous, she kept on going.

It was after 2:00 p.m. before Lindsay could get away. Slipping on her boots in the coatroom, she heard Phyllis behind her reaching for her coat. "So what's the plan for Christmas Day, Lindsay? Are you folks at home?"

"No, we're having Christmas dinner at the Steffensens." Hoping to avoid further discussion on that point, she added quickly, "And you're going to Clarenville?"

Phyllis leaned closer to Lindsay and whispered, "Yes, we are. My goodness, dinner at the Steffensens', what ever will you wear? Those people, you know, are rather stuffy. Steven will have to wear a suit. Shirt and tie. So will Jordy."

"Oh, I'll find something." She wanted to change the subject rather than argue that they were not "stuffy." "The morning coffee and sale was a success. Did they do okay?"

"Yes, I don't think they did as well as last year, but the weather wasn't good this time. Lindsay, I wanted to thank you again for filling in. Don't know what we would have done without you."

"Oh, you're kindly welcome. We had a good laugh, and I met some interesting people." She tucked her scarf tightly around her neck and slipped on her gloves. She made a motion to leave, but Phyllis caught up with her.

"I'm glad you got a chance to chat with Reverend West. I hope you don't mind, but I passed along your name to her. I'm on a committee with her to write church history. It has to do with the anniversary of Methodism in the province. You're such a good writer, and I mentioned that your mother was a lifetime member of the UCW, and several of her friends as well. Perhaps you could interview them?"

"That might be interesting."

"Great. No doubt she'll be in touch. You know how hard it is to get people to volunteer."

Yes, thought Lindsay, *it's easier when they're conscripted.* "Okay, I won't be surprised when she calls. Actually, Phyllis, my mother mentioned Reverend West to me some time ago. Mom and Carrie's aunt Frances went to school together."

"Really! Her mother lives with her, you know. Just the two of them. Carrie's father died a few years ago."

"Carrie's father?" she asked, hoping for more.

"Yes, Marshall. She talks about him quite fondly. They say he was very active in the church down in Falcon Cove."

"Phyllis, how old would you say Carrie is?"

"I know exactly. She turned fifty last year." She zipped up her coat, pulled her gloves from her pockets, and pushed the handle of the large wooden door with rectangular glass inlay.

"Fifty. Are you sure?"

"Yes. The first time I met her was when we had our first committee meeting last fall. We were joking about our ages, and she said that she had just reached the half-century mark. She said that putting it that way sounded so old. I told her to wait until she turns sixty! Then she'll be a senior. Ugh." She feigned a shiver.

Lindsay laughed, said goodbye to Phyllis, and ran to her car. As she waited for the windshield to defrost, she thought about Phyllis's words. *Fifty. That would make her too young to be the baby Hannah had when she was seventeen. Hannah would be only sixty-seven, and Mother said that Hannah was just a few years younger than she and Elsie were.*

When Lindsay arrived home, she found her husband replenishing their Christmas tree with fresh water. "Steven," she called from the front porch, "you're not going to believe who was there! Carrie West. Reverend Carrie West from Falcon Cove."

Steven slowly got up from the living room floor, wiped the edge of the watering can with a paper towel, and met his wife in the doorway. "Hannah's daughter." He chuckled. "Listen to me, sounds like I know the woman." Steven placed the watering can on the storage shelf near the basement stairs. "So she's the baby that Hannah had while she worked at the Sinclair house?"

"If she is, according to Mother, or should I say, Frances, Charles Sinclair is her father. But there's a wrinkle in that theory. Phyllis says her father is Marshall West. She said Carrie talks about him fondly. But not only that, Carrie is only fifty. That makes her too young to be the child that Hannah had with Charles Sinclair."

"Ah, what a tangled web," Steven observed with a laugh.

"Maybe Phyllis has it wrong. I don't know. All we do know for sure is that Hannah and Charles had a baby, and that baby may or may not be Carrie. Do you realize what that means?"

"They had ecumenical sex?" He chuckled. "Charles was Anglican, wasn't he? Hannah obviously is United Church. Nothing like it. That's what you and I have, Lindsay, ecumenical sex," he said with a broad grin and a raised eyebrow.

"Steven, for heaven's sake. This is serious. That woman I met this morning could be Joe and Lauren's aunt."

"Yes, Lindsay, my darling, I hear what you're saying. Or she may not be. In any event, the question is, should you be the one to break the news?"

* * * * *

Joe and Sandi arrived at Lauren and Alan's house on Saturday night to a warm and inviting smell of mulled wine and burning birch logs in the stone fireplace. It was the usual Friday night group joined by Jaclyn and Kurt. The occasion was decorating Lauren's Christmas tree, always, as Kurt noted, the beginning of the Christmas season.

The home was beautifully decorated for Christmas. The window ledges in the living room were trimmed with rows of alternating paperwhites and miniature cypress trees in small glass cups enhanced by deep dark soil and artificial snow. Across the mantel lay a thick cedar swag adorned with silver and white candles and bright lime-coloured ornaments. The dining room table was set with a poinsettia pattern of Royal Albert china and red linen napkins. A chunky white pillar candle covered in hurricane glassware sat in the middle of a silver service tray on a bed of evergreen, berried juniper, boxwood clippings, and silver sprayed pine cones. The only task left was to decorate the eight-foot tree that stood in the corner between the fireplace and the window.

Quentin finished his glass of Pepsi and reached for the first string of lights. "I know I am going to regret this because Blondie will be barking orders at us in no time, Alan, but I guess it's time to put on the lights. You signed up legally, Alan, but I don't know my excuse." He climbed the ladder with the end of the lights in one hand.

Alan held the end and joined the next set and laughed at Quentin's sarcasm. "Quentin, I really don't mind doing this, you know, if you'd rather get something to eat first."

"No, no, let's get this done," he said. "God knows Blondie likely has us on a timer." He knew there was nowhere else he preferred to be, but would never admit it. He carefully attached the plastic clips of each bulb to the ends of branches. After a few minutes, he moved the ladder and continued the pace. Lauren supervised from the floor by suggesting changes to bulb colour as he went.

"Lauren, if you want to change the colour of the light bulbs, you'll have to get up here and do it yourself," he called down from the top rung.

"I really don't like ladders, Quentin."

"Ah, but it's okay for me to risk life and limb."

"I bought you your favourite cheezies," she teased, and picked up the full bowl on the coffee table for emphasis.

Within a couple of hours, the tree was decorated completely with Lauren's tartan bows. Quentin refused to have anything to do with them, as it was, in his view, Lauren's attempt to genderize the tree.

"Lauren, I love your dishes," Sandi said, as they filled their dinner plates.

"Thanks. Grandmother Steffensen gave me the whole set the first Christmas that Alan and I were married, along with some other dishes belonging to her mother. I know they don't fit in with the decor, but they mean a lot to me."

"My Grandma Martel gave me dishes, too. I have them packed away most of the time, but yesterday I took out the silverware. I used to clean it for her when we visited in the summertime and at Christmas. Hopefully, someday I'll be able to put them all in a cabinet where I can look at them every day. By the way, Jaclyn and Kurt, thanks so much for inviting us to Christmas dinner. I understand my mom volunteered to bring dessert. She makes the best plum pudding in the world. I really hope everyone likes it."

Quentin was enjoying his Angus beef strips but took time to give his approval. "I think I could probably gum that down. Tell your mother to start picking plums, Sandi."

Jaclyn laughed. "You're very welcome, Sandi. By the way, I hear that Jordy is going to do his work term at Steffensen Publishing after Christmas."

"Yes, and Doris is thrilled," Kurt said. "She hugged him when he helped her with her computer this week. As soon as he left, she told me if I had any compassion in me at all, I'd hire him after Christmas. I learned a long time ago not to argue with Doris." He picked up his cup of mulled wine. "Joe, how's the work on the Sinclair house going? We drove by there earlier. It's amazing what a difference a few new windows can make."

Joe nodded. "Yes, it'll be even better with a new entrance, which should be done by the end of the week if the materials arrive. Gregory called me to see what's taking so long. Believe me, I'll be happy to put an end to his nagging and send him a bill."

Sara spoke up. "You know, it still puzzles me that Charles left the house entirely to Emily."

"I know it's tradition in many jurisdictions for the eldest son to inherit the house," Alan said. "Not so the case here, I believe, because land wasn't worth much, according to the history I've read. It may be that the Boland family decided to pass on the property to the eldest daughter. That would explain Emily getting the house."

Quentin stood at the dining room table filling his plate with a scoop of English trifle that was surrounded by an assortment of cookies—lemon shortbread, hazelnut linzer thumbprints, and anise crisps.

He almost missed the double chocolate squares. Listening intently to the conversation behind him, he noted that Kurt remained quiet.

"Dad, as much as the Sinclair family is not my choice of conversation topics for Christmas, what do you make of this latest information that Hannah West is mentioned in Grandfather's will?" Joe asked.

Kurt shook his head. "I'm afraid I can't shed much light on it."

Joe sat forward and rested his elbows on his knees. "Curious, isn't it? It's one thing to give her money for child support, but after all these years, that child is in his or her fifties now. Why keep the connection?"

Kurt laughed. "Remember, you're talking about the Sinclairs," he said, and hoped that would end the topic of conversation. He didn't get his wish.

Sandi hesitated. As she was new to the social circle, she wasn't sure how kindly Kurt would take to her interference. As innocently as she could, she simply said, "Mom met Reverend Carrie West at a morning coffee at church. She's in the city for some church meetings."

Lauren brightened momentarily. "Hannah's daughter? Wow! She could be . . ." Then she paused. "I guess I can't walk up to the woman and say, hello, your father is my grandfather."

"Presuming this Reverend West *is* the child of Hannah and Charles," Alan said.

Kurt reached for his wineglass and said softly, "Perhaps not. We may never know."

Lauren laid her plate on the coffee table and wiped her hands. "If Carrie West, or whoever the child is, knows that Charles Sinclair was her father, she'd also know that he passed away in August. It was in the news."

Jaclyn glanced at Kurt, and they made a knowing eye contact. "Maybe she does know and won't have anything to do with it. After all, this person, the baby that Hannah had, whether she is the minister or someone else, has lived a life, perhaps married with children, and maybe has no interest in bringing out into the open who her father is. There's more at stake here than tarnishing the reputation of Charles Sinclair. There are other families to consider."

"Never thought of that, Jaclyn," Joe said. "You're right. News that Grandfather actually fathered another child could potentially do more harm than upset just Mother and Emily."

Kurt tried to end the conversation. "That's why I have suggested that we let it go. If this lady, Hannah, or her child wants to come forward, there's nothing anyone can do to stop them. But it doesn't seem to be the case." He stood. "Now, Lauren, if you don't mind, I'm going to put on some coffee."

"Sure, Dad, I'll help."

In the kitchen, Lauren stood next to her father at the counter as she filled the filter with coffee and he poured fresh water into the top container. "You know, Dad, it's really too bad, all this about Grandfather and Hannah and her daughter and everything. If Grandfather did have a relationship with her sometime in his life, it makes sense why he left her some money."

"Yes, it's sad, sweetie," Kurt said, dismissively.

"You really do think it's best to forget all about it, don't you?"

"Yes, Lauren, I do. For the sake of everyone."

In the doorway, Joe heard his father's words. He thought he knew his dad very well, but this time his directive to put the issue at rest was spoken with unexplained conviction. For the first time in his life, he suspected Kurt was keeping something from them. He wondered what it was, and, more importantly, he wondered why he couldn't tell them.

* * * * *

Later that night at home, Quentin propped up his two feather pillows and got into bed. He reached for his current murder mystery, read for a while, tossed it on the side of the bed, and leaned over to turn off the lamp on the night table. The sound of the gusting wind drew his attention to the window. Flashing yellow lights of a city salt truck flickered through the room. For a while, he lay awake staring out the window at a street light in the distance. Tree branches now covered in ice moved up and down in the wind. He thought about

Kurt's words that evening and what he had said during the night of the tropical storm in September. *I will put you in an awful position of knowing something that Lauren and Joe do not.*

Quentin's mind reeled as he turned over in the bed and wrapped his right arm around the pillow. *Emily inherited the house from her parents as their eldest daughter. Why not both daughters? The house had to be inherited by a relative of the Boland family. Charles, he knew, had good reason to comply with that wish. What if it had nothing to do with Emily being the oldest, as Alan had suggested? What if it was passed on to the one and only daughter related to the Bolands? The house was not inherited by Virginia's oldest daughter,* he realized. *The house was inherited by Virginia's only daughter. And that was why, the last time he spoke to Charles, he was adamant that the house should go to Jeanne, but that it would not be easy. Jeanne's mother was someone else.* Quentin closed his eyes. *Hannah?*

* * * * *

On Christmas Eve, Jeanne stood at the base of the terminal escalator mindlessly taking in the sights at the airport in front of the arrival doors. She rolled her eyes in disgust at the Christmas trees and lights in the waiting area and wondered why they bothered to decorate a public place that people passed through quickly.

Her plan to spend Christmas on her own, with her favourite wine and a collection of new English novels, had been ruined. Instead she was awaiting the arrival of Emily and Gregory. Emily by herself would have been bad enough, but Emily *and* Gregory was more than she could stand.

Just two days before, Emily had called late in the evening just as Jeanne was getting into bed. "I know you're not expecting us, but I thought, since it is our first Christmas without Father, we can spend some quiet time together. I don't think we should socialize too much, do you? After all, what would people think?" Emily was starting to babble, and Jeanne tuned her out.

"Whatever you wish," she said weakly, as much as she could muster. She squeezed her eyes shut in anticipation. "When will you be arriving?"

"On Friday. That's as early as Gregory can finish up at the clinic. Oh my, but that's Christmas Eve, isn't it? I do hope the weather co-operates. I wouldn't want to be stuck in a snowstorm."

Jeanne looked away and shook her head. She refrained from pointing out that the flight was direct from Halifax to St. John's, so there was no possibility of getting stuck anywhere in between. "Fine, then, I'll be out at the airport to meet you."

"Thank you, Jeanne. That'll be wonderful."

She hung up and cringed at the thought. *Why must the world insist that we spend the twenty-fifth of December in a group hug?*

Now, she glanced at her watch and noted the first few passengers deplaning before catching sight of Emily laden with bags and a large leather purse. Gregory took up most of the doorway with his swagger and his grey trench coat resting on his shoulders. She felt a brief moment of sympathy for the flight attendants. *At least with Gregory with her, they can't stay long.* She tried to reassure herself as she watched them come down the escalator. Their greeting took its usual superficial tone. Gregory did not seem interested in being there and promptly announced he would be leaving again on Boxing Day. "Going south for a week, to get out of this hellish weather."

That's one, thought Jeanne. "The luggage is this way," she said. She directed them to the nearest carousel and wondered if she should encourage Gregory to head out on the next flight.

On the drive home, Emily bubbled like an excited adolescent. "This was a wonderful idea." Her hand reached to Jeanne's hand on the steering wheel and squeezed it, forcing Jeanne to quickly overcompensate a turn. "Just wonderful."

Jeanne glanced at her sister and wondered for the thousandth time how they had come from the same gene pool. "Uh huh."

"I hope we haven't been too much trouble for Leah."

"Actually, I sent Leah home yesterday."

Emily looked at her, wide-eyed. "You did? Why?"

"For Christmas. The woman does have a family to care for."

"Well, not to worry. We won't make a mess. Besides, I am looking forward to relaxation."

As opposed to what you usually do?

"I would like to drop into my house just to see how the renovations went since I was there last," Gregory bellowed from the back seat. "I am hoping to talk to Joe if he's not too busy. I want to get the place on the market ASAP. Jeez, I hope he'll take care of that for me. 'Course, if he's any kind of a businessman, he'll do it as long as I pay him enough." He looked away and grunted.

Jeanne immediately noticed that he referred to the house as his own and caught his smug expression in the rear-view mirror. Emily was noticeably quiet. She stared down at the pristine grey mat of the car and moved her foot to toy with the small bit of slush that had dropped from her boot.

"Did you leave heat on, Jeanne?" Gregory asked, and leaned forward for emphasis. "I wouldn't want the place to be damaged by the cold. Makes resale difficult."

Jeanne turned left onto Exeter Avenue and left again into her driveway. She heard his question, but any words in response would have simply stuck in her throat.

* * * * *

In the Martel home, Sandi was wrapping Joe's Christmas gift, a photo collage of a heritage home he had restored, when Lindsay entered the living room pushing the vacuum cleaner. Sandi noticed the worried look on her mother's face. "You okay? You look like something terrible happened."

"No, I'm fine, Sandi." She laid down the vacuum attachments and sat in the armchair next to the tree. "I hate bringing this up again." She hesitated. "Did you tell Joe and Lauren that I met Carrie West?"

"Yes, and, like you, they wish there could be some way to talk to her. Then again, how would one bring up the topic?"

Lindsay took a few deep breaths of her favourite aroma, freshly cut fir tree. "Sandi, I've been meaning to tell you something about Carrie that Phyllis told me that morning at church. It turns out that Carrie can't be Charles's daughter, not the child that he fathered. She's too young. She's only fifty-one now. That would make Hannah only sixty-eight years old right now. I'm sure Mother said she was in her mid-seventies."

Sandi sat back, her eyebrows raised. "Ah, so much for her being a Sinclair. Well, this is interesting. She's not Joe's aunt after all."

"No, I guess not," Lindsay replied wistfully, as she looped a stray piece of tinsel around a branch and moved a crystal star ornament to fill in a blank spot.

"But it answers one question and opens up another one entirely."

"Yes, it does. Are you going to tell Joe?"

"I'll tell him today when I meet him for lunch." She glanced at her watch.

"Do you think he and Lauren will pursue it further?"

"I don't see how they can unless they start going back through historical records to find out what happened to the baby, and I can't see Joe doing that. Perhaps Lauren might. But then again, what would be the point?"

Steven heard their conversation from the kitchen. "I wouldn't put much faith in those old records. Sometimes they falsified things just for the sake of appearances."

"Phyllis said that Carrie is definitely the daughter of Marshall West, no doubt about it," Lindsay said.

"Then, I guess it ends there. We'll probably never know." Sandi secured the bright green bow and reached for a gift tag.

"I hope it does," Steven said. "I'll remind you both once again that we should never have gotten involved in this mess in the first place. It's really none of our business. Leave what's in the past right where it belongs."

"Steven, my mother told me about Hannah. That was innocent enough."

"Maybe so. But let's leave it there, shall we? Whatever you do, don't mention it tomorrow night at the Steffensens'. It's hardly conversation for Christmas Day." He refrained from mentioning that, in his view, it was nothing more than idle gossip.

"I'll tell Joe, but we won't mention it tomorrow. It's what Kurt wanted all along, anyway."

Steven looked puzzled. "He does? Why's that, Sandi?"

She shrugged. "I dunno. Joe says his father doesn't like to talk about it. He changes the subject immediately. I noticed it the night we were decorating Lauren's tree."

"Interesting," Lindsay observed. "How about Joe's mother? Has he talked to her about all of this?"

"Same thing. She flatly refuses to discuss it."

Steven closed the dishwasher door, fully realizing that, despite his advice, his wife of thirty-four years had no intention of letting this go.

* * * * *

Jeanne left Gregory at the dining room table gobbling a second bowl of seafood chowder and headed upstairs to find Emily unpacking her suitcase. "Settled in okay?" she asked, and closed the door behind her.

"Fine, thanks, though I may need an extra blanket. The windows seem to be drafty."

"Of course." Jeanne reached for a white wool blanket on the top shelf in the closet. "Emily, in the car Gregory referred to Father's house as his. What did he mean?"

Emily laid the blanket across the foot of the bed. "Oh, that. I told him that as soon as the estate is settled, he can have the house to sell. To be honest, Jeanne, I don't want to have to deal with real estate agents, offers, and all of that."

"You gave him the house?"

"Yes. Why? What's wrong with that?"

Jeanne walked away and shook her head. "So that's how you handle things?" she spoke imperiously.

"Why, Jeanne, what ever do you mean?"

"You know *damned* well what I mean. I asked you to take care of Gregory, to get him to back off."

"Please, such language. Jeanne, you were raised better . . ."

"Raised? By whom?" she sighed and manoeuvred around Emily's suitcases to get to the far side of the room. "I go away for a few weeks, I ask you to do a simple thing, and what do you do? You give him the bloody house!"

Emily slumped on the bed and gave a half cry. "Jeanne, I am not used to this kind of abuse."

"Oh, no, I'm sure you're not. What in the world possessed you to give over the house to Gregory?"

"I asked him not to make inquiries about Mrs. West, just to let it go. He demanded to know why. I said it would hurt a lot of people. He demanded answers. I didn't know what to tell him. I assume it was a woman that Father had a relationship with. One of many, Mother said, although frankly why Father would single her out, we'll never know."

Jeanne stood by the window and stared out into her garden, now dormant for the winter and covered in snow. She felt drained. Could a week go by without hearing about that woman? And now, the mere thought of spending the next few days in the house with Emily and Gregory crushed her even more. "Jeanne, are you listening?"

Jeanne was jolted back to the reality of the room. "Yes."

"I was saying that I don't know why Father left that Mrs. West money. After all, she was hardly a friend of the family that I'm aware of."

There was a prolonged pause.

Jeanne inhaled slowly and held her breath. "She's my mother," she uttered slowly.

"Pardon?"

"I said she's my mother." This time she spoke with emphasis. She turned back slowly. "Hannah Parsons West was my mother, or, I should say, is my mother. She's still alive. That's why Father left her money, Emily. As some sort of payment, I imagine, for keeping quiet all those years. Whatever the reason, now you know." She sat on the small corner chair. "Why do you think Virginia left everything, the house and its contents, to you? Didn't you ever think to question that?"

"Everyone said it was because I am the eldest."

"*Everyone* was wrong." Her voice quivered.

"Jeanne, I'm so sorry. I didn't mean to upset you. It's just that, well, I've always thought of you as my sister, my whole sister." She gasped for air and dabbed her eyes with a tissue to keep her tears from spilling down her clothes. "Oh my, oh my. I don't know what to do. I don't know what to say, Jeanne. Except I'm so sorry."

Jeanne stood, walked back to the bed, and faced her sister with a glaring look. "There is nothing for you to say or do or apologize for. And if you truly feel sorry for me, you'll promise that it will never leave this room. Do you understand?"

"Yes."

"Emily? Are you listening? Never to go out of this room!"

"I understand. I promise. I'm so sorry." She sat fixed in one spot of the queen-sized sleigh bed and rubbed one foot across the plush green carpet, her hands clasped on her lap.

Jeanne sighed heavily, walked across the room, and closed the door to the walk-in closet. "Fine. We'll let Gregory sell the house. That's all we can do. It's just a house."

"Where we had such wonderful memories."

"You did, Emily. You did." She turned to leave.

"Jeanne?"

"Yes."

"Do you mind if I ask? When did you find out who she was?"

"I found out her name on my wedding day. The same day Virginia told me that she wasn't my mother. I was getting dressed in my bedroom just putting on my bridal gown. You were downstairs with the others. She came into my room and complained because one of the girls had almost destroyed one of her precious dishes, that Spode bowl. Anyway, almost in the same breath, she said that my mother lived in the bay, in a small outport, a fisherman's daughter, one of nine children. She said her name. Hannah Parsons."

"Oh my." Emily placed her hand on her chest. "How ever did

they cover it up? I mean, the doctor who delivered the baby, I mean delivered you, knew that this woman, Hannah, was your mother. Yet he deliberately signed the birth certificate with Virginia's name on it?"

Jeanne nodded.

"No one wondered at the time?"

"Emily, you know as well as I do, in those days, who would dare ask questions? The staff certainly wouldn't. And friends, well, even if they suspected, they would let it go. Virginia told me she went away for the winter and came back with a baby. Simple as that."

There was an uncomfortable silence. Then Emily spoke. "Have you ever heard from her or met her?"

"Yes, a long time ago. A week after Joe was born. I had just come home from the Grace Hospital. She came here to the house to see her grandson for the first and last time. I have not seen her or heard from her since then." She stood in the doorway and paused, grasping the door handle. "Remember what I told you." And she left.

* * * * *

On Christmas Eve, Joe, like most employers, shut down his business at noon. Shortly after, he and Sandi stepped gingerly through the slush on Water Street intersections, hurried along the salt-encrusted sidewalks, and looked for a place to eat lunch. The restaurant that they chose was very busy, but the wait staff hurried to keep up with demand. They found a table in the corner and quickly ordered.

Sandi poured milk into her coffee and laid a napkin across her lap. "It feels so good to have some time off. I'm looking forward to next week. You'll be over tomorrow morning for breakfast?"

Joe nodded. "Although I'd rather we wake up together."

"As would I, but let's not spoil my dad's Christmas, shall we? He still thinks I'm twelve," she said with a smile. "By the way, I have a wrinkle to the story of Hannah and her child. We all thought that Reverend West was the baby that Hannah had with your grandfather."

"She isn't?"

"Nope. Her father is Marshall West. He died a couple of years ago. Leave it to my Aunt Phyllis to have the scoop. The woman should have been a private investigator instead of a teacher. Anyway, Carrie is not old enough to be that baby."

"So what happened to Hannah's baby?"

"Dunno. Maybe she put the baby up for adoption. That's Mother's guess. You might want to pass that along to Lauren."

"Will do. So I guess we'll never know what happened to that child," he said. The waitress placed an order of chicken quesadillas in front of him. "Now, let's enjoy our lunch and head home. Your Christmas present is waiting in my apartment."

* * * * *

As much as she was not in the mood to do so, Jeanne knew that it was one of the few days of the year that she had to cook. She was grateful to Leah for leaving her recipe for roasted stuffed cod with mustard caper sauce and steamed winter vegetables. She had also made gingerbread and left a small container of lemon sauce next to it. At the last minute, Jeanne took her Christmas china from the buffet in a half-hearted attempt to make the table look festive.

The three sat quietly until Jeanne broke the uncomfortable silence by informing Emily and Gregory that they were all invited to her friends', the Kavanaghs', for Christmas dinner.

"Oh yes, that'll be wonderful," Emily remarked.

Jeanne sighed at her sister's overuse of *wonderful* and topped up her glass of wine.

Gregory sat with his knife in one hand and his fork in the other. He looked like a character in a children's book. "Jeanne, do you know if Joe has any special plans for this evening or tomorrow? As you know, I'm leaving bright and early on Boxing Day, so I need to get the house squared away before I go."

"It's Christmas Eve, Gregory. I assume he will be spending time with his friends or his girlfriend. I understand he's become quite close to her family, the Martels. And he's going to Kurt's tomorrow, as usual. Joe and Lauren said they would drop by tomorrow after lunch, though. I'm sure he'll be happy to talk business then." She knew the opposite was true.

Gregory gulped his wine and drained the last of it from the bottle into his glass. "Well, I have to make the most of the time. I think I'll drop over to my house as soon as I finish eating and see what kind of shape it's in."

Emily was noticeably sullen during dinner, so Jeanne suggested she should rest a little after eating. She was glad to be alone as she cleared the dishes and tidied the kitchen. Switching on the lamp in the living room, she curled up in the corner armchair and turned the cover of a new novel, an early Christmas present from a friend. An hour later, she heard Gregory return. He said hello as he walked by the living room toward the kitchen and announced he was planning to make coffee. Knowing he would never find anything, Jeanne tucked her bookmark into her novel and went to the kitchen, where she found him slamming doors searching through the cupboards for coffee.

"Coffee's here in the refrigerator, Gregory," she said, and passed him the container.

"Thanks. The new windows are nice at the house. Have you seen them?"

"Yes. The contractor did a fine job."

"The front entrance is interesting. Not what I would have done. Joe spent a lot of money on it, but I suppose it looks appropriate given the age and style of the house. I know nothing about these things."

Jeanne chose not to agree out loud with the obvious.

"By the way, Jeanne, I noticed a few things around this house that belonged to Grandfather. The stand by the front door and the chair in the living room. You brought them up here from the house?"

"Yes, I told your mother. She thought it was a good idea during the winter."

"I suppose. And where are all the dishes?"

"In storage boxes, downstairs."

"Good, then they can be shipped directly to Halifax."

Jeanne stood in the kitchen and faced him.

"Shipped to Halifax?"

"Yes, to my place. It all belongs to me—the house and its contents. Of course, God knows I don't want much of it. I'll probably trash it or sell the antique furniture. Did you want to buy any of it?" he asked, apparently unaware of her churning resentment.

"No, I do not," she said vehemently. "And I was not aware that giving you the house also included its contents." A rage burned inside. She clasped her hands and pursed her lips to keep them from shaking visibly.

"Why not? It's Mother's inheritance." He was back-on to her, carelessly measuring spoonfuls of coffee into the coffee maker. "While we're on the topic, I've been wondering about this West woman in Grandfather's will. Mother keeps insisting that I let it go, but I'm curious. Do you know her?"

"No."

"Huh," he snorted. "Must have been one of his women."

Jeanne stood by the counter and braced her hands against the edge. She turned and grasped Gregory's arm and held it firmly, despite the fact that he was twice her size. "How dare you!" she exclaimed with a piercing stare. "How dare you say such things about your grandfather! He did so much for you. Where did you get these ideas that he saw other women?"

"From my grandmother, his own wife! When she was sick in hospital, she told Mother and me one night that Charles had women on the side." He gave a haughty laugh. "Not quite the words she used, but you get my drift."

"And you believe her? You have proof?"

"Proof? Who is this Hannah West I read about in the will if not one of his snacks?"

"You have no idea who she is, and you have no right to spread such malicious lies about a man you should be grateful to."

His head went back with a laugh. "Grateful? For what?" He shook off her arm and walked away shaking his head. He grabbed a coffee mug from the counter and poured his coffee. "Now, I don't suppose you have some brandy around I can have with this?"

Jeanne ignored his request. She approached him again. "Save that smug look for the nursing staff, Greg, it has no effect on me." She took a deep breath. "Let me tell you something. Your grandfather paid for your education, every last cent. That's what you have to be grateful for."

His expression had changed to one of shock. "My father . . ."

"Your father what? Sent you the money? Now there's a joke. *My* father sent the money to Emily. I was there and watched him write out each and every cheque. I remember he used to ask me if I thought it was worth it, whether you'd actually graduate from medical school. I told him to just send the money for Emily's sake, to keep the peace. Now he's gone, and you can't thank him. So deal with that, Dr. Gregory." *I hope the guilt haunts you for the rest of your days.*

She turned to make the quickest exit from the kitchen through the dining room. There, to her surprise, she saw Emily slumped in a chair at the end of the dining room table with her head lowered. "Emily?"

She looked up.

"Are we going to church?"

She nodded, but did not speak.

"Good. I'll be ready shortly."

CHAPTER 9

On Christmas morning, Quentin woke to the voice of a radio announcer who seemed reluctant to inflict the news on his listeners. He laughed at the man's attempt to find something good to say about a weather forecast that called for freezing rain, ice pellets, and high winds well into Boxing Day. *It's all right, you don't have any control over that either. You're forgiven.*

Shortly after nine, as he was making coffee in the kitchen, he heard a key turn in the front door and knew it could only be one person. "Sara?"

"Yes, it's me." She kicked off her boots, dropped her coat and gloves on the chair in the hall, and headed for the kitchen. "Mornin'. Merry Christmas! You're up early," she said, and gave him a gentle hug.

"Habit. A Christmas habit, I mean. I think that sometime during the night the ghost of my mother kept telling me it was all right to get up. Here, have a coffee."

They clinked coffee mugs and toasted the season.

"When are you going to Kurt's?" Sara asked.

"If Jaclyn had her way, I'd be there now."

"Fine. Why don't I drop you off on the way to my parents'?"

"Little early, don't you think?"

"Hardly. You know Jaclyn. She's been up shaking her presents for an hour by now, and Kurt never sleeps past seven. They're expecting you." Sara turned to the window and watched frozen droplets form vertical chains on the outside. "Joe is having breakfast with the Martels, so he'll be late getting there. Then he and Lauren are going to visit Jeanne around lunchtime."

Quentin stood from the table and placed his empty coffee cup in the sink. "Now there's family obligation carried to the extreme. Visiting Jeanne. Okay, give me a few minutes to get ready."

"Take your time. Given my destination, I'm in no rush."

* * * * *

Outside the Steffensen home, tree branches bent with the weight of ice forming on each tip. Last night's five-centimetre snowfall had morphed into a thick slush on the driveway and steps as the temperature rose in the early morning hours.

Kurt was just coming downstairs when he heard a car door. He opened the front door to Quentin. "Merry Christmas! Come in out of the mess."

"Merry Christmas!" He stepped past Kurt into the foyer. "Sara dropped me off. She figures she'll be back during the afternoon or early evening at the latest, as soon as she can escape."

"I know she's not looking forward to the day with her family," he said as they walked toward the living room.

Quentin bent to place a bag of gifts under the tree. "I have no idea why she does this every year."

"Hope, Quentin. Sometimes, with relatives, people just live in hope that maybe it'll be different this time. No matter how often it's the same."

"I s'pose, but it's a hard way to spend the day," he said, and sighed heavily. "So where's Jaclyn? Not up yet?"

Kurt laughed. "Oh yes, she's up. I caught her earlier trying to secretly open her gifts before I knew what she was doing. She'll be down in a few minutes. Meanwhile, I was thinking about getting a fire going."

Quentin knelt in front of the hearth, and crumpled newspaper.

"Too bad everyone can't be here today. I mean your parents and the rest of them up in Halifax."

"Yeah, it's not the same, is it? But Mother, Father, and Jeanette will be here tomorrow. And Peter and Katie and the lads promised to come down for a few days after New Year's. Katie felt obligated to spend Christmas with her parents."

Quentin stacked four birch logs on top of each other and reached for the matches. He had given a lot of thought to his next question, but finally decided to risk it. "Kurt, I've been thinking about all this business with Charles and the house and Hannah and so on."

"Uh huh."

"I know Lauren would get on my case for bringing up a touchy subject on Christmas Day, but while there's just the two of us here . . ."

"Go ahead, Quentin. What's on your mind?" Kurt watched as the small flame burned underneath.

"You told me a while ago that you were keeping something from Joe and Lauren, and you said it was a decision you had to live with. I've given this some thought and, well, I think I know who Hannah's baby is."

Kurt stared at him, then closed his eyes and lowered his head. "Yes. I figured you might."

"I assumed that Charles and Virginia left the house to the only daughter related to the Bolands. That would make sense. After all, Charles would go along with whatever the Bolands said."

Kurt nodded. "And you know why?"

"Let's just say I know enough, and suspect more." Then being careful not to divulge his suspicions, he changed the direction of the conversation. "Kurt, one cannot help but wonder what difference it makes. So Charles fathered a baby with another woman over fifty years ago. He's gone, and his reputation is hardly important to anyone anymore. As for Jeanne, why does it matter if it comes out? These days nobody gives a hang about that stuff."

Kurt peered at his young friend and searched for words to explain what appeared to be absurd. "Everyone has to have something to define who they are, Quentin. For Jeanne, it's her family's

name and her father—that's all she has. She believes the embarrassment of her friends finding out about her mother, who she is
and where she's from, would be unbearable. It sounds ludicrous
to you and me in this day and age, but, for Jeanne, it's her whole
world."

"Are you going to tell Joe and Lauren about Jeanne and Hannah?"

"I'll tell them when I can figure out how. Soon, I assure you."

"Okay," Quentin said, quietly. "I'll leave it to you."

"Thanks, Quentin. I appreciate it."

The confirmation of his suspicion did not come as a surprise to
Quentin. Nevertheless, it left a burning question in his mind. Why
had Kurt agreed to keep a promise to Jeanne that the secret would
never get out? They managed only to be civil since the divorce. Surely
he didn't owe her anything. Yet, here he was, risking his relationship
with his son and daughter for Jeanne's sake. Because it was Christmas
Day, he decided to let it go for the moment.

* * * * *

"Lauren, you know I don't want to do this." Joe watched his sister wrap herself in a sapphire blue wool coat and turn the collar up
around her neck.

"I know. You say that every year. But it's Christmas, and we have
gifts for her. C'mon. Let's get going." She turned back to kiss Alan
goodbye. "I won't be long."

"Okay, Alan." Joe opened the door to let his sister precede him.
"This is your last chance. Are you sure you don't want to come with
us?"

"No. No thanks," he chuckled with a wave of the hand. "I have
no desire to deliberately spoil my Christmas Day. Have a nice time."

"Yeah, right. See you in a while."

Alan watched Lauren and Joe run through the freezing rain to
Joe's Audi, his winter car. He adjusted the large balsam wreath on the
outside of the door and was grateful that he did not have to face his
mother-in-law that day. Instead, he closed the door and headed for

the study to fulfill a more pleasant task, to chat with his brother and mother in Cochrane, Alberta.

There were few cars on the parkway as they headed east. Joe sprayed windshield wash to melt the ice pellets as they gathered on the edge of the window. "Did you tell her what time we'd be there?"

"Yes, I talked to her after the church service last night. I don't mind Mother or even Emily, but, dear God, I hope Gregory is still in bed."

Ten minutes later, Joe carefully pulled into the driveway on Exeter. They stepped gingerly over the slick pavement stones. Before Joe could ring the bell, Jeanne opened the door. "Merry Christmas!"

"Merry Christmas!" Lauren responded, and ducked in quickly out of the rain. "Unfortunately, it's not very Christmassy outside. Wouldn't want to be a six-year-old with a new toboggan this morning."

In the living room, they found Emily enjoying the Queen's Christmas message on television. Joe stood in the entrance while Lauren sat across from Emily and tried to engage her in conversation about the Queen. Through the double French doors, Joe could see Gregory eating alone at the end of the dining room table.

"Join me for something to eat, Joe," he called, and waved his hand across the spread on the table in front of him. "I bought some cold cuts and bread and stuff yesterday rather than starve to death. Your mother doesn't eat enough to keep a bird alive."

"No thanks, Gregory. I just finished brunch at the Martels. And we have a big dinner planned for tonight."

"Well, here, at least sit down and have a coffee. I want to talk to you about the house."

"You've been down there?" Joe pulled out a chair and filled a cup half full of what appeared to be more like black tar instead of coffee.

"Uh huh. Last evening. It's nice, quite nice. The contractor did a fine job. Now, I want to sell it." He slurped the remaining drops of coffee from the mug.

"With the contents?"

"No, no," he shook his head, and wiped his face with a green linen napkin. "I'm having that stuff shipped to Halifax, unless, of course, there's something you want. Or you, Lauren. Need any furniture for that huge shack you have up the west end?" He spoke with his mouth full and waved his fork in the air. "Take what you like."

"No thanks, Gregory. Alan and I are fine with what we have."

"Your mother has all the dishes here, so go through it and pick out anything. My plan is to dump it."

"Dump it!" Lauren exclaimed. "Good heavens, Gregory. Surely there are people who could use it. Why don't you give it to the Goodwill Centre or a women's shelter, somewhere like that?"

"Because, my dear," he said in the best patronizing tone he could muster, "I have neither the time nor the interest. If you want to do it, go ahead."

Lauren looked at her mother, her eyes pleading. "Mother, Aunt Emily, there are dishes and cutlery and linens that others would appreciate. I work with the women's centre here. I'm sure they could use the linens."

"It's not my decision," Jeanne said dismissively.

"You can take what you want, Lauren. Give it to those people who need it," Emily said softly.

"Joe, back to selling the house." Gregory reached for the coffee carafe and refilled his mug. "I was hoping to put it on the market as soon as possible, in January. I'll be in Florida for ten days. I was hoping you'd take care of it for me."

Jeanne walked through the dining room on her way to the kitchen. "The people who do that are called real estate agents, Gregory, not architects." She spoke as if she was explaining it to a child. Joe was surprised at his mother's tone but, in a rare moment, appreciated it.

"I'm well aware of that," he snapped, "but I need someone to oversee the entire process."

"Best to hire a real estate agent and a lawyer, Gregory. They'll take care of your best interests," Joe said. "I can recommend a good agent, if you like."

"Sure, write down the name before you leave." His tone indicated he was not pleased with his cousin's refusal to do it.

"Not a problem." Joe took a sealed envelope from his pocket along with a pen. He wrote the name of his friend, Graham, who was a real estate agent, on the back of it. "There you go, Gregory. Here's the name you wanted, and, now that my work's complete, here's my bill for services rendered."

Gregory was startled by the invoice. He turned the envelope over but did not open it.

Joe stood and took his coffee mug to the kitchen, poured the overly strong coffee down the sink, and placed the cup in the dishwasher. His mother stood beside him. "I will be very glad to put him on the plane tomorrow morning," she whispered.

"Indeed."

"Will there be many at Kurt's tonight? Has the family come down from Halifax?"

Joe shook his head. "No, most of them arrive tomorrow. There are eleven of us tonight. The Martels are joining us."

"What ever for?" she asked with great surprise.

"Because Sandi and I want to be together."

"Oh my, Joe," she said with a disapproving tone, and looked away.

He stared at her. "What it is? What's the problem?"

She sighed heavily. "I wasn't impressed with that young woman when I met her at your apartment. She didn't seem like your type. Her hair was a state and her hand was beaten up. She seems rather rough and ready, as they say. And her mother's apparently a bit of a gossip."

"Anything else?"

She did not respond.

"Good, because I'm not interested in your assessment of the Martels. Now, I'll get Lauren. We have to be over to Dad's to help with dinner."

He passed Lauren her coat and pulled her hair out from under the collar. He wished Merry Christmas to Emily and Greg and turned to open the door.

Lauren stopped and gave her mother a gentle hug. "If it's all right with you, I'll come by next week and look at the dishes and the rest of it."

"Certainly, as you wish." She closed the door behind them, and felt very alone.

* * * * *

Lindsay lost the argument to leave Mollie at home. According to Jordy, she was invited with the rest of the family. As they pulled up in front of the Steffensen home shortly before 6:00 p.m., Lindsay reminded Steven and Jordy again to keep an eye on "that dog," but her concern was relieved when Jaclyn and Kurt greeted them.

"I have a warm blanket for Mollie right in here," Jaclyn said, and Mollie followed her to the fireplace, wagging her tail at the sight of a new rawhide chewie.

Steven hung up his overcoat and smiled to himself. *If only Mother and Father knew where I'm having Christmas dinner tonight!* Lindsay took in the details of her surroundings: three plush sofas in a square and the softest deep green leather armchairs she had ever seen. She chose one of the chairs across from Kurt. Always fascinated by human nature, Lindsay took advantage of the casual conversation to size up her host. He was, she thought, a classic example of sophistication, realizing, as she turned the word "sophisticated" over in her mind, that it was an old-fashioned term. She studied Kurt's clothing up and down and noticed that his socks stayed up perfectly. Looking over at Jordy's socks which were crumpled around his ankles, she made a mental note to tell him about it tomorrow. She was relieved to see that Kurt was wearing a wool V-neck navy pullover. She wondered where he'd bought his shirt, which had a narrow stripe of navy blue, the exact same dye lot as the sweater. Her hostess wore a pretty kelly green dress with three-quarter-length sleeves. A diamond bracelet sparkled on her right wrist.

Lauren had arranged the dinner table in shades of red and gold. On a snowy white linen cloth sat eleven place settings of Royal Copenhagen china and stemware. A line of white candles of various heights separated guests on either side. Snippets of holly and miniature red roses held together with red and gold striped satin ribbon enhanced each setting next to the wineglasses. The top plates were filled with Sara's salad—a blend of spinach and radicchio, goat cheese, and walnuts, drizzled with honey and strawberry vinaigrette.

Dinner conversation was as Lauren requested: light and positive, memories of Christmas past contributed by everyone around the table. There would be no talk of Sinclair secrets tonight. Despite Lindsay's earlier directive to Jordy that gluttony was a sin, he filled his plate twice, having chosen to take his host's suggestion over his mother's. Lindsay shook her head as she noticed him glancing at her when he reached for the platter of turkey.

After dinner, Lindsay studied the paintings and photographs on the mantel as she listened to Sandi describe how she had made Joe's Christmas gift that was on display next to the ten-foot tree. Across the room she noticed that Kurt, Steven, and Quentin were in an intense conversation about government deficits and was grateful that Lauren was chatting with Sandi. Otherwise she would have reminded them it was inappropriate conversation for Christmas Day.

One photo caught Lindsay's attention, so she stood to get a better look. It was unmistakably a photo of Joe, Quentin, Sara, and David, taken when they were about six years old. She heard Sara behind her. "That's a great picture. I remember the day it was taken. Kurt took us to Monty's in the Square for ice cream. We sat on a bench across the street."

"It's amazing how much Quentin hasn't changed, Sara. Neither have you." She looked around. "This is a beautiful home."

"Would you like to see the rest of the house? Kurt and Jaclyn won't mind."

Lindsay followed Sara across the living room, through Kurt's study and Jaclyn's art room. She ran her hand across the mahogany rail on the way upstairs and stopped to view the paintings along the wall. "Sara, how do they keep this place so spotless? I feel like our house is a mess by comparison."

"They have a housekeeper, Patricia. She'll be back on the twenty-seventh. But it's not always like this. When the whole family's here, it's another place entirely. Kurt loves it. If he had his way, we'd all be living here."

At the top of the stairs, they turned left. Lindsay marvelled at the decor of the five bedrooms and adjoining bathrooms. Her first thought was that she certainly wouldn't want to clean it. Returning to the top of the stairs, Sara stopped and pointed to the room facing her. "This is the Henderson room, as you can see by the name on the door."

Lindsay laughed and ran her fingers across the small gold letters. "That's great. He put his name on it."

"Quentin stayed here when he came home from university. He's covetous over it."

Lindsay entered and looked around at the spacious surroundings. "It's gorgeous. Sara, do you have your own room?"

She shook her head. "No, I have stayed here from time to time in one of the guest rooms, but my room, the one I lived in, is across the way at David's house."

"Oh yes. Sandi mentioned that you lived with the Gilchrists for a while."

"They were my salvation, Lindsay. My father thought that university was a waste of money for a girl. You know the argument. Anyway, Joe, Quentin, and David would have none of that, so when it was time for me to go to university, my father said the best he could do was to put my bed in the basement and let me live there. My older brother, Gary, and his wife moved home when Karen was pregnant. They needed my room for the baby."

"What did you do?"

"At first I thought I would try to get a job and find my own place. But Elizabeth, David's mother, insisted that I move into their house with them. I'll never forget that day. The guys had all my stuff moved from my house to the Gilchrists' within an afternoon." She laughed. "They even helped me hang up my clothes in the closets and then took me out to buy supplies for university. I guess they didn't want me to change my mind. Ken and Elizabeth, both doctors, were gone most of the time, so it was a perfect place to study. They refused to charge me anything, and Kurt paid my tuition. I tried to pay them all back when

I graduated, but they wouldn't let me. I don't know what I would have done without them."

Lindsay could see that the young woman was truly at home in this place. "Sara, surely your family is proud of you now. Here you are, a full-fledged engineer with a graduate degree in naval engineering."

"Lindsay, I don't think they know what I do. As far as they're concerned, I screwed up my life when I left Ray last year. I walked away from a husband who's a lawyer."

"That's really sad. I'm so sorry. I'm sensing that today was particularly rough. Did something happen?"

Sara sighed. "The usual. But I guess it just hurt more this time. I cleaned up the dishes by myself because my mother and my sister-in-law both have the flu, and by four o'clock they had to go back to bed. My father came into the kitchen and asked me if I was coming over here tonight. I said yes, and he responded, well, I won't say how he said it, but he suggested that I owed Kurt Christmas sex."

Lindsay gasped and closed her eyes. "Oh my God, Sara! You don't deserve to be accused of something like that."

"You're right, Lindsay. I don't. That's why it was my last time. I swear, my last time. It's funny, when I phoned David earlier at his grandparents', he asked me why I was going to my parents' house. Quentin asked me the same thing. I guess I hoped that it would be different. But today I realized for the first time that they'll never change."

Lindsay squeezed her hand. "But you have another family to count on. C'mon, we better get back downstairs before they eat all the dessert!"

In the kitchen, Jaclyn and Sandi had centred each piece of Lindsay's plum pudding with butter brandy sauce on white full-lace china plates. Kurt placed a thin wafer cookie next to each piece. "There you go, a perfect blend of English and Norwegian tradition, Lindsay," Kurt explained. "The wafer cookie is a Norwegian Christmas favourite."

Later that evening, Lindsay slipped out to the kitchen and quietly rinsed the dessert dishes. She couldn't help but think that her pension would not cover the cost if she broke them.

"Jaclyn will be upset with you for washing dishes, Lindsay. Just leave them," Quentin said, as he came into the room behind her.

"I don't want to leave them with all of these dishes to do."

He reached for her hand. "Sara and I will help them before we go home. Now, come back to the living room."

"Okay, just place these over on the counter, please, because they're clean." She handed him a stack of plates. She stood at the counter and admired the slender young man. "Christmas Day is different from all other days of the year, isn't it, Quentin?"

"How so?" He closed the cupboard doors and turned back to her.

"It's one day when we all seem to focus on memories."

"Memories, Lindsay, can make you feel warm or cold, depending on what they are." He wiped the counter unnecessarily.

"True," she responded, looking at her new, wounded friend. "And they are not enough. Remember that when you are older. For my age group, it seems that's all they have, memories, no plans."

Quentin gave her a half smile.

"Quentin, do you mind if I ask you something?"

"Sure."

"What do you make of Hannah and Mr. Sinclair? Are you surprised no one has heard from that child for all these years?"

"I guess it depends on whether he or she sees an advantage in coming forward. Perhaps owning up to being the child of Hannah and Charles is not worth it."

Lindsay wanted to pursue Quentin's line of argument, but chose not to do so, given the time and place. Instead, she asked, "Did you come into the kitchen for a reason?"

"Yep, another helping of your plum pudding. Sara wants more as well, with extra sauce," he responded with a grin, and reached for two clean plates.

* * * * *

When Gregory left on the early morning flight on Boxing Day, Jeanne wondered how she would keep Emily entertained for another few days. After breakfast, she found her sitting in the solarium staring ahead, but clearly not focused on anything in particular. Even for Emily, despondent behaviour was unusual.

"Not much to look at this time of year," Jeanne said, as she sat across from her and placed her half cup of coffee on the small table beside her. She reached for a *Canadian Living* magazine and mindlessly turned the pages. "Are you feeling okay? You're not worried about flying back alone, are you? I know you don't like flying."

"I'm fine, Jeanne." She folded her hands in her lap on her heavy wool skirt and pulled the matching jacket together over her light blue turtleneck. She continued to look away as she spoke. "I've been thinking about that woman, Mrs. West, your mother. How much she has disrupted our family. It's so disappointing, so unfair. You know, I've read about women like her."

Jeanne looked up and returned the magazine to the table next to her. "Women like her?" Jeanne asked in disbelief.

"Yes, young women who seek out older rich men as a way of improving their life situations. You know what I mean."

"Emily, you don't know her. You've never even met her. How can you make such a judgment?"

"I'm not judging. I'm just saying that's what I'm thinking, that's all." She finally turned and stared directly at her sister. Her voice remained calm and soft. "I don't mean to hurt your feelings. You are my sister, I mean, my half-sister, and you always will be." She smoothed her skirt. "Certainly, I don't mind acknowledging that publicly, if I have to."

Jeanne thought to say *How gracious of you*, but chose not to.

Emily continued. "However, now that I've thought about it, I understand perfectly why Mother and Father left the house to me. After all, I was their only child, that is, the only child that they had together, so I was entitled to it. And furthermore, I was entitled to do with it as I pleased, including giving it to Gregory." She punctuated her words by tapping her hand on the armrest of the chair.

Jeanne sat, unable to answer. She swallowed hard in an attempt to push the hurt away.

"Yet you told me what to do, or should I say, ordered me to do. And you knew all along, Jeanne, that you had no claim on that house." Years of conditioned politeness kept her from raising her voice.

Jeanne summoned her words. "We both have the same father. He's the one who passed away. He's the one who could leave the house to whomever he wished. It was his will."

"Father was expected to do as the Bolands wished, Jeanne, you know that. And he did. He had very little choice."

"But I'm saying that ultimately it was his decision."

Emily leaned forward, her eyes squinting. "Father was at the mercy of the Bolands all of his life. He started with nothing." Her tone was biting. "He was fortunate enough to have my mother fall for him at a very young age, and he married her quickly before she could change her mind. Her family gave him money to start in business and, over the years, they gave him more to stay in business."

Jeanne's throat tightened in anger. "He worked hard all of his life, Emily. You and I both know that. He worked so hard, and he was successful." She thought seriously about telling Emily how very wrong she was. The truth about her parents' relationship. But she fought back the words.

"Indeed. But would he have been successful if it were not for Mother? *My* mother? And how did he repay her? He had a relationship with a young teenager, a coarse, uneducated girl from the bay. Such a disgrace! Yes, Jeanne, I may admire the man for his success, but I certainly *don't* admire him for what he did to his marriage, to his wife and daughter." For the first time in Emily's life, she felt that she had something to hold over her younger sister, the sister she had always privately resented for being her father's favourite. But Emily was not prepared for Jeanne's ammunition.

"Lots of men intentionally destroy their marriages, don't they, Emily?" Jeanne recoiled.

"What?" she asked angrily.

"Winston, Gregory's father. He destroyed your marriage, or should I say relationship, since I have no knowledge that you were ever married."

"Leave him out of it," she demanded. "This has nothing to do with my relationship with Winston."

But Jeanne knew that, in a convoluted way, it did. And she left it there, in the air between them. She looked at her sister in a new way for the first time. She appeared to be shaking a little, and her eyelids were puffy. Her grey hair was held back with a thin hair band revealing earlobes that no longer held earrings. She wondered how much of a toll this had taken on Emily. Had Gregory said something or done something to make it worse? They sat in silence, and Jeanne realized that for the first time she felt sorry for her sister.

* * * * *

Lindsay treated herself to sleeping in that morning. It was after ten o'clock before she wrapped herself in her thick velour bathrobe and headed downstairs.

In the kitchen, Steven looked up from his cereal. "Good morning! Sharon phoned about a half-hour ago. I told her you were still in bed. She said your mother was wondering what happened to you last night."

"I know. I promised I'd call because I thought we'd be home early." Lindsay reached for the phone and dialled. When her mother answered, she asked her about her Christmas Day and explained that they got home just after midnight, when it was too late to phone. Edna wanted all the details of the house, their clothes, and the meal, but Lindsay kept the details to a minimum, emphasizing the great time they had.

Toward the end of the conversation, she broached a familiar subject. "Mother, I know this is off topic, but before I go, just a thought about Hannah West. Is Carrie the baby that Hannah had when she worked for the Sinclairs?"

"What, Mr. Sinclair's daughter? Oh my, no. Sure, I remember when Carrie was born. Frances had a baby shower for her sister. No, Carrie's father is Marshall West."

"Yes, that's what Phyllis said, but I thought maybe she had it wrong. Oh well, I'm glad that saga is over with. It was stirring up a bit of trouble. I just wanted to clarify it."

"Some things are best left in the past, Lindsay. Besides, it all worked out. Hannah's first little girl got the life that Hannah wanted for her. She certainly wouldn't have done that well if she had lived in Falcon Cove."

Lindsay restrained her surprise. "You know what happened to the child?"

"Yes, of course. Hannah left the little girl with her father."

"Her father? But you said her father was Charles Sinclair."

"Yes, that's right. He and his wife, Mrs. Sinclair, raised her like she belonged to both of them. Poor maid had no choice. Heartbreaking, it is. Heartbreaking. I can't imagine . . ."

"Excuse me, Mother. Sorry to interrupt you, but I need to get this straight. Hannah left her baby with the Sinclairs?"

"Yes."

"And you told me that Hannah went there to help take care of little Emily."

"Yes, I suppose she was only three or four. Perhaps not even that old."

"So Hannah's baby was their second daughter. Her name is Jeanne."

"Yes. That's all they had, wasn't it, the two girls? Those were difficult times, Lindsay. The Depression was on. Oh my, the poverty, but, of course, the Sinclairs were wealthy."

But at this point in the conversation, Lindsay did not want a history lesson. Flabbergasted by what she was hearing, she dug for further detail, fascinated by how much the present was an overlay of the past. "I understand that," placating her mother, "but how did the woman, Mrs. Sinclair, all of a sudden show up with a new baby? Wouldn't people be wondering why they hadn't seen her pregnant?"

"Lindsay, women didn't show off in those years when they had babies. For goodness' sakes, most of them, the rich crowd I mean, stayed inside all the while they were expecting. I imagine Mrs. Sinclair went off on a holiday somewhere on the mainland for a few months, and came back with a baby. No one would have thought much of it at the time. And certainly no one bold enough to ask questions."

Not wanting to let on about the possible repercussions of this news, Lindsay simply said, "Well, it's all very interesting, isn't it? Different times indeed. So Joe and Lauren Steffensen actually do have an aunt, after all, and a grandmother."

"Those are her son and daughter? Yes, but now, Lindsay, if they don't know it, it's because no one wants them to. So keep that to yourself."

"Uh huh." She chatted for a while about their plans for the week, but her mind was not on the conversation. When she hung up, she sat for a moment at the kitchen table and looked out the window to the blue sky above just opening up through white puffy clouds. *Where do I go with this?* she thought. She mindlessly folded the green tartan placemat on the table in front of her, over and over, into a small square, and wondered about the gentlest way to proceed, or whether she should.

CHAPTER 10

"Mother, these blankets are lovely," Lauren said as she folded two Scottish plaid woollen throws. "There are several more here in the box." She returned them to the carton, taped it securely, and marked it *Goodwill*. On the morning after New Year's Day, Jeanne and Lauren sifted through the cartons of linens and kitchenware that had been trucked to Jeanne's basement from the Sinclair house.

"Some of these boxes are marked *Family Heirlooms*. What did you want to do with those?" Lauren shifted the six specially marked boxes from the others.

"Just leave them," Jeanne said, seemingly content to sit back and direct her daughter. "I'll ship those to Emily, and she can distribute the stuff to our cousins. But there were two silver service sets that I looked at earlier. One belonged to the Bolands. It's pure silver, and I'll send that to Emily. The second one was a wedding present to your grandparents. You can have that, if you wish. Of course, it doesn't really fit the style of your home, so don't feel obligated."

"That would be wonderful! I'll be happy to take it. Thanks." Lauren opened the last box. "There can't be too much left at the house, is there?"

"I shipped the furniture to Halifax, except for what I kept here. There are still a lot of books, but I'm afraid they're of little value. I've contacted the local archives at the university to see if they're interested in any of it, especially the photographs of communities around the province back in the 1930s and 1940s, and someone's coming by next week to take a look. Of course, all of Father's business papers are still as he left them. Other than that, it's pretty bare."

"Joe says that Gregory plans to put the house up for sale as soon as he returns from Florida this week. He's already been in touch with the real estate agent. Gregory's not wasting any time." She reached for the scissors she was using to slit the packing tape. She looked around at all the things that she had never been allowed to touch as a child, now tucked away in a series of numbered movers' boxes to be given away to anyone who could use them. She glanced at her mother, sitting across from her with a stack of linen tablecloths and Battenburg lace napkins on her lap. It was a challenge to read her face. Lauren guessed that packing this away was a very difficult task for her, but, if it was, she certainly wasn't showing it.

"It must be sad to see the house you grew up in being sold," Lauren said.

"There's nothing much I can do about it," Jeanne commented dismissively. "I guess most people would ask what I would do with it, anyway. I already have a house."

"I realize that, Mother, but I also know how much that house meant to you."

"What I miss is going over to the house to see my father. It's my last connection to him. He loved that home. It represented who he had become, all he had accomplished in his life." She passed the tablecloths to Lauren and indicated that they should be placed in the Goodwill box. "The last few months, I slept over there most nights. Father couldn't do much, but we had wonderful conversations." Her smile brought Lauren's immediate attention. "I learned a great deal from him during those last days. Those were good talks." She patted down her perfectly tailored navy wool pants and adjusted the collar of her sweater. "I'll never forget them. Or him."

Lauren was surprised at her mother's sudden willingness to reveal her feelings, although she was not convinced that her words represented her sentiment. She waited to hear more, but Jeanne chose to end the topic.

"Did you go to Quentin's yesterday for dinner? That's the usual plan for New Year's Day, isn't it?"

"Uh huh. It was great. Grandma and Granddad were there. Aunt Jeanette is gone on a ski trip, but the Martels joined us, too."

"My goodness, they are getting in with Joe, aren't they? First Christmas Day, now New Year's. It must be serious."

"Yes, it is. Joe's walking on air these days."

Jeanne stood up. "Well, that's nice," she said, as she resisted the urge to pass judgment. "I'm sure they are, too," she added under her breath.

* * * * *

As much as the latest information about Hannah and her daughter played on her mind all week, Lindsay decided to keep it to herself and Steven until after New Year's Day. She didn't see much of Sandi and Joe during the week, at least not alone, and it was not something she wanted to blurt out in a passing conversation. Lindsay got her opportunity to deliver the news when Sandi and Joe arrived at their house around noon.

In the living room, Steven was telling Joe how much he had enjoyed talking with his grandparents the day before. "Married almost sixty years. Now there's a goal for us, Lindsay. And, Joe, they certainly appear to be in remarkably good health for their age."

"I hope I'm in as good a shape when I'm their age," Lindsay commented, and quickly added to Jordy, who was entering the room with a plateful of roast beef sandwiches: "Not a word out of you, young man."

"Nah, that one's too easy, Mother."

As she passed along a plate and a napkin to Joe, Lindsay gave Steven a knowing glance. "Joe, I know I really started something when this all began a few months ago, and I certainly didn't realize where it would lead. It has to do again with the baby that Hannah had."

Joe nodded, and laid down his glass of ginger ale. "Sure, Lindsay, what is it?"

She played with her fingers nervously. "I was talking to Mother in Corner Brook a few nights ago. I mentioned to her that I had met Carrie West at church. Mother confirmed that Carrie is Marshall West's daughter, just like Phyllis said." Lindsay hesitated. "Joe, apparently Hannah's child was kept by your grandparents to raise. That's what Mother is saying, and she got that from Elsie. Hannah had the baby and gave her to the Sinclairs."

Joe's eyes widened as he processed her words. "Are you serious? Really! Then that means . . . that means that the baby that Hannah had is Mother?"

"That's right. It does," Lindsay responded softly, as she ran her hand through her hair. "I'm sorry, Joe, I know this comes as a surprise. I probably shouldn't have been the one to tell you."

"I had no idea." He stood and walked around, his hands on his hips. Then he turned around. "Well, this is a shock. I really don't know what else to say."

Lindsay looked back and forth between him and Sandi. "Joe, this would have been best coming from your mother . . ."

"Lindsay, it's all right." He reached out for her hand and squeezed it gently. "You did the right thing, and I appreciate knowing. To be honest, the more I think about it, the more I realize that it explains a lot, doesn't it? Mother's relationship with Grandmother, for instance." He shrugged. "I should say Virginia. Gee, I just realized I have a new grandmother."

"And a new aunt," Lindsay added.

"Yes, that's right." He wiped his hands with the linen napkin. "An aunt I didn't know I had. I guess my only question is why we weren't told about this."

"That I can't answer, except to speculate that maybe Hannah promised to keep it to herself, at least until you and Lauren had grown up. Your parents likely just went along with that decision."

"I wonder why Frances seems to think it's okay now," Sandi speculated. "If what you're saying is correct, Mom, Hannah would have sworn Frances to secrecy as well, wouldn't she?"

"I don't know, Sandi, my darling. We're all just guessing."

Joe collected his plate and glass. "Okay, well, where to go from here? I guess I had better relate this information to Lauren. I suppose I'm going to have to talk to Mother, too. I don't know how she'll react."

Steven spoke up. "Do you think she already knows?"

"Good question. There's only one way to find out. Thanks for the lunch, Jordy. Sandwich was great!" He turned to Sandi. "Would you like to come with me to Dad's? I'll phone Lauren and ask her to meet us there." Seeing a distressed look on Lindsay's face, he hugged her tightly. "Thanks, Lindsay, I mean that. You did the right thing by telling me. Okay?"

She nodded and whispered, "Okay," but inside she questioned her decision.

* * * * *

A piercing northerly wind and heavy grey sky sent drifts of snow grains across the crosstown arterial road that afternoon. As they turned left onto Waterford Bridge Road, Joe and Sandi speculated about who knew this information and what the repercussions would be. By the time they arrived at Kurt's, Lauren and Alan were there already and were chatting about the Sinclair house and its potential sale.

"Good afternoon, all."

"Good afternoon, Joe, Sandi, it's wonderful to see you again." Christian demonstrated his old-world manners by automatically standing and waiting for Sandi to be seated. Sandi gave him a warm smile as she sat. She noticed his cashmere pullover and wool pants of classic English tweed. When Joe sat beside his grandfather, Sandi agreed with the mother's earlier observation that their resemblance was indeed remarkable. She could not help but think this would be Joe in fifty years, and her heart skipped a beat.

Alan, who was sitting in the large armchair next to her, reached for a handful of chocolate-covered cashews from the bowl on the coffee table in front of him. "Joe, you have something to tell us? You were rather cryptic on the phone," he said with a grin, popping in one cashew at a time.

Joe sat back and lodged his feet on the deep green leather ottoman in front of him. He hesitated and looked around at his family, wondering about the reaction to come. He sighed heavily. "Well, everybody, this is some interesting news, although I'm sure there will be repercussions from it getting out. We just came from the Martels'. Lindsay told us . . . about . . . the baby that Hannah had. Grandfather's baby as well. Apparently, the baby was kept by Grandfather and Virginia."

Lauren was wide-eyed. "What? Kept? You mean the baby was, I mean, is Mother?"

"So it seems," he answered.

Lauren's left hand went to her mouth in disbelief. "So Virginia raised the little girl as her own. How in the world did that remain a secret? Didn't everybody realize that she wasn't pregnant? I don't understand."

Catherine, sitting next to her granddaughter, touched her arm. "Not necessarily, my darling. Remember, very different times. Virginia could have simply gone away for the winter, ostensibly to visit relatives or some such. Stayed away long enough to come back with a baby. No one talked about such things, especially in those social circles. Oh, maybe some of her friends suspected, but again, they would be too polite to ask. The baby could have been born at home, and a couple of weeks later, Virginia would show the little one to her friends, as her own. She would not have been the first, nor the last, to pull that one."

Sandi spoke up. "Yes, I can see that happening, but what about the doctor? Wouldn't he have had to fill out a birth certificate stating the names of the parents?"

There was a silence until Kurt spoke softly. "He would have, Sandi. You're correct. But as a close family friend, he may have simply written in Virginia's name, and justified it as being the best thing for all concerned."

"Who would have been the doctor?" Joe wondered out loud.

"He wouldn't be alive now," Kurt quickly pointed out.

"True."

Lauren sat up and suddenly became excited at the implications of the news. "That means we have a grandmother that we didn't know about. Good heavens, Joe! She's still alive and living in Falcon Cove."

"And it explains why Grand—" He corrected himself again. "Why Virginia was always so nasty to Mother and to us, Lauren. Obviously, she resented Mother for being the result of her husband's indiscretion with the 'help,' as she would have likely called her."

"Oh my." Lauren swept her soft bangs from her face and sighed heavily. "It also explains why Mother didn't inherit any share in the house, for one thing, that is, if the Bolands had anything to say about it." Lauren squeezed her husband's hand. "I have another grandmother, one I don't know yet." She smiled broadly.

"And an aunt," Sandi offered.

"That's right, an aunt. Aunt Carrie. Wow, this is incredible news." Her blue eyes sparkled.

But Alan was cautious. "Lauren, I know this is a surprise, a pleasant one, but remember, now, the woman has remained out of your life for thirty years, one would assume intentionally so. She may not want to be a part of it now. Please don't get your hopes up."

"Maybe she's keeping to herself because she believes we don't know about her, or maybe she doesn't know how to get to know us."

Alan tilted his head as a visual way of reinforcing his advice.

Kurt's silence was evident to all seated around the room, especially to Joe.

"Dad, the big question is, do you suppose that Mother knows? What do you think?"

Kurt hesitated. He looked at the expectant faces of his son and daughter. In his peripheral vision, he could see his mother and father, both with their heads down, as if they, too, knew the truth, though he knew they didn't. Only Jaclyn sitting next to him knew, and then only recently. Suddenly, the secret seemed so trivial and his reasons for keeping it inane. How would he convince them that at the time, so many years ago, he felt he was doing the right thing? Whatever their reaction would be, he knew there was no turning back. He ran his hand through his hair and squeezed the back of his neck, as if he was trying to quell a serious cramp. Finally, he nodded and said quietly, "Yes, she does."

"Are you sure?" Joe asked.

"Yes, I am." He paused, sighed, and leaned forward, rubbing his hands together. "Because I remember when she was told."

There was an uncomfortable silence rarely experienced before in this family gathering. Kurt's eyes met his son's, an expression of anticipation now changed instantly to a hard stare and furrowed brow.

"Because you knew as well?"

Kurt nodded.

"Since when?"

"Since Jeanne and I were first married." He took a deep calming breath. "Actually, the day we were married. Virginia told Jeanne on our wedding day that she was not her mother. She said that her mother was a young girl 'from the bay,' as she put it, who came into St. John's to work for them. She went on to tell her that Charles was her father and that he had only a brief relationship with the young girl, Hannah."

Lauren sat back with her elbow resting on the armrest, her three fingers at the side of her face. "How unkind, how cruel is that? Clearly, she was just being vindictive. She must have deliberately chosen that particular day, so that Mother would always remember it not as her wedding day but as the day she found out about her biological mother."

"Exactly. It was about an hour before the ceremony. Jeanne didn't tell me until the next day. She was shocked, needless to say, but she also said it explained a lot about her life. She never was very close with Virginia."

As he listened to his father's explanation, Joe got up and walked to the other side of the room. He leaned one elbow on the edge of the mantel and rubbed his face with his hand. He looked back at Sandi and, seeing an obvious look of concern, smiled to reassure her that he was okay. He did, however, want answers.

Christian spoke before Joe had a chance. "It does explain Virginia's behaviour over the years, no doubt about that. But of course, it doesn't excuse it. She had a daughter and two wonderful grandchildren by marriage that she certainly didn't get close to. I can't help but wonder what kind of hell their relationship must have been. Virginia's and Charles's."

Catherine nodded. "Indeed. Imagine that conversation when Charles told Virginia about Hannah and the baby. I wonder what the price was?"

"The price?" Lauren asked.

"Yes, my sweet. No doubt Virginia would want something in payment for what he did to her. Her husband cheated on her only a few years into their marriage. What alternatives did she have? Divorce was virtually impossible. The church saw to that. She had to stick it out for life, and she knew it. She'd have to make it worth her while."

"Divorce wasn't possible until Newfoundland became part of Canada, was it?" Sandi asked.

"Pretty much. But even if one got divorced, either through Parliament or eventually the court, it was considered scandalous. Most families whose children got divorced believed they had failed as parents. It was so embarrassing they wouldn't mention it in public. The Bolands certainly wouldn't have. So Virginia had no choice but to stay with Charles and raise another woman's baby. Given how much they depended on community approval, they never would have allowed that to get out."

Lauren sat back and folded her arms. "I guess there's a lot of the story we'll never know. In the meantime, I have a grandmother who is still alive, and an aunt."

Joe looked at her. "There's a lot more to this, Lauren," he said quietly.

"I know, but anyone would be better than Virginia, Joe. That's the first time I called her that. *Virginia.*"

Joe shook his head and walked toward the window and looked out at the snow swirling around the shrubs now tied tightly with burlap for protection from the winter. One question ran over and over in his mind. *Why didn't you tell us?* He wondered why his father hadn't trusted him with the information, why he had denied him and Lauren vital information all these years. He could ask, but sitting there were the two people, beside Sandi, that he loved more than anyone else. His grandparents. The two people he always emulated and trusted. The two people who, having experienced the reality of losing loved ones to war, taught their grandchildren always to find the answer to a disagreement through talking and listening. How he wished it were that simple. But the disappointment, the disillusionment within him, caused his chest muscles to tighten and his heart to pound. He wondered if it simply wasn't best to say nothing at all until he could get alone with his father. He could not upset his grandparents. He could never live with that. He searched for words.

He returned to the sofa and felt the warmth and comfort of Sandi next to him. He breathed deeply several times to induce calmness. Finally, he managed softly, "Dad, let me be the one to ask the obvious question. Or two questions, actually." He looked around the room, then back to his father. "Why didn't you tell us this before? And, secondly, would you have ever told us, if Lindsay hadn't uncovered the truth?" His voice was remarkably restrained, but his expression melded hurt and disappointment.

Kurt knew his son as well as anyone could. He had never before been the object of that look. And for the moment, he knew and was thankful that Joe was holding back. "To answer your second question first, yes, I planned to tell you. In fact, I planned to do it very soon, after New Year's was over and life got back to normal."

"And my first question?"

"I had a good reason. I made a promise."

"To Mother," Joe assumed. Another deep breath. "Dad, when did you ever feel like you owed Mother anything? You've barely been able to get along with her since the divorce. And you only did so because of Lauren and me. Now you're trying to tell us that you did this for Mother? To be honest," his voice quivered, "I find that very hard to believe."

Kurt shook his head, then looked down at the floor in front of him. "I promised Jeanne in the beginning, yes. I thought as the years went by she would want to look for her mother. I actually had a way of doing so. Charles told Jeanne at one point that her mother was living in Falcon Cove. There was a man who works for me whose family was from a community near Falcon Cove. I asked him if he ever heard of the Parsons family. He said yes, that there were nine children and they were a wonderful, caring family. As the years went by, we learned that Hannah had gotten married and had a little girl. Part of Jeanne wanted to know her, but, at the same time, who she had become prevented that from ever happening. She worried about what it would do to her parents, to Charles and Virginia, I mean. Being their daughter was a big deal. It meant a lot in this town in those years and she didn't want to lose that. For the Bolands, and for Jeanne, what everyone thought of them was more important than anything else." He welcomed a glass of ice water from Jaclyn.

"That hardly seems like something you'd go along with. Since when did you care about appearances?"

Kurt struggled to make eye contact. "Joe, I know it sounds ridiculous now. But we were in our twenties at the time. I was green in business, to say the least. I was building a reputation in the community, difficult enough given that my father is Norwegian by birth. To some extent I was considered an outsider, even though I was born here. Heck, people had a hard enough time learning my surname. Jeanne argued that she didn't want to do anything to bring scandal to the family, ours or the Sinclairs. Times were a lot different then than they are now. It mattered where you came from. Of course, today, no one gives a damn who your parents are. Thank God."

Hoping he could soften the progress of the conversation, Christian spoke up. "Kurt, you and Jeanne, did you ever meet Hannah? Was there any contact at all, or did she choose to stay away completely once she left the baby here and presumably returned home?"

Kurt sighed and rested the glass on the table in front of him. "I remember one day in early December, just after Joe was born, I came home from work. Funny how one's mind works. I can remember the strong smell of the Christmas tree that I had bought at the Square and put up in our living room." He leaned back. "Anyway, there was a woman in the house sitting next to the tree. Jeanne was upstairs with the baby. I knew who she was immediately because there was such a strong physical resemblance to her daughter. She introduced herself as Hannah West and told me she was there to see her grandson. She had been there most of the afternoon. She was soft-spoken and gentle, and her eyes glistened when she saw Joe and held him. She looked at him like he was the most precious thing she had ever seen. We wanted her to stay for supper, but she had to go because she was meeting her daughter at one of the stores in Churchill Square. But, before she left, she asked us, no, she pleaded with us, to keep it all a secret. She explained that her parents were still alive and her husband's parents were as well, and that they would be crushed if it came out that she'd had a relationship with a married man, one that had produced a baby. She had told her mother, and that was all. She also said she worried about what it would do to Charles and Virginia. In her opinion, it would only bring hurt to everyone. She believed her grandson would be embarrassed by his grandmother when he grew up."

"Oh my, so sad and so different from the world today, isn't it?" Catherine offered. "No doubt the poor woman was very humiliated, and my guess is, intimidated by both of you and her surroundings. So she felt the best solution was to stay away. Can you imagine the excruciating pain that must have caused her?" She shook her head. "How many stories are there similar to this one? These young girls had no choice but to make very difficult decisions. Being away from home was tough enough."

Kurt nodded. "We could see how painful it was for her when she was at the house that day. It had obviously taken a lot out of her just for her to come by without anyone knowing about it. Imagine, she returned to her daughter only a block away that evening, knowing all the while that she had just left her other daughter. And that the two of them presumably would never meet."

"It's impossible for us to understand it," said Lauren, almost in a whisper. She shuddered as goosebumps ran up and down her arms. "Dad, clearly Virginia did not see Emily and Mother in the same light."

"No. Over the next few years as we were together, I started to notice how much Virginia resented Jeanne and our children, and me, for that matter. Not that I cared what she thought of me. She was one very strange woman. Jeanne told me horror stories about how Virginia treated her when she was growing up. She wasn't physically abusive, but she was certainly emotionally abusive. Jeanne was everything Emily was not. She was smarter in school, as well as prettier and more popular. Jeanne devoured books and Emily rarely read. Jeanne carried herself so well at social functions, could 'work a room' beautifully, as they say. Emily stumbled over her words. And then to top it all, Jeanne married me. Not that I'm much of a catch, but I guess I was more desirable than poor Winston Masters, the man Emily got entangled with. As you two grew up and did well, Virginia came to resent Jeanne and all of us even more. Jeanne tried to keep the peace for her father, and Virginia knew enough not to go public, as it would destroy her own marriage. But, oh boy, privately, she could be nasty."

He ran his hand through his hair as he remembered. "Joe, I'm sure you've never forgotten the time when Lauren was small and Virginia scalded her hands as she tried to clean them in the sink upstairs. How's that for cruel? Take out your anger with your husband on an innocent five-year-old? That was the turning point for me. I pitched Virginia out the door that day and told her not to come back unless I was home. She hardly spoke to me afterward. Not that I cared."

He turned to his mother and father. "Virginia even resented the clothes that you folks sent down from Halifax because we couldn't get anything like that here. And even worse, the things you brought back from England."

"I had no idea, Kurt. If we had known, we wouldn't have made it worse," Catherine said regretfully.

"And deny Lauren and Joe the things you wanted them to have? That's not fair to any of you."

Kurt looked around at the eyes fixed on him. "There were several times when I insisted that we break off with them entirely, and Jeanne would have, too, except for the fact that she cared for her father so much. Probably because she was making up for what Virginia didn't give him, some kind of affection or care. And she always said that contacting Hannah and bringing it out into the open would be breaking a promise to her. I pushed the matter several times. I remember one Sunday afternoon, you two were teenagers, Charles called me into his study and told me that if I didn't co-operate and get along better with Virginia, he'd do what he could to destroy my business. Fortunately, it was a false threat, because by that time, I was fine on my own, thank you very much. I had established my own credibility."

"Okay, but that's over ten years or so ago. You divorced Mother. What's stopped you since?" Joe pressed for more.

"My promise to Hannah. I figured if she wanted to come forward, she would. But she hasn't. She still has family where she lives, and a daughter, Carrie. She must still be embarrassed by it all. I'll never forget the look on her face that day, Joe, when she pleaded with us to keep it to ourselves. I promised her I would. I realize now that we should have tried to work this out, somehow."

"Okay, but you said a few minutes ago that you planned to tell us soon. What changed your mind?"

"Well, when I heard from Lindsay that her mother knew and that Mrs. Mackenzie had gotten the story from Frances, Hannah's sister, I realized that keeping it from Hannah's family was no longer an issue. Obviously she has told them, or at least her sister. I suppose she's okay with others knowing about it now that both Charles and Virginia are gone."

"Fair enough, Dad. But you could have told us, and we would have kept it a secret for the sake of our grandmother."

"I know, I know. And again, I'm truly sorry. Hannah's been through a lot in the past ten years. Her parents passed away, then her husband had a long and difficult battle with cancer. Jeanne felt the last thing she needed on her plate was all of this coming out. Believe me, I planned to tell you before either of you had children. I wanted you to know, so they would. I intended to tell you, but Lindsay uncovered it all first. I'm glad she did, because now it's all out in the open."

While Joe felt for Hannah, he was not convinced that he had the whole story. But for now, with his beloved grandma's hand resting on his arm, he let it go. He sat back, waved his hand, and simply said, "It's all out now. Done and dusted."

"Yes," Kurt responded. "And I guess the best thing would be to let Jeanne know that it is out, as you say. What happens after that, we'll leave to her and Hannah to decide." He straightened in the chair as Jaclyn and Alan came into the room. Attention focused momentarily on the lemon shortbread that Sandi had brought as Jaclyn placed the plate on the table in front of them. Alan laid a tray of tea and cups next to it.

Christian smiled and reached for one. "Kurt, as long as our cardiologist is not within view, you and I can have one or two, I suppose."

Kurt nodded and held up the cookie with a smile. "Dad, David knows I'm eating this cookie even though he's thousands of miles away skiing in Colorado. But I'm going to have it, anyway."

"Yuuummmmyy." Jaclyn savoured every mouthful of her favourite type of cookie—not that she would ever turn down anything labelled a cookie. "Sandi, I suppose this is a family recipe. A deep, dark secret?"

"Jaclyn," Sandi laughed, "even if the recipe were a secret, I think we'd all agree that it's time it came out! Enough secrets!" Her comment brought the relief of laughter around the room. "Actually, my Grandmother Martel got the recipe when the Second World War was on. She heard it on BBC Radio one Sunday night. She taught me how to make them one Christmas when I was only about twelve years old. Since then, I've even given them as gifts because they are soooo good."

"Well, thanks to your grandmother and thanks to you, Sandi. These really are delicious," Catherine declared.

Alan returned from the kitchen with a mug of freshly brewed coffee. "Catherine, these girls who came in here to work in St. John's, in service, I guess they weren't very qualified in terms of workplace skills?"

"No, most of them were only in their teens. We had young women working in our house." She gently stirred her tea. "You must remember that this was not simply moving into St. John's to get a job. It was a lot more than that. These girls had never left their communities before. The farthest they had ever been was to the next community. They went from living in a place with maybe two or three hundred people to a city with thousands. From oil lamps to electricity. From grassy paths worn down by generations of walking to constructed roads. Streetcars and buses. They saw food and drink they had never seen before. Moving pictures in theatres. Huge churches with beautiful windows and powerful organs. It was all new. Add that to the mix of living in a strange home with hot running water and sewage and having all kinds of responsibilities thrust upon you. And no one to protect them."

"Made of sterner stuff," Jaclyn commented. "And an indomitable faith."

"Indeed, Jaclyn. And yet an in-service job was often considered embarrassing." Catherine shook her head in amazement. "I know those who worked for my parents were very talented young women. They could knit, sew, fix things. Unbelievable. I remember one young girl got engaged while she was working for us and we gave her a bridal shower. She was a wonderful person. As you say, Jaclyn, unquestionable Christian faith. But you know, there were horror stories, too. Some girls were not treated very well in these homes. Some were even physically abused."

They listened to Catherine's descriptions with interest. Lauren asked questions, but Joe sat in silence. When Kurt stood to click on the Christmas lights, Joe finally spoke.

"I guess, Lauren, we should go talk to Mother." Glancing at his watch, he said, "Sandi and I are due at Quentin's for supper in a few hours."

"Okay, let's see if she's home now." Lauren stood.

Knowing how difficult their meeting with Jeanne would be, Kurt volunteered. "Why don't I give her a call? And I'll come with you, if you like."

"Fine," Joe answered. "But I'll drop Sandi off at her place first. There's no reason why she has to take this on, too."

Outside in the driveway, as they sat in Joe's Audi waiting for the windows to defrost, Sandi could sense Joe's disappointment. As he shifted the gears into drive, he sighed heavily. "Sorry, Sandi, but I think there's more to the story. I think he's keeping it from us. I didn't push it, not with Grandma and Granddad there."

The sun had dropped below the horizon shortly after 4:00 p.m. and the city lights were already on. Joe returned to the east end of the city by the same route as they had come. Snowdrifts were forming on the inside lanes of the parkway. The sky had a greyish whiteness and a ring around the moon indicated precipitation.

"Joe, I know this is all a shock to you. My Grandma Martel used to say that life happens in epiphanies. But your father obviously had good reason, or at least it was a good reason, as far as he believes."

He nodded. "I know. I'm not as much angry as I am disappointed. I'll talk to him sometime soon, privately. In the meantime, hopefully, I should be back for you within the hour. Frankly, I could use a few hours of Quentin's humour tonight."

CHAPTER 11

Jeanne opened the door to Kurt, Joe, and Lauren, not knowing what to expect. Kurt's brief phone call an hour before had simply informed her that Joe and Lauren wanted to talk to her because they knew the truth about Hannah. With only a few glib social niceties, they took off their coats, hung them in the hall closet, and followed her to the living room. Jeanne chose the comfort and security of her favourite chair. She sat and waited.

Kurt remained standing. "Jeanne, as I mentioned on the phone, Joe and Lauren have learned that Hannah West is your mother, and that you and I chose to keep that from them. I have told them, as best as I could, why we did that." His voice lowered. "But perhaps it would be best if you explained it as well." He sat on the edge of the nearest sofa, next to Lauren.

"Very well," Jeanne said, her voice shaking. "May I ask first how you found out?"

"That's not important," Joe said.

"Joe!" Lauren whispered his name under her breath. "Mother, I mentioned to you before that Sandi's grandmother is from Falcon Cove. She and Frances Parsons are good friends."

"Your Aunt Frances," Kurt interrupted.

Jeanne gave him a sharp look.

"So Mrs. Mackenzie told her daughter, Lindsay. It was all quite harmless," Lauren explained.

"These women have nothing else to do with their time?"

Joe shook his head. "That's not it at all. Lindsay met Carrie West at a church function. They talked about the fact that their respective mothers are from Falcon Cove. There. Done. So back to the question, why did you decide to keep this from us?" His reaction was more rooted in the fact that she was questioning Lindsay's motives than in the secret she had kept.

Jeanne looked at Kurt, but found only a blank look. She stood and walked to the window and looked outside. "It's always my fault, isn't it, Joe? No one else can be responsible when you are wronged in some way other than me." She turned back to him. "I didn't tell anyone about my mother because my mother begged me not to tell. She didn't want anyone to know. Yes, it would be embarrassing for me and for my father, but did you ever stop to think what it would do to her and her family? She was married and had a child with him. She had parents, aunts, uncles, and cousins. She didn't want them to know because of how they would see her. She had a relationship, willingly, with a married man."

There was prolonged silence.

Finally, Joe spoke. "But neither one of you saw fit to entrust this to Lauren and me. Doesn't say much for what you think of us." He had said the words, but Lauren's glance suggested he should not have.

The line was a bitter blow for Kurt, but Jeanne showed little response. Instead, she studied her son and daughter like she was looking at them for the first time. "As I said, my mother, your grandmother, felt it was best that you did not know. She asked us not to tell you. I know that must be difficult to accept."

Joe sat back. "Fine."

Lauren looked at each of them. "This still doesn't completely explain why Grandfather left the house to Emily. You are his daughter. He could have left it to you. What did the Bolands hold over him?"

Jeanne looked to Kurt for help. Surely after all these years of knowing each other, he could read her face.

"The Bolands had a lot of money, Lauren. Charles did not, at least not in the beginning," Kurt explained. "When Charles and Virginia were married, they gave him money to start his business and, over the years, they contributed to the expansion of some of his business ventures. I guess he felt that he owed them, so he did what Virginia wanted. He gave Emily the house." Slowly, he stood. "Unfortunately for you, Jeanne, he misled you along the way."

"Yes," she managed weakly.

Joe glanced at his watch and sighed. "Okay, so where are we on all of this? Virginia was not our grandmother, nor your mother. You both have known this for years and you kept it quiet out of respect for Hannah West. Charles felt he owed the Bolands, so he did as they requested, or demanded, I should say. But none of that now justifies why Lauren and I can't contact our grandmother." He leaned forward. "For God's sake, don't you think you'd be better off with your mother, your real mother, in your life? It would be a damn sight better than sitting here by yourself, or even worse, tolerating Emily as you appear to do."

"Why? Because I am so pitifully alone? Is that it? I don't have the life we're all supposed to have? And who's responsible for that, Joe?" She paused and looked around the room at her family that once was. "Would that life were so clear, Joe, as you want it to be. Your definition of what is right. Your standards. It's too bad that I probably won't live long enough to see you when reality hits." She took a deep breath. "And, by the way, you have no idea how my days are filled. I hardly ever see you or hear from you. So don't sit there in judgment of what you think I do, or don't do."

Joe looked away, but Lauren was feeling a sense of compassion for her mother that her brother did not. "This has been a difficult day for all of us. I assume you thought this would never come out."

"I'm fine, Lauren, as long as it stays right here in this room. But that is likely not going to happen. What do you plan to do, now that you know?"

Lauren adjusted her silk scarf. "I haven't thought about it yet. I just found out I have a grandmother and an aunt I didn't know about. I guess at the very least I would like to meet them."

Moments later, at the door, Kurt turned back. "Jeanne, it's better that this has come out."

"Of course."

He knew she was hurting, a deep hurt grounded in the worst kind of disillusionment, one created by family. She was doing well not to show it. He wondered if there was something else that had happened. He would mention it to Lauren. "Take care, Jeanne," he said, and closed the door behind him. But his words meant very little to her.

* * * * *

Alone, standing in the hallway, Jeanne felt chilled to the bone, so she reached for her brown cardigan from the hall closet and wrapped it tightly around her. Her life seemed to be unravelling and she was powerless to stop it. Mindlessly, she walked around her house. She was not prepared today for either Joe's words or Lauren's questions. She knew others would soon know the truth. There was little doubt about that, despite her efforts to keep it from them. Her friends would hear that her father had had a relationship with a young girl, and she was the result. They would know as well that her father's money had come from the Bolands. That revelation was worse. Charles Sinclair, the self-made wealthy businessman, was not self-made after all. On top of that, if Lauren and Joe had their way, she would have to face Hannah and Hannah's other daughter.

She moved slowly back into the living room and sat on the armrest of the first armchair she reached, mindlessly rubbing her fingertips back and forth across the seams. Where had this gotten her, keeping this secret all those years? She circled the pattern of flowers on the chintz upholstery with her right forefinger. She remembered the last few weeks of her father's life and the night he died. *The house is yours, you know that.* She expected tears now, but none came. She even tried to force them to come. Nothing. She felt neither anger nor sadness. Just a deep well of emptiness.

She fell back in the chair and squeezed her eyes shut. *So what,* she thought, *so what if it does come out? Perhaps it should. After all, you deserve it. You lied to me. Deliberately. Just hours before you breathed your*

last breath, you looked into my eyes and promised me that the house,
our beloved home, would be mine because I deserved it. Why should I
care what the community thinks of you? You were a fraud.

She stood, walked to each window on the first floor, and stared outside, but saw nothing. This house that Kurt had built for her, for them, for their family, now her alone. Moments later, she found herself downstairs, sitting in the chair Lauren had sat in that morning to go through the boxes of Sinclair household goods. She pulled along the first box marked *Family Heirlooms* and opened it. She removed the sheets of packing material and found two crystal vases side by side. She took out one, looked at it briefly, and returned it to the box. She pushed that aside and reached for the second box. It had only one item, a Spode porcelain bowl, about ten inches wide and five inches high. It had brilliant blue and gold coloration, in an intricate pattern, and a gold trim. She held it in her hands and turned it over slowly. She remembered it well. It was Virginia's most prized possession, inherited from her great-grandmother in England, dating back to the early nineteenth century. She remembered how guests in their home viewed it behind the glass door of the dark wood buffet. Virginia had proudly taken it out to show the lieutenant-governor's wife one evening.

Jeanne thought back to the day she was married, a warm and sunny July day. Eighteen-year-old Annie, who worked as a housekeeper, had helped her get into her dress and assured her she was the most beautiful bride she had ever seen. Annie left the room quickly, fearing that Virginia would find her away from her assigned chores. Moments later, the door opened and Virginia walked in, complaining that one of the young girls almost had an accident cleaning the dishes in the cabinet downstairs. Taking only a few breaths, she went on, "By the way, Jeanne, there is something you need to know. Perhaps I should have told you this before now. But it really doesn't make that much difference." She paused, then spoke as if reading a mindless script. "I'm not your real mother. I didn't give birth to you." Jeanne, who was back-on, turned away from the mirror and made eye contact with Virginia, who continued without so much as a quiver. "Your father had a . . . well, a young girl who worked for us had a baby. Charles's baby. She couldn't take care of you. She was too poor, so you were left with us." Then, as if she had done nothing more than give a weather report, Virginia turned away, paused momentarily to straighten the bedspread and needlessly push back her hair, then closed the door behind her.

Now, years later, Jeanne held the very bowl that Annie had been dismissed for "almost" dropping that day. She lost her job for not holding a bowl properly as she dusted it. *Did it make you feel good, Virginia?* she wondered. *Did you sleep better that night? Did you relish telling your friends about the incompetent "help" and how quickly you dismissed them? How much more important was that bowl than me?*

Slowly, she ran her fingers around the base of the bowl. Not a scratch, not an indentation. She could picture Virginia so clearly—tall and emaciated, with short brown hair always swept back, as if she wanted to deny it existed. Her clothes, her speech, her life were orderly to the point of obsession.

Charles's words about Virginia came flooding back. He had once described how he met Virginia, and Jeanne recalled that his description did not match the woman she remembered. Charles told her that his young wife was full of life and energy, that as a young teenager she rarely sat still. But over time, as the years passed, she developed an obsession for orderliness. It was as if keeping the cutlery in perfect formation on the dining room table also kept her life and others around her in line. As she grew older and the girls grew up, she developed a brooding, introspective nature. Her face, once bright and full of life, became drawn and pale. She and Charles, always separated by bedrooms, eventually separated in their daily lives, except for weekends of entertaining expected of them by a socially stratified community. They maintained a facade right up until her death.

Jeanne turned the bowl over in her hands again. *Now I am expected to be the "help," is that right? Pack this up and send it to Emily so she can show her friends the beautiful things that her mother owned.* She stood, still holding the bowl, and turned to go upstairs. But something stopped her there. She looked down at the carpeted floor, then at the bowl. For a moment she remained fixed in place as she thought. Then she walked to the door that opened to the attached two-car garage, turned the handle, and pushed it open. Cold air rushed toward her as she stepped forward. Standing in the middle of the second parking space, she looked down at the bowl and held it in the palms of her shaky hands for a final time. She bit her lower lip in anger. Then she opened her hands and let it drop, watching it smash into minute pieces on the grey concrete beneath her. The crash was the only sound in the house. She swallowed hard, and after a moment she moved to the far side of the room and picked up the small blue-handled broom and dustpan that hung on the wall. Slowly, she swept the pieces in one motion onto the pan and dumped them in the plastic garbage can by the door. She replaced the cleaning tools, satisfied, and without regret she returned upstairs.

* * * * *

Kurt pulled his car into the garage attached to their home, turned off the ignition, and sat momentarily thinking over the events of the day. This was not how he wanted the news to reach Joe and Lauren, and something in Joe's eyes suggested that he would not forget easily. The reactions of his son and daughter caught him by surprise. Lauren was the one who wore her heart on her sleeve, yet she was seemingly taking it all in stride, anxious only to meet her real grandmother. Joe, on the other hand, appeared shaken and certainly not so accepting of the news. Kurt reached for his gloves. *Perhaps*, he thought, *he just needs some time.*

Inside, he welcomed the warmth of their home. He found Jaclyn and Catherine sitting in the kitchen placing silverware back in its wooden chest. He pulled out a chair and joined them, giving a loud sigh.

"How did things go at Jeanne's?" Jaclyn asked.

He shook his head. "As one would expect. Jeanne is not thrilled that this information is out. 'Course, that's not surprising." He stretched his arms. "But I'm not concerned with Jeanne."

"Joe," Catherine said, softly. "You're worried about him."

"Yeah, not so much that he was upset. Joe, as you know, rarely gets angry. It's more than that. He seems hurt by it all. Disappointed. Makes sense, since we kept it from him. Still, it's not the reaction I expected. Lauren—she's just concerned about her grandmother."

Jaclyn touched his arm. "But remember, now, you promised Jeanne's mother."

"I know, my love, but right now, as I sit here, that seems like a pretty lame argument."

There was silence around the table. Kurt leaned forward and placed his elbows on the edge of the table. Beside him, Catherine studied her son carefully. She knew him better than anyone, and right now she knew if there was any way he could make it better, he would. That was the Kurt she knew, the man she was always proud of. Always wanting to fix it, to make it better. The man who stepped forward when Quentin's parents died, the man who paid Sara's legal fees when she wanted to divorce quickly.

"Kurt," Catherine began, "I've thought about this from time to time over the years, and what happened here today brought it to the surface again." She ran her fingers across the edge of the linen napkin in front of her and folded it several times. "Charles Sinclair, the Sinclair family, and, for that matter, the Boland family, Virginia's family, there was a lot going on behind the scenes that is not common knowledge. Charles's relationship with his in-laws, from what I recall, was tenuous at best."

"I always had that impression. He never spoke of them in good terms, and when he did, Jeanne remained silent." Kurt looked puzzled. "What are you thinking?

"This is all speculation, I mean, just what I heard Mother and Father and others say, when I was growing up. The city was a very different place then. The social circle of people who were well-off financially was quite small and everyone knew everyone else's business, though they rarely talked openly about it. Sort of an unwritten code. My father's work life was nearing the end when Charles was at his peak. But I remember that Dad would come home from listening to Charles at some business organization. Charles would complain about workers, how lazy they were, and my father would shake his head. He would say to Mother and I, 'Charles Sinclair doesn't know what unions will do to his world. No one is going to put up with his treatment, not in the world of today.' That was the sixties. Workers weren't going hat in hand anymore looking for work. No one deferred, not like they once did."

"And Granddad was right."

"When it came to business, and people, he usually was." The voice behind him was Christian, just entering the kitchen and overhearing his wife's words. He joined them at the table.

Catherine continued. "The more I think about it, the more I wonder if the most important secret here is not the fact that Charles fathered a child by another woman. Heavens, that kind of scandal went on all the time. Nobody talked about it, that's all."

Jaclyn laughed. "Still goes on."

"Absolutely!" Catherine smiled and nodded. "So that's what leads me to believe that there is more to this, something else that Charles and his family didn't want to get out."

"Such as?" Kurt asked.

Catherine hesitated and looked out the window across the back lawn at the snow whipping through the shrubs now dormant for the winter. "The Bolands had lots of money. Mr. Boland, I think his name was Clarence, that's Virginia's father, was a hard old cuss. And he knew he had a daughter who likely would never find a husband, at least not without some help."

Jaclyn's green eyes widened. "Help? Catherine, you mean . . . her father . . . found her a husband."

Catherine laughed. "Well, not so much found, as secured the arrangement. Rumour had it that Mr. Boland enticed Charles into making it a permanent arrangement."

"In exchange for?" Jaclyn asked.

"In exchange for financial backing for the rest of his life."

"Dear God, Mother," Kurt said with a smile, "how desperate would a woman have to be to marry Charles?" He paused. "Hang on, now, I'm talking about Virginia. Poor soul. She couldn't take care of herself, let alone a family or a household. And certainly she was never able to work outside the home."

"Exactly. Virginia was helpless. She didn't have much to do with bringing up Emily or Jeanne, as I recall. Charles came along, with his Scottish accent, and Virginia thought she had the moon."

Christian grinned. "The accent, Catherine, that was enough to attract her to Charles?"

"Of course, my darling, some women fall for the uniform, some for the accent." She winked at Jaclyn.

"So that's why you agreed to see me? My accent?"

"Of course! Norwegian, the language of love. To paraphrase, 'a loaf of bread, a jug of wine, and thou Norwegian accent.' That's all it took."

Jaclyn and Kurt enjoyed the laughter. Catherine reached out and squeezed Christian's hand to signify she was teasing. Jaclyn thought of all the times that she thought Christian's soft-spoken voice was just perfect. She was not alone.

"So Mother, what you're suggesting is that the Bolands kept Charles in business. In return, he stayed with Virginia."

"I suppose they referred to it as a substantial dowry, but yes, the principle was the same. Times were hard in the 1930s. Very likely Charles needed money to keep going. From what I recall, he didn't have much to start with."

"That certainly was a lot to keep a secret, wasn't it," Jaclyn said, "but then, there was more than one secret that had to be kept. Even that doctor, whoever he was, the one who delivered the baby. He deliberately falsified records."

Kurt and Catherine's eyes met in acknowledgement that they both knew the truth. Kurt turned to his wife. "It's no secret who he was, Jaclyn. I didn't want to disclose his name in front of the others. But I will tell them. It was Alexander Hamlyn. Dr. Hamlyn. You remember him, Mother?"

"Indeed I do. And his son, Jonathan, Jeanne's lawyer, is very much like his father."

"Ah yes, of course," said Christian with amusement. "It's just as well to find the humour in all of this, folks. After all, it's all done and dusted, as Joe said earlier. Some people did some pretty stupid things. Nothing new to report there. I guess the question is, how much do Jeanne and Emily know about their father?"

"If Jeanne knows about what Mother just said, she and Charles did a damned fine job of keeping it from me all those years," Kurt observed. "Or someone did. It's one thing to father a baby with a woman other than your wife. That might have been scandalous then, but hardly now. But this news. His reputation would certainly be tarnished in the community. Of course, he's gone now. But Jeanne and Emily are still here. Hmm . . ." he sat back as the others looked at him and shared the same thought. "I wonder if Hannah knows?"

* * * * *

Joe and Sandi took a while to recount the story to Quentin and Sara in front of a crackling fire in Quentin's living room. Quentin munched on Cheezies and drank Pepsi, only nodding on occasion to indicate he was listening. He refrained from commenting until they had finished.

"At least it's all out in the open now."

Joe raised his eyebrows in surprise. "That's it?"

"What else is there?" he asked in a matter-of-fact tone. "Look, we knew from the get-go that Charles had another woman in his life and we knew that she had a baby. Today you find out that the baby was your mother. Okay, so you have a grandmother you didn't know you had. You get a do-over, a mulligan. And, as a bonus, you get an aunt. Cool. Mind you, you'll have more Christmas shopping to do . . ."

Oh Lord, thought Sara. *Quentin, this is not the time to be flippant. Joe doesn't need that.* She interrupted. "Joe, Kurt must have given you a good reason for keeping this from you. What exactly did he say?"

"He said that he promised Mother because she didn't want to upset her family or bring scandal to them. Then, he promised Hannah, who didn't want her family to know."

"Well, that sounds reasonable, doesn't it?"

"Yes, absolutely, Sara, except that Mother's parents are gone and Dad divorced her fourteen years ago, so he hardly owes her anything. As for Hannah, clearly the family knows, because her very sister is telling friends. So the two arguments don't hold water anymore . . . if ever."

"The main thing is, you know now," Quentin said.

"Quentin," Joe said, "you obviously haven't been listening to me at all. We weren't entrusted with this rather important information. I'd expect that from Mother, but from Dad I'd expected more." He stood and walked away.

"I heard every word you said. But nobody's died."

"You sound like this isn't a surprise. Did you know already?" He turned back and glared at his friend.

Quentin drew in his breath and held it momentarily. "Fine. Yes, I knew, sort of, but only for a few weeks. I suspected it that night when I heard Alan say that the house was left to their eldest daughter. The Boland family wanted the house to go to a relative of theirs. I've known that for a long time. I realized then that Emily was the only daughter related to the Bolands."

Sandi and Sara exchanged puzzled looks that questioned how Quentin knew about the house "for a long time" and obviously before the rest of them. Sandi looked at Joe, who evidently had not picked up on the comment.

Quentin continued. "Now you know the reason, Joe. It explains why she treated you and Lauren like crap all those years. Isn't it good to have answers? It's no big deal."

"Big deal, Quentin?" his voice rose in frustration from the far side of the room. "The big deal is that Dad didn't even bother to tell us. He didn't trust Lauren and me enough to tell us the truth. And that sure as hell bothers me. I let it go today because Grandma and Granddad were there, but don't you think we had a right to know who our grandmother is?"

"Kurt would have told you and Lauren. He said he would."

"When did he say that? You weren't there today."

"He told me Christmas Day, actually. I asked him about it. And he told me he planned to tell you, and I believed him. I have no reason not to."

Joe held up both hands for emphasis. "And did you ever consider telling me?"

"As I said, I knew Kurt would. That's all I needed to know."

"That's an easy way out," he responded in disgust.

Quentin caught sight of Sara's pleading expression and, as always, could not deny her wishes. He stood and walked over to Joe. "Listen to me."

"I'd rather not."

"Well, you're going to." He grabbed Joe's arm to prevent him from turning away. "Your father did what he did because his wife asked him to and because Hannah, your grandmother, asked him to. He kept a promise. In many ways, these days, that's an admirable thing. Whether or not you agree with all the reasons behind it, that's not your place to judge. Okay, so you think your father should have told you. Perhaps he should have. Kurt's a well-intentioned person. That almost goes without saying. God knows, I've admired him all my life and I always will, because I know whatever he does, he does because he firmly believes it's the best option. And that's a rare thing today, as well." He let go of Joe's arm and his voice was quieter. "He's not perfect, Joe."

"I know that."

"Good. Then get past it."

"Quentin, I wish it were that simple. He obviously doesn't think much of his son and daughter to keep this from us."

Quentin looked down at the floor and back at his friend. "Listen to me. Are you willing to damage your relationship with your father because of this? Because if you are, it would be the stupidest thing you ever did." His tone was cutting. He sighed, looked away momentarily, squinting his deep brown eyes. He looked back at his friend, his eyes glistening. "At least you have a father who's alive and you have a chance to forgive him."

* * * * *

Later that night, in their king-sized poster bed, Alan tucked the thick duck down duvet around his wife's shoulders and noticed she was still awake. "Can't sleep, Lauren? It's after eleven."

"No," she sighed, "it's been quite a day. Guess I can't get everything out of my mind."

"Thinking about your grandmother?"

"Dad, actually. It made sense, his reasons for not telling us, at least while he and Mother were married. But after that, after their divorce, I don't see why he was willing to go along with it. I mean, he didn't trust Joe and me enough to simply tell us and swear us to secrecy, which we would have gladly done for Grandmother's sake." She shifted her head and pulled her hair out from the pillow. She ran her hand across Alan's chest and sighed. "I guess I'm missing something. Or perhaps Dad's content to tell us only so much. I'm fine with that, I suppose. I have to believe that he does things with the best of intentions. I have to, Alan. He's my dad. I can't face tomorrow knowing he doesn't trust me."

Alan kissed her lightly on the top of her head. "Perhaps he needed the secret, Lauren. Perhaps by its power it served a purpose. In any event, you go to sleep now. You have to work tomorrow."

Lauren closed her eyes but stayed awake for a long time. *A purpose*, she thought. *A price*. Perhaps she'd never know.

CHAPTER 12

By mid-January, Joe welcomed the opportunity to sleep in later than he normally would on a workday. Shortly after 9:00 am., having promised to take his grandparents to the airport, he backed out of his parking garage below his condominium and headed west up Duckworth Street to Waterford Bridge Road. A few minutes later, he found his grandparents just finishing breakfast, their suitcases waiting in the hall. His father and Jaclyn had already gone to work.

He poured himself a cup of coffee, took a croissant from the microwave, and joined them at the kitchen table. "I wish you both would stay longer, at least until all this news about Hannah West comes out and Mother decides what she's going to do. You know Lauren. She won't stop until she has our grandmother sitting at the dinner table next Christmas."

Christian smiled. "We're only an hour or so away by plane if we're needed. Besides, this will take a while to unfold. I doubt that Jeanne will act quickly, if at all. It's not like she's going to head out to Falcon Cove in January."

Joe laughed, but Catherine looked concerned.

"Joe, there's one thing here that's more important than all that information about your mother and Mrs. West. That's you and your father. Whatever happens, you must not let anything interfere with what you have with your dad. It's too important to him, and to you."

"I know."

Catherine sliced her apple cinnamon muffin into four pieces and spread butter on each piece. "Yes, I know you do. But still, you're preoccupied with what happened." She wrapped her fingers around the warm mug of coffee. "I know all of this is news to you, but it seems to me that you're more bothered by your father's role in all of this."

"Grandma, I'm sorry, but it's hard to understand. Why didn't he tell Lauren and me? We would have kept it to ourselves. You know that."

"Yes, I do, but Kurt had his reasons."

Joe exchanged looks between his grandparents. "Yeah, and I'm guessing what it was. He used the information. Am I right? It was something to hold over her."

Catherine sighed and looked at Christian as she decided how much she should disclose. "That's between you and your dad. Let him explain it to you. He will. For what it's worth, he feels terrible for not telling you. He really does."

Christian reached his hand to Joe's shoulder. "As soon as you can, talk to him. And remember, Kurt rarely does anything without a very good reason. Just like his son."

* * * * *

Kurt anxiously returned to his office that morning to plan the next few months. Reluctant to say goodbye to his mother and father, he promised to visit them in Halifax before too long. But the coolness that remained between him and Joe still weighed on him heavily. He knew he should act on his parents' advice and tell Joe the whole truth and, more importantly, make it right.

He was never one to take his troubled mood out on his employees, and most of the staff of Steffensen Publishing saw Kurt as his usual congenial self. Doris McKinlay noticed that occasionally he seemed preoccupied, so she tried more than usual to keep him from unnecessary aggravation. Kurt declined to point out that she was hovering. Meanwhile, Jordy's work and wit were a welcome addition to the office, and Kurt made a mental note to let him know before too long how much he appreciated him that January.

Later in the afternoon, he finished talking to his parents, who had arrived safely back in Halifax, and swivelled in his chair to watch the harbour lights come on. A dusting of snow covered the Southside Hills and Signal Hill. Outside the entrance to the harbour, whitecaps dotted the greenish blue North Atlantic. The winter season, above the other three, made him fully aware of this place, an island captured by the bitterly cold Labrador Current, cut off from the rest of the continent.

Standing next to his desk that afternoon, Doris gathered files and reminded him of tomorrow's busy schedule. "Doris," he mused, "I must be pretty transparent. My mother, instead of asking me how much money I made today, as she usually does using her best sarcasm, she told me to get some sleep tonight."

"You're as transparent as sandwich wrap, Kurt," Doris declared with a chuckle. "All of you Steffensens are, 'cept your father, of course. He's a real man." She smiled at his predictable response when he rolled his eyes. "I'm assuming this has to do with family, not business," she said. "Your lack of sleep, I mean."

"Yeah, wish I could talk about it, but it's best not to—at least not yet."

A light tap on the half-opened door caused both of them to look up. Joe pushed the door open. "Good afternoon."

For Kurt it was a welcome sight. In the past, Joe had made it part of his daily routine to drop by during the slow days of January, but given the way they had parted a week ago, he wasn't certain that the habit would continue. "Well, good afternoon! What brings an architect out on a day like this? I thought you were taking a few days off before things get busy again."

"I'm working on that international project I told you about. Thought I'd take advantage of the quiet. Michael's gone to Bermuda for two weeks and business is predictably light." He slipped off his jacket and tossed it across the sofa along with his leather gloves. Doris tapped her fingers on his cheek, like she used to do when he was a little boy, and gave him her best grin as she left the office, closing the door behind her.

"I'm glad you're here. I appreciate the distraction." Kurt glanced at his watch and stood up. "Ah, time for high tea. And as a bonus, I have some chocolate-dipped macaroons."

"What! How did you get your hands on those on a workday? They're usually reserved for special occasions. Does Jaclyn know?"

He nodded. "She's the one who gave them to me this morning. She's worried I haven't had much appetite lately."

"You okay?"

"Oh yeah, fine. Just a lot on my mind." He flicked the switch of the kettle.

"Like what?"

"You know, the way we left this business about your mother and Hannah. You didn't seem satisfied with the answers."

"I'm sorry. Didn't realize I was so obvious. Am I that easy to read?"

Kurt nodded. "Just ask Doris. She described all of us Steffensen men, except Dad, of course, as transparent as sandwich wrap." Kurt shifted a file across his desk, picked up his good pen, and toyed with it. Having thought about it all week, he realized that the truth couldn't possibly affect his relationship with Joe any more than not knowing. In the privacy of his office, he would attempt to explain. "Joe, I assume you held back in front of Mother and Father. So, whatever you need to know, just ask and I'll try to clarify it all."

Joe sighed loudly and sat back. "Dad, I admit it bothered me a lot that you kept this from us. I was equally surprised that Quentin knew, granted, only for a short time. As usual, he brought me back to reality. He said I was making more of this than I should."

"Your reaction was understandable."

"Maybe so. I appreciate you trying to protect Hannah and even Mother, while she was your wife. What I don't get is why you simply didn't take Lauren and me aside years ago and tell us the truth. You know we would have kept it within the family. Even if Quentin and

Sara and David knew, they'd have no reason to tell anyone, and they wouldn't, especially if you asked them."

"I know, I know." Kurt sighed. "All that makes perfect sense. You're right."

"Okay, so I guessed something else this morning, and Grandma and Granddad didn't deny it. You needed that information, didn't you? You planned to use it, or you already have."

Kurt nodded. "Uh huh."

"Why? What for?"

Kurt stood and filled the teapot, moved two mugs to the desk, and returned to his leather chair. "Call it leverage, Joe, a negotiating tool. I used it to deal with your mother. I made a promise to myself when Jeanne and I got divorced that I wouldn't gripe about her in front of you and Lauren. After all, *I* divorced her; you didn't." He rubbed both hands across his face and leaned his elbows on the desk. "But yes, you're right. I needed that secret to use when necessary."

"For the divorce?"

"It made it easier to ensure she wouldn't contest it. I simply reminded her what I knew. I knew she was angry with me for leaving. She could have manufactured all kinds of things and told her friends."

"She could have, or she did?"

Kurt waved his hand. "Doesn't matter now. I didn't give a hang about it, myself, but I didn't want you and Lauren, especially Lauren, hearing stories about her father, especially since they weren't true."

"Yes. Anything else?"

"Lauren wanted to move to Halifax to attend private school and be with you, Mother and Father, and Peter and Katie. I made sure that Jeanne didn't put up much of a fight. In the summers, when you both came home from Halifax, she insisted that Lauren stay with her. Lauren said she didn't want to because you and Quentin were staying with me."

"And she stayed with us. Funny, I wondered about that at the time. Mother didn't seem to push the issue."

"No, with good reason. Once you graduated from university, I thought again about letting it go and telling you, but Lauren and Alan started going out together and Jeanne didn't approve of that relationship. It seemed like we were heading for an uncomfortable week before the wedding when all the Matheson family arrived from out west. I wanted it to be perfect for Lauren, so I told Jeanne to back off or else Lauren and you would find out about Charles and their real grandmother."

Joe shifted in the seat and crossed his right leg over his left knee. "I thought it was something like that. That explains it."

"I'm sorry. Well, actually, no I'm not. I'd do it again in a heartbeat. But you probably think I was being cruel."

"I assume you felt you had no choice."

Kurt continued. "It seemed that every time I'd decide to tell you, something came up. Last Christmas, a year ago, Jeanne dropped by the house with gifts for you and Lauren early on Christmas Eve. She was flying to Ontario for the holidays. Everyone was at our place for brunch, the whole family. Quentin answered the door and Jeanne's first words to him were, 'Oh, I see Kurt is still taking in orphans for the Christmas season.' I didn't find out about it until that night when Peter told me he had overheard her."

Joe looked away in disgust. "How did Quentin respond?"

"Didn't bother Quentin, or at least he said it didn't." Kurt chuckled. "Apparently he told her I was being very Dickensian. Sounds like something Quentin would say, doesn't it? But it sure as hell bothered me. Totally uncalled for. I told her to apologize when she came back after Christmas. I doubt she ever did."

"No, I expect not," Joe said softly, in amazement.

Kurt leaned forward. "Joe, I guess some people would call what I did blackmail. But I know your mother and what she's capable of. As I said, I would do it again. In any event, it's come to an end now."

"Are you worried now that you don't have anything to hold over her?"

"I just hope she doesn't take on Sandi and her family." He raised a questioning eyebrow. "Am I assuming correctly that your relationship is going in the right direction?"

"That's the plan," Joe answered with a smile. "But you don't need to protect me, or Sandi, for that matter."

"I know, but Lindsay and Steven are great people. God knows what Jeanne would say to Lindsay given the chance, especially out of earshot from you or me."

Joe shook his head. "Dad, believe me, if she goes up against Lindsay and Sandi, she'll be taking on two formidable forces. I wouldn't worry."

"Good. Let's hope it doesn't come to that. In the meantime, be on your guard." He refilled his mug. "The fact is, your mother's never forgiven me for leaving her, and she likely never will. But your families, your children, should be able to at least get along with their grandparents, and not need to have backup every time they visit their grandmother. Right now, I need to know whether you're all right with what I told you."

Joe smiled. "Yeah, I'm okay. The question is, are you going to explain this to Lauren? Or did you want me to?"

"Not unless it's absolutely necessary, Joe. There's no need. Lauren seems to get along okay with her mother. God knows that's very gracious of her. She's your Grandmother Thorburn reincarnated. She can get along with absolutely anyone. So let's just leave it, unless it comes up. Okay?"

"Sure. Thanks for telling me all this." Joe reached across the desk at the plate. "I'll have one of those macaroons now."

"And I'll have the rest," Kurt responded, feeling his appetite returning.

* * * * *

Alone in his office later that evening, Kurt cleared his to-do list as Doris had requested before she had left for the day. Checking the time, he made a quick call to Jaclyn to tell her he would be home by six thirty. He contacted a service for a long-distance phone number. As he listened to it ring, he realized he hadn't even thought about what he was going to say when she answered.

"Mrs. West?"

"Yes."

"Hannah, this is Kurt Steffensen calling. You may recall that we met . . ."

She interrupted. "Yes sir, a long time ago."

"Over thirty years."

"Yes."

"Hannah, are you able to talk right now?"

"Yes, my daughter is at the church."

"Okay, well, I am very sorry to phone right out of the blue. It's just that we have a situation that I would like very much to resolve." He leaned back in his chair.

"Oh?"

"A series of events has occurred over the past few months, well, since Charles Sinclair passed away, that frankly affects you, and I thought you should know."

"I see. If you are talking about the bequest, then I'd like to say that I didn't ask for anything or expect anything."

"No, no, this has nothing to do with the money. Suffice it to say that some friends of my family got some information regarding Charles and you, and they eventually pieced it together that you are Jeanne's mother. Now, our son and daughter, Joe and Lauren, have been made aware of this, and they felt that someone should tell you."

"It's . . . um . . . kind of you to call, but I really don't know what to say." Her voice reflected her nervousness.

"I wanted you to know also that they didn't learn it from me. However, when they confronted me about it, frankly, I was compelled to tell them the truth. I hope you understand."

"Yes, of course. I'm sorry for the position you were put in."

"It's been a long time. Times have changed, Hannah. I think we should deal with this now."

"Mr. Steffensen, I know it must have been very difficult for you to finally admit it to your children. How old are they?"

"Please call me Kurt. They are both in their thirties. And, Hannah, let me point out that they are more than my children—they are your grandchildren."

"Yes." She swallowed hard.

He paused, and thought carefully. "It's likely that they will want to meet you sometime soon."

"Yes, I understand that they must be curious."

"This is not about curiosity," he said softly. "Joe and Lauren are caring people. They have a grandmother they didn't know about."

"Yes, I'm sure they are wonderful young people."

"I understand from a friend that you don't have any other grand-children?"

"No."

"So wouldn't this be nice for you and for them to meet and get to know each other? I'm not saying where it has to go from there. But I'd really appreciate it if you would just give them the opportunity."

"Kurt, I'm sorry. This is all too much for me." Her voice cracked and her breathing became shallow. "What will people say about all of us? I have a brother and sister-in-law here, and nephews and nieces and cousins. I'm worried most about Carrie. She's a minister and she's well-respected here in the community. I don't want to do anything that will bring gossip. It's a small place."

"Yes, Hannah," Kurt said softly, and wished once again that he had his father's people skills. "I understand all of that. Believe me, Joe and Lauren are not out for sensationalism or gossip, or to hurt you in any way. They would just like to meet their real grandmother. They didn't get along well with Virginia. She was difficult at the best of times. Now they have found out that they have a grandmother and an aunt, and they'd just like to meet you. They wouldn't have to acknowl-edge you publicly as their grandmother, if you didn't want them to."

"Please, Mr. Steffensen, sorry, Kurt, I'd really rather not talk about this." She gasped for a full breath of air. "I will give it some thought."

"What about your daughter, Carrie? Would it be all right for them to meet her? Or does she know?"

"Carrie knows some of the story. I guess I will have to tell her everything. In the meantime, can we just let it go for now?" She tried desperately to get out the words in an articulate manner.

Kurt was exasperated, but felt bad. "Yes, of course, I am so sorry to have upset you this way. Please, just think about it. I'd appreciate it."

"Yes, I will."

"Thank you."

"Kurt, before you hang up," she said, and took another deep breath, "would you please tell me, how is Jeanne?"

"She's fine, Hannah, considering it's been a difficult year. Losing her father was very hard. They were close. Then she learned that her sister, Emily, inherited the house and she, in turn, gave the house to her son, Gregory. As I understand it, Gregory's intention is to put the house up for sale very soon. So as you can imagine, it's been a rough time. Now this has come out and Joe and Lauren, quite rightly, have a lot of questions."

"I understand. Yes, a difficult time indeed. Thank you for calling, Mr. Steffensen, and thank you—for everything."

Kurt hung up the phone and sat back. *Not much further ahead*, he thought, *except I have answered one question. Carrie knows the truth.* He would begin by telling Lauren and Joe, and they could work from there.

* * * * *

"Mother? You feeling okay?" Carrie found her sitting by the kitchen window, watching snow flurries lightly touch down on the windowsill and melt. The lights of the community twinkled in the distance.

"Yes, fine, why?"

"Well, it's Thursday evening. I haven't heard the Scrabble game rattle."

"Oh, yes, sorry Carrie." She jumped up. "I've had a few things on my mind I have to talk to you about. Get the Scrabble game. I'll clear off the table and put on the kettle."

Carrie returned with the dark red cardboard box, removed the tattered cover, and took out the notepad and pencil to keep score. She watched as her mother opened the cardboard square and the small wooden racks for the game tiles. She methodically turned over each tile, but Carrie noticed her hands were shaking.

Nervous about what was coming, she waited a moment to ask. "So, what did you want to talk to me about?"

Hannah stood. Carrie thought her mother was getting tea, but instead she was getting her purse from the counter. She took out an already opened white envelope and returned to the table. "First of all, I got this cheque yesterday in the mail. It's from that lawyer I told you about. Mr. Hamlyn, in St. John's."

Carrie opened the cheque and stared at the sizable sum. "Oh my heavens! That's a lot of money. Were you expecting that much?"

"To be honest, I didn't know what to expect, Carrie. But I have to put it in the bank tomorrow morning."

The boiling kettle sang, and Carrie jumped up. "Well, the crowd at the bank will wonder if you won the lottery." She took two mugs from the rack of wooden pegs and placed them on the counter.

Hannah gave a half-hearted smile. "They've never said anything in the past. I always go to the manager to help me. Frank's been very kind and private."

"In the past? You mean you've gotten cheques before?" She placed the cups on the table and turned back to the cupboard to find something sweet. She found a package of gingersnaps. She quickly tore off the plastic on the end and pulled out the tray.

"Over the years, Charles sent me some money and I put it straight into savings. It helped pay for your education, Carrie. After all, he didn't say how I should spend it."

"I had no idea. The bequest certainly is very generous. He must have had a conscience after all."

Hannah wondered at her daughter's remark, but let it go.

"You said there were two things you wanted to tell me?"

She nodded as she switched the places of several tiles on the little wooden rack, trying to form a word. "Yes. This morning the phone rang while you were gone to the church. It was Mr. Kurt Steffensen in St. John's, the man who used to be married to Jeanne. I think I mentioned him before."

She nodded. "What did he want?"

"He called to tell me that his son and daughter, Joe and Lauren, have just learned that Jeanne is—that I'm her mother."

"Oh my!" Carrie exclaimed. "How did that happen?"

"He didn't give me the details and they haven't told anyone else, as far as I could understand. They don't intend to, and neither does Kurt. But he said they would like to meet me, and you, too. I guess they're curious about us. But he called to let me know that, when they brought it up, he had no choice but to confirm it. He felt sorry."

"I think it's to his credit that he's kept it in this long."

"Carrie, life is never simple."

"I'm well aware of that. But asking two parents to keep the identity of their children's grandmother from them is difficult, to say the least. I know exactly why it was done. I'm just saying that it couldn't have been easy, that's all."

Tears filled her eyes. "No, it wasn't easy, Carrie, and it wasn't easy for me, either."

"Oh Mom, I'm so sorry. I didn't mean to say that it was only difficult for them. I can't begin to understand what you went through. What did you tell him?"

She shook her head. "It's too embarrassing, Carrie. I can't face those people. I simply can't. I'm sorry." She searched for her handkerchief. "Besides, heaven knows what else will come out once they start."

"You have no need to apologize, none whatsoever." Carrie straightened the board and stared at the seven letters in front of her, then quickly started the game with the word *snowy*.

Hannah wiped her face, took a deep breath, and reached for her letters. Moments of silence went by. "Carrie," she said quietly, "what do you plan to do?"

"I have to go into St. John's in a few weeks. If it's all right with you, I might meet with Jeanne's son and daughter. But I promise it won't go any further than that." Her voice was reassuring. The last thing she wanted was to put any undue stress on her mother, and she'd have to make certain that everyone understood that.

CHAPTER 13

Unusually mild temperatures in eastern Newfoundland at the end of January were short-lived. February brought cold northerly winds and snowstorms, one after the other up the eastern seaboard, like trains arriving on schedule. For three weeks in a row, snow began late on Friday afternoons and continued well into Saturdays. The regular Friday night dinner group battled icy roads and snowdrifts, but on Quentin's directive, nothing was to stop Friday night, not even the "weather gods."

On the last Saturday morning in the month, Steven wheeled the snow blower from the garage and began to work on a five-foot snow-drift that had formed overnight across their driveway. Inside their back porch, Lindsay wrapped her wool scarf tightly around her neck and reached for her "shovelling" gloves. The phone rang just as she put her foot in her left boot. To her surprise, the caller was Carrie West.

"I'm calling, Lindsay, because I haven't been able to get in touch with your sister-in-law, Phyllis. I have some transcripts of interviews here for her to edit for our church history project and I want to drop them off on Thursday when I come to St. John's. Do you know if she's away?"

"Yes, she is, Carrie. Phyllis and Robert are in Florida for a month. Given our weather this morning, I wish I were with them."

"How true. It's the same down here. This is the most snow we've had in years."

"Is there something I could help with? Phyllis won't be back until early March."

"Perhaps, if you don't mind, could I drop off the package at your home?"

"Certainly. If you're going to be at the church office on Elizabeth Avenue, we live not far away, on Stoneyhouse Street near Churchill Square."

"That's great. I appreciate that. I should be finished by eleven, so any time shortly after that."

"Good." Lindsay took a deep breath and braced herself to ask a question. "Carrie, before we hang up, do you mind if I ask? Ah . . . this is something personal."

"No, not at all. What is it?"

"I understand that your mother has been talking to Kurt Steffensen. He's a friend of our family. Our daughter, Sandi, is seeing his son, Joe. Do you know Kurt?"

"I've never met him," she said tentatively, "but I do know what you're talking about." She gave a sigh of relief. "You are obviously aware of the circumstances that brought our two families together."

"I am. And I wanted to let you know that Joe and Lauren would really like to meet you. This has all come as such a surprise to them. They hardly know how to react. But they would like to chat for a while, if you wouldn't mind. I think they'd really appreciate it."

"My mother has told me that she prefers to stay out of it, Lindsay. She has her reasons, and I respect her wishes. The last thing I want is for her to be hurt by all of this. But she also said I could make up my own mind on what I wanted to do."

"I understand fully. If it's okay with you, I could ask Joe and Lauren to drop by on Thursday. What do you think?"

"Oh my," she said, with nervous anticipation, now that it was becoming a reality. "Yes, I guess that's okay. It's important, though, that they do understand that this is to be kept private."

"Not a problem. I'll explain that. You can count on them."

"Thank you, Lindsay. I'll see you on Thursday morning."

Lindsay hung up, somewhat satisfied with her little diplomatic

mission. As she finished dressing, she wondered about Hannah's re-
luctance to see her daughter and meet her grandchildren for the first
time. Was there more to this story? Something that only Hannah and
Jeanne knew? Dismissing the thought, Lindsay grabbed her shovel,
and went outside to clear the walkway. As she began, Joe and Sandi
pulled up in front of the house, just as she was telling Steven about her
upcoming visitor.

* * * * *

On Sunday afternoon, Kurt did two unusual things. First, he
decided to visit Jeanne, and, second, he chose to do it alone. Given
his mission, he decided it was best to go solo. He had put it off long
enough.

His conversation with Hannah had not gone as he had hoped;
still, he felt more optimistic than he had previously. Perhaps Carrie
was the way to her mother. He knew as he turned off the parkway onto
Allandale Road that, ultimately, Jeanne would have to be the first to
act, and he wondered if she would. He knew if there was any chance
of persuading her, it would have to be face to face. He appreciated
Jaclyn's willingness to give up their valued Sunday afternoon together,
but, as he parked in front of Jeanne's home, he wondered if he was
taking one step ahead or two steps back. He longed for the comfort of
his favourite living room chair, a good book, a roaring fire, and a glass
of wine. He sat momentarily in his car and stared at the house in front
of him, the house he had built with pride when he and Jeanne were
first married. He wondered how to approach her. He always believed
he had her figured out, that he knew how she thought. Now, he was no
longer so sure. And that had him rattled. He wondered which Jeanne
he would encounter today.

"Whoever you have clearing your driveway, Jeanne, they do a
great job!" he declared as he entered the front door and removed his
boots, camel hair overcoat, and brown leather gloves.

She stood and waited. "Yes, two young men. They're very reliable.
Leah recommended them. One of them is married to her niece."

He followed her into the living room and sat in the large chintz armchair in the corner, immediately determining that it was not as nice as the one he was missing.

"I'm surprised you've come by yourself. You don't usually." She sat across from him on the matching sofa, adjusting the cushions.

"Joe is playing tennis this afternoon with Sandi."

"I see." She peered at him. "Kurt, you look tired, if you don't mind me saying."

"I am tired. We're busy at work, and there's been a lot happening in the past few weeks, as you know. Actually, that's why I'm here. I took a step, hopefully, in the right direction. You may not see it that way. But I thought you should know."

She focused on him, waiting. Mindlessly, she buttoned and unbuttoned the last pearl button on her green cashmere cardigan.

"I phoned Hannah," he stated, and sat back, bracing for a predictable response.

"You . . . did . . . what?" Her brow furrowed. "What ever for?"

"To bring some resolution to all of this, Jeanne. It's gone on long enough, and I'm not going to sit back and allow Joe and Lauren to have unanswered questions any longer." In his head he could hear his father's voice cautioning him to be less abrasive.

She sighed heavily. "Kurt, you may think your goal is admirable. Heaven knows you think that you were put here to bring about world peace, but Hannah West is not interested in building any kind of a relationship with us, and you should know that. Personally, I'm not prepared to welcome her and her daughter into my life, either. You're building up Lauren and Joe's hopes for nothing, only to have her say she's not interested. And neither am I."

"I think there's a way around this, to make it better for everyone."

"Why, so you can be a hero for Joe and Lauren?"

"No, Jeanne. I'm no one's hero. Nor do I have the aspirations you mentioned. But I've seen a hurt in their eyes that you and I are responsible for, and I think we have to take care of it. Granted, it may not be easy, but we owe them that, for keeping this from them for so long."

Jeanne clenched her fists around the edges of the cushion and called up her inner strength. "It was done for good reason. And as you recall, we promised Hannah that we would. We agreed to that."

"A long time ago. But everything's changed since then."

"Not for me, it hasn't," she contradicted him quickly. "Life is always so simple to you, isn't it, Kurt? Joe is so much like you. Is this what comes from growing up in that perfect Steffensen home? Knowing exactly what to do all the time, without thought to the consequences?"

"We're not perfect. Nowhere close."

"It's certainly the image you all try to portray. Joe and Lauren think that their grandparents walk on water." She brushed the knees of her wool pants needlessly.

"Only because of how they were treated by them all their lives. Only because they knew they were cared for. They can hardly say that about Charles and Virginia, can they? Now they want a chance to meet their biological grandmother. That's only reasonable. And if she wants nothing to do with any of us, fine, we'll let it go. But they have to try."

There was a prolonged silence between them. The clock ticked on the mantel.

Finally, Jeanne spoke. "Then you can begin by telling me what she said when you talked to her."

Kurt relaxed a little. "She was surprised to hear from me. I explained what happened, though I didn't give her the details, just the result. I told her that Joe and Lauren want to meet her, and Carrie as well. She said it was up to Carrie what she wanted to do. She's leaving that to her."

"Then Carrie knows?"

"She does now. We were at the Martels' last night for dinner, and Lindsay told us that Carrie phoned her on Saturday and asked if she could drop off some materials for Lindsay's sister-in-law this week. Apparently, Carrie plans to be in St. John's on church business. Lindsay has already told Joe and Lauren that Carrie's coming. I think the plan is to meet her at the Martels'. She said that Carrie seemed happy to meet them."

"And then what? We all get together for Easter Sunday dinner?" Jeanne said with biting sarcasm. She crossed her legs and sat back in disgust, shaking her head.

"I don't know, Jeanne. They'll take it from there. You and I don't have any right to say one way or the other. It's just a get-together."

She digested his words, then stood and walked to the dining room window. Angry at the loss of control over the situation, she turned back and glared at him. "What I don't understand in all of this, Kurt, is the role that this Lindsay Martel is playing. It's none of her business. It never has been. Yet she's put her nose in where it certainly does not belong. And she won't give up, no matter who gets hurt. What the hell is wrong with that woman? Joe figures she acted in good intention, but I find that hard to take in."

Kurt shook his head. "Jeanne, there is nothing wrong with Lindsay. She found out innocently from her mother about Hannah and Charles because her daughter happens to be seeing our son."

"There's nothing innocent about it. She's been out to tear down my family from the beginning. I don't know if she's jealous or she doesn't have anything else to do. Perhaps both. Maybe it's her upbringing." Her hands folded over and over in front of her and her face reddened. "In any event, someone has to tell her to step away from it."

"You're wrong, Jeanne. Lindsay is a kind-hearted person and, believe me, she's doing everything she can to make sure no one is hurt."

"Too late. The hurt is out there. Why doesn't she just leave it alone?"

Kurt remained calm. "Because she wants to help Joe and Lauren and Carrie."

"Bring them together for a big family hug, is that it?" she asked sardonically, standing in front of the picture window.

"No, she wants to put them in a position where it is their choice, not someone else's. Listen to me, Jeanne. Your father has controlled this from the beginning. Hannah made a promise to him that she would stay out of it, and he's still controlling it from the grave, and it has to stop."

Jeanne turned away and focused on the photo of Charles with her on her wedding day. *It always comes back to you, doesn't it, Father? You let me down after a lifetime of devotion. Just like Kurt did.* She looked across the room at her former husband, but he avoided her gaze. *You walked away after twenty years with the flimsiest of excuses,* she thought. *I didn't get along with your friends, the people you work with. We had grown apart, you said. Now there you sit, wanting to turn my life upside down once again. And you get to walk away with everybody's understanding. Damn it! Why don't I hate you?*

She moved toward a chair and sat gingerly on the edge of the cushion. The clock on the mantel chimed three times. She reached for the cup of tea, now cold, on the table next to her and sipped it. In a tone of crushing defeat, she said, "My father lied to me. He told me the night he died that he was leaving the house to me. He assured me. But he deliberately lied, after all I did for him. I took care of him. I spent hours with him every day when he complained that time was long and there was nothing to be here for. He told me last summer that he didn't know what he would have done without me. Even when Virginia was alive." She looked over at Kurt. "So, I guess he didn't mean that, either. He didn't mean anything. It was all a lie just to get me to take care of him. Funny, I can remember one time he gave the newspaper boy twenty dollars to run to the store for him. I told him he was being quite generous, but he grinned at me, a strange grin, and said, no, it would keep him coming back. And I guess that's why he promised me so much. To keep me coming back. So perhaps I should phone Hannah myself and tell her that, should I? The man she's been protecting all these years was an utter and complete fraud."

"Jeanne, Charles was sick for many months. His life with Virginia wasn't easy."

"I don't want your pity, Kurt, or excuses for Father, so stop right there."

"It's not pity, and I'm the last person in the world to make excuses for Charles Sinclair. I'm trying to help you make sense of it, that's all."

Kurt studied the woman sitting across from him. Seemingly she had aged years in only a few weeks. Her words describing her father were markedly harsh, and he couldn't help but wonder why. *Utter and complete fraud. Does she know more about her father? Is that what she is scared will come out? Something more than fathering a child? Is Mother right about the hold the Bolands had?*

He stood, pushed his hands into his pants pockets, then moved toward her. Jeanne sat with her head down. "Jeanne," he said quietly. "Is there more? Is there more about Charles than all of this business with the baby?" He sat on the edge of the sofa next to her chair, hesitating to touch her with his hand.

She did not look up. "What do you mean?" Her voice quivered.

"Charles. Do you know something else about his life? How he made his money?"

"He made his money working hard. It's as simple as that."

"I understand that the Bolands gave him money from time to time, when a business venture failed, and he needed it. I remember that when we were married." She did not respond. "Charles, for that matter the Sinclair family, didn't have much when he started out. Charles was in business in the 1930s. Hardly a decade to become rich. He was lucky to survive, especially on this island. The money had to come from somewhere. The Bolands?"

She nodded. "Yes, Virginia's father gave him money on occasion."

"Must have been rough. I'm guessing that he'd hold it over Charles."

"No," she answered, momentarily squeezing her eyes, "Father did the one thing that Clarence Boland wanted him to do."

"What was that?"

"Marry his daughter."

Kurt's nodded. "Yes, I thought so."

She twisted uncomfortably on the sofa. "They gave him a substantial amount for those years. Clarence believed it was unlikely that any man would come along for Virginia. She was hardly wife material by the standard of the day. She couldn't boil an egg, and God knows she needed someone coming behind her cleaning up. She made herself homely-looking. So when Clarence met Father and he realized he had acumen for business, he proposed to finance his initial venture, the furniture and dry goods store downtown, and keep him comfortable, in return for Father marrying Virginia."

"Quite the price to pay," Kurt observed.

Jeanne smiled. "More than he realized at the time, or at least that's how he explained it to me." She reached out and touched his arm. "I've known so many secrets, Kurt, since I was a teenager, I can hardly tell sometimes what came out and what didn't. The last time I was at the house, I was thinking about it. All the things I overheard from the vantage point of the stairwell as a child. Scandals and crimes beyond measure that have never come out. I never breathed a word of it because somehow I was led to believe that those people were important, that was how they lived, and they needed to be protected. Then, last spring, one Sunday afternoon, I sat with him in his study and he told me about Clarence Boland and the rest of them. He described in detail the very afternoon that Clarence proposed the deal and he agreed to it." She chuckled. "He even remembered the weather that day. He told me about his life with Virginia. He lived with her, but it was hardly a marriage. They pretended to be married and barely spoke a sentence or two a day to each other. Virginia seemed content with that, but Father was miserable. When he reminisced about Hannah, though, he smiled. A broad smile. The nicest memories."

"Did he ever talk about when you were born? The arrangement they made with Hannah?"

She shook her head. "Not much. I think it was embarrassing for him. Some of it I already knew. I overheard years ago, when Father was talking to Virginia about it. They had an argument, a big one. That's when I learned that the attending doctor was Alex Hamlyn."

"Jonathan's father?"

"Uh . . . huh."

"So that's why he's always been so protective of you, willing to do whatever you want. He didn't want you to disclose that his father falsified a birth certificate."

"That's a long time ago. It doesn't matter anymore."

"Still, it was a lot to take in."

Jeanne felt momentary warmth in his caring voice, the voice she had fallen in love with so many years ago. His aftershave was so familiar. She closed her eyes and let the feeling envelope her. She missed it so much her heart ached. Then, she opened her eyes and traced the seam of her sweater to the armrest next to her and Kurt's left hand resting there. His left hand. And a platinum wedding band embedded with diamonds. A ring placed there by another woman. She stood, steadied herself, and moved toward the window, deliberately standing with her back to him. "I'm tired of all this, Kurt. Very tired."

Kurt stood slowly. "Jeanne, does Emily know about her mother and Charles? That he was given money for marrying her?"

She shook her head. "No, and I'm not going to tell her. And I know I have no right, but I'm asking you not to as well. She'd be crushed. Irrevocably. And she doesn't have much. Gregory is a handful, to say the least."

He stood in awe at her concern for Emily, a sister whom by all admission irritated her beyond words. Here was a glimpse of Jeanne that he thought was gone, buried forever under a lifetime of disappointment and disillusionment. "Certainly," he responded, "as you wish." He glanced at his watch. "I should be going, Jeanne. The reason I came, well . . . I just wanted you to know that Lindsay Martel has invited Carrie to their home. That's why I came here today. And we'll see where it goes from there."

"This Mrs. Martel woman fancies herself some sort of diplomat, I guess," she said quietly.

"Let's just leave that there, shall we?" He walked down the hall and retrieved his coat and gloves. "I just have one question because it may come up. If Carrie wants to see you, will you agree to meet her?"

"I doubt very much if that will happen."

"You haven't answered my question. Will you talk with her, for Joe and Lauren's sake?"

Jeanne sighed. "Yes, I suppose, although I can't imagine what we would have to say to each other."

"Fine. That's all I wanted to know." Kurt turned to leave, but stopped and looked back, puzzled. "Jeanne, is there any more about the house? Or its contents? I haven't heard anything lately, since Lauren donated so much to the women's centre."

"Yes, as a matter of fact there is. Emily phoned this morning. She said that Gregory is upset that we didn't send all the stuff from the house to him. He claims he wanted all of it, and Lauren gave it away."

"What's he talking about?" Kurt's voice was raised. "I understood that he didn't care what happened to it. Didn't he tell Joe and Lauren on Christmas Day to do whatever they wanted with the stuff?"

"Yes, I heard him. So did Emily. But now, she says, he didn't mean *everything*. That they could just pick out something they liked and send the rest to him. Seems he's discovered he can sell it."

"Good God! The man is deranged."

"I guess this is Emily's way to get back at me. I told her at Christmastime about Father and Hannah—that she is my mother. Emily's interpretation was that Hannah took advantage of her situation."

"That's ridiculous. Besides, Emily is hardly in any position to judge anyone. So, what does Gregory want Lauren to do? She's given away most of the linens."

"I have no idea. Get it back, I suppose. Emily says he's threatening to take her to court."

"Fine, I'll match his lawyer with mine, and we'll see who comes out of this one. Does Lauren know about this?"

"No, I haven't told her."

"Let me. We're going over there tonight. I'll take care of it." He stood to leave. "By the way, any news on the house? Has anyone made an offer?"

"It's been sold. Emily said that someone made an offer just as it went on the market. The money's already been transferred."

"Ah, likely someone who had told the real estate company to be on the lookout for that kind of place. They must have plans for it."

"Yes, well, Gregory got the full asking price, apparently. No negotiating. He's laughing all the way to the bank."

"It's amazing how cocky he gets from afar. Let him go, Jeanne. His kind has a way of eating you out. He's toxic." He walked to the door and put on his coat. "So long. We'll talk later."

"Yes, no doubt." She was tempted to advise him that their relationship had changed somewhat now that the secret about her mother was out, but she decided to let him find out another way.

Kurt backed out of the driveway and pulled down the sun visor to shield his eyes from the setting sun as he drove up the parkway to the west end of the city. He was still thinking of his nephew. *You're taking on the wrong person this time, Gregory*, he thought. Suddenly, Kurt had a renewed burst of energy.

* * * * *

That same Sunday afternoon, Sandi and Steven headed out for their first walk around Quidi Vidi lake since Christmas. Despite the cold temperature, today was the first day for a long time that they enjoyed sunshine and calm wind.

As they waited at the crosswalk, Sandi explained to her dad why Kurt had kept the information about their mother from Joe and Lauren.

"I have to say, Sandi, I can't blame the man." He shifted Mollie's leash from one hand to the other to make way for other walkers. "As far as I'm concerned, he did what he had to do."

"Joe feels a lot better now that he knows."

"Is he looking forward to meeting Carrie on Thursday?" Steven asked, zipping up his winter coat to the neckline.

"Yes, but I guess he's a bit anxious about it, too. It might be only a one-time thing if it's left to Hannah."

"That's too bad, but they're going to have to respect her wishes, Sandi. It's only fair."

"Exactly. I doubt that Jeanne will help matters. From what I understand, Jeanne is not the most conciliatory person in the world."

"That's an understatement, given that Kurt had to use this business to get her to be co-operative over the past few years. But I guess those days are over now, so everything is open season for Jeanne."

"What do you mean?"

"She no longer has to worry about Kurt having anything to hold over her. My advice is to be careful. The lady might decide that you are not the right person for her son. This time there's not much Kurt can do."

"Joe told me the same thing last night." She tightened her scarf. "Don't worry. I can handle Jeanne."

He reached out and squeezed her hand. "I have every confidence that you can, my darling. After all, you're Lindsay Mackenzie's daughter." He chuckled. "Put her up against Lindsay. Now there's a force to be reckoned with. After thirty years of teaching, Lindsay'll back down from absolutely nothing." He tucked in an end of his scarf that had become loose. "God, that air is cold, even without much wind. You okay?"

"Yeah, but I'll be glad when we turn at the end of the lake."

They stopped periodically so that Mollie could greet some of her canine friends. Finally, they crossed the bridge at the far end near Quidi Vidi Village and turned to walk west toward home.

"So, young lady, you've had a relatively uneventful new year so far, certainly compared to Joe's life."

"Indeed. We were laughing about it last night. Seems we take turns with catharses in our lives. Good thing, I suppose, as long as we're together."

"Ah, is that a hint?"

"We're together now, Dad. That's all I'm going to say."

"And if Mr. Steffensen wanted to make it a more permanent thing?" Stephen stopped long enough for Mollie to sniff at a Styrofoam container. He shook his head and grinned at his daughter. "You don't have to answer that. That's a question for your mother to ask."

"She already has. A hundred times." She stared pensively at the setting sun in the western sky.

"You okay? Tell me you don't have regrets about leaving Shawn."

"Absolutely not, Dad! Just thinking about Jeanne, that's all. Sara, Quentin, Alan—they all seem to be *very* cautious around her. Sara says she can blindside you when you least expect it."

He tucked her hair in under the scarf wrapped twice around her neck. "Don't you worry. I've always got your back," he promised.

"Thanks, Dad." She knew he meant it.

* * * * *

On Thursday morning, Lindsay shovelled the front steps just in time to welcome Carrie as she pulled into the driveway.

"Lindsay, it is so nice to see you again," Carrie said as she walked up the steps. Inside, she removed her coat and boots. "Ah, it's so good to get inside."

"I'm glad you could come. Joe and Lauren said they'd be here around eleven thirty." Lindsay invited her into the kitchen and offered her tea or coffee. "Please, have some blueberry crumble cake. Save me from it. I have to keep something sweet in the house for Jordy and Steven. That's my son and husband. Unfortunately, the sweets are there to tempt me."

Carrie reached for piece of cake and laid it on a side plate in front of her. "I can't resist dessert. Thanks so much." She reached for a fork. "Lindsay, I hope Joe and Lauren don't have their hopes up about Mother. The past few years have been very difficult for her. She's been through a lot. Dad was sick, and I was living in Ontario at the time."

"I understand, and so do Joe and Lauren. Let's just see how it goes." Lindsay placed cream and sugar in front of her. "By the way, Carrie, have you ever met Jeanne?"

She shook her head. "No, I saw her once in the distance at the Arts and Culture Centre. I was there with a friend for a concert and my friend pointed her out."

They chatted about Carrie's project on church history as they waited for Joe and Lauren to arrive. Carrie stood as they walked into the kitchen. "It is so nice to meet you both. I hardly know what to say."

Lauren gave Carrie a warm hug. "I'm glad we finally get to meet you."

"Sit down, everybody," Lindsay said. "I'll get more cups."

They talked for almost an hour, and Lindsay was finally convinced that she had done the right thing in bringing them together. When the conversation seemed to wind down, Lauren touched Carrie's arm and dared to ask, "Carrie, do you think it's possible for us to meet our grandmother?"

Carrie's face grew serious. She played with her napkin as she searched for the right words. "This is very difficult for my mother, Lauren. Let me just say that she's very embarrassed. Having a baby for a married man in those years was certainly considered a terrible thing. Her hope was to keep it private for Jeanne's sake and for you, your brother, and her family as well, of course. She asked your mother and father not to tell anyone, and she promised your grandfather that no one would ever know. They agreed on that. That was a solemn promise that she made to the Sinclairs. She doesn't want to break that promise."

Lauren tipped a little milk into her hot tea. She looked into Carrie's eyes. "Carrie, our parents kept this from us until now. It's taken us a while to figure out why. Is your mother still worried that her family will find out?"

"Yes, I guess that's part of it."

Lindsay had stayed in the background for over an hour and did not want to interrupt. But there was a point to be made, so she interjected. "Carrie, for what it's worth, I should mention that the information I got about your mother and Charles came from my mother. And to her from your Aunt Frances. So the story is out there . . ." she explained cautiously.

Carrie raised an eyebrow at Lindsay's revelation. "Yes, you're right, Lindsay. I should have thought of that. Since Frances knows, then it might be that everyone else does, and they've just kept it to themselves. Interesting." She turned back to Lauren and Joe. "Mom doesn't know this, or at least she hasn't said so. She said she told her mother and father, that's all. But as you say, Lindsay, if Frances told your mother, she's not too worried about keeping the secret within the family."

"Carrie, would you mind telling us about her?" Joe asked. "Even if we never get to meet her, it would be nice to know."

Carrie smiled. "Well, she and my father were married for almost fifty years. She cared for him right up to the day he passed away. They had a wonderful life together. They weren't well off, though they managed to get me through university. They had a lovely home and everything they needed. Dad was a terrific carpenter. Self-taught. He could build anything. My mom never worked outside the home after she left the Sinclairs, but the church was her life. She has experienced a lot of loss in her life: her parents, her younger sister a few years ago, and twin brothers in a boating accident about fifteen years ago."

"That's terrible. So sad," Lauren said.

"Indeed. But through it all, my mother has had amazing Christian faith. She's an inspiration to us all. As much as she'd love to meet you, it would be difficult. She finds leaving and saying goodbye so hard. There are times she's wished she never saw people in the first place because she has to leave them."

"I cry buckets at weddings and funerals and airports. Good grief, Alan goes to Ottawa on business for two days and I'm an embarrassment at the airport."

Carrie was laughing. "You must have inherited that from her. A friend of mine who is a psychologist calls it being *tender*. It's just the way some people are."

"Carrie, would you please tell her for us? We're here if she wants to see us."

"I will. Thank you," she said sincerely. "That's the nicest thing I can tell her."

Carrie glanced at her watch. "It's almost one and I have to watch the time. I have a meeting at a downtown church. It's been so nice to meet you both. I don't know what will happen, but I guess we'll leave that right now for Mother to decide. Before I go, Joe, I wanted to ask you a question about architects, if you don't mind."

"Certainly."

"We need a new church hall in Falcon Cove. The one we had fell into disrepair during a windstorm a couple of years ago. We lost most of the roof. It was only a wooden structure to begin with, and my father used to say that they only used one nail to build it." She laughed. "Anyway, we've come into a little bit of money to be put toward a new hall, and I'd like to do it right this time. Are architects expensive to hire?"

Joe laughed. "I should say no, but, in all fairness, it depends on what you need done. Carrie, I'll be happy to look at your plans or draw some up, if you like."

"You would? Oh my, that's wonderful. I've been told by someone in authority—" She glanced at Lindsay with a smile. "—that you're the best there is."

"Lindsay might be a tad biased. Here's my business card, and I'll write my home phone number on the back. And Lauren's as well. Call us at any time."

"Thank you. Thank you both."

Lindsay walked her to the front door and passed along her coat. Holding her scarf and gloves, she said softly, "Carrie, for what it's worth. Jeanne lives very nearby."

Carrie smiled. "Whew, Lindsay, that's a lot of emotion for one day. I don't know if I can take that on. Thanks for everything."

* * * * *

"Hot cross buns, Quentin! Yum!" In Quentin's kitchen on Friday night, Sandi had spied a tray of the special rolls dotted with currants and white icing in the shape of a cross next to the breadbox. Plastic wrap stuck to some of the icing. Only one had been removed.

"Yep, those and Tim Hortons' Roll up the Rim contest: first signs of spring." Quentin lifted a roasting pan from the oven. "Help yourself."

Sara came around the corner rubbing her cold hands. "You'd never say it's close to spring outside. We're a long way from budding trees and daffodils. But I did win a coffee at Tim's this morning. That makes it palatable."

As the regular Friday night group sat around the table and passed slices of roast pork, applesauce, and steamed vegetables to each other, the first topic of conversation was a description of Joe and Lauren's morning with Carrie.

"She sounds easy to get along with," David assessed, as he spooned applesauce onto his plate. "By the way, Quentin, we are eating uncharacteristically healthy tonight, aren't we? Giving up trans fats for Lent?"

"I'm saving myself for Easter week," Quentin responded with his usual sarcasm. "Besides, I bought chocolate truffle cheesecake for dessert."

"Ah, sounds more like you." He turned back to Joe and Lauren. "Any possibility of meeting your grandmother?"

"Not likely, right now," Lauren explained. "She's still having a difficult time with all of this. We're just going to see what happens. But she didn't rule it out completely when she was talking to Dad on the phone. Now I just have to figure out what to do about Gregory." She laid down her fork and took a sip of wine. "He wants all the stuff that I gave to the Goodwill Centre and the women's centre. He claims that he didn't say that I could take it all and give it away. He hinted at legal action."

Joe shook his head in disgust. "Leave it to Greg. That is nonsense. I was there when he said you could do whatever you wanted with it. He was planning to dump it all."

"That's when you suggested giving it away to those who could use it."

"You're expecting rationality from Gregory?" Alan asked. "The guy's crazy if he thinks he's going to get anywhere with this."

Quentin reached for his wineglass. "Speaking of which, are you willing to sign an affidavit to what you heard Gregory say, Mr. Steffensen?" He spoke as if he was questioning a witness in front of a jury.

"Yes, why?"

"Because I'm Lauren's lawyer. I'll be the one representing her in court if it comes to that."

"Do you think it will?" David asked.

Quentin grinned. "Nah, I'm counting on ol' Gregory not having the stomach for thousands of dollars he'd have to pay out in legal fees. I trust he can do the math."

* * * * *

Carrie woke in her hotel on Saturday morning with every intention of getting on the road early to drive back to Falcon Cove. As she ate breakfast in the hotel restaurant, she made a list of the few items she needed to pick up on her way out of town. On her coffee refill, she played the conversation with Joe and Lauren over in her mind. She had been distracted at the church meetings yesterday, not that she found budgets fascinating, anyway. But her mind kept returning to her mother and their last conversation about Charles and Jeanne.

She paid her bill, brought her things to the car, and wondered how she could have acquired so much in only a three-day visit. She still had to stop at the Avalon Mall on her way home. She turned the ignition and waited patiently as the front and rear windows defrosted. There had been heavy frost last night, but the morning sun helped to melt it quickly. She thought back to Lindsay's suggestion that she might visit Jeanne. She sighed. *I wonder if she is home this morning? You coward*, she admonished herself, *how many more times are you going to try to summon the courage to meet your half-sister, only to chicken out at the last minute?* She remembered the first time she considered it. She had pulled up in front of Jeanne's house on Exeter Avenue during a trip to St. John's about a month after her father had passed away. Two days before, her mother had told her about her relationship with Charles. That day she ended up turning her car around, driving east a few blocks, and sitting in front of Quidi Vidi Lake in the north parking lot. She ate a ham and cheese sandwich and stared at the gulls and ducks for an hour.

Now things were different. Jeanne knew there was a possibility, if not a probability, that she would contact her. It wouldn't be a shock. Surely, she would find the right words to say. Her oldest parishioner, Millie, who was 103 and living in the senior citizens home near Falcon Cove, always said she was a joy to talk to. Carrie prayed today she was right.

Windows clear, she turned right out the parking lot and headed east down Elizabeth Avenue. At the first set of lights, in front of the university, she considered turning left and heading out of town, making her escape while she could. But the light turned green and she continued on, through another intersection, past the Square, and right onto Exeter. She saw Jeanne's car in the driveway. It was fate, she decided.

She pulled in and quickly glanced at herself in the mirror. The only makeup she wore was lipstick. It would have to do. *Good heavens, Carrie*, she chided herself again, *you're not auditioning for a Broadway show*. She released her seat belt, opened the door, and stepped out into the warm sunshine.

A woman answered the doorbell, but Carrie knew it was not Jeanne. She was dark-haired and dark-eyed, and Carrie guessed she was about her age. "Could I help you?"

"Yes, I'm . . . ah . . . looking for Jeanne Sinclair."

"May I ask why?"

"Please, just tell her it's Carrie. Carrie West. I'd like to speak to her, if she wishes. She knows who I am."

Leah turned back to see her employer walking toward the front door. "It's okay, Leah, have the lady step in."

Leah did so and took her coat. They simply exchanged hellos, and Carrie followed her to the living room.

"You don't seem surprised to see me," Carrie said.

"Not really. Kurt mentioned that you were in town, and my daughter, Lauren, called this morning for another reason and said that she had met you. Please, have a seat." She waved her hand at the sofa.

"I met Joe as well," Carrie added, and made herself as comfortable as she could possibly be. "Jeanne, you have a wonderful son and daughter. They are so personable and talented. They must be your pride and joy."

"They have both done well."

Carrie took a moment to assess her surroundings and quickly determined that every piece of furniture had to have been shipped in, because she had never seen anything like it in local stores. "You have a lovely home. Have you lived here all the time, since you moved away from your—from your father and Virginia?"

"Yes, with the exception of a few months. Kurt had this house built for us a year after we were married. It was a newly developed area then. St. John's housing was booming in the fifties. This was one of the first houses on this street. Joe and Lauren both grew up here. We were a family for about twenty years. But then Kurt decided to leave."

"I'm sorry."

"Everything happens for a reason," she said dismissively, looking away.

Carrie was surprised at her resignation.

Jeanne made eye contact once again. "I guess you really have to believe that line, given the work you're in."

Carrie, taken aback by the statement, could only laugh. "You make it sound like I'm a used car salesman and I'm pushing sunroofs."

Jeanne pursed her lips and forced back a smile. There was something forthright about this woman that she liked.

"Jeanne, I'm not going to presume to say how you feel about all of this. I will tell you that it's been hard for me, mainly because of my mother."

"Let's just say it was unexpected and difficult, given my father's recent passing," Jeanne returned.

"We have something in common, you and I. I lost my father almost two years ago. And you just a few months ago. It seems we were both very close to our fathers."

Jeanne nodded.

An uneasiness filled the room.

"Mother has never gotten over losing Dad. She says it's easier with me there, but sometimes I wonder. I've never been able to read her feelings very well. She doesn't talk openly about them. She wasn't raised to express her feelings to anyone else. She was raised to keep them inside."

"I was as well." Jeanne surprised herself at this admission to a stranger, and even more surprised that she decided to continue. "I remember when I was dating Kurt. The first time he told me he was in love with me, I hardly knew what to say. He was the first and only man to do so. I finally said it back to him, but I really didn't understand what it meant, except that I enjoyed being with him. Then I met the rest of his family, the Steffensens, and they were completely opposite from what I was used to. They hug each other a lot, and tell each other how much they care, that sort of thing. It was really uncomfortable for me. Still is."

"I understand." Carrie searched for words that wouldn't come.

"Carrie, may I ask, when did you find out about me?"

"Only since Dad passed away. You're probably going to think this is strange, but Mother told me one night while we were playing Scrab-ble. We do that a lot. It's when we talk without having to make eye contact, I guess. I only got pieces of the story at a time. Just enough for one game." She laughed, turning her head to the side. "First, I heard about when she worked in here at the Sinclair house. Then she told me about finding out she was going to have a baby. She certainly didn't give me the details of that. Then another night, I asked her about the baby, and she told me how she thought her little girl would be better off with her father and his wife. I didn't argue with her. I knew all too well the kind of life that Mother had before she married Dad. Her parents were wonderful, I assure you. They worked hard, but they had a large family of their own to feed and clothe. Mother said she felt that the baby would have a better chance getting ahead if she left her in a good home. That's all she told me at the time. Later, I learned that you had been married to Kurt Steffensen and you had two children. I've heard the Steffensen name. Who hasn't, in this province?" She shifted in her seat, self-conscious about her comfortable but casual chinos. "So, when did you find out about me?"

"I knew where you lived. I don't know if you are aware of this, but your mother came to visit me just after Joe was born."

Carrie nodded. "Yes, she just told me that a few weeks ago, when she told me about Kurt's phone call."

"Are you aware that my father contacted her several times over the years?"

"Yes, I only learned that recently as well."

"As did I. Apparently, he sent her money from time to time. I found the cancelled cheques."

"She showed me the final cheque from the estate. I was surprised. I don't know how you feel about it, whether you think it should be yours . . ."

"I'm fine." Jeanne jumped in quickly. "What she does with the money is entirely her decision."

"From what I can gather, she plans to give it to our church for upkeep and to go toward a new church hall. But she wishes it to re-main quiet."

"Not a problem. I have no one to tell."

"I don't know if you knew this, Jeanne, but your father sent Mother his pocket watch and the hymnary a few months before he died."

Jeanne sat up. "No, I did not know that. How strange for Father . . ."

Carrie tried to straighten the collar of her blouse. "Yes, she cherishes them. She has the watch tucked away in a jewellery box. She will take good care of it."

There was a lull in the conversation. The clock on the mantel chimed. Carrie looked over to see a line of photos near the clock. There were graduation photos of Joe and Lauren and a much older photo in a silver frame. She stood to look at it. "You and your father?"

"Yes, taken the week I got married."

"He was a fine-looking man. Very distinguished." She tried to picture her mother with him, but couldn't.

"Yes, he was."

She replaced the photo and slowly sat down again. "Jeanne, I couldn't help but notice that a few minutes ago you said 'your mother.' She's your mother as well, you know. I may as well say it. That makes us . . . sisters." There, she'd managed to get out the words that she knew would be difficult. *We are sisters.*

Jeanne gave a blank expression. "I've only met her once, for a few hours, and this is the first time I've met you. We've spent only, what, a half-hour together? Sisters are supposed to know each other all their lives. And be . . . close."

"I don't think there are any rules, as such. Are you and Emily close?"

Touché, thought Jeanne. *She's either made a lucky guess or she's done her homework.* "No, not really."

Leah interrupted with coffee and warm lemon bread, lightly buttered.

"Leah, I neglected to introduce you to this lady. This is Carrie West. Reverend Carrie West. She's . . . a friend of the family, the Sinclair family, that is."

"Very nice to meet you, Leah."

"Pleasure to meet you."

"Leah worked for the family for a year or two just before I got married. Then she left. Shortly after that, Joe was born and I hired her to take care of him, and later his sister."

"And precious little angels they were," Leah said.

"Well, Leah, maybe sometime if I visit again, you could share some stories of them when they were children. I've only recently met them both. I must say, they are an impressive pair."

Once Leah was out of the room, Jeanne stood and walked to the window, pushed back the sheer curtains with her hand, and surveyed the front garden. She disliked this time of the year. Her garden was yearning for warmth that wasn't coming.

"Jeanne," came Carrie's voice behind her, "tell me about your father. Please."

Jeanne turned around to look at her. She sat and broke a piece of lemon bread into smaller pieces. "What would you like to know? The family was originally from Scotland and came to Newfoundland in the late 1800s. He was a highly successful businessman. Self-educated. He grew up here, in the east end of the city. When I was growing up, I remember him working very long hours, and he was tired at the end of the day. He walked in powerful circles and had a lot of influence. Politicians took his advice. In those days, politicians were simply that. Not businessmen. They listened to my father," she said proudly, her head erect. "He took care of his family to the best of his ability. Men didn't play with their children in those days, not like today, though he used to read to me when I was little. I learned to love books from him."

"Did he ever mention our mother?"

Jeanne did not feel like responding. She had let her guard down once in this conversation. She wondered how far she should go. She hesitated.

"Please, it's important to me," Carrie pleaded.

She sighed. "Yes, several times, but only to me. The conversation was personal, and Father was not one for talking about personal things. He asked me not to repeat it to anyone. But he did care for her,

I know that." She stopped there, not wanting to reveal the depth of his affection for Hannah.

"I see." Carrie twisted around again on the sofa and sat back. "It's just that I wonder a lot, and I can't ask Mother because it would be too embarrassing for her to talk about. I've wondered if he took advantage of her. She was a young girl with no life experience. I suspect he did, but I shouldn't say that without any proof."

Jeanne returned her small plate to the coffee table and sat a seemingly long time without speaking. The question, if asked just a few weeks ago, would have alarmed her. *Did my father take advantage of Hannah?* She would have railed against the suggestion and told this woman to get out of her sight.

Carrie could feel her heart beating quickly. "Perhaps I only want to believe that because I can't deal with Mother being with another man willingly. I always believed that my father was the only one in her life." She had shocked herself by making such statements to a woman she didn't know. Looking across the room, she realized that at that moment the two sisters had a great deal in common.

Jeanne stared at her hands and finally spoke after a prolonged silence. "Have you ever had your faith shaken?"

"Yes, of course, many times." Carrie was taken aback by the question and wondered about its source.

"I have always loved my father. Strangely, I still do. I guess I always will."

"Strangely? Why do you say that?"

"Because of what he did to me." She made only momentary eye contact with Carrie. "He lied to me. The day he died. He told me he left the house to me. That the house would be mine. But that didn't happen."

"Your sister, Emily, inherited it?"

"Yes. And everything in it."

"I see. And that's caused you to question your father's feelings for you?"

"Why wouldn't it? If he could boldly lie to me, there on his deathbed, why wouldn't he have lied to me all my life? How can I believe anything he ever said to me? He let me down." Jeanne clasped her hands. "As to how he felt about Hannah, I really don't know. He said to me during the last few months of his life that he thought about her a great deal. But I don't know, Carrie. He may have told your mother just about anything to get what he wanted. It worked with me. It likely would have worked with her."

Carrie sipped her tea. "Could I ask . . . does Emily know the truth about us and her father?"

Jeanne nodded. "Yes, I told her at Christmastime when she was here."

"How did she respond?"

"She said it was disappointing. To be honest, she seemed to feel it was more Hannah's fault than his, that they had a relationship at all. I guess it's difficult to accept that about her father."

Carrie studied her sister sitting only a few feet away. She saw a woman whose faith in everything—her husband, marriage, family, children, her sister, and her father—all had been shaken to its very foundation and swept away like the spring tides sweeping the shoreline around Falcon Cove. But knowing how guarded she was, she wondered how far she should try to enter her world. She tucked away her minister's role, and became a sister.

"You shouldn't assume, Jeanne. Circumstances drive people to change their feelings. Don't assume because your father let you down at the end that he didn't care for you. I'm sure he did," Carrie said. She reached for the small embroidered cushion beside her and held it in her lap. "My father was a wonderful man. He could build anything without any plans in front of him. People said it was a natural gift. He was quiet. Rarely talked about anyone. He used to tell me we don't know what anyone else is living. I remember when I told my mother and father about choosing the ministry. They were surprised, but happy, I guess. I wondered what other people would think of me. My dad said, 'No point in letting what others think bother you. After all, when you look in a mirror, there's only one face looking back.'" Carrie chuckled at her dad's words and wished she could talk to him now. "As I said, Jeanne, your father cared for you. If he hadn't, he wouldn't have confided in you as much as he did."

"Perhaps that's true," Jeanne replied. "I really don't know. Let me ask you, did your mother care for him?"

"She has never said. I know she respected and admired him a great deal. I think she was in awe of him. But did she actually love him? She's never told me. In fact, she's likely never told herself."

CHAPTER 14

Driving home alone on the highway that Saturday afternoon, Carrie did what she usually did on a long drive by herself: she sang hymns. She began with Lenten hymns, but by the time she reached Butter Pot Park, a campground not far from the city, she felt they were too gloomy, so she switched to Easter Sunday hymns. Once she entered Terra Nova National Park, two hours later, she decided that even the Almighty, with His infinite tolerance, had tuned her out. Her mind was on the upcoming conversation with her mother rather than singing in tune. An hour later, she turned right at the junction to Falcon Cove and followed the winding two-lane road to her home. A strong easterly wind had pushed offshore slob ice into the harbour for most of the week. The sun was lending some warmth, though in the distance, heavy grey clouds signalled the likelihood of rain by nightfall.

Carrie pulled her car up by their house and noticed a line of small floor mats across the back rail drying in the sunshine. Her mother had been busy spring cleaning. Inside, a delightful aroma of homemade turkey vegetable soup welcomed her, the steam wafting through the kitchen.

"I'm back! Smells good in here!"

Hannah closed the door to the upstairs behind her. "Thought you'd want something right away. How was the drive?"

"Dry roads. No moose. Lots of coffee. All good. How's everything here?"

"Dr. Jeffries called. Our Millie down in the seniors home took a turn and she wants to see you. He thought you should wear your clerical clothes. Poor ol' dear, just had her birthday. My guess is the Good Lord has already set a place for her."

"Mother, you're shocking!" Carrie said with a laugh. "I'll pop down there as soon as I have a bowl of soup—if it's ready," she said, and laid her parcels on the floor by the kitchen door.

"Sure is." She filled a bowl and put it on the table. "What's the news in St. John's?"

Carrie sat at the end of the table, buttered two Purity cream crackers, topped them with a slice of cheddar cheese, and picked up a soup spoon. "Meetings were boring, but I s'pose we accomplished what we set out to do, in a lot longer time than was necessary. Otherwise, I met some wonderful people. I'll tell you all about it later."

Hannah turned from the stove. "Oh? Then you met Jeanne's children?"

Carrie nodded. "It'll take a while, but I'll tell you the condensed version now." She reached for the salt and pepper shakers. "I met Lauren and Joe on Thursday morning at Lindsay Martel's. It was quite pleasant. Joe is an architect, and I even had the nerve to ask him about a plan for the church hall. He seemed happy to help. Lauren is a lovely young woman, a lawyer. Pretty as a picture." She paused. "Then I went to visit Jeanne today just before I left. It was an impulse. I hadn't planned to."

Hannah sat in the kitchen chair at the far end of the table. "I see," was all she could manage. She patted the dishcloth that was folded neatly in a square beneath her hand.

"I'll tell you more about it later, okay? Don't worry, it was all very friendly. Nobody upset or angry. All quite civil."

Her mother nodded, but remained at a loss for words.

They sat in silence while Carrie quickly finished her soup. Then she stood, and put her bowl in the sink. "That was delicious. I have to get changed and get going. I won't be long."

"Okay. While you're gone, I'm going to walk down to Iris's with some soup. She's got that miserable flu that's going around."

By the time Carrie arrived home just under two hours later, the sun had set and darkness was falling quickly. She was surprised to find that her mother was still not home. She reheated the soup, changed her clothes, and unpacked her suitcase. Still no sign of her. Glancing at the clock on the stove, she decided to phone her aunt and uncle. Perhaps they had invited her to stay for supper.

She dialled their number and her uncle answered on the first ring. "Uncle Toby, it's Carrie calling. Is Mother still there, or has she left?"

"Your mother? She was here, my dear, dropped off some lovely soup, but she left an hour ago. She's not back yet?"

"No, and I'm getting worried. It's dark and it sounds like freezing rain on the kitchen window."

"Perhaps she dropped in somewhere else. Likely Adelia's place, and you know how they can talk when they get together." But guessing he was not reassuring her, he added, "I'll put on my coat and go out. Maybe someone's seen her walking up the road. Don't worry, Carrie, my dear. Han's walked that road for seventy-odd years. She can smell her way home."

"Thanks, Toby." She sat at the living room window with a mug of soup and waited. She could only see four or five houses away. The wind was gusting and ice pellets clicked on the window. Every minute seemed like an hour.

* * * * *

In the Falcon Cove cemetery that evening, Hannah tucked her coattail underneath her and sat sideways on the grey concrete edge of her husband's grave. She rested her right hand on top of the headstone and read his name over and over, as if she couldn't believe it was there. The cold mist and wind sent a chill down her back. From the cemetery hill, she could see ice across the bay and a heavy sky. As the mist changed to droplets, she pulled the collar of her corduroy coat tightly around her neck and adjusted her hood.

"I'm here, Marshall," she said in a whisper. "I need to tell you that it's all come out." She choked on the words. "And I don't know what to do. You said we'd deal with it if it ever happened, but you're not here to show me how. And I don't know what to do." Tears brimmed in her eyes, then trickled down her face. She sobbed. "How am I supposed to face those people? What am I going to say to them? I did a terrible thing. I had a baby for a married man. So wrong, so very wrong. I promised Charles I wouldn't tell, but they won't let me keep my promise. Now it's all a mess."

The rain pelted harder now, mixed with beads of ice stinging her face. She sat for a few moments listening to the sound of waves in the distance. She lowered her head, squeezed her eyes shut, and thought back to that night so many years ago, that night in the Sinclair house when Virginia was gone away with her two sisters and little Emily was asleep. She and Charles were the only two adults in the house. He asked her to keep him company, so she sat by the fire and listened intently as he told her about his childhood growing up in Aberdeen. As the fire dimmed, Charles reached out to her, touched her hair, and told her she was so very pretty. The only man to ever do so. She had never forgotten that night, the sound of the birch crackling, the flickering light, the touch of a hand, a gentle kiss on her cheek, and then . . .

Suddenly, the easterly wind whipped up around her and jolted her back to reality. She looked up at the darkened sky and back to the words of the headstone now almost obscured. "I have to go home now, Marshall," she whispered. "Carrie will be worried. Good night. I'll be back tomorrow."

She eased her way up from the icy concrete, scraping the palm of her hand and turning away from the grave. Night was closing in, and she found it difficult to pick her way down the rocky path to the main road. The town truck had left two large ruts that were filled with muddy water and slush. She squinted to focus and stepped around them. The smoother rocks in the path were already slippery, and she struggled to maintain her footing. Finally, after ten minutes had passed, she saw the wooden sign that marked the main road perpendicular to the cemetery road. As she moved gingerly around the corner, she neglected to look down and suddenly caught her boot on the edge of the asphalt. Her ankle twisted to one side and she fell against a nearby alder bush. The ends of the branches jabbed her wrist and arm. Grasping one end of a branch to steady herself, she stepped forward, but her ankle throbbed in pain. She stared into the darkness, helplessly looking for someone, anyone, who could help her, but there was no one in sight.

"Oh my," she whispered to herself, "all the times I've walked this road. I never hurt myself until they paved it." Wincing in pain, she placed only enough weight on her right foot to move her left one ahead. Ice pellets struck her face and trickled underneath her collar. She kept her head down, glancing up only long enough to note each town landmark—the post office, the abandoned courthouse, the crossroads. Step by step. Another few minutes passed. She limped slowly, counting each step, if only to convince herself that she had to be getting closer to home. From out of the darkness in front of her, she heard a voice. The street light was enough to illuminate the lone figure coming in the distance. She recognized Carrie's light green raincoat flapping in the wind and heavy rain.

"Carrie!" she called out. "It's me. Here."

"Mother?"

Behind her, another familiar voice. "Hannah, my dear, I'm right behind you."

She stopped and glanced around to see her brother, his winter jacket zipped to his chin, just catching up to her. "Toby, thank God!" He was close to her now, so she leaned out and grabbed his arm. "I hurt my foot. Stupid me."

"C'mon. I'll get you home. Take your time. That's Carrie coming, look."

"Mother, what happened?" Carrie had caught up to them, breathless. "Where have you been?"

But she found it too hard to say much as the cold wind gusted in their faces. "I'm all right," she managed.

Finally, they reached the door of their house, pushed it open, and welcomed the warmth. Carrie helped her with her coat and Toby let her lean on him as she got to the wooden kitchen chair. She sat and elevated her injured foot as Carrie placed a cushion beneath it.

"I just twisted it, that's all."

"Carrie, she should see a doctor," Toby said, as he took off his cap and hung it on the back of the chair. His ruddy complexion glistened with rainwater.

"No, no," Hannah objected, and raised her hand in protest. "I'll be fine. We're not risking life and limb driving down to the hospital tonight. I'll rest my foot and, Carrie, if that soup is hot, I'll have some of that to warm up my insides."

Carrie looked at her uncle, exasperated. "You know there's no telling her what to do."

"Uh huh. Been like it all her life. Her mother before her, same way."

"Carrie, how's poor Millie? Worse off than I am, I'm sure."

Carrie stirred the soup as it heated up and shook her head. "She's fine. Turns out she ate something she shouldn't have. Pork fat, she thinks. Her daughter dropped off a plate of fish at lunchtime. She was upset because she can't eat like she used to. Once Dr. Jeffries and I told her we have the same problem, she calmed down. I said a prayer for her appetite."

Carrie placed the soup in front of her mother and retrieved a warm quilt from the living room sofa. "What were you thinking going out on a night like this?"

"I went to the cemetery. I had to talk to your father."

"First of all, Dad is in a better place than that cemetery, and, second, what ever for?"

"Because I don't know what to do, Carrie. I don't know what to do." She looked over at her brother pleadingly. "You may as well know, Toby," she said, as she pulled the soup bowl toward her and wrapped her fingers around its base. "It's about what happened when I was a young girl, when I worked in St. John's."

Sitting on a kitchen chair across the room, Toby rested his elbows on his knees and rubbed his hands for warmth. "What ever are you talking about, Han? The baby, you mean?"

Carrie had been standing by the counter, but quickly pulled out a kitchen chair and sat down. "Then you know?"

He nodded. "S'pose I do."

"Oh my, we didn't know that. This is all my fault, Uncle Toby. If I hadn't agreed to meet the Steffensens in St. John's this week . . ."

"Steffensen? That's that businessman, isn't it? He was married to Jeanne Sinclair once. Aren't they gone abroad?"

Hannah looked up, her eyes widening. "You know about Jeanne?"

"I know she's your daughter, if that's what you mean."

"How long have you known?"

"I dunno. Since you had her, I s'pose. Mother told us. That's a long time ago now."

"You've never said anything to me. I knew Frances knew. And Pop. But Mother said she wouldn't tell the boys. Said they wouldn't understand women's things. Why haven't you ever mentioned it?"

"Sure, it's no one's business, is it? No one's at all."

"I did something terrible, Toby."

"You lived your life, Hannah. That's all any of us can do. Besides, that's a long time ago. Why bring it up now?"

"'Cause Jeanne's children are grown up and they want to meet me, Toby," Hannah choked out her words.

"I s'pose they do, for goodness' sakes. You're their grandmother. Nice change for them, I'd say, from that uppity bunch they're used to. What do you think, Carrie?" he asked with a grin.

"I think you're absolutely right, Uncle Toby." She laughed at her uncle's view of life, and was filled with relief. "And I think you're absolutely wonderful."

"Well then, now that's been declared, I'll be on my way." He put on his jacket, zipped it to the top, then reached for his cap and put it on securely. "Now then, Han, lie down and get that foot better. They won't be able to have service tomorrow if you're not there. And stop worrying about that other stuff." He headed for the back door. "Carrie, would you phone Iris and tell her I'm on my way and that your mother is safe and sound?"

"Will do." She saw her uncle to the door and returned to the kitchen and made a quick call to her aunt. She pulled up a chair next to her mother and examined her foot carefully. "It's a bit swollen, but I don't think it's fractured or broken."

"I'll be okay for church tomorrow morning."

"Uh huh. Do you feel better? Now that you know Toby and the others know?"

She nodded. "I had no idea that he knew. No one ever mentioned it." She finished her soup, thinking about her brother's matter-of-fact way of looking at life. *I was so worried that they all would know and never forgive me. I neglected to forgive myself, and that got in the way.*

For the next hour, Carrie recounted the conversations she had with Joe and Lauren, and then with Jeanne. She gathered the dirty dishes, motioned for her mother to stay where she was, and stood up to rinse them in the sink. "Jeanne's very pretty. Her clothes are exquisite, and her house, oh my, every detail is perfect. I don't know where she got her furniture, but it's certainly not local."

"You'd expect that."

She poked the bowls into the dishwasher. "Still for all, Mom, she appears to be a lost soul. She misses her father a great deal, and she thinks he let her down because he left the house to his other daughter. I got the idea that she doesn't get along with Emily; yet Emily inherited the house, even though Jeanne took care of him for years. He told her the house was hers."

"I'm sure he had good reason." But privately she reflected on what it was.

Carrie hesitated about asking the next question, as she believed it was unlikely her mother would respond. "Jeanne told me about Charles. What he was like as a father. Although, to be honest, her description sounded like he was a very lonely man."

"He was. He had a wife, in name, but not much else."

"I see. This may surprise you, but we both wondered how you felt about him."

Hannah adjusted the pillow under her foot and thought carefully. As much as she wanted to say the truth, she wanted Carrie to continue believing that she only truly loved her father. "Carrie, my dear, I was seventeen at the time. I didn't have a clue what I was doing. It was all so new and exciting. Going to St. John's. He was older than me, wealthy and important. I got caught up in the fact that he even looked at me. Then, when he actually spoke to me, well, like I said, I could hardly believe it. Young and foolish, that's what I was. Nothing more. I know now that he likely didn't mean any of it, but I'm a lot older and lived a life. A good one."

Carrie realized how much her voice was like Jeanne's. "You really think that?"

"Sure, why?"

"I dunno. You seem to cherish his things, his watch, his hymnary. I thought you really cared about him."

Hannah had a faraway look in her eyes. "I guess in some way I did at the time. He was charming, Carrie; that's what he was, charming. But the man had a miserable life with Virginia." She pursed her lips. "He deserved better."

Carrie looked surprised. "How did you know about his life with Virginia?"

"I ran into Alva Green years ago, back in the seventies. We were at a church festival in Gander. Had a long conversation on Sunday afternoon, and she told me things I didn't know at the time."

"Like what?"

"The Bolands, that's Mrs. Sinclair's family. They were the rich ones. Mr. Boland helped Charles out financially over the years, when he needed it."

"Okay. But there's nothing much wrong with that. Charles was their son-in-law."

Hannah nodded. "But sometimes, accepting money comes with a price, Carrie."

"I see. So he felt he owed the Bolands." Carrie tucked the bread away in the wooden box and swept the crumbs into the sink. "That must have been difficult for him. My, I have a different impression of him than I first had. I guess at the beginning I didn't want to because I thought he rivalled Dad for your feelings. But now I understand what you're saying."

And at that moment Hannah decided that Carrie should never know how Charles felt about her, so she said, "Carrie, my dear, there's one thing that Charles Sinclair truly loved, and that was his money, and making money. Fortunately for him, he was successful. But his personal life, that's another story. Mrs. Sinclair, Virginia, she played at being his wife, that's all."

"Do you miss him?"

She laughed. "I haven't seen him in many, many years. I can hardly miss the man. I miss what I was then. I was brave back then. Or I think I was. The things he sent me have sentimental value. They help me remember a time when I was young, not afraid of anything, and wanting to get out of here and find out what life was like out in the world. I got attention from the last man on earth I expected would ever notice me."

Being careful not to make eye contact with her mother, Carrie cleaned the kitchen counters mindlessly and let her talk. It was the most Hannah had confided in Carrie in all their years together. Finally, when she seemed to have run out of things to say, Carrie asked, "Mother, should you ever meet Jeanne and talk to her, will you tell her all of this?"

Hannah shook her head. "I wouldn't do anything or say anything to destroy her opinion of her father. What I know about her father or Mrs. Sinclair is better left unsaid. Poor Jeanne has had enough to deal with over the years." She wiggled her foot and declared it was on the mend.

* * * * *

Quentin knew that if his mother were alive she would be very upset to see him working on Good Friday. But it had been an extremely busy week, mainly because it was a short one. In the middle of it, he had to make an unexpected business trip. He promised himself a vacation very soon and planned to persuade Sara to join him.

When he left his office late on Thursday evening, he grabbed a pile of mail that Beth Ann, his assistant, had stacked on the corner of his desk and pushed it into his leather briefcase. Quentin hated unfinished business, so on Friday afternoon, he decided to take care of it with a strong coffee and his two hot cross buns, warmed in the oven with melting cheddar cheese. He laid both on his desk in his study and reached for the first envelope.

He read through the document carefully. He took some legal-size empty envelopes from his files and one that contained several other documents. The latter envelope was simply labelled *Charles Sinclair—real estate*. He separated the copies, then placed the original in an envelope and sealed it. He took the last bite of his lunch, licked the excess cheese and icing from his fingers, and wiped them on a paper towel he had laid under the plate. He reached for his phone and dialled Jeanne's number.

An hour later he pulled his navy Cressida into her driveway. The air was remarkably cold despite the deep blue sky and brilliant sunshine. *Ice offshore*, he thought, as he manoeuvred around patches of dirty snow on the lawn and stepped onto the clean walkway to the front door. Jeanne opened it within seconds.

"Hello, Jeanne. Thank you for seeing me, especially today."

"I must admit, I am a bit surprised." She waved him inside, and closed the door. "No one is working today, and I assume this is not a social call."

"No, it isn't."

"Well, if you are here representing Gregory, I've had enough of him to last me a lifetime. So whatever it is, contact my lawyer."

"No, no," he chuckled. "I am certainly not here representing Gregory. May we sit down?"

"Certainly." He followed her to the living room and sat on the nearest sofa. He laid a large envelope on the coffee table, opened it, pulled the contents out, and left them there.

"Jeanne, I am here representing—your father."

"My father?" her brow furrowed. "How can that be? My father's lawyer was Jonathan Hamlyn."

"Well, technically, Jonathan is your lawyer, and Emily's, I guess.

This is a separate matter. I've come to tell you that the Sinclair house has been sold."

"I know that already. Why should that matter to me? It's Gregory's house."

"Not anymore."

"Who bought it?"

"I did."

"You did! What ever for? You have a house, just down around the corner from here. Didn't Kurt's mother buy it for you?"

He ignored the question about Catherine. "Yes, I do have a house." He leaned forward and rested his elbows on his knees. "But I was instructed to purchase the Sinclair house, and I simply carried out that instruction. Let me explain. A couple of years ago, just after Virginia died, I met Charles in Jonathan Hamlyn's office. Jonathan had called and asked me to come down for a brief meeting. Charles told me that Virginia and her family wanted the house to go to Emily. He didn't explain much, except to say that it was originally a Boland house and they wanted it passed down to her eldest daughter."

"Father was willing to go along with that?"

"For a while, yes. Of course, he had the right to do whatever he wanted with the house, but it was obvious that the Bolands would pressure him to do as they wanted. I didn't question it then, but Jonathan explained to me later that the Bolands had given your father a substantial sum to keep his businesses going over the years and, so, in a way, he felt he owed them. He would have to will the house to Emily." Quentin ran his hand through his straight black hair. "But he also gambled that Emily would want to sell it, especially with Gregory behind her looking for every dollar. He was right, of course. Emily transferred the deed of the house over to Gregory and he hired a real estate agent to sell it. What no one knew is that your father put a considerable sum of money in trust for me to buy the house. He had no idea what the market value was or how much Gregory or Emily would try to sell it for, so he asked me. I checked it out, and he assured me the money was there to cover it. Apparently, he sold a lot of property somewhere else in the province, and this was the proceeds.

As soon as it went up on the market, actually before, because I happened to know the real estate agent—he went to school with Joe and me—I made an offer, the full asking price plus a little more to make it enticing."

"I don't understand. Why would Father want you to buy the house?"

"It was the only way he could think of to ensure that you would get it. And he wanted the house to be yours. As for why me in particular? Jonathan couldn't do it himself, being the family lawyer, and, well, Jonathan had apparently convinced your father of my reliability. My guess is that your father was looking for a low-profile lawyer, someone who didn't walk in his own social circle."

Jeanne paled as the blood drained from her face and she processed the information. Her throat went dry. She swallowed hard. "He told me," she whispered, "the night he passed away, that the house was mine. When I heard later that Emily had inherited it, I assumed he had lied to me."

"No, he didn't lie to you. He told me that he wanted to take care of you and that he wanted you to have the house. He felt it was only fair, since you took care of him all those years." Quentin reached for the envelope. "So there it is. I have transferred the deed to you. The house legally belongs to you now. In the envelope you will find copies of all the transactions, including notes of the meetings that I had with your father, signed by him and me. I must admit it was an unusual contract to draw up, but it is one of my few talents. I have the originals that I am going to drop off to Jonathan on Monday morning for safekeeping. I think you would agree that's best?" He stood and passed her the papers.

"Yes, of course." Her shaking hands took the documents. She glanced at them, but rather than read them carefully, she simply placed them on the cherry wood table beside her.

Quentin continued. "There was some money left over. I overestimated what Gregory would ask by about $20,000. Your father figured you would need to renovate it, new windows, new roof, that sort of thing. Fortunately, Gregory took care of all of that before he tried to sell it. Good advice from Joe, but Joe, of course, had no idea at the time that he was getting Gregory to pay to renovate your house." He smiled and received one back. "So you can put that money to other good use, I'm sure."

"Yes, I can. Thank you," she replied, knowing exactly what she was going to do with it.

He stood to leave. "Then that takes care of it, Jeanne. That part of Charles's estate is settled, and you'll be hearing from Jonathan next week. I'll be going. If you have questions about any of the papers, don't hesitate to call me. I've placed my business card in there, and I've put my home phone number on it as well."

She stood to follow him to the front door. "Quentin, surely I owe you for your services? You've done a lot of work here."

"Oh, I was paid. It was all taken care of."

"One other thing," she asked.

"Sure, what is it?"

"Does Gregory know that you bought the house?"

"Oh yes. I had no problem allowing the real estate agent to tell him. At the time, I simply said it was an investment. Quite plausible."

"But he's going to throw a fit when he hears the truth."

"So? Let him. At least he'll implode in Halifax. He won't make a mess here."

His wit made her laugh, the first time in several days. "Indeed," she said. "It's just that this business about the stuff from the house. I wouldn't want to make it worse. I have no problem testifying, if need be.

Quentin tossed his head in laughter. "That's been taken care of as well. Don't worry."

"Thank you, for all of this." She held the edge of the door. "Quentin, I know you and I . . . over the years . . ."

"Jeanne, it was a simple legal transaction. I was paid quite well for my efforts." He stepped outside. "So long."

She closed the door behind him, squeezed her eyes shut, and took a deep calming breath. For a moment, she leaned against the back of the door. *The house is yours, you know that.* The words resonated through her mind once again; this time they brought a smile. She shook her head and whispered, "Dad."

In the car, Quentin realized for the first time how relieved he was to get that nasty bit of business over with. Owing something to Charles Sinclair was more than he could stomach. He glanced at his watch and realized that he had to hurry to get home, finish his paperwork, and get over to Joe's for Friday night dinner. *But then,* he thought, as he turned into his driveway, *they can wait for me for a few minutes, especially since I have the Friday night story of the century.*

* * * * *

Joe was whisking milk, seasoning, and tomato paste into the lobster bisque when Lauren and Alan arrived at his apartment shortly after 6:00 p.m. Jordy, who had been urged to join the Friday night group, cleaned and sliced strawberries at the counter next to him recounting the April Fool's joke he'd played on Doris MacKinlay earlier in the week. In the dining room, Sandi was placing wineglasses on the table.

Joe turned to greet his sister and brother-in-law. "Gorgeous day."

"Certainly was. We went for a walk around Bowring Park with Grandma and Granddad, Dad and Jaclyn. Everyone was out." Lauren laughed. "We were like a community of bears coming out of hibernation."

"A hug," Jordy said with a chuckle.

Lauren turned to him. "What?"

"A hug. It's a hug of bears, not a community of bears. That's what happens when you work at a publishing company. You learn new words every day," Jordy explained, as Lauren enjoyed a laugh.

"Lobster, Joe? This is a treat," Alan said, as he hung up their jackets. "Special occasion?"

"Well, it's Easter, so I figured we should have something special. Besides, I don't often have a day off to cook. Sandi's made a really nice dessert, too. Strawberry shortcake, the Nova Scotian version."

"Yum. I'll have to walk across the island tomorrow to work this off," said Lauren.

Quentin rushed in around seven, the last to arrive. He removed his jacket and tossed it on the back of a chair. "Sorry, everyone. Busy day."

David looked up. "Even I did early rounds today, Quentin. What's your excuse? Nothing's open. You couldn't have been working, because Kurt's home. And we're all here, unless you played squash by yourself."

Somewhat out of breath, Quentin poured himself a Pepsi, stuck several pieces of lemon in it, and headed for one of the armchairs. "I had work to do at home and an appointment to keep. Something I wanted to get out of the way. It's been stuck to my fingers for almost two years."

"An appointment?" Sara asked. "Today?"

"Yeah, I'll tell you in a minute because it's unquestionably the Friday night story for this year, if not the decade or century. But let me take care of something else first." He leaned forward and placed his glass on the table in front of him. "Lauren, you owe me for one lunch. Here's the receipt."

"Oh, what ever for?" She picked up the crumpled receipt and noted that it was from a restaurant in Halifax.

"The case that Gregory was putting together against you? He's changed his mind."

"*What?*"

He swallowed a mouthful of Pepsi. "Yeah, I had a little chat with him over lunch, and he's decided it's not worth it."

"When did this happen?"

"Wednesday. I popped up to Halifax to see him." Quentin described the trip to Halifax like it was down the street, not an hour and a half by plane. "There was no sense trying to get through to him on the phone. My phone call didn't represent billable hours for him. So I flew up Wednesday morning, knowing he couldn't resist a free lunch at the Sheraton, and I flew back Wednesday night. So here's my bill for lunch." He grinned and sat back with a look of self-satisfaction. "Guess

I could charge you for the airfare, too. Lunch was $54.83 plus the tip. I had an Angus beef burger with sweet potato fries. Yum! That's the first time I had sweet—"

"*Quentin!* Never mind what you ate! How did you persuade Gregory to change his mind?" Wide-eyed, Lauren was waving her hands for answers. The others laughed around her at her animated response.

"I pointed out to him that he would spend more in legal fees than the stuff that you gave away was worth. At first, he didn't believe me. He had an itemized list, something about a Spode bowl valued at several thousand dollars?"

"I never saw any Spode bowl. Besides, all the expensive stuff was sent to his mother, except for a few items that Mother kept and gave to me."

"Anyway, I told him that I had an affidavit from Joe and one from Jeanne and I planned to nag his mother to get a statement from her. Since they were the two daughters of the deceased, it's not likely that a judge would side with Gregory's nonsense."

"That did it?"

"Yeah, that and a stray comment about his father's misdeeds. Oh, and a reminder that it would be best for him to stay on the good side of Kurt if he hoped for any Steffensen inheritance to come his way down the road."

"Yeah, right," Joe said, and almost choked with laughter as he stood in the kitchen door and took it all in. "No doubt Gregory's is the first name in Dad's will. I'm just glad it's over with. C'mon, let's eat."

Lauren hugged Quentin as she moved to the dining room table. "Thanks, Quentin. You're the best. And I will pay your expenses, including your airfare."

"Nah, consider it a freebie, Lauren. It's been a bonus week." They moved to the table in front of the large bay window that looked out at the hotel across the street. Joe placed a large white Fitzsu tureen at the centre and an assortment of bread and cheese nearby. He dished up bowls of lobster bisque, and David poured their favourite Chardonnay.

When he was not forthcoming, Sara prompted Quentin, who was enjoying his lobster and crusty rolls. "We're waiting, Quentin, for the story of the week, or did you say year. There's more to it than getting Gregory to stand down?"

"Oh yeah," he answered, slathering his roll with butter. "I bought a house."

"You did what?"

"I bought a house."

"Why? You already have one."

"A guy can invest, can't he?"

"Quentin, you know very little about houses," Joe said, feigning exasperation. "And you didn't ask me about it. Which one did you buy?"

"Didn't need to ask you. You just renovated it. I bought the Sinclair house."

"*What?*" The word was shouted in unison around the table, and they stopped eating.

Quentin laughed. "Calm down, the lot of you. Actually, I bought it with someone else's money. And then, I gave it away."

They waited.

"Okay, okay." He put up his hand, then reached for his napkin. "I bought it using money that Charles put away in a special account before he died." He went on to explain the arrangement. "I agreed to buy the house as soon as it went on the market, and to put the house in Jeanne's name. It was a way of getting around the inheritance. Gregory got his money, Jeanne got the house. Charles did what he said he was going to do. He left it to her. 'All's well,' as the old bard said."

Lauren looked puzzled. "Quentin, what I don't understand here is why Granddad didn't simply will the house to Mother! As I understand matrimonial property, he had the right to do as he pleased. Virginia's interest in the property died with her. If he wanted to leave it to Mother, he could have."

"You're right, but the Bolands didn't see it that way. They wanted the house to go to a relative. And Emily was the only daughter who was. Apparently, the Bolands were the money behind your grandfather. Charles didn't want to risk that one of them, likely Virginia's nosy sisters, knew about Jeanne and Hannah. Rather than take a chance it would all go public, and Jeanne would be embarrassed, he left the house to Emily as they wanted, and did an end run around it."

Lauren sat in shock, shaking her head. "Quentin, I don't know what to say. I guess the first thing that comes to mind is why would you do work for Grandfather, or Mother, for that matter? Did she know?"

"She does now. I told her today and gave her the deed." He reached for the ladle to refill his bowl.

"Wow! What did she say?" David asked.

"She said 'thank you,'" Quentin answered.

"After all she's said to you over the years. Why?" Joe asked.

"Charles was a client, Joe. Simple as that. I was paid quite handsomely for my work. Just another client." He smiled, and shrugged his shoulders. "Actually, I donated the legal fees to charity, that women's shelter you've been going on about for months, Lauren. I guess if there's an added bonus, I'm thinking maybe it'll keep Jeanne at bay for a while. You know, something to make her feel like she owes me."

Lauren suddenly stopped eating, laid down her spoon, and looked directly at her brother sitting across the table. "That's it, isn't it?"

"What?"

"What Quentin just said. 'Keeping Jeanne at bay.' That's why the secret about Mother and Hannah was so important to Dad. That's why he didn't tell us. He used the information to get Mother to agree with what he wanted over the years, likely starting with their divorce."

Joe hesitated, but finally nodded in agreement. "Yeah, you're right."

"At the time of the divorce, she told me there was no point in contesting it because she wanted out as much as he did. I didn't believe her then. I'm guessing there were other times?"

Joe nodded. "A few, over the years. You wanting to go to private school, stay with us in the summer, that sort of thing."

"Ah, makes perfect sense. And Dad explained all of this to you?" Lauren asked.

"Yeah, a few weeks ago. He told me to tell you if it came up. But he wasn't keen on letting you know, because you seem to get along with Mother better than the rest of us, and he didn't want to do anything to make that relationship worse."

She shook her head. "It's okay. Thanks for telling me now."

Alan was taking in the conversation. "Joe, the week of our wedding. It was a great week, but I always had a sense that Kurt was making sure Jeanne kept a still tongue, as they say. Am I right?"

"Alan, yes, I'm sorry." Joe was reluctant to confirm his suspicions.

"It's okay. I'm grateful to him."

Seated next to him, David wondered, "Joe, do you think this whole business about Hannah will change her in any way? Perhaps now that it's out, she'll have a different perspective on things?" he asked.

Joe shrugged. "I have no idea, David. She scored a victory today. She got the house she wanted, and expected to get. We'll see."

Lauren added a simple statement that surprised them all around the table. "I'm not so sure we have a right to expect her to be any different from what she's always been." She made eye contact with her brother and David to emphasize the point.

Later in the kitchen, as Sandi and Lauren cleaned dishes and placed them in the dishwasher, Sandi noticed that Lauren seemed particularly quiet. "You okay, Lauren? Seems like you have something on your mind."

"Nah, just thinking about my mother, that's all, Sandi." Sara entered the kitchen in time to hear her comment. "I know this is going to sound stupid, guys, but there are times I feel sorry for her." She chuckled. "My dad says I'm a lot like my Great-grandmother Thorburn. She could see a multitude of sides to every story."

"Probably what makes you such a good lawyer, Lauren," Sandi said.

"Thanks." She closed the door to the dishwasher and pressed the start button. "Mother has done some pretty cruel things over the years. Sara knows all too well."

Sara nodded and sat at the kitchen table.

"Heck, the day before my wedding, she changed my bouquet to

white roses because they are *her* favourite flowers. Uncle Peter knew the florist and was able to get it changed back at the last minute to what I wanted. She did it likely to be vengeful, or so I thought at the time. The more I think about it, the more I realize how alone she was that week. There was a big crowd of us at Dad's, all having a great time, and she wasn't a part of it."

"She could have been with us, Lauren, if she was either bit gracious. But let's face it, she doesn't like the Mathesons very much. Perhaps it was just as well she wasn't there."

"I know. She's frustrating, I agree. But I keep thinking where it all started. I remember one time when I was about fourteen, I came home from tennis early one afternoon and I overheard Dad telling her how cold and unfeeling she was, that she never showed any affection. I remember thinking at the time how right he was. She never was one for hugging us or expressing her feelings in any way. Then, shortly after that, I walked by their bedroom and I saw her sitting on the bed, and she was crying. She looked so pitiful, even helpless. At the time, I didn't know what to think, but I've thought about that day a lot in the past few months. She learned from the best, didn't she, when it comes to being cold and unfeeling. Virginia. And her father was hardly home to counteract it, and even if he was, I doubt he would have been any better. Not like my dad or the whole Steffensen family. As for private school and coming home in the summer, I guess I can't help but wonder, is it unreasonable for a mother to want her daughter to be with her? I dunno. Does any of this make sense?"

"Perfect sense, Lauren. And I think Jeanne is very fortunate to have you for a daughter. You've got more patience than most," Sandi observed.

"I don't know, Sandi. There are times I think I could wring her neck." She laughed. "Now, enough of this. Let's take out the strawberry shortcake. I am so looking forward to your recipe."

Sandi sliced each shortcake in half and scooped spoonfuls of strawberries across each one. Topping the dessert with fresh cream, she smiled. "What's everyone's plan for Easter Sunday? We have Uncle Robert and Phyllis coming for dinner, don't we, Jordy?"

"Uh huh. Phyllis. Not one to aid the digestion." He looked around the table with his charming grin. "Don't suppose anyone would consider taking in a stray for Sunday?" he asked, digging into the layers of pastry, strawberries, and cream, and toasting the delicious taste with his fork.

* * * * *

The next morning, Jeanne sat in her solarium and surveyed the garden through the windows. "Leah, it's actually quite warm. I think I'll have lunch out here. Garden's not much to look at, but most of the snow is gone, at least."

She took her chequebook and an envelope and sat in the sunshine at the small round table draped with a bright yellow flowery tablecloth. She wrote a cheque for $20,000 to Bethel United Church, Falcon Cove, placed it in the envelope, and sealed it. She reached for a single postage stamp, then stopped as Leah laid a steaming bowl of seafood chowder in front of her.

"Well, this is a treat. Thanks, Leah. Are you going now?"

"Yes, if it's okay. Did you want me to mail your letter on my way home?"

Jeanne hesitated. "No, that's okay. Thanks anyway. I'll take care of it. I have several things to do this weekend. By the way, do you have family coming in from out of town for Easter?"

"Oh yes, all hands. My sister and her husband are driving in from Glovertown. The weather is going to be nice, so the roads will be dry for the next few days."

"Good. Happy Easter, Leah! Enjoy your family!"

* * * * *

On Saturday afternoon, Sandi declared that the return of Joe's Porsche was his acknowledgement that spring was definitely close by.

"So, where are we going?" she asked, as she got into the passenger side.

"Thought we'd check out the hill to see if it's changed much since last fall. Remember?" He glanced at her and saw her smile acknowledge the memory of that day in October when they walked the trail around the hill for the first time. Joe drove up Signal Hill Road and pulled into the parking lot at the top facing the city. The cold wind made him question his choice of clothing, but Sandi quickly reassured him that he would be warmer once they started walking. She was right. Joe soon forgot about the chill of the damp Atlantic air as they took in the spectacular view. A large iceberg was grounded near the entrance to the harbour, and a line of ice bordered the horizon as the sun illuminated the aqua cast. Soft wisps of clouds feathered the sky, a private showing for the only two souls on the trail.

They walked down the steep decline with their fingers tightly interlocked. Winter snow and spring runoff had left the usually even surface rough and treacherous. They picked their way carefully, slipped once or twice on the loose gravel, and held on to each other tightly. At the far end of the trail, at a point closest to the sea, they sat on a wooden slatted bench facing the water. Behind them in the distance they could hear the sounds of the city on a busy Saturday afternoon. The wind was picking up, but the air remained warm enough to be comfortable. Strands of Sandi's brown hair escaped the pearl clasp. Dampness caused her face to be framed with unruly soft curls. She sat back next to him and leaned back so he could wrap his arms around her. She lodged her right leg across the edge of the bench. Joe gently massaged her shoulders. They did not look at each other, but straight ahead toward the east, to the nearby iceberg, and beyond, to the horizon and a larger berg floating freely down the coast. Though he had not planned for this moment, Joe knew it was unquestionably the perfect one.

"Sandi?"

"Mmm." She turned her head slightly to look up at him.

"Where do you see yourself ten years from now?"

She laughed. "God willing, tenured. Just kidding." She brushed back the hair from her eyes. "Here, I guess. With you, I hope. What about you?"

"I kinda hope I get that big northern climate housing project done by then," he said with a laugh. "Seriously, where will I be? With you. No matter where I am or what I'm doing, with you. That's all that matters."

Joe looked to his right at the waves washing the Narrows and focused back to her. "Sandi, I love you with all my heart. You know that, don't you?"

"Yes, and I love you, too, Joe. I can't imagine life without you."

"Then, you should never have to find out." He paused and took a deep breath.

He looked at her with a questioning smile. His hands continued to smooth back her hair, his fingers stopping to play with her tiny pearl earrings. "Sandi, could I be your husband?"

She responded immediately. "Yes, I'd love to be your wife." She looked into his deep blue eyes. He leaned forward to kiss her ever so lightly.

She twisted around, stood up, and reached both hands for his. Tears glistened in her sparkling brown eyes. "I love you, so much."

"And I love you," he replied, "more than all the world."

They kissed and hugged each other tightly.

As they headed back up the trail, Joe said, "Sandi, we have to do this right. Marriage, I mean. Not like people talk about marriage today. The guys I went to university with used to talk about having a 'starter wife.' Good grief! Like they expected it to be temporary. Ours has to be different, somehow. Something special."

She laughed at his description. "I can do one better. My girlfriends at Dal used to describe their boyfriends as fixer-uppers. Guys to be worked into shape in order to become husbands. No, my love. We've been friends from the beginning. It'll be different."

"Absolutely."

"Let's go home," he whispered. "I have something for you." Then, locking hands tightly again, they began the steep ascent up the hill.

Minutes later, inside Joe's apartment, Sandi slipped off her hiking shoes and heavy sweater. "Well, Joe, at least it was a lot warmer today than the last time we walked that trail."

"Yes, although I enjoyed that day back in October. I'll never forget it. Like today."

Sandi watched as he walked to his desk, opened a drawer, and took out a small velvet case. "I dearly hope you like it and that it fits."

With that, he slipped a perfect Tiffany diamond on the fourth finger of her left hand. It had a platinum band of sapphires and diamonds.

"Joe, it's the most beautiful ring I've ever seen. I love it."

"I'm glad you like it. I bought it in Boston. I debated the style for hours."

He locked his arms around her waist and held her tightly. Then he smiled. "I guess we should let everyone in on our news, huh?"

Sandi turned her head to look up at him, her eyes widening with a question. "That can wait till later, can't it? Remember what we did the last time after we walked around Signal Hill? Maybe we should make that a habit." She reached for his hand and, taking it in hers, led him in the direction of the bedroom. "From now on, we'll refer to it as 'walking up Signal Hill.'"

"Great, we have our own euphemism! It'll be a wonderful excuse to be late!"

* * * * *

On Easter Sunday morning, most of the pews in Bethel United Church in Falcon Cove were filled with regular members of the congregation, and several visitors. The church served residents of three nearby communities and, on this special Sunday, many of them drove to Falcon Cove. As it was a warm morning, a church usher opened several side windows in advance of the service to let a cross breeze cool down the sanctuary before people arrived. The smell of furniture polish, oil soap, and lilies pervaded the room.

In the vestry, Carrie peeked out through a side window into the sanctuary and was pleased to see a full church. She made a mental note to welcome any visitors, but not to make much fuss, as her father had once said that some people are easily embarrassed by attention.

As it was a spring-like day, Carrie decided to encourage her congregation to look forward to a busy summer full of energy and life.

Strains of familiar Easter hymns filled the sanctuary. Carrie entered quietly and closed the door behind her. The congregation stood briefly as she spoke the Invocation and welcomed them all to the service. The choir stood and sang two verses of "Christ the Lord is Risen Today." Carrie took a moment to look around at the familiar and unfamiliar faces. Despite her limp, Hannah had made it to church, with her best friend, Adelia, sitting next to her. Following decades of tradition, they wore new coats and had their hair perfectly curled the night before.

After the opening prayer, Carrie reached for her brief notes of announcements tucked in her hymnal. She thanked those who had placed lilies in memory of loved ones and asked for a moment of silent prayer in memory of them. She reminded the stewards of their upcoming meeting and the women of the spring sale. She commented for a moment on the newness of the season, the beginning of nature after a long, cold winter. She even added a personal touch that, despite her "orange thumb," as she called it, she had managed to coax some daffodils up two or three inches in her garden, a true testament to her belief in the Almighty. The congregation laughed.

She paused for a moment to survey the congregation before she welcomed the visitors. Halfway down the left side, her eyes stopped and fixed on a woman exquisitely dressed in a blue and white linen dress with three-quarter-length sleeves. Her matching coat and silk scarf in bright shades of blue hung neatly across the back of the pew. Three strands of pearls graced her neckline. She sat alone, her eyes fixed on the altar.

Jeanne.

The surprise of seeing her sister was so great for Carrie it took her a moment to realize that the church was completely silent. The congregation waited for her to speak. She laid down her notes.

"On this beautiful Easter morning," she began slowly, "I welcome you all to God's house. And we welcome, in particular, visitors who have joined us today. Just so that we may make our welcome more personal, would you please take a minute or two now to greet persons standing near you as brothers and sisters in Christ? And if you are visiting us, please identify yourself and sign our guest book. Also, if you have time, you are welcome to join us for coffee and sweets in the room off the front vestibule before you leave this morning."

With that, Carrie looked down from the altar and saw her mother, Adelia, Aunt Iris, Uncle Toby, and other regular members greeting those around them. There was a low chatter throughout the sanctuary and the occasional audible laughter.

Hannah turned around to her left and noticed the striking woman two rows behind her, clearly a visitor but somehow familiar. She stretched out her hand. Jeanne was looking toward the front and was surprised by the greeting. She turned her head and heard soft-spoken words. "Happy Easter! Welcome to our church and to our home. My name is Hannah, and it is so good to have you here." Jeanne reached out her hand, which Hannah immediately clasped and squeezed gently, suddenly recognizing the woman whose hand she held. And Jeanne looked into the eyes of her mother and smiled.

ACKNOWLEDGEMENTS

I am grateful to many people for their support during the writing and publishing of this novel. My co-workers and wonderful friends, Roxanne McHugh, Valarie James, and Jillian Gosse, were my initial readers. They encouraged me to keep writing and to submit the manuscript for publication. Their smiles inspired me to continue! Many thanks as well go to Roxanne McHugh and Fay Whelan for their feedback on the cover and for listening whenever I needed to vent my frustration.

My sincere appreciation goes to my sister, Audrey Oake, for her editing during the initial writing process. She was meticulous. Iona Bulgin copy-edited and provided me with constructive feedback on the first draft. My good friends, Ted and Bart, have always been there for me, whatever I do. We take care of each other.

A special thank you goes to the staff of Flanker Press, namely Garry Cranford, Jerry Cranford, and graphic designer Graham Blair. They were willing to take a chance on a new writer and brought me through the publishing process in a professional manner. I also appreciate the suggestions of their editor, Robin McGrath.

I am forever grateful to Albert, my husband, who probably knows the characters in this novel as well as I do and never seems to tire hearing about them. Without his encouragement, ideas, and support, this book would not have been written. He taught me to "write for myself." Special thanks to him as well for taking my photo and building a website!

As a young girl, I got to know several very special women who worked in service in St. John's during their formative years. Their stories demonstrate their courage, talent, and determination to make a meaningful contribution to their families and communities. They are truly an inspiration to succeeding generations.

While in-service work in Newfoundland and Labrador is a matter of historical record, the events, places, and people in this book are purely fictional. Any similarities to real people or places are coincidental, and any errors are my responsibility.

Trudi (White) Johnson was born and grew up in St. John's, though her family's roots are in Bonavista Bay. She graduated from Memorial University with a B.A., B.Ed., and M.Ed., and taught for ten years in the K-12 school system in White Bay and Labrador City. She returned to Memorial in the 1990s and completed a doctoral degree in Newfoundland and Labrador history, specializing in matrimonial law and inheritance practices. Currently, she is an associate professor in the Faculty of Education at Memorial University, where she enjoys teaching pre-service teachers and researches effective teaching and teacher efficacy.

In addition to writing fiction set in Newfoundland, she likes to garden, read murder mysteries, and obsess about hockey and baseball. Through her writing, she hopes her readers will come to understand the special connections that we all have to our past and appreciate how those who came before us shaped our lives. She is currently working on a sequel to *From a Good Home*.

Trudi lives in St. John's with her husband, Albert. She can be reached at her website: www.trudi-johnson.com.